ALIEN INFLUENCES

Also available from Millennium

The White Mists of Power
Heart Readers
Traitors
Facade

ALIEN INFLUENCES

KRISTINE KATHRYN RUSCH

MILLENNIUM
An Orion Book
LONDON

This edition first published
in 1994 by
Millennium
An imprint of Orion Books Ltd
Orion House, 5 Upper St Martin's Lane
London WC2H 9EA

A CIP catalogue record for this book is
available from the British Library

ISBN: (Csd) 1 85798 104 9
(Ppr) 1 85798 105 7

Millennium
Book Forty One

Typeset at The Spartan Press Ltd, Lymington, Hants
Printed and bound in Great Britain by
Clays Ltd, St Ives Plc

For my sister, Sandra L. Hofsommer,
with thanks and love

Acknowledgements

Thanks on this one go to Jerry Oltion for the discussions of hard v. soft science fiction; the Tuesday night writers group, who manage to keep me honest; to Ed Ferman for believing in the Dancers from the beginning; to Mike Resnick for the idea behind 'Alien Influences', the short story; and to Dean Wesley Smith for suggesting this novel in the first place.

John

He first saw the Dancer when he was a toddler. He was inside the dome, rose bushes on both sides. The Dancer stood on the dirt street, surrounded by a crowd of people. He knows this is a memory, not an incident someone has told him years after the fact. No one speaks to him of the Dancers. When he mentions their name, people turn away, embarrassed, as if he still has blood on his hands.

In his memory, his hands were pudgy. He sees them raised in supplication: I want . . . I want . . .

He had no words, only the desire. The Dancer stood before him, impossibly tall, trapped and flighty against the molded plastic of the dome. It was like him and not like him. It had two arms and two legs, but they were stick thin and shiny black. Its cinnamon smell overpowered the roses. It moved as if it were in water – all grace and light.

I want . . . I want . . .

It hummed and whistled, then stopped when it saw him. A little boy was reflected in its large silver eyes. Twin little boys, pudgy arms reaching – reaching –

Sometimes he dreams of the Dancer standing before him, and he wakes, hands outstretched, muttering –

I want . . .

I want . . .

Part One

Justin Schafer

They brought him in after the fifth murder.

The shuttle dropped him on the landing site at the salt cliffs, overlooking the golden waters of the Singing Sea. Apparently something in the shuttle fuel harmed the vegetation near the small colony, so they developed a landing strip on the barren cliff tops at the beginning of the desert. Winds and salt had destroyed the plastic shelter long ago, so he wore the required body scarf and some specially developed reflective cream. Before she left, the shuttle pilot pointed out the domed city in the distance. She said she had radioed them to send someone for him. He clutched his water bottle tightly, refusing to drink until he was parched.

A hot, dry breeze rustled the scarf around his face. The air smelled of daffodils, or so it seemed. It had been so long since he had been to Earth, he was no longer sure what daffodils smelled like.

Everything around him was golden, or bright, dazzling white. The sun felt like a furnace; the heat reflected off all the nearby surfaces. He had read that, in some seasons, temperatures went beyond human endurance.

The desert spanned between him and the domed city. A narrow footpath wove its way over the slight dunes, appearing to lead to the city itself. The dome reflected the sunlight. From this distance, it looked small, about the size of his thumbnail, but he knew it housed over a thousand people, homes, and the Salt Juice plant.

He took a deep breath, feeling the dryness in his throat. It had been a long time since he had been off Minar Base. Even longer since he had been hired to do any on-site evaluations. He had prepared by meditating and by reading everything he could find on Bountiful – which was very little outside the production figures for Salt Juice. Still, he woke each morning in a panic, afraid that he was not up to the task they had hired him for. He had tried to be taken off the case, but Bountiful had insisted. They wanted him, a fact that bothered him more than anything else.

To his left, salt continually eroded down the cliff face, little crystals rolling and tumbling to the white beach below. The Singing Sea devoured the crystals, leaving a salt scum that reflected the harsh light of the sun. Perhaps this was where, decades ago, the miners had begun their slaughter of the Dancers. The Dancers were a protected species now, about one one-hundredth of their original numbers.

This place had quite a few protected species, but most lived far away from the colony. The only known Dancer habitat was at the edge of the domed city. All the materials sent to him on Minar Base pointed to the Dancers as the cause of the murders. The colonists wanted him to make a recommendation that would be used in a preliminary injunction, a recommendation on whether the Dancers had acted with malicious intent. That idea left him queasy and brought the dreams back.

Justin glanced back at the barren, whitish brown land leading to the dome. Colonists who escaped this place called it the Gateway to Hell. He could understand why, with the endless heat, the oxygen-poor air, and the salt-polluted water. Just before he left the base, he had spoken with an old man who had spent his childhood on this planet. The old man's skin was shrivelled and dried from too many hours in an unkind sun. He ate no salt, and he filled his quarters with fresh, cool water. He said he was so relieved to become an adult because then he could legally escape the planet. He had warned Justin to stay away.

'Justin Schafer?'

He turned. A woman stood at the edge of the trail leading back to the dome. Her body-length white sand scarf fluttered in the breeze. She had dark skin and wide brown eyes. 'I'm Netta Goldin. I'm taking you to the colony.'

'We're walking?'

She smiled. 'The ecology here is fragile. We have learned to accept a number of inconveniences. Be sure to stay on the path.'

His fingers tightened around the water bottle. He hoped they didn't have to walk far. He was already breathless from the poor air, and he was out of shape. He had neglected his body in the years since Minar.

The reflective white cream gathered in the lines on Netta's face, making her appear creased. 'I hear they brought you in from the base near Minar. Minar is supposed to be lovely.'

'It is.' A shiver went through him. Minar had been lovely, and he hated it. 'Your name is familiar.'

'I'm the head of the colony.'

He remembered now. The scratchy female voice on the corded message. 'Then you're the one who sent for me.'

She adjusted his scarf hood. The heat increased, but the prickling on his scalp stopped. 'You're the best person for the job.'

'I deal in human aberration. You need a specialist.'

'No.' She threaded her arm through his and walked down the trail. The salt crunched beneath their feet. 'I need someone who knows human and xeno psychology. You seem to be the only one left on either nearby base.'

'I thought you were convinced the natives are doing this.'

'I think the deaths have happened because of interactions between our people and the Dancers. It's clear that the Dancers killed the children, but we don't know why. I want you to investigate those dynamics. I also want this done fast. I want to do something about the Dancers, protect my people better than I am now. But I understand that you need to investigate the natives in their own environment, so we have taken no action.'

The wind played with his sand scarf. A runnel of sweat trickled down his back. Small, white plants he had never seen before – with prickly spines and a tough look – grew in small clumps in the salt and sand mixture. 'I'm not licensed to practise xenopsychology.'

'That's a lie, Dr Schafer. I researched you rather heavily before I went to the expense of bringing you here. The Ethics Committee suspended your license for one year as a formality. That was nine years ago. You're still licensed and still interested in the field.'

He pulled his arm from hers. He had sat by the sea on the first morning in Minar, too. He had been thirty years old and so sure he could understand everything human or alien. And he had understood, finally. Too late. 'I don't want this job.'

'You're the only one who can do it.' She clasped her hands

behind her back. 'All the other xenopsychologists in the quadrant have specialized in one species or refuse to do forensic work. Besides, no one is better at this than you.'

'They charged me with inciting genocide on Minar.'

'And acquitted you. Your actions were logical, given the evidence.'

Logical. He should have seen how the land encroached, poisoned, ate away human skin. He later learned that Minaran skin oils were also acidic, but didn't cause the same kind of damage. The original colonists had died first because of land poisoning, not because the Minarans were acting on an old vendetta. All the work the natives had done, they had done to save the colonists. He had ascribed a human motive, the ultimate sin in xeno work. It had been the wrong human motive and it had decimated a sentient race. 'I don't want to make the same mistake again.'

'Good,' she said. The wind blew her scarf across her face. She brushed the cloth away with a cream-covered hand. 'Because then you won't.'

ii

Once he got inside, the dome felt huge. Houses ran along the unpaved streets in a strict grid pattern. Each lawn had plants he recognized, and the dome itself was a Texas summer blue. The dome protected them from the intense heat, and he was grateful for it. Netta had shown him to his quarters and instructed him to appear for a meeting within the hour.

The meeting room was part of the Command Central base on the western end of the dome. Several buildings made up Command Central; from leaders' offices to a huge communications centre. The meeting room was part of a building that housed the city's library, records systems, and data bases.

Justin went inside, following the wide corridor. All of the buildings he had seen lacked windows, and that, combined with the dome looming overhead, gave him a vague touch of claustrophobia. The artificial lighting was pale after the brightness of the sun. The building was made of old white terraplastic – the kind colonists brought with them to form temporary

12

structures until they could build from the planet's natural materials. Wood and stone were not scarce commodities on Bountiful, yet it was almost as if the original colonists had been afraid to use anything native.

He pulled open the door to the meeting room. It was done in white. Chairs lined the windowless walls, and four long, white tables were set up in a square. Three people sat at the edge of the table nearest the door, beside a small, old-fashioned holojector unit that pointed at a blank wall.

Justin recognized the faces from the materials Netta had given him in his apartment. Davis, a thin, wiry man, led the laboratory team. Sanders, head of the medical unit, had hands half the size of Justin's. He stared at her, wondering how someone so petite could spend her time shifting through the clues left in a dead body. And of course, Netta. Her hair was dark, her skin bronzed by Bountiful's sun. Netta had brought them all to brief Justin. The only person missing was the head of colony security.

The cool air in the meeting room smelled of metallic processing. Justin walked to the chair that Netta had pulled back for him. He swallowed hard, ignoring the aches in his body. The walk had been longer than he expected, and he really wanted a rest before submerging himself in the problems of the colony. Despite the reflective cream and clothing, his skin had turned a blotchy red. His scalp itched. Little raised bumps had formed beneath his hair. He was afraid to touch them, afraid they might burst.

'Thank you for coming,' Netta said. 'I know you must be exhausted.'

He probably looked it. He sat in the chair. It and the table were made of the same hard plastic as the walls. The chair did not bend with his weight. This room had not been designed for comfort or beauty, and its plainness was more distracting than decorations would have been.

'I wanted to get started on this as quickly as I can,' he said. Because then it would be over quicker. Nothing about this job excited him. He didn't want to investigate alien motives for murdering children.

A small man, his hair greased back and his face darkened by the sun, entered. He dumped papers and holochips on the table in front of Netta.

13

'Thank you,' she said. She pushed her chair back and caught the small man by the arm. 'Justin, this is D. Marvin Tanner. He heads the security forces for this area. If you have any questions about the investigative work prior to this time, you should direct those questions to him.'

Tanner's gaze darted around the room, touching everyone but settling on no one. His hands shook as he moved. Justin frowned. Tanner had no reason to be nervous. He had worked with the others.

Unless he was afraid of Justin, or something Justin would uncover.

'Most of what I will tell you is in your packet, for your own personal review later,' Netta said. 'But let me give you a general briefing now before we show the holos.' She let go of Tanner's arm and he sat down next to Justin. Tanner smelled of sweat, and something sweet, almost like pot fumes, but marijuana could not be grown in this soil. Besides, he was the head of security. He should eschew the available vices.

'They found the first victim less than three weeks ago,' Netta said. 'Linette Bisson was eleven years old. She had been propped against the front door of her home like a rag doll. Someone had removed her hands, heart and lungs.

'The next victim, David Tomlinson, appeared a day later. Same MO. Three more children – Katie Dengler, Andrew Liser, and Henry Illn – were found during the last two weeks. Again, the same MO. These children all played together; they were the same age. And, according to their parents, none of the last three were terribly frightened by the deaths of their friends.'

She paused and glanced at Justin, looking for a reaction. He had none. Most people didn't realize that children often had no concept of death and the things they feared were not the things adults feared. He was not surprised that the children were not affected. They might not understand.

'The Dancers mature differently than we do,' Sanders said. Her voice was soft and as delicate as she was. 'They do grow a little, but their hearts, lungs and hands work like our teeth. The old ones must be removed before the new ones can grow into place. They have developed an elaborate rite of passage that ends with the ceremonial removal of the adolescent's organs.'

Justin leaned back. The hard plastic of the chair bit into his

14

skin. He felt out of his depth. He needed to know Dancer physiology, psychology and history. He turned to Netta. 'You said the Dancers interacted with the colonists.'

She nodded. 'For decades, we've had an informal relationship. They develop the herbs we use in our exports. We haven't had any trouble, until now.'

'And the Dancers were allowed inside the dome?'

'We restricted them when the killings started, and now they're not allowed in at all.'

'We also set up dome guards,' Tanner said. As he moved, his body odour became overpowering. 'The dome doors have no locks and can be operated from the inside or the outside. We had done that as a precaution so no colonist would die trapped outside the dome.'

Colonists. Colony. The word choices bothered Justin. The language was evolving differently than he would have expected. The 'colony' had been settled for nearly a century. Gradually it should have eased into 'city' or 'settlement'. The domed area had no name, and even people like Tanner, who had lived in Bountiful their entire lives, felt no sense of permanence.

'We have some holos we'd like to show you,' Tanner said. He got up, and pulled the chips from the pile he brought in. Justin held his breath as the breeze from Tanner's movements swept over him. He adjusted the holojecter at the edge of the table. He moved chairs away from the wall, leaving a wide, blank space. He pressed the switch, and a holo leaped into being.

Laughter filled the room, children's laughter. Twelve children huddled on the floor, playing a game Justin did not recognize. The children all appeared the same age, except for one, who sat off to one side and watched. He appeared to be about eight. The older children would pound their fists on the ground three times, then touch hands. One child would moan or roll away. The others would laugh.

Tanner froze the image. 'These are the children,' he said. He moved near the images, stopping by a slim, blonde girl whose face was bright with laughter. 'Linette Bisson.' Then he moved to a solid boy with rugged features who was leaning forward, his hand in a small fist. 'David Tomlinson.'

Tanner moved to the next child, his body visible through the

15

holos in front of him. Justin shivered. Seeing the living Tanner move through the projected bodies of dead children raised the hackles on the back of Justin's neck. Superstition, racial memory . . . His ancestors had believed in ghosts.

So did he. Eager Minaran ghosts.

Tanner looked at a dark-haired girl who frowned at the little boy, sitting alone. 'Katie Dengler. Beside her, Andrew Liser and Henry Illn.' The boys were rolling on the ground, holding their stomachs. Their mirth would have been catching if Justin hadn't known the circumstances of their deaths.

Tanner went back to the holojecter.

'Who are the other children?' Justin asked. At least eight were not accounted for.

'You'll meet them,' Netta said. 'They still run together.'

He nodded, and watched. Tanner switched images, and the projection moved again. The children's clothing changed. They wore scarves and reflective cream. A middle-aged woman with sun-black skin stood beside them. 'Do as I say,' she said. 'Nothing more.' They turned their backs to the room, and walked past trees and houses until the dome appeared. The woman flicked a switch, and the dome rose. The children waved, and the dome closed behind them. The younger boy ran into the picture, but an adult suddenly appeared and stopped him.

Tanner froze the image. Justin stared at the boy, seeing the dejection in his shoulders. Justin had stood like that so many times since Minar, watching his colleagues move to other projects while he had to stay behind. He pushed himself back just a little. He had to stay impartial on this one. He couldn't let himself get involved personally.

'We think this is the first time the Dancers met with the children,' Tanner said.

'Who is that boy?' Justin asked.

'Katie Dengler's brother, Michael.'

'And the woman?'

'Latona Etanl. She's a member of the Extra-Species Alliance.' Netta answered that question. Her voice dripped with bitterness. 'She believed that having the children learn about the Dancers would ease relations between us.'

Justin glanced at her. 'There have been problems?'

16

'No. The Alliance believes that we are abusing the Dancers because we do not understand their culture.' Netta leaned back in her chair, but her body remained tense. 'I thought we had a strong cooperative relationship until she tried to change things.'

Justin frowned. The Alliance was a small, independent group with bases on all the settled planets. Theoretically, the Alliance was supposed to promote understanding between the colonists and the natives. In some areas, Alliance members spent so much time with the natives that they absorbed and practised native beliefs. On those lands the Alliance became a champion for the downtrodden native. In other lands, the group assisted the colonists in systematically destroying native culture. And sometimes the group actually fulfilled its mission. The Alliance representatives he had known were as varied as the planets they worked on.

'How long ago was this holo taken?' Justin asked.

'Almost a year ago,' Tanner said. But the children weren't as taken with the Dancers as Latona thought they would be. I believe that was the only visit.'

'What has changed since then? What has provoked the Dancers?'

Netta glanced at Tanner. She sighed. 'We want to take control of the xaredon, leredon, and ededon plants.'

The basis of Salt Juice, the colonists' chief export. Salt Juice was one of the most exhilarating intoxicants discovered in recent history. It mixed quickly with the bloodstream, left the user euphoric, and had no known side effects according to the initial tests: no hangovers, no hallucinations, no addictions and no dangerous physical reactions. Justin had read in the most recent literature that Salt Juice's harmlessness was being questioned, but those studies were years from completion. For the time being Salt Juice brought a small fortune into Bountiful. 'I didn't know the Dancers controlled the herbs,' Justin said.

'They grow the herbs and give us the adult plants. We've been trying to get them to teach us to grow the plants, but they refuse.' Netta shook her head. 'I don't know why, either. We don't pay them. We don't give them anything for their help. They wouldn't lose anything by teaching us.'

'And the negotiations broke off?'

'About a week before the first death.' The deep voice

17

surprised Justin. It belonged to Davis. Justin had forgotten he was there.

'Let me show the final image,' Tanner said. 'It's of the first death. You can see the others if you want in the viewing library. This one begins the pattern carried through on the rest.'

Justin licked his lips. He didn't want to see, but he couldn't say that. He had no options. They had bought his contract and he had to make a ruling in this case.

A ruling meant he had to study all the parts, including the murders.

Tanner clicked the image. The scene was grim. Linette, her hair longer and sun-blonde, her skin darker than it had been in the first projection, leaned against one of the windowless, inlay doors. Her feet stretched in front of her; her arms rested at her sides. Her chest was open, dark, and matted with blood. Tanner froze the projection, and this time Justin got up, examining the holo from all sides. The stumps at the end of her arms were blood-covered. Her clothing was also bloodstained, but that could have been caused by her bleeding arms. Blood did coat the chest cavity, though. Whoever had killed her had acted quickly. The girl's eyes were wide and had an inquisitive expression. Her mouth was drawn in a slight O of surprise or pain.

'The wounds match the wounds made by Dancer ceremonial tools,' Davis said. 'I can show you more down in the lab if you want.'

Justin nodded, feeling sick. 'Please shut that off.'

Tanner flicked a switch and the image disappeared. Five children, dead and mutilated. Justin had to get out of the room. He had received too much information, had seen too much. His stomach threatened to betray him. The others stared.

'This packet and the facts you've given so far should be enough for me to get started,' he said. He stood and clutched the chair for support. The plastic was cool beneath his palms. 'I'm sure that I will return with questions.'

He let himself out of the room and took a deep breath. The image of the child remained at the edge of his brain, mingling with that of other dead colonists on a world ten years away.

He heard rustling inside the conference room, and knew he had to be gone before the others emerged. He hurried through the dimly-lit corridor. Sunlight glared through the cracks

18

around the outside door. He stopped and examined the almost inch-wide space between the door and its frame, forcing himself to think about things other than holographic images. Clearly the people who lived inside the dome had no fear of the elements or of each other. Anyone, or anything, could open that door by wedging something inside the crack.

He felt better outside the room. The people inside made him nervous. They had discovered what they could through instruments and measures and other 'scientific' things. He had to crawl inside alien minds and see what had caused such murders. If the colonists had suspected a human killer, they would have brought in any one of a dozen other specialists. Instead, they brought him.

He had to see the Dancers clearly, without dead Minarans clouding his vision. If the Dancers killed with malicious intent, the colony had to be protected or moved. He would simply approach things differently this time. Instead of going to the leaders of the colony, he would go to Lina Base Security, and appeal to the territorial powers. That might prevent slaughter. The dancers, with their small population, were easier prey than the Minarans.

He stepped outside and blinked at the blue-tinted light. The dome filtered the sunlight, deflecting the dangerous ultraviolet rays, and allowing only a modicum of heat inside. Roses grew beside the door, and young maples lined the walks. Patches of grass peeked through, hidden by bushes and other flowering plants. The care that the colonists had not placed in their homes, they had placed in making the interior of the dome look like Earth. It felt odd to stand there, among familiar trees and lush vegetation, and to know that just outside the dome, a different, alien world waited.

But beneath the scents of roses and fresh grass, another lurked. That sickly sweet odour he had noticed on Tanner. Perhaps it was the scent of this part of Bountiful. Perhaps it belonged to something in the colony that he couldn't yet identify. Whatever it was, it would bother him until he found out.

He crouched beside the roses. No odd fertilizers, nothing here that obviously created the smell. He put his hand in the brown soil. Perhaps it was less alkaline that the salt cliffs had led him to believe. Or perhaps the colonists had imported the soil, as they had imported everything else. He saw no reason to live in a new place if he were going to try so hard to make it look like the place he had left. That attitude was a difference between Justin and the colonists. He would collect thousands of differences before he was through. The problem was whether thousands were enough – or if they meant anything at all. The differences he had to concentrate on were the differences between human and Dancer thought. Something that should have taken a lifetime of study, he would have to discover in a few days.

iii

That night he dreamed of the Minarans. Their sleek seal bodies dripped with water. They hovered around him, oversized eyes reproachful, as if they were trying to warn him of something he would never understand. They reached out to touch him, and he slapped their fingered fins away. Shudders ran through him. They had caused the murders. But if he told the colonists, they would slaughter the Minarans – the fat mothers, the tiny males, and the white pups that, not much earlier, the children had watched as if they were pets. Minaran blood was colourless but thick. It still coated his hands, leaving them sticky and useless.

Justin blinked himself awake. A fan whirred in the darkness; the blanket covering him was scratchy and too hot. He coughed, and tasted metallic air in the back of his throat. The one bedroom apartment Netta had given him felt small and close.

He had done nothing right since the Minaran trial. He should have resigned from psychology, let his licenses lapse, and bought back his contract. He had had the money then. He wouldn't have had to serve out his time on Minar Base, the planet hovering in his viewscreen like an ugly reminder. Instead he stayed, wrote abstracts and papers, conducted studies, and worked with an intensity he hadn't known he had. His colleagues ignored him, and he tried to ignore himself. Just before she left him, Carol accused him of idolizing the Minarans. She said that he hid in his work, that he had buried his emotions in the search for the cause of his own flaws. Perhaps he had idolized the Minarans. He certainly had stored his emotions far from himself. But he knew the cause of his own flaws. He didn't hide in his work. He liked to think he was atoning.

He rolled over. The sheets were cool on the far side of the bed. Maybe his sense of guilt allowed him to let his contract safeguards lapse so that someone like Netta could buy his services for the next year. The darkness closed around him. When he shut his eyes, he saw the Minarans.

He could, he supposed, cancel the contract and head to Lina base for re-education, never to practise psychology again. But the work was all he had. Perhaps he was atoning. Or perhaps he simply hadn't learned . . .

iv

Justin rose early and drank his coffee outside, watching the colony wake up. He sat on the stoop of the apartment building, looking over some sort of evergreen bush at the street beyond. All of the houses had the same design; a single-storey rectangular shape, with a door in the centre, and no windows at all. They were evenly spaced on square lots. Only the plants out front marked the difference in care and ownership.

The apartment building was square also, but had a second storey. The apartments were clearly for guests. He had heard no one in the building during the night, and no one had passed him on the way to work.

The streets were full, however. Adults carrying satchels and briefcases walked by, chatting. Others wore work clothes and carried nothing. A few wore sand scarves and helped each other apply reflective cream. They all seemed quite joyful. Laughing, joking, giggling. He had never seen people so happy to go to their jobs. Work seemed to start at the same time. He would have wagered that the workday ended at the same time too.

They didn't need split shifts. Most of the workers processed and shipped Salt Juice. The rest maintained the stores on the south end of the colony or worked in Command Central. They all seemed quite self-sufficient – not surprising, considering their heritage. They had gardens and rarely ordered much beyond staples from Lina Base.

He stood, and went inside. The apartment didn't seem as tiny

21

as it had the night before. The living room had a couch and two easy chairs, upholstered in green and obviously shipped in from Lina Base, a desk with a computer set-up and one wall converted into a 2-D screen, with disks and holochips stored in shelves on the sides. The apartments had been designed for traders who came to deal in Salt Juice. They were obviously given the best the colony had to offer.

The tiny kitchen had water purifiers, air cleaners, and an ancient compressor cooker. Cheap paintings, reproductions from works he had seen on Minar and Lina Bases, covered the white plastic walls. He would have preferred windows.

He put his mug in the air cleaner. Then he went back out. The last of the stragglers had gone up the street, and in the near silence, he heard a squeal of laughter, followed by a child's voice. He followed the sound. It didn't seem too far away. The laughter came again and again, guiding him to it. He walked in the opposite direction of the workers, past terraplastic homes with no windows, large gardens that passed for lawns, and fences dividing property. The fences caught his attention: another need to mark property, or did the colonists feel the need to block each other out?

The laughter grew closer. He turned and saw a small corner park, marked off by a waist-high white gate, and three weeping willows. Flowers grew like vines along the gate and, inside, on the grass, about ten children sat in a circle, playing the game they had played on the holo.

One child stood back, leaning on the plastic gate. He was tall for his age – the gate came to his chest – but the longing expression on his face made him seem even younger than he was. Justin wondered if his own face used to look like that on nights after the Minaran trial, when he passed his colleagues in the middle of a heated round table discussion. He suppressed a sigh and stood beside the boy. It took a moment to recall his name. Michael Dengler.

'What are they playing?'

He glanced at Justin, seemingly surprised that someone would talk to him. ''Race.'

The children pounded their fists on the ground three times, then made different hand gestures. They laughed. The muscles bulged in their arms. They had to be in some kind of exercise

22

program. The girl rolled away, stood up, arched her back, and growled. 'Limabog!' 'Arachni!' 'Cat!' 'Illnea!' the children called. At each name the girl shook her head. Finally someone yelled, 'Bear!' She nodded, joined the circle again, and the fist pounding started all over.

'How do you play?' Justin asked.

Michael's frown grew until his entire face turned blood-red. 'I don't,' he said.

The hair on the back of Justin's neck prickled, and for a moment, he heard the hushed whispers of former friends gossiping about his failures. He swallowed, determined to distance himself from the boy. 'Don't you play with friends your own age?'

Michael stopped leaning on the gate. 'You're one of the strangers here for the Salt Juice, aren't you?'

Justin gave a half-nod, not bothering to correct Michael's misconception.

'You got kids?'

'No.'

Michael shrugged. 'Then it stays the same. I'm the only kid my age. My mom and dad didn't follow the rules.'

The children burst into laughter and another child rolled away, this time approaching the group on all fours. Apparently this colony still followed the practice of having children in certain age groups, then spacing the next group at least four years away. It was a survival tactic for many new colonies.

'So you want to play with the older kids,' Justin said.

'Yeah.'

Justin could hear the wistfulness in the boy's voice. He watched from outside; Justin had written papers about other people's work.

Michael glanced at the children, his hands clenching. 'They won't let me play until I grow and learn to think like a big kid. Mom says they should take me for who I am.' He looked at Justin, mouth set in a thin line. 'What do you think?'

Such an easy question, asked of the wrong person. Justin had always thought for himself, and it had gained him respect and a following – until Minar. After that, he stood at the edge of the round table discussions instead of leading them, waiting for someone to pull back a chair and let him in. If he had said he was sorry, opened himself up for dissection, perhaps he wouldn't have been standing friendless in an unfamiliar colony.

'In an ideal world, your mom is right,' Justin said. 'But sometimes you have to do what the group wants if you're going to be accepted.'

Michael crossed his arms in front of his chest, his fists still clenched. His body language made his thoughts clear: he didn't want to believe. Justin turned away. Once he would have felt the same, but things had changed. Standing outside the group, watching, was more painful than playing inside.

'Could you explain the game to me?' Justin asked.

'No!' Michael spun, and started down the pathway. 'Maybe they will. They talk to grown-ups.'

He ran away. Justin almost started after him, then let him go. The boy had reached Justin because Justin saw a similarity between them. Michael didn't have a lot to do with the investigation.

The children laughed as if they hadn't noticed Michael's outburst. Justin took Michael's place at the gate and watched, to see if he could learn the game from observation before he tried to talk with the children.

v

By midday, the dome filter had changed, giving the colony a sepia tone. The children had refused to talk, running when Justin approached. He would have to get Netta to arrange a time for him to talk with them. Then he walked to the office of the Extra-Species Alliance, hoping to talk with Latona Etanl.

The office was clearly marked, one of the few buildings with any identification at all. Tulips and lilies of the valley blossomed across the yard, and two maple trees shaded the pathway. The office building itself was made of terraplastic, but it seemed larger, perhaps because of the windows beside the door.

Justin mounted the stoop and saw, through the window, a woman get up from her desk. The door swung open, and he found himself staring at the woman from the holos. He recognized her sun-blackened face. It took him a moment to realize she wasn't wearing a sand scarf. Her long black hair went

24

down to her knees and wrapped around her like a second skin.

'Ms Etanl,' he said, I'm – '

'You're Dr Schafer. I've been waiting for you.' She stood away from the door, and he stepped inside.

The room had the rich, potent aroma of lilies of the valley. A bunch of flowers were gathered in a vase by the window and other vases rested on end tables beside the wide couch and easy chairs that filled the rest of the space. A hallway opened beyond the desk, leading to other, smaller rooms. The sepia-coloured light shining through the windows made the outdoors muddy and the interior even brighter than it should have been.

'Your offices are lovely,' he said to cover his surprise at her greeting.

'We like to have pleasant surroundings,' she said, and he thought he heard a kind of condemnation in her voice. 'Care for a seat?'

She moved over to one of the easy chairs and waited for him to follow. He sat on the couch, sinking into the soft cushions. She sat down at the edge of her seat, looking as if she were going to spring up at a moment's notice.

'Ms Etanl – '

'Latona.'

'Latona. I'm surprised you knew who I was.'

'The colony's small. And Netta told us you would come.' She adjusted her hair over her legs as if it were a skirt. 'She blames me for taking the children out of the colony. She thinks I started the Dancers on this.'

Latona hadn't looked at him. 'What do you think?' he asked.

She shook her head. 'I don't think the Dancers are capable of such killings.'

'From my understanding,' he said slowly, 'Dancers don't kill their young. They perform mutilations to help adolescents reach maturity. Could something have happened in the one meeting that would have made the Dancers try to help human children?'

She finally looked at him. Her eyes were wide and black, the colour of her hair. 'You haven't seen the Dancers yet, have you?'

He shook his head.

'You need to. And then you can ask me questions.' She took a deep breath, as if hesitating about what she was about to say. 'I'll take you if you like.'

'Now?'

She nodded. 'We have protective gear in the back.'

His heart thudded against his chest. He hadn't expected to see the Dancers yet, but he was ready. A little thrill ran down his spine.

They got up and she led him down the hall to one of the back offices. As she walked past an open office door, she peeked inside. A man sat behind a desk, his bald head bowed over a small computer screen. 'Daniel, I'm taking Dr Schafer to see the Dancers.'

Daniel glanced up. He was younger than he had originally appeared – about thirty or so. 'Would you like a second?'

She shook her head. 'Not unless he thinks we need one.'

She was asking a question without directing it at Justin. He shook his head. 'If she thinks the two of us will be fine, I'm not going to second-guess her.'

Daniel smiled, showing a row of very white teeth. 'Latona is our best. She's studied the Dancers her entire life.'

Latona had already started down the hall. Justin nodded at Daniel, then followed her. The room she entered was the size of a small closet. She flicked on a light and pulled two sand scarves from pegs. She took out a jar of reflective cream and handed it to Justin. He applied it. The goo was cold against his fae, and smelled faintly sweet. Then he wrapped the sand scarf around himself, and waited as Latona did the same. She tied a small pack to her waist. Finally she pulled two pairs of sunglasses out of a drawer and handed him one pair.

'Put these on after we leave the dome,' she said.

They left through a door on the back side. The sepia tone of the dome seemed to have grown darker. Latona led him across the yard along an empty pathway until they reached the dome. Two men stood beside the structure, looking bored. Latona nodded at them.

'I'm taking Dr Schafer to see the Dancers.'

'Netta permit this?' one of the men asked.

Latona sighed. 'She doesn't have to. Dr Schafer is off-world.'

The man looked as if he were about to say more, but his partner grabbed his arm. He pushed a button and the dome door slid open. Dry heat seeped in, making the air inside the dome feel as plastic as the buildings. Justin followed Latona outside and heard the doors squeak closed behind them.

Sunlight reflected off the white cream on his face, momentarily blinding him. The wind rustled his sand scarf. He already felt overdressed. The air smelled of salt, daffodils and promises.

Latona tugged her hood over her face and headed into the wind. He bent and followed, wishing he could see more of the desert. But the wind was strong and blew the sand at a dangerous rate. He put on the glasses, thankful for the way they eased the glare.

'Netta hates it when I visit the Dancers,' Latona said, 'but she can't stop me. I'm not officially a colony member. Neither are you.'

'Why did you bring the children out here?' The sand was deep and thick, and he was having trouble walking. There were plants on either side, half-covered in white sand.

Latona followed no visible trail. She headed away from the dome, away from the landing pad. If he squinted and looked ahead, he saw a dark shape outlined against the horizon. 'There are a lot of creatures here the colonists ignore. Little sand devils that burrow tunnels below the surface, birds with helicopterlike wings, and insects. Daniel is studying the birds to see if they're intelligent. Micah, one of my other colleagues, has determined that the sand devils are not. But the Dancers are intelligent, in their own way.'

The sand became thin and packed, almost a mudlike surface. He glanced back. The dome was a small bubble in the distance.

'The early miners hated the Dancers and killed them. The killing stopped, though, when the colonists discovered Salt Juice.'

'This is history,' Justin said. 'I want to know about now.'

'I'm getting to now. The Dancers grow the herbs for Salt Juice and although the colonists have tried, they can't. So they need the Dancers as another intelligent species. The colonists take the plants without recompense, and the Dancers just grow more. I know some of the colonists think the children's deaths are retaliation.'

'What do you think?'

Latona shook her head. 'That's a human reaction. The Dancers are a different species. They have very alien thought

27

processes.'

The dark shape on the horizon had resolved itself into a grove of trees. They stood at the same height, and their tops were canopied, providing shade.

The wind had eased but his skin felt battered. He brought a hand up to his cheek and felt sand on the cream. Sweat ran down his back, and his throat was dry. 'You have water in the pack?'

Latona stopped, opened the pack, and handed him a small plastic bottle. He saw others lined in rows of six. He put the bottle to his lips and drank. The water was warm and flat, but the wetness felt good. He handed the bottle back to Latona, and she finished the water, putting the empty bottle into her pack.

'We're almost there,' she said. 'I want you to do what I tell you and nothing else. The Dancers will come when I call them, and will touch you. They're only trying to see what you are. Their fingers are more sensitive than their eyes.'

They stepped into a shadowy darkness, and it took him a moment to realize that they had reached the trees. They had dark, spindly trunks, wind-whipped and twisted. Sand caught in the ridges, making the trees look scarred. The tops of the trees unfolded like umbrellas, the rope-like leaves entangled and braided to form the canopy. Latona took her hood down, removed her glasses, and whistled.

Dark shapes approached. Justin let his hood down and pocketed his sunglasses. The creatures weren't walking, although they were upright. They almost glided along the hard-packed sand, and had long, twig-thin bodies with shiny black skin, two legs, two arms, and wide, oblong heads with large silver eyes. It was easy to see why the colonists had called them dancers; they moved with a fluid grace, as if they made every step in time to a music that Justin couldn't hear.

His heart pounded. The Dancers surrounded him and Latona, and touched them lightly. He clutched his hands into fists, fighting the feeling of being trapped. Latona held her head back, eyes closed, and Justin did the same. Fingers with skin like soft rubber touched his mouth, his nose, his eyelids. He didn't move. The Dancers smelled of cinnamon, and something tangy, something he couldn't identify. The bumps on his scalp burned as the Dancers touched them. He wanted to move his head

28

away, but he didn't.

He heard whistling and low hums. The sounds seemed to follow a pattern and felt, after a moment, as familiar as a bird's call. He opened his eyes. Latona had stepped away from the Dancers a little. She was gesturing and churring. One of the Dancers touched her face, and then whistled three times, in short bursts.

'He said they would be pleased to have you visit their homes.'

Justin pulled away from the Dancers. Even though they were no longer touching him, he could still feel their rubbery fingers against his skin. He glanced at Latona, and then at the Dancers again. They had no visible, recognizable sexual characteristics. He didn't know how she knew the speaker's gender. 'Thank him.'

She did. They walked with the single Dancer through the canopied trees. Justin's heartbeat slowed. He was growing calmer. If the Dancers were going to hurt him, they would have done so when they met at the edge of the forest. Perhaps. He was assigning human logic. He shook his head and tried to clear his mind.

The air grew cooler as they hit areas without sunlight. The white sand turned into dirt, and small plants grew beneath the trees. His eyes adjusted to the darkness, and he saw clothlike material stretched around trees like handmade tents. The Dancer continued talking, touching things as if he were giving a tour. Latona did not translate.

They followed him inside one of the tents. There the tangy cinnamon scent was stronger. Justin touched the tent material. It felt like waterproof canvas. Rugs made from leaves covered the ground, and in the corners sat glass jars that cast a phosphorescent glow around the room.

'He says he would like to welcome us to his home.'

'Tell him we're honoured.'

She responded and Justin examined the glass jars. They were crude. The glass had bubbles, ripples, and waves. The light inside moved as if it were caused by something living.

Their host whistled and churred. Latona watched Justin.

'What is he saying?' Justin asked.

She glanced at the Dancer as if she hadn't heard him. Then she smiled. 'Right now he's saying that if he were a good host, he would give you a jar, but the jars are valuable, too valuable to give a guest who will disappear before the day ends.'

'Tell him that I plan to return – '

She shook her head. 'It doesn't matter.' She slipped out of the tent. 'You need to see the rest of the homes.'

He followed her into the shaded darkness outside. 'Shouldn't you thank him?'

'No.' She led him toward more of the tentlike structures. Dancers emerged, hands reaching for the humans' faces. Latona ducked. Justin did too. He was a bit more at ease, but he didn't want them to touch him again.

From appearances, the Dancers seemed to be hunter-gatherers. The entire area lacked permanence. The ground was untended and wild with no signs of cultivation. But then, Justin didn't know what he was looking for. For all he knew, the canopied trees were an edible, renewable resource.

'This is it,' Latona said.

Justin stared at the tents, the scattered possessions. The Dancers huddled around him like shadows in the late afternoon sunlight. 'Which ones are the children?'

'The children live elsewhere. Let me ask permission to see them.' Latona turned to a Dancer beside her and spoke. The Dancer whistled and churred in response, gesturing at Justin. Latona nodded once, and then the Dancer walked forward. 'Come on,' Latona said.

Justin followed. The hard-packed mud curved inward, as if feet had worn a smooth path through the trees. There were no tents here, and the plants had grown waist-high, their foliage lush. Justin realized then that the land behind them had been tended, that the Dancers had done the opposite of the colonists. The Dancers removed vegetation except for the thin, spindly trees.

Sunlight broke through the overhead canopy. They reached a sun-mottled area where the undergrowth had again been thinned. There the canvas material had been tied to the trees sideways to form a fence. They approached the fence and stared over the edge. Inside, small dark creatures scrabbled in the dirt, tussling and fighting. Some sat off to the sides, leaning on the fence – sleeping, perhaps. Toward the back, larger children lay on the ground, their skin gray in the filtered sunlight. Their

30

fingers seemed claw-like, and their eyes were dark, empty and hollow.

Justin nodded toward the children. 'Are they ill?'

'No,' Latona said. 'They've hit puberty.'

'Do these children ever interact with adults?'

'Not really. The adults treat them like animals. Education into the life of a Dancer begins after puberty.'

Justin shivered a little, wondering at life that began in a cage under a harsh sun. The gray-skinned children did not move, but lay in the sunlight as if they were dead.

The Dancer churred and hovered over them. Justin glanced at it. Latona spoke briefly, then said, 'We have to leave.'

The Dancer corralled them, as if pushing them away from the children. Latona took Justin's arm and led him in a different direction. The Dancer watched from behind.

'This is a quicker way back to the dome,' she said. Some of the cream had melted off her face, making her appear lopsided and slightly alien.

The gray-skinned, sickly looking creatures with the clawed hands haunted Justin. 'You never told me why you brought the children here.'

'I wanted them to learn respect for the Dancers.' Latona kept her head down. They moved out of the trees.

'Why? The arrangement seemed to be working.'

'They're living beings,' Latona snapped. 'Humans have a history of mistreating beings they don't understand.'

'And you think the colonists are mistreating the Dancers?'

'Yes.' Latona pushed a ropy branch aside and stepped into a patch of sunlight. Her sand scarf glowed white. 'But I don't know what the Dancers think.'

'That's why the Alliance is here, to find out what the Dancers think?'

'And to negotiate an agreement over the Salt Juice herbs.'

Justin frowned. He stepped into the sun, and the heat prickled along his back. 'But there is no agreement.'

'You can't negotiate with the Dancers,' she said. 'They have an instinctual memory, and a memory for patterns that allows them to learn language and establish routines. Past events have no meaning for them, only future events that they hold in their minds. It poses an interesting problem: if we negotiate a treaty with them, the treaty will not exist because they will have forgotten it. If we plan to negotiate a treaty in the future, as their language and customs allow, the treaty will not exist because negotiations haven't started yet.'

'Their language has no past tense?'

'Not even a subtle past. They speak only in present and future tenses. They also have a very active subjunctive. Their lives are very fluid and very emotional.'

'And when one of them dies?'

'He ceases to be.' She glanced at Justin, her lips set in a thin line. 'And then they skin the body, eat the flesh, throw the bones to the children, and cure the skin. They stretch it and mount it until it becomes firm. And then they use it to form their tents.'

Justin shivered. 'What's in the jars?'

Netta shrugged. 'We don't know. They won't let us take any for study. Although they offer to, as they did with you.'

'Where did the jars come from?'

'The miners made them. The Dancers used to live closer to the salt cliffs.'

Justin's mind felt cold and information-heavy. Heat rose in waves from the sand. 'What did the children think of the Dancer children?'

Latona shrugged. She took out the cream and reapplied it. 'They seemed fascinated. Who knows what would have happened? But Netta banned any child contact with the Dancers.'

'Before the murders?'

'Yes.' Latona handed him the cream. 'I'm not supposed to bring them back.'

Justin nodded, done asking questions. He drank the water Latona offered, then looked across the desert. The dome seemed small and far away. He wrapped his scarf around his face and followed Latona, too tired to do anything other than walk.

vi

Latona promised to show Justin a time-lapsed holo of the Dancer puberty rite. He left the apartment the next morning, unable to comb his hair because some of the bumps had burst, leaking pus on his scalp. His skin, which had been a light red the night before, had eased into an even lighter tan. It would take many hours wearing reflective cream under the sun before his skin colour even approached that of Netta or Latona.

He had barely missed the morning work rush. He walked along the pathway, staring at the yards and the windowless plastic homes. These people made the most euphoric drug in the system, and they were stay-at-homes who created beautiful yards, but refused to look at their handiwork from inside the house.

The yards had different flowering plants from different climates and different seasons. Roses seemed to predominate, but some blocks preferred rhododendrons, while others had hyacinths. All of the flowers bloomed, too, the tulips with the pansies, the daisies with the sunflowers. It seemed odd that a colony with such botanical expertise could not learn to grow native herbs from seeds.

A movement caught his eye. He turned. The children stood outside a building. It was square, windowless and white, like the others, but smaller than any other building he had seen in the colony. There was only grass around it.

The children were talking seriously. Even though Justin couldn't hear the words, he recognized the tone: they were angry. A slender girl slashed her hand against the air, and a tall boy caught it, as if to deflect her argument. They moved just enough to let him see inside the circle: Michael Dengler stood there, looking tiny and confused. The girl gestured at him, and Michael shrugged.

Justin walked toward them. The tall boy looked at him and frowned. The children backed away, as if he were an enemy: then, as a group, they turned and ran.

Justin stopped and watched them go. Only one child glanced back as he ran. Michael Dengler. Justin waved. Michael didn't wave back.

Justin waited until they were out of sight, then walked to the building. He avoided the path and walked across the grass. It was spongy and poorly cared for, unlike the other plants in the area. He stopped outside the building, and stared at it.

A whir of motors came from inside. A single step went to the door, a small footprint in the centre of the plastic. Justin stepped around the print and tried the knob. The door opened easily, and a blast of cool air coated him.

Along with the smell. It was tangy and antiseptic. He recognized the smell from every morgue he had visited. Beneath the antiseptic odour was the faint scent of rot. A shiver ran down his back.

Dim fluorescent lights made everything in the room look gray. A white plastic table was the only furniture. Equipment rested beside the sink, and the walls were covered with huge cabinets. The room had originally been used for emergency cold sleep. Now it housed the dead.

He pulled open a drawer. The sound echoed in the small space. Katie Dengler lay there, her grotesque arms at her side. Someone had wrapped rope leaves loosely around her torso, but through them, he could still see her bloody chest laid open, a hole where her heart should have been. His gorge rose. He made himself swallow as he closed the drawer.

The children had had no place here. Yet nothing appeared to be off-limits to them. Nothing except the Dancers.

Suddenly he wanted out of the building. He left and drank in the processed air of the dome as if it were fresh. Odd that they hadn't buried the bodies yet. But this colony was still following initial settlement procedures. Such procedures called for cremation instead of burial – a precaution because the ashes to ashes, dust to dust philosophy of putting a body into the ground might not work in an alien environment. The bodies were to be kept in cold storage until the investigation was complete.

He shuddered. It was one thing to see holos. It was another to look at the body. The girl had been alive once. Michael's sister. Someone who tormented him and played with him, and probably loved him. Justin frowned. Michael had been very concerned about his status with the other children, but he hadn't exhibited any of the signs of a grieving child. No circles under his eyes, no signs of recent nervous habits. Latona had been right. The children seemed to have no understanding of death. Perhaps the argument outside the morgue was the beginning of that understanding.

Justin smoothed his hair and patted his clothes, as if the movement would wipe the stench of the morgue from him. He made himself walk the remaining few blocks to the offices of the Extra-Species Alliance.

A woman sat at the desk. She was petite, with close-cropped hair and wide eyes. 'Latona couldn't be here,' she said, 'but she told me to show you the holo, and she said she'd answer any of your questions this afternoon.'

Justin nodded, feeling relieved. If Latona had been there, he would have had to ask her about the burial customs and her suppositions about the children. He was glad that the opportunity slipped by him. He wanted the experience to be private for the moment.

He followed the woman into another closet-sized room with a holojecter set up. She flicked on the jecter, flicked off the lights, and left him.

Dancers filled the room, less frightening without their tangy cinnamon scent. They circled around a gray-skinned child, huddled on the desert floor. The circling seemed to last forever, then a Dancer grabbed a ceremonial knife and slit open the breastbone, reached in and removed something small, blackened and round. Probably the heart. The Dancer handed the black object to another Dancer who set it in a jar. Then the Dancer slit again, removing two thin, shrivelled bits of flesh from the child's interior. The child didn't move. Another Dancer put the flesh into a jar beside the heart. Finally the first Dancer lifted the child's hands by a single finger and sliced once along the wrists. The hands fell off, and the child's arms fell to its side. The Dancers carried the child to a tree and leaned the child against it. They wrapped the child's chest with rope leaves and as they placed the arms on the child's lap, he could see small fingers peeking out of the hollow wrists like human hands hidden in the sleeves of a jacket one size too big.

The Dancer child did not bleed. Latona's comparison to a human child losing its baby teeth was an apt one.

Justin sighed. At the end of Katie's arms were stumps and bits of bone. No fingers hidden in her wrists, waiting to replace that childish version of her hands. Hadn't the Dancers been able to see that? Or didn't they understand? He had trouble comprehending a mind with no conception of the past.

He made himself focus on the holo. The time-lapse was becoming clear. The child's hands grew; its skin grew dark like

35

that of the other Dancers. Gradually, it moved on its own, and the adult Dancers helped it crawl to a nearby tent. Then the holo ended.

He replayed it three times, memorizing each action, and confirming that there had been no blood.

Things weren't adding up: things Latona had said, things he had seen. He shut off the jecter and left the room, thankful that the woman was not at the front desk. He needed to read his briefing packet to see if the information in there differed from the information Latona had given him about the Dancers.

He hurried back to his apartment and sat in the front room, reading. Latona was right. The Dancers showed no ability to remember things from visit to visit or even within visits. During the murders by the miners, the Dancers returned to the sites of the deaths and continued to interact with the miners as if nothing had happened. They never tried retaliation, and they never mutilated any of the miners.

Dancer preadolescents were gray and motionless, looking more dead than alive. The human children Latona had taken to the Dancers were fluid and energetic, as lively as the little creatures he had seen scrabbling in the dirt.

He set aside the packet, not liking what he was thinking. The Dancers were a protected species, so they could not be killed or relocated without interference from Lina Base. The colonists were great botanists and had been trying for years to learn the way to grow the Salt Juice herbs. The Dancers were impossible to negotiate with, and they guarded the seed jealously. What if a colonist figured out how to grow an herb from seed? The Dancers were no longer necessary; were, in fact, a hindrance. The murders allowed Lina Base to send in one expert instead of a gaggle of people – and also put the expert on a strict timetable. Netta had requested an expert with a flawed background, known for his rash judgments. Justin's impetuous decision-making had led one colony to spray an alkaline solution in an acidic ocean filled with intelligent life. Perhaps this colony wanted him to make another bad decision, and they would use that as an excuse to murder the Dancers.

He leaned his head on the back of the chair. He had no evidence supporting his theory, had only suspicions as he had with the Minarans. He stood up. He had to go to Command

Central and send for more help. He could not make this decision alone.

vii

A knock on the door startled him out of a sound sleep. He was lying on the packet on the couch in the apartment's front room. The knock echoed again. It souded loud in the nearly empty room. Before he could respond, the door eased open and spread a wide patch of yellow light across the floor.

'Dr Schafer?'

He squinted and sat up, reaching for a light. As the lights came on, he closed his eyes, wincing even more. 'Yes?'

'We have another one.'

He blinked. His eyes finally adjusted to the brightness. D. Marvin Tanner, the head of the dome's security, stood in the doorway. He seemed calm, except for the odd shaking Justin had noted before.

'Another one?'

'Yes,' he said. 'Netta sent me to get you. We have another dead child.'

That sickly sweet odour he carried with him like perfume filled the air. His flat tone sent a shiver down Justin's back. The security officer on Minar had come to him in the middle of the night, hands shaking, mouth set in a rigid line. His voice would crack as he spoke of the dead and his own feelings of helplessness. Tanner didn't seem to care. Perhaps that was because this was no longer his investigation. Or perhaps he was one of those borderline psychopaths himself, the kind that went into law enforcement because it provided them with a legal way of abusing others.

Justin frowned, swallowing hard. That smell had got into his mouth. He could taste the half-burnt scent. He rubbed a hand over his face before something else hit him: Tanner should not have been able to get into the apartment. Netta had assured Justin he had the only key.

'What happened?' he asked.

'You'll be able to see,' Tanner said. 'No one is allowed to work the scene until the entire team has been assembled.'

37

Justin got up and followed Tanner outside. The dome filter had changed again, this time to one that left everything looking gray and grainy, probably the colony's equivalent of dawn. Shadows seemed darker, and the dome filter leached the colour from the plants. Only the white plastic was unchanged, but startling for the contrast against the physical environment.

People had stepped to the edges of their gardens and were watching the men pass. The street seemed unusually quiet. Justin waited for someone to say something or to follow them. No one did. The people stared as if Justin and Tanner were a two-man funeral procession and everyone else were distant relatives, there only for the reading of the will.

Justin and Tanner turned the corner and arrived at the murder scene. A dozen people stood in a half-circle on the cultivated lawn. Netta and Saunders crouched near the door. Justin pushed through the people and walked up the sidewalk.

'Netta?'

She turned, saw him, and moved out of the way. This body was headless. Justin stared for a moment at the gap where the head should have been, noting as calmly as he could that no blood stained the white plastic door. This child was smaller than the others. Its chest had been opened, and its hands severed.

'You need to see this, too, Justin.' She walked down the steps and rounded the building. He followed. There, in between two spindly rose-bushes, the head rested. He stared at it, feeling hollow, noting other details while his stomach turned. Michael Dengler's empty eyes stared back at Justin. His mouth was caught in a cry of pain. His severed hands were crossed in front of his chin, but Justin couldn't see his heart or his lungs.

The last time Justin had seen him, he had been running with the other children. Justin crouched down beside him, wanting to touch his face, to soothe him, to offer to take his place. Justin's life was empty. Michael's had just begun.

'Michael Dengler.' Netta's voice startled Justin. He took a deep breath. 'His sister, Katie, was one of the earlier victims. His mother is over there.'

A woman stood at the very edge of the semi-circle, her hands clutched to her chest. The silence was unnerving. Justin could hear himself breathe. The rose scent was cloying. He turned back to Michael and thought, for a moment, he was staring at himself.

'This is the first time we have ever found the missing body parts. We have to confirm, of course, that the hands are his, but they look small enough,' Netta said.

Justin made himself concentrate on Netta's words. Michael Dengler was dead. Justin was part of the investigative team. He had to remain calm.

'I need a light,' he said. Someone came up behind him and gave him a handlight. He cupped his hand around the metal surface and flicked the switch, running the light around the head. The boy was pale, the pale of a human body that had never ever tanned. 'How old was he?'

'Eight.'

Eight. Too young for puberty, even on the outside edges of human physiology. If he had been female, maybe. But even that was doubtful. This was a little boy, a child, with no traces of adulthood – and no possibilities for it. *Mom says they should take me for who I am*, he had said. *What do you think*?

Professional, Justin reminded himself. He had to be professional. He took a deep breath, stood up, and dusted his knees.

'Someone needs to talk with the mother,' Netta said. 'I think you're the best choice.'

Justin's heart froze. He didn't want to deal with someone else's emotions. He wanted to go back to the apartment, close the door, and cry for the little boy who had lost everything. Justin didn't want to talk with the mother, even if he was the best choice because he had been trained in a helping profession. Helping. He made a small, quiet sound. He had never been able to help himself. How could he help a woman who had lost two children by murder in less than a month?

'Go on,' Netta said. Her words had the effect of a strong push. His movements were jerky as he walked over to Michael's mother.

She was half Justin's height, in her early thirties, her eyes dark and haunted. 'Ma'am,' Justin said. 'I'm Dr Schafer.'

'He's beyond doctors now.' Her voice sounded rusty, as if she hadn't used it for a long time. She smelled pungently of sweat – not the healthy kind, but the kind that appeared when the body was under great stress.

'Yes, he is, but you're not. Let me talk with you for a moment.'

39

'Talk?' The word seemed to snap something inside her. 'We talked the last time, and talked and talked. I have two more babies, and I want to leave this place. I wanted to leave before, with those crazy aliens out there, killing and killing. You want my whole family to die?'

Her words echoed in the stillness. He didn't want anyone to die, especially her son. She pushed away and walked to the edge of the steps, staring at what remained of Michael. Justin watched her for a moment, and could think of nothing to say to comfort her. He wasn't even sure she needed comforting. There was something reassuringly human about her pain.

He was the one who needed to remain calm. His hands were shaking and the back of his throat was dry. He had missed something in the shock of Michael's death. Something was not making sense. He went to Davis, who was examining the ground near the rosebushes. 'Leave the weapon this time?' Justin asked. The killer had, each time in the past, removed the body parts and left the weapon, a thin, flensing knife chipped from native rock. Davis pointed. The knife sat on the other side of the bush, away from Michael's head.

'It's smaller than I thought,' Justin said.

'But powerful.' Davis leaned over. 'See the edge? It's firm. Anyone could use this knife. If the victim is unconscious, the killer doesn't need much strength.'

'Not even to cut through bone?' Justin shuddered, thinking of Michael screaming as the knife sliced his skin.

Davis shook his head. 'It's a Dancer knife. They do this stuff all the time. We've had people cut themselves in the lab, losing fingers, just handling the things.'

Justin's odd feeling remained. He glanced around. The houses were close together, the lawns well tended. How could a Dancer sneak in here, steal a child, and return it in such a grisly condition without anyone seeing? How could a Dancer get past the dome guards?

He stood up and took a deep breath. He had to get away from the roses. Their rich scent was making him dizzy. And he hated the silence. He pushed past the semi-circle of people to the street and glanced once more at the scene in front of him.

Poor little Michael Dengler. He had wanted so much to grow

up, to be part of the group. Justin shook his head. At least he had been able to be with them that one last time. At least he had got part of his wish.

viii

He leaned against the desk at the office of the Extra-Species Alliance. The cool plastic bit into his palms. Latona stood in front of him, her arms crossed in front of her chest. She had contacted him as soon as she heard about Michael Dengler's death.

'Dancers do not behead their children,' she said. 'I can show you document after document, holo after holo. It's not part of the ritual. A beheading would kill the child. Someone is killing them. Someone human.'

A chill ran down Justin's back. She had come to the same conclusion he had. 'But the other children died. Perhaps the Dancers thought that the beheadings might work?'

Latona shook her head. 'They don't learn as we do. They think instinctively, perform rituals. Beings with rituals and no memory would not experiment. That's not within their capability.'

'But couldn't they modify – '

'No.' Latona leaned toward him. 'Dr Schafer, they remove the lungs and the heart to make way for larger organs. They remove the hands to make for sexually mature genitals. They mate with their hands. The head remains – their heads are like ours, the centre of their being. They can't live without the head, and the Dancers do not kill each other. They never have, not even mercy killings. They have no concept of it.'

And when they die, they cease to be. He shivered. 'Why would someone kill children like this?'

Latona shook her head. 'I don't know. I wish I did. Maybe the children know. Maybe they've seen something strange.'

He nodded. The children. Of course. If anyone had seen something, the children would have. They were the only ones free during the day. He ducked out of the office. He had to talk to Netta.

41

Netta's office was a small room in the back of Command Central. He had already been in the building once in the last 24 hours – to send for extra help before Michael Dengler's death. Lina Base had promised assistance within the next few days; they had to pull people off other assignments and shuttle them to Bountiful. During that visit, though, he hadn't seen Netta's office. He wasn't prepared for it.

The room smelled of roses. Plants hung from the ceiling and crowded under grow lamps attached to shelves on the far wall. Salt Juice ad posters from various nations, bases and colony planets covered the white wall space.

Netta sat on a large brown chair behind a desk covered with computer equipment and more plants. 'You have something to report?'

'No.' He had to stand. She had no other chair in her office. 'I would like to make a request, though.'

She nodded, encouraging him to continue. She looked tired and worn, as if Michael Dengler's death affected her as much as it had affected his mother.

'I would like to interview the older children.'

'Why?' Netta sat up, suddenly alert.

'I think they might know something the rest of us don't.'

She templed her fingers and tapped them against her lips. 'You've seen the reports and the holos, and Latona has taken you to see the Dancers. I'm sure you have enough to make a preliminary recommendation without bothering the children.'

'No, actually, I don't.' He looked around for a chair or available wall space, anything to lean on to ease his discomfort. 'Some things aren't adding up.'

'Everything doesn't have to add up for a preliminary ruling,' Netta said. 'I want quick action on this, Justin. Another child died yesterday. I need to protect my people from these Dancers.'

'And what happens if I get an injunction against the Dancers? That removes their protected status under Parliamentary law. Michael Dengler died inside the dome. His killer might not be native to this planet.'

Netta's lips turned white. 'I brought you here to make a ruling on the Dancers' motivation, not to solve a crime that has already been solved. Those children died by Dancer methods. I need to know what methods I can use to protect my people from those creatures.'

'I want to talk to the children,' Justin said. The office was unusually hot, probably for the plants. 'I want office space by tomorrow, and the children brought to me one by one. I'm doing this investigation by the book, Netta.'

Her eyes widened a little, and for a moment, he felt his suspicions confirmed. Then she reached over and tapped a few lines into the computer. 'You'll have a room and a place, and someone will bring the children to you,' she said.

'Thank you,' he said. Then he took a deep breath. 'You aren't paying the Dancers for the Salt Juice herbs, are you?'

Netta leaned away from the computer, her fingers still touching the screen. 'Why?'

'I'm wondering what they'll lose now that you've discovered how to grow your own herbs.' His hands were shaking, revealing his nervousness at his guess. He clasped them behind his back.

Netta studied him for a moment, as if she were tempted to find out where he had got the information. Her eyes flicked to the left, then down. It seemed as if hundreds of thoughts crossed her mind before she spoke. 'We think the seeds have a religious significance for the Dancers. We don't know for sure. We don't know anything about them for certain, despite what the Alliance says.'

A curious elation filled him. He had guessed right. The colonists had learned the secret of making Salt Juice. The Dancers were dispensable.

'The Dancers are dangerous, Justin,' Netta said. 'I don't think you need any more proof of that. I want some action in the next three days on this. I need quick movement.'

He nodded, thinking of the team shuttling in. They would arrive soon. Netta would get her movement, although it might not be the kind she wanted.

x

The room she had given him to interview the children was the same one in which they had held their initial briefing. It was too

43

big and very cold. A table sat in the middle of the room, his chair on one side, a child-sized chair with booster on the other – a setup guaranteed to make the child uncomfortable. He made sure the computer took meticulous notes, but the first half dozen interviews ran together in his mind.

'What is the game you played?' he asked.

''Race.' The boy was tall with dark hair.

'How do you play it?'

'You pound your fist on the ground three times.' This time the speaker was a girl, a redhead with sun-dark skin. 'After that you either make a fist, lay your hand flat, or put up two fingers. If you do something different from most of the group, you have to imitate something, and we have to guess. If we can't guess it, you're out.'

'Did the Dancers teach you the game?'

'No.' Another little girl, this one with black curly hair.

'What did the Dancers teach you?'

'We only saw them once.'

'Why didn't you want Michael Dengler to play?'

The fat boy scrunched up his face. 'He was too little.'

'But he was with you the last time I saw him.'

The blonde girl shrugged. 'He followed us around.'

Justin didn't get much information from them, and what information he got was the same, except repeated in different words. By midday he was tired and discouraged. He planned to see only a few more children and then quit, ready to let the team take over when they arrived.

The next child who entered was named Beth. She was tiny for an eleven year-old, with long black hair, dark eyes, and brownish black skin. She sat stiffly on the chair, ignoring the anatomically correct dolls he had placed beside her, after pausing momentarily to examine the doll that had been altered to represent a Dancer.

He poised a hand over the computer screen to highlight anything of importance. Such a standard gesture usually made people more comfortable. But nothing seemed to ease these children. And he knew their answers by heart.

'Let's talk a bit about what's going on,' he said.

'I don't know anything,' Beth said. Over her soft voice, he heard six other voices murmuring the same thing.

'You'd be surprised what you know.'

The others had shrugged. Beth's lower lip trembled. He watched it, trying not to take too much hope from such a small gesture.

'I understand you've met the Dancers.'

She nodded. 'Latona took us.'

'What did you think of them?'

'They're kinda spooky, but neat. They grow up fast.'

A new response. He tried not to be too eager. 'What makes you say that?'

She shrugged. He waited in silence for her to say something. When she did not volunteer any more information, he asked, 'How often have you seen the Dancers?'

'Just the once.' Back into the rote response. Her eyes were slightly glazed, as if she were concentrating on something else.

'Did you know Michael Dengler?'

She looked at Justin then. Her eyes were stricken, haunted. He had to work to meet her gaze because the pain was so deep. 'I always played with him when the others weren't around,' she said.

Justin nodded once to let her know he was listening and interested.

'John and Katie say we aren't supposed to be nice to him because that means he'll keep following us. I told John that Mikey was too little, and John said that little didn't matter. He said he knew a way to make him grow faster. But he's not going to grow at all, is he, Dr Schafer?'

'No,' Justin said. Her use of the present tense bothered him.

'The Dancers do,' she said. 'They grow into adults.'

Justin's hands had turned cold. 'Do you want to be an adult, Beth?'

'Not any more,' she whispered.

xi

Justin's entire body was shaking when he returned to his apartment, a jecter under his arm. He no longer trusted himself after the mistakes with the Minarans. He had to double-check every suspicion, every thought. The remaining children he had

45

interviewed said nothing about the Dancers, nothing about growing up. But Beth's soft voice kept echoing in his head.

John said that little didn't matter. He said he knew a way to make him grow faster. But he's not going to grow at all, is he, Dr Schafer?

None of them grew, Beth. The experiment failed.

Justin pulled out the holos and the file. He stared at the 2–d photos, examining the colour closely. Then he watched the holos. Katie Dengler's face was as pale as her brother's on the day she left to see the Dancers for the first time. When she died, her skin was as dark as Latona's. All the other children had pale skin in the earlier holo, and dark skin at the time of their death. They had got the dark, dark tan from the harsh sun. They had been outside the dome – a lot. Justin's skin, despite its off-planet weakness, had turned only a light brown. The children's skin was almost black.

The dome guards were new since the death before Michael Dengler's. The dome doors were easy to use and didn't latch. The children were unsupervised except for occasional school days, when workers could be spared to teach. No one watched the children, so the children went off to watch the Dancers.

Do you want to be an adult, Beth?

Not any more.

The Dancers wouldn't remember from time to time and would show the ritual to the children over and over again. The children could take the knives without the Dancers realizing it. The Dancers' lack of a past probably meant that they lost a lot of things over the years and thought nothing of it.

John said that little didn't matter. He said he knew a way to make him grow faster. But he's not going to grow at all, is he, Dr Schafer?'

'None of them are,' he whispered. The old man he had seen before he left, the old man who had lived in Bountiful as a child, had said he could hardly wait to become an adult because then he could legally leave the planet. Shuttle pilots rarely checked IDs. They figured if a person was large enough to work on any of the nearby bases, they would ferry that person off-world, away from a colony, away from home.

Away from a sterile place with no windows, lots of rules, and no real place to play.

Justin shut off the jecter and hugged his knees to his chest.

46

Then he sat in the darkness and rocked, as the pieces came together in his mind.

Sometime toward morning, he decided to go to Command Central. The building was only a few buildings away. As he walked, he listened to the silence of the community. The dome filter was a thin gray, as it had been the morning of Michael Dengler's death. The colony itself was quiet, with no indication of people waking.

His back muscles were tight, and an ache throbbed in his skull. He lacked the skill, the expertise, and the authority for this case. He had to contact Lina Base, push to get the help here as soon as possible. If his suspicions were right and the children were mutilating each other in an attempt to grow up, then something had to be done, quickly. Some of the children, like Beth, were beginning to realize that the experiment didn't work. The others, though, the others who answered him by rote, still believed in what they were doing.

The children must have visited the Dancers daily since Latona took them the first time. Young minds were particulrly susceptible to new cultures, and these children had absorbed the Dancers' beliefs, modified them, and interpreted them in a new way. If Dancer children became adults by losing their hands, hearts, and lungs, then human children would too. Maybe, they must have thought when they carved Michael Dengler, human children grew taller if their heads were removed.

John said that little didn't matter. He said he knew a way to make him grow faster. But he's not going to grow at all, is he, Dr Schafer?

The children experimented, the adults took the bodies away, and placed them in a safe place, as Dancer adults did. Not enough time had lapsed for the children to understand that the experiment hadn't worked. Only Beth had realized that things weren't going the way they should be. Perhaps the change in ritual had got her thinking. Perhaps that day in front of the morgue, when he had looked at Katie Dengler, the children had been looking at her too. Unlike Dancer children, no limbs were growing in place of the severed ones. That could have been

47

enough to show Beth that something had gone wrong.

He walked over to Central, spoke briefly with the man who monitored the equipment, and then took a private console. Each console was housed in a booth of white plastic, walls so thin that he could shake them apart. He jacked in his private number, sent a signal to Lina Base, and requested that help arrive immediately.

'Good work, Dr Schafer.'

He turned. Netta stood behind him, her arms crossed, a half-smile on her face. She was rocking back and forth on her feet, her skin flushed. She seemed very pleased to catch him. 'The tech let me know you were here.'

'I'm sending a private communication,' he said. His hands were shaking. Her attitude disturbed him.

'And it's perfect. When they arrive, I'll tell them that you ran into an emergency, you slapped an injunction against the Dancers, and they rose in a frenzy of slaughter. No one will question the fact that you're gone.'

He gripped the console. 'You've been killing the children?' It didn't make sense; why would she behead Michael Dengler?'

Netta shook her head. Her smile grew. 'The children gave me a problem when they started killing each other. I solved it – and another one with your help. There won't be any more killing, and there won't be any more Dancers.'

His throat was dry. He stood slowly, bowing his head, playing the docile prisoner. 'Where are you going to take me?'

'I'm not going to take you anywhere,' she said. 'I think right here will be— '

He pushed past her and leaped into the main room. Two guards stood behind her, startled by his sudden movement. He ran down the slick plastic floors, past the tech who had betrayed him, and through the open door.

The dome filter was losing its gray. Some of the sunlight peeked through, illuminating the pathway. His heart caught in his throat. He was out of shape, not used to running.

Damn her. Damn her for using him. For using all of them. The children killed each other in a misguided attempt to imitate the Dancers, and she let the deaths occur. Then she discovered him, with his flaws and his history, and the loophole in the law that allowed one person to make a decision for an entire species. She manipulated them all and, in that manipulating, she caused the deaths of more children, including Michael Dengler.

Michael Dengler. His wistful face rose in Justin's mind. Netta would act before the shuttle came. He had to stop her.

He ran through the twisting streets until he reached the offices of the Extra-Species Alliance. He pounded on the door. Daniel opened it. He looked sleep weary. Justin pushed past. The computer screen on the main desk was blinking. 'I'm looking for Latona,' he said.

She stood at one of the side doors, her long hair flowing around her. 'A message about you just came across the net. Netta says you have decided that the children are killing each other in an imitation Dancer ritual, and you believe all the children under the dome should die.'

So Netta knew how close he had been to the truth. She had to have been monitoring him. 'Netta's trying to figure out a way to stop me. I contacted Lina Base for help.'

'I'm not going to help you kill children,' Latona said.

'I'm not trying to hurt children. I'm trying to save your Dancers.'

'The Dancers?'

'Listen,' he said. 'I don't have time. I need someone who can talk with the Dancers. We need to get them out of here.'

'Why would Netta hurt the Dancers?'

'Salt Juice,' he said. 'She doesn't need them any more. You got me on this track when we talked about Michael Dengler. There is a human killer, which means someone is trying to pin this thing on the Dancers.' Justin decided the entire truth was too complicated to explain at the moment.

'But Netta— '

I don't think Netta is working alone.'

'She's not.' The voice came from behind them. Daniel still stood in the doorway. He stepped into the front room. His hands were empty. 'Some of the dome leaders have been trying to cancel our contracts here. The negotiations have grown too cumbersome. They want to harvest their own Salt Juice plants, but the Dancers won't let them near the plant site. And even though the colonists know how to grow from seed, they still need the atmospheric conditions and special soil of the Dancer lands.'

49

Latona whirled. 'You never said anything about cancelled contracts.'

Daniel shrugged. 'I was working with it. So was Lina Base. It would have worried you and interfered with your work.'

'Shit.' Latona grabbed her sand scarf and a small laser. 'Will you stay here, Daniel, and stall them?'

He nodded. 'I'll also contact Lina Base and tell them we need emergency personnel now.'

'They know,' Justin said. 'Netta plans to use that as an excuse to make up some story, something about an emergency that requires the colonists to kill the Dancers – and do it all with my permission.'

'All right,' Daniel said. 'I'll make my message explicit. Colonists trying to illegally kill Dancers. Need emergency assistance. Good enough?'

'If the assistance comes in time,' Latona said. 'Come on, Dr Schafer.'

He followed her outside. 'They flashed that message. I won't be able to get out.'

'There're other ways out of the dome.' Latona hurried to the dome edge and touched a seam. A small panel slid back, and bright sunshine slipped in. If the children wanted to avoid the doors, they could have used these panels. 'You don't have a sand scarf.'

'We don't have time to get one. Let's go.'

They slid through the dome opening and into the light. The heat was searing. It burned into his skin. Latona threw him her cream and he rubbed it on as they ran. Perhaps this was the way the children went when they studied the Dancers. He would ask Latona sometime.

It took forever to cross the hot sand. Finally they reached the canopied trees. When they did, Latona let out a long, shrill whistle. His skin was crackling and dry. He already saw heat blisters forming beneath the surface.

The Dancers appeared, hurrying through the trees. Latona stepped back as they tried to touch her. She spoke rapidly. One of the Dancers spoke back, gesturing with its hands. She shook her head and tried again. The Dancer repeated the gesture.

'What?' Justin asked.

'I've told them to leave,' she said. 'They don't understand that

50

there is somewhere else to go. They don't remember. All they know is here.'

He peered through the canopied trees. Air cars shimmered in the distance. Perhaps it was his overactive imagination. Netta had implied that they didn't have air cars on Bountiful. He had to do something. He and Latona had to get the Dancers out of the area, if only for a short time. The shuttle would arrive within a few days. The Dancers needed that much of an advantage. 'Give me your weapon,' Justin said.

'Why?'

'Have them show us the plants.'

'But— '

'Now! I think we've been followed out of the dome.'

She spoke to the Dancer. The Dancer churred in response, then grabbed Latona and pulled her through the trees. They walked the path they had walked before, the one that led to the children's pen.

'The plants are all around us,' Latona said.

'Give me your weapon,' Justin repeated.

'What do you want to do with it?'

'I want to start these plants on fire, to show the Dancers how unimportant they are.'

'But the children— '

'There'll be time to get the children out of the pens.'

She bit her lower lip.

'If you're worried, tell him what we're going to do. Have him send others to the children.'

She spoke to the Dancer. He made a whirring sound. Latona reached down and touched a plant with the laser, searing the leaves. The Dancer whistled shrilly, and others ran down the path.

'Tell him that we're not bluffing. Tell him that we have to destroy the plants, and that they have to leave. I don't care what reason you give them. Just get them out of here.'

Latona spoke quickly. The Dancer listened, then repeated Latona's sounds loudly. Justin's ears felt as if they were being pierced. He grabbed the weapon from Latona, studied it for a moment, saw the finger control on the side and the open mouth along another side. He pointed the mouth at the plants and pushed the control. Heat whooshed out of the mouth, catching

51

the leaves and sending fire along the plants. The Dancer beside them screamed and ran down the path. Other Dancers were running too, like the shadows of animals running before a forest fire. In the distance he saw the Dancers lifting children from the pen and tucking them under one arm as they continued to run.

The heat was getting under his skin, making his body ache. The smoke felt faintly sweet. That same sickly sweet he had smelled on Tanner. Justin giggled, feeling giddy. The canopy was keeping the smoke in the forest. They would pass out if they didn't escape. He grabbed Latona's arm and pulled her with him.

When they reached the desert, he saw no air cars. Hallucination, then. But he did see a band of people in sand scarves, walking determinedly across the sand. He remembered watching other colonists walk like that, carrying laser weapons to beaches that lined their island home, and blasting small, seal-like creatures until clear blood coated the sand, while seeding shuttles circled overhead, dropping alkaline solution into the acidic ocean. He sank down against a tree. His whole body itched. He didn't want to watch again.

Latona slipped away from him. The smell had grown cloying, and the giddiness had grown with it. He wondered where he would stay until the ship arrived. He glanced at his skin. It was black. Large lumps had risen under the surface, with pus bubbles on top. They would be painful when they burst.

'They're gone,' Latona said.

Justin looked at her, then at the colonists. They were getting closer.

'The Dancers,' Latona said. 'They're gone.'

He felt relief run through him like a cool draft of air. He took a long breath to speak, and toppled face forward into the sunbaked sand.

Part Two

John

John huddled against the shuttle's window. The plastic was scratched, the metal rims cool against his cheek. He refused to look outside. The blackness of space haunted him and made him feel even more alone. He had never left Bountiful, although it had once been his dream. But he had wanted to go on his terms and in his own way. Not trapped inside a small shuttle that barely held eight children, with a guard at the door, another blocking entrance to the pilot's area, and a third clutching a laser in the back.

His parents had looked unusually grim as they watched him pack. His mother had actually touched him, running her hand along the side of his face and then cupping his jaw. He hadn't pulled away. For a moment, he thought he had seen some caring in her eyes. But then she let go and he felt a coolness where her hand had been. She had turned to his father for comfort it seemed, initially. Then their embrace turned into something else, as it always had. John had waited for the authorities alone, sitting on the front steps, listening to his parents' laughter echo from inside the house. He hadn't even had a chance to say goodbye. He wasn't sure he wanted one.

Beth slept beside him, her small body curled against the plush blue upholstery, her black hair pulling out of its ponytail. Even in sleep, deep circles made her eyes look bruised. She had cried when she saw him, and he had held her cradled in his arms as if she were the most precious thing he had ever touched.

'They're all dead,' she had whispered. 'We killed them.'

He had stroked her soft hair and rocked her, murmuring, 'Dancers don't remember.'

He wished he were a Dancer.

The other children shared seats as well: Verity wrapped her arms around her knees, staring at nothing, her red hair and sun-darkened skin making her look foreign in the shuttle's artificial light. Pearl sat beside her. Pearl's dark scalp shone through her white-blonde hair, making her look as if she were going bald. Dusty kept her face pressed against the window, her too-thin back to the group. She hadn't looked at them since the authorities rounded everyone up.

Max sat beside her, staring at the carpeted floor. He bit his lips until they were scabbed and bleeding as if he were trying to prevent himself from saying something. Allen slept in the seat behind Dusty, his small mouth open and moist, his pudgy hands balled into fists. He had cried too, and wouldn't let anyone near him, although Skye had tried. She still sat next to him, looking small and fragile next to Allen's bulk, one hand resting on his shoulder as if to give him support. Occasionally her brilliant blue gaze would meet John's and, in it, he saw the despair he felt.

He couldn't sleep. When he closed his eyes, he heard Michael Dengler scream, felt the blood spurt all over him. Michael had died, like the rest, like his sister Katie who had started it all.

It should have worked. They could move like the Dancers, and talk like the Dancers, even think like the Dancers if they really tried. Why couldn't they share the Dancers' rituals?

Why didn't they grow up?

He rubbed his eyes with the heel of his hand. It was beyond him. Latona's look after the Dancer forest burned. The doctor, the man who had found them out, on a stretcher – the sun blisters on his scalp, his skin swollen and deformed by too much heat. The parents, pulling their children away, expressing concern, embarrassment, and hatred. He had heard Dusty's mother scream at her for taking part in an ugly, nasty business, then he had braced himself for the crack of the hand on Dusty's face. When it came, he had winced as if he were the one who had been hit.

The fourth guard came out of the pilot's area. He was tall and slender, his silver suit molded to his body. His head brushed the ceiling. He leaned over and whispered to the guard in front of the door. That guard was a heavyset man with muscles that bulged as he moved. He took the light cuffs off the wall, stood and walked down the aisle.

'Landing,' he said to John. 'We don't want no trouble.'

John swallowed against a dry throat. The guard picked up

Beth's limp hands, attached the watch-sized device to her wrists, then turned it on. Two bands of red light encircled her from her thumbs to her forearms. As he dropped her hands, she snapped awake. The light was painful if it brushed against skin. John had discovered that before they left Bountiful.

He held out his hands. The guard snapped the device to John's wrists, fingers brushing John's thumbs. The guard's fingers were cold. He shied away at the touch. John glanced up, saw a slight flush against the guard's cheeks. Something flashed through the guard's eyes before it disappeared. Fear?

John scared the guard?

But John was just a twelve-year-old boy. A twelve-year-old boy who had failed to grow up.

The guard flicked the switch and the lights came on, sending a slight tingle through John's hands even though he was careful not to brush anything. He held his arms over his lap. The position would get tiring all too quickly, but it was better than that burning pain the restraints could cause.

Beth held her hands in the same position. Her cheeks looked hollow. Sleep clung to her eyelashes. 'What's going on?' she whispered.

The guard glanced at her as he moved to the other seats, but did not answer.

'I guess we're there,' John said.

Beth nodded. She watched the guard put the restraints on the remaining children. John turned away, and found himself facing the portal. His own reflection stared back at him through the scratched plastic: a lean boy's face with dark eyes and darker hair, high cheekbones and a suggestion of fullness around the mouth. In a few years, he would look just like his father. His father, the man who smelled like Salt Juice and never spoke. His father, who hadn't even come out of his bedroom to bid his son goodbye.

The light of the free-floating base seemed to draw the shutttle in. Bay doors opened like tiny eyelids in the base's centre. As they got closer, John realized that the base was huge: ten times the size of the colony he had left or maybe more. People everywhere. And no one had told him what would happen next.

Allen screamed. John turned. The guard was bent over Allen holding out the cuffs. Allen licked his lips and blinked against the artificial light. Skye was pressed against him, the cuffs already on her hands.

'It's okay,' John said, letting his voice carry. 'We'll be okay.'

Allen's eyes seemed to focus. He nodded and held out his hands. The guard cuffed him. A tear trickled down Allen's cheek. 'What are they going to do with us, John? I want to go home. I want to see the Dancers.'

'Me, too,' John said, choosing to ignore Allen's question. If he had the answer, he would be calmer himself. But he didn't know. No one would talk to him.

No one would even look at him.

He could barely look at himself.

He had known something had gone wrong when a week had passed and Linette hadn't changed. By then, Dancer children showed some signs of life, a bit of finger showing through the hole in the wrist, a kind of awareness behind the eyes. If anything, Linette had looked paler, as if that cold the adults kept her in was leaching everything from her, even the ability to change.

'What are they going to do to us?' Beth whispered.

'I don't know.' John swallowed, hard. They looked to him for all the answers, just as they always had. From the time they could talk, this group had been together, and he and Katie had led them. No one had taken care of them. They had run wild, going home only when they were forced to.

Steven and Scott, two of the older kids, had said there once was a school, but the teacher had disappeared into the Dancer forest, and no one thought to start it up again.

One of the men who had imprisoned the children had said none of this would have happened if the children had had some structure. Latona had nodded. She had tried. She taught them about the Dancers – and took them to the forest that first time. John had liked her. She had never smelled of Salt Juice.

John's arms were getting tired. The shuttle banked and turned, blocking his view of the base. He turned away as the blackness faced him again. All the other children had told him about their fears. They had cried or let him see the terror in their eyes. Only Pearl had said nothing. She had glanced at him across the room, her eyes flat, her expression so old that she seemed ancient. When she realized he had seen her, she mouthed, 'Useless.'

He had nodded. He hadn't leaned on anyone either. From the minute the authorities found them near the morgue, he had been Dancer. He would flow. He would change with each moment, as if the past hadn't existed.

Only his eyes burned, and he knew if he blinked wrong, the past would flood up in a wave of tears.

The shuttle's hum – a sound he had grown used to – rose to a higher pitch, digging into his ears. Something dragged against the front, slowing the shuttle, making his stomach feel as if it had moved into his chest. The guards had braced themselves against the doors, their faces impassive. John's heart pounded and his mouth was dry. He glanced at Beth. She was staring straight ahead, her lips in a tight line, her chin shaking.

'Do you understand what you have done?' asked the man with no hair and skin so pink he must never have seen the sun. 'You have killed six children. Do you know what that means? It means they are dead. They will never breathe again. Never play again. Never talk again. They have ceased to exist.'

'They will be all right,' John said, 'if you just wait.'

'No,' the man said. 'They're humans, not Dancers.' He pulled open Linette's drawer and yanked John over. 'Look inside her chest. Do you see anything there? New heart? New lungs? No. It's empty. Because humans do not grow new organs when the old ones are removed.'

Two slight bumps, a large bang, and the shuttle stopped moving. Behind him, Skye whimpered. She must have hit her cuffs against her wrists. The shuttle's hum stopped completely, making John's ears ring. No one spoke for a moment. He glanced behind him. The other children sat like he and Beth did, backs rigid, arms extended in front of them, as if the guards were going to rope little leashes to their wrists and lead them out of the shuttle in a group.

In essence, they already had. The locks would tighten and send bolts of pain through the arms of anyone who tried to make a wrong move. They had all learned that shortly after the authorities captured them.

Latona had protested the harshness the guards were using as the ship got ready to leave Bountiful. 'Word from on high, ma'am,' one of the guards said. 'They're to be treated like the murderers they are.'

61

'But why?' Latona had cried.

'Because the government don't want no one else imitating aliens. We got enough troubles without that.'

The other children hadn't heard that interchange, but John had. And he knew, from that point on, that life would be even more difficult than it had been before.

The guards in front trained their lasers on the group. The outside door pulled open, letting in cooler air and the sound of many voices. John cringed. He didn't know what they were going to do to him.

'Stand up,' said the guard nearest the door.

Beth and John stood in unison. He assumed the others stood with them because he heard no cries of pain. The cool air smelled dusty, tangy, harsh with chemical cleaners. The urge to sneeze rose in him. He breathed shallowly until it went away.

Flow.

Move forward.

Live only in the moment.

He was a Dancer, and Dancers had no past.

'You will move in a group,' the guard said. 'You will make no sudden movements. You will do as we tell you. Walk down the stairs, across the floor to the open double doors directly in front of you. You will answer no questions and speak to no one in the crowd.'

He didn't ask if they understood. From what John had seen, the guard didn't care. If he had to shoot a child, he would. They were nothing to him. He cared even less about them than their parents did.

'Move!' the guard said, swinging his laser.

John and Beth moved first, side by side. For a moment, John's feet touched the carpet, and then he reminded himself: he was a Dancer. He felt himself rise just above the floor, his body gliding forward. Beth glanced at him, fear on her face, before it faded and she joined him.

The two guards went down the stairs first. John followed, and nearly lost his control. The room was huge – larger than any room he had ever seen, maybe as big as all of Command Central combined. Four visible sets of metal stairs led to metal walkways and rooms on a second floor, just like in the Outsiders' apartments. Mingled with the scents he had noted earlier were the scents of sweat and perfume. People spanned the length of the floor, with more pouring in from side doors. Bright lights blinded him and he had to blink as voices rose in questions:

' . . . did you kill them . . . ?'
' . . . feel to slice someone's hands . . . ?'
' . . . any remorse . . . ?'
' . . . murderers . . . '
' . . . children . . . '
' . . . did you know what you were doing . . . ?'
' . . . murderers . . . '
' . . . children . . . '
' . . . Dancers . . . '

John was breathing through his mouth. He made himself stare at the double doors, open, their destination. The doors were brown, not white like doors should be, and they were pressed against their frames. Another set of guards formed a trail through the crowd, holding the people back, including those with small, hand-held pieces of equipment that they kept shoving forward like offerings.

The guards had reached the bottom of the steps. John followed, having to walk because Dancers never encountered steps before. When he reached the bottom, he glided through the openings. Lasers were pointed at him, their snub noses looking dark and threatening.

Gasps rippled through the crowd as he passed.

' . . . look . . . '
' . . . What's he doing . . . ?'
' . . . aren't on the floor . . . '
' . . . flying . . . '

The locks tightened on his wrists. Searing pain ran up his arms, through his heart, and into his brain. 'Walk like a human being!' one of the guards snapped at him.

The pain made him land on the floor, then sink to his knees. Someone bumped him from behind.

' . . . children . . . '
' . . . murderers . . . '
' . . . Dancers . . . '

People closed in around him. Their strange shoes – made of soft material and pointed at the toes – pushed against his hands. The lock tightened on his wrists.

'Get up!' the guard yelled.

He didn't want to get up. He didn't want to move. Let them trample him. He didn't want to be in this place.

'. . . dead . . . ?'

'. . . just children . . . '

'Get up!'

Hands grabbed his shoulders, fingers digging into his flesh, pulling him back and away. A voice rose above the others, shrill and high. 'John! John! Don't kill him. Please . . . '

Beth's voice. She needed him. They all needed him. They wouldn't know what to do without him.

(They wouldn't be there without him.)

The floor beneath his hands was steel and shiny. Layers of grit coated his palms. The chemical smell was stronger here, mixing with the scent of unwashed feet and plastic shoes.

The pain shooting through his arms was the only thing that made him feel alive.

The hands slid under his armpits and pulled him on to his feet. The faces were closer to his, skin tones of varying colours, eyes too bright, cheeks flushed.

'. . . pass out with remorse . . . '

'. . . feel to kill your best friend . . . '

'. . . murderer . . . '

'. . . child . . . '

'John.' Beth touched his arm, then her face spasmed with pain. A tear trickled out of the corner of her eye, but she ignored it. 'They want us to go through those doors.'

And then what? No one had told them. No one had explained the size or all the people or the smells. No one had said he would have to be so far away from the Dancers.

Save me. He projected the message, projected the emotion, just as he had done so many times before. Only this time, there was no answering chirrup, no dark face peering at him with concern.

A hand pushed at the small of his back, and he stumbled forward, the crowd parting so that he and the others could pass. He glanced beside him, and saw the guard who had been manipulating him: one of the guards from the ship, the big one who had put the restraints on them.

'. . . are your parents . . . '

'. . . where are the other . . . '

'. . . all alone . . . '

The pressure on his wrists eased, leaving the memory of pain echoing through his nerve endings. He was breathing shallowly, unable to block out the voices, the hands shoving small square pieces of equipment at him – recording devices like Latona had – was this what they did for the vidnets that he had seen tapes of? How many people would see him?

Behind him, he heard sobbing. Deep, choking sounds that were growing louder with each step John took. The voices continued around him, but he forced himself to focus on the tears. His body wanted to moan in unison, to shake with the same kinds of sobs.

'. . . look too young . . . '

'. . . Schafer's been wrong before . . . '

'. . . children . . . '

Finally he could take it no longer. He turned. Allen was behind him, eyes focused on the ground, the sobs making his entire body quiver. Skye was trying to quiet him. Each time she touched him, her entire body jerked as the guards messed with her wrist locks.

Allen had been crying ever since he found out that the other children were dead. John stopped and the pain returned, harsh and shattering. He breathed against it, moved slightly into the future as the Dancers had taught him, and pressed his body against Allen's. He rested his chin on Allen's shoulder, his cheek against Allen's damp one. Allen's body shuddered against his. 'Come on,' John whispered in Allen's ear. 'We'll stay together. It's always been us anyway. No one else.'

The other children crowded around them, becoming a circle against the crowd. Allen's quivering stopped, his breathing heavy and moist. John felt cocooned in the middle, safe for the first time since he had left Bountiful.

'Separate!' the guards were shouting. The pain in John's wrists was becoming unbearable. Skye whimpered. 'Separate now!'

'We're a team,' John said. Hands pulled Pearl back, then Beth, then Skye. Allen grabbed for John, then yelled when his wrist locks flashed blue. Allen almost sank to his knees, but John caught him with one hand and pulled him up by his elbows. 'Be

65

strong,' John said. 'You're a Dancer.'

Allen nodded.

A guard pulled John away, and pushed him forward. The crowd had grown silent. They had backed away, as if they were expecting to get hurt somehow. Their eyes had grown wider, and that eager quest for knowledge had faded.

John's wrists were swelling against his restraints. He turned around, glanced at Beth, and they walked forward, their feet making hollow sounds against the steel floor.

A woman stepped in front of him, holding up her square vidnetcorder. 'Young man, what is your bond to the other children?'

The guard pushed her back, but her question opened the door. The voices grew again.

' . . . strange link . . . '

' . . . executed them . . . '

' . . . purpose behind the deaths . . . '

The doors were closer. Behind them was a white wall with no people in front of it. The white looked like relief. John had been craving white. All the colours were assaulting his eyes, like the voices assaulted his ears. The whole upper half of his body ached. Maybe, when he got through this crowd, he could sit down.

' . . . to do with Salt Juice . . . '

' . . . What caused such . . . '

' . . . never heard of before in the history of colonization . . . '

A man stood near the door. He watched, hands clasped in front of him. He had long dark hair and big black eyes. He studied John, and in his face was a hint of compassion, a hint of warmth. John watched him like a thirsty man watching a distant pond.

' . . . only a child . . . '

' . . . six dead . . . '

' . . . murdered . . . '

Hands brushed him, and he didn't flinch. Corders pushed against his face. He kept his gaze on the man in front of him, until they stood side by side. The man nodded and smiled just a little. His lips moved, but John heard no voice through the others. But the lips said, *You'll be all right.*

John let out a small sigh. His body was still quivering to

Allen's rhythm. He went through the doors and into the empty hallway, his feet tripping on the light brown carpet. The others followed and the door slammed shut behind them, dampening the voices.

The air in the hall was cool, almost cold. Sweat ran down the side of John's face. He took a deep breath. The hall was four people wide, but felt small after that huge room. The guards secured the door behind him. There were more guards than he had realized: two per child. Without speaking, two grabbed his sore arms and dragged him down the hallway. The other boys followed. The girls went in the opposite direction.

'No!' The voice belonged to Skye. She was screaming. 'I have to go with Allen. He needs me. No!'

John glanced back. She was still beside the double doors, her entire body locked in a struggle with the guards. A third guard, protecting the door, raised his laser.

'He'll be all right!' John shouted to her. 'He's with me!'

His gaze met Skye's and he could see the pleading. Allen's breakdown had frightened them all. His guards' hands dug deeper into the sore flesh of his upper arms. They lifted him off the floor and carried him through the corridor. Skye's guards picked her up as well and took her down the other hallway, where the girls had disappeared.

He was shivering with the cold, the only warm parts on his body now were his sore arms and hands. The sweat had frozen into his skin, making it feel crusty and tight. The guards carried him around a corner. Here the corridor branched off into a series of rooms. Allen's guards yanked him into one room, John into another.

'No,' he said. 'I need to be with Allen. Please.'

The guards said nothing. They tossed him on to the floor. He landed on his arms and the pain made him cry out. One guard bent over and released the cuffs, pocketing them. Then the guards left, locking the door behind them.

He lay there a moment, trying to catch his breath. The pain was subsiding in his arms, but his wrists were red and swollen. Had they damaged something? He didn't know.

The room was the size of his room back home. The carpet was plush and warm against the chill. The pile was thick and red, the fibres softer than the bedclothes he had used. The burning in the back of his eyes grew stronger, and he had to blink it back.

They had turned away from him, his parents, when they found out. They had never liked him much, always complained about everything he did, but he had thought, somehow, that when he really needed them, they would be there, they would at least acknowledge him as their child. Instead, they had stared at him as if they had never seen him before. Then they had pulled him to their side, his mother's hands like claws digging into his flesh. It probably looked like a loving family to the man from Lina Base, but it wasn't. John still had marks in his shoulders from his mother's fingernails.

When the man left John in their custody, his parents had sent John to his room. Then they had made themselves dinner and, shortly after the meal, they were giggling and laughing as if the whole thing were one big joke. He knew if he came out of his room, he would get slapped around. They wouldn't want him there, a reminder of all that had gone bad in their lives.

It was as if Salt Juice had destroyed their vision. They only saw each other because they shared the high.

He clutched at the carpet. At least his fingers worked. He made himself concentrate on the ceiling above. It was white, with a glazed surface. The walls were brown and appeared to be made of strips of wood. Paintings were bolted to the walls, portraits of the blackness with an occasional dot of light. Furniture stood around him, four upholstered chairs that blended the browns and reds. To the side, two stairs led to a mirrored door. He glanced at it, saw himself in the middle of the floor, his eyes wide, his face pale underneath his tan, his hair sticking up in tufts. He looked no better than the others had.

A small hiss echoed in the room, the sound of an automated program beginning its run. He recognized it from the library in Command Central. There, he had listened to all the programs he could find, trying to learn like Steve and Scott said the others had, trying to create his own school, so that he could teach the others.

The hiss turned into a whir which resolved itself into an automated voice: REMOVE YOUR CLOTHING IN PREPARATION FOR AUTODOC EXAMINATION.

They couldn't make him. They couldn't make him do anything. He would sit here, motionless, until he saw Allen again.

He had promised Allen that they would remain together.

FINAL WARNING; REMOVE YOUR CLOTHING IN PREPARTION FOR AUTODOC EXAMINATION.

John's hands were shaking. His fingers were as puffy as his wrists.

An alarm sounded, a harsh buzzing that made him jump. The door opened and he scuttled backwards, tingles of pain running through his hands as he pressed them against the carpet. His back hit the wall and he stopped.

A guard stood before him, a big guard, one he had never seen before. His shoulders were broad, his hair the white blond Linette's had been after they had visited the Dancers for a month. The guard slammed the door behind him.

'Take off your clothes,' he said. 'Or I will do it.'

The shaking in John's hands had moved through his entire body. 'I need to be with Allen.' Even his voice shook. 'I promised.'

'Take off your clothes,' the guard said. He crossed his arms in front of his chest. His silver uniform strained against his muscles.

'I won't do anything. Just let me be with Allen.' John had never heard that pleading tone in his own voice before.

The guard was across the room in a flash. He grabbed John's shirt and ripped it off, then grabbed the waist of John's pants. John screamed and flailed, but the guard's grip was too tight. John couldn't get away. Within a few moments, he was naked in the cold.

The guard threw John toward the mirrored door. John watched his own frightened face get closer until he slammed into the silvering. Blood, reflected and real, smeared on the glass as he slid to the carpeted steps.

'Now get inside the autodoc.'

John wiped his mouth with the back of his hand. He glanced at the guard, standing in the middle of John's ripped and strewn clothing. John's heart was pounding against his chest. He stood, slowly, and opened the mirrored door.

Inside was a small, dark, hot cubicle, a square box with nowhere to sit down. He stepped in and stood, not knowing what to expect next.

'Close the door,' the guard said.

John grabbed the slim hole behind the mirror and pulled the door closed. The darkness was complete. No light even marked the edges of the door. It was like his room at night, before the banshees came, before he discovered how to think like a Dancer and move sideways.

The hiss started and made him jump. Then the whirring and the automated voice.

PLACE YOUR HANDS AT YOUR SIDES. DO NOT TOUCH YOUR ARMS TO YOUR BODY. DO NOT MOVE OR THE PROCEDURE WILL HAVE TO START AGAIN.

Light strobed beneath his feet. When it touched his skin, it had a warmth that startled him. The light played across his toes, his arches, then up his legs, touching his privates. Then it shoved inside him, at his bottom, and he stifled a scream. The light moved out, traced a pattern on his torso and arms, then shoved inside his mouth.

He closed his eyes, trying to distance himself from the invasion.

KEEP YOUR EYES OPEN the automatic voice said. DO NOT MOVE.

He opened his eyes and stared at the blackness in front of him. The lights stabbed his pupils, and the heat on the eyeballs was more than he could bear.

He screamed and slammed into the wall. The lights shut off, and he was alone, in the dark.

Then he heard a click, and the door swung open. Cold air streamed in. The room was empty. The guard was gone, and so were his clothes.

He stepped out gingerly, goosebumps rising on his exposed flesh. On one of the upholstered chairs rested some folded white material. John picked it up. It was a jumpsuit, made of some kind of natural fibre. The weave was open and loose, like the library tapes had told him such stuff would be. He put the suit on, grateful for the warmth.

Only then did he realize that the pain and swelling were gone from his arms. He glanced into the mirror. The blood that had been on his cheek was gone. He tongued the corner of his mouth. The bruise was gone too.

A shiver ran down his back. Nothing like that had ever happened to him before.

He sat on one of the chairs and drew his knees up to his chest. His toes were little blocks of ice. He wished they had given him something for his feet.

Poor Allen had probably just gone through with the same thing. His fear must have reached a fevered pitch by now. Everyone was probably terrified, even more now that they were without John.

And he had promised them that they would stay together.

He had to find a way to make that work – for himself, as well as for them.

ii

They moved him through a back door to a small room with white walls and no windows. A white plastic cot with slats instead of a mattress took up most of the floor space. Its bottom, top, and left side all touched the walls. A small hole in the floor served as his toilet. When they closed the door, he could no longer see its outline in the wall.

The guards hadn't listened to his pleas to see the others. The guards hadn't spoken to him at all, just dragged him down the carpeted corridor until they reached this room.

There they had left him. Alone.

The lights were bright, made even brighter by the shiny white plastic all around him. The floor was cold against his feet, and he wondered if he would ever be warm again. He sat on the cot, and was surprised to find the slats comfortable.

Then he lay back and closed his eyes. His lids provided little shade against the brightness. Instead of darkness, he saw an orange colour that became brown when he placed his arm over his face.

It was like home. It was just like home. He wondered how he ever could have considered white to be a relief. He was surrounded by it now, and it would drive him crazy – especially since he hardly had any room to move.

The cell was silent except for the hum of the air processor built into the walls. He thought about yelling, but knew no one would come.

They all believed he was a bad guy, that he had done

71

something wrong. And apparently he had. He hadn't expected anyone to die. He had just been trying to help them. He and Katie.

They had tried so many things. The afternoon Henry had heard about the shuttle landing, and they had hiked across the desert to the Singing Sea to ask the pilot to take them along. She had chuckled. 'You guys don't look old enough to go anywhere without your parents' consent. Tell you what. I'll be back next week. If you're here with Mom and Dad, I'll take you anywhere you want to go.'

She had known that they were trying to get away from their parents, not taking a trip with their parents' approval. Later one of the Salt Juice buyers had said that pilots saw that kind of thing on colonies all the time. Only grownups could leave. It was a good rule, designed to protect families from the horrendous cost of paying for an illegal trip on a shuttle.

They had met other shuttles, forged documents, asked every pilot they could find, and they met with the same response. *You need your parents' consent.* John's parents had laughed at him when he finally asked.

You'll see the Outside soon enough, his father had said. *Then you'll understand how wonderful everything is here.*

Wonderful. Nothing was wonderful. Each day was the same—

There was a clunk coming from the direction of the door. John uncovered his face and sat up. The door's lines appeared in the wall, then the door slid backwards, opening into the narrow corridor. John got to his feet. Finally, they were going to let him out. He wasn't going to be trapped in this small room forever.

A guard stood at the side of the door. Another brought a white chair and plunked it inside. He glared at John. 'Don't get any ideas.'

John swallowed, his feet absorbing the cold from the floor. A woman slipped in around the guard. The guard stepped out and the door slammed shut – all except for a small viewing slit near the ceiling.

The woman was slender and agile next to the hulking guards. Her dark hair brushed her collar. She wore a blue shirt, and even bluer pants. She was the only spot of colour in the room, and that calmed John.

72

The woman extended her hand. 'My name is Dania Zinn. I'm your attorney.'

John stared at the woman's hand for a moment, noting her small, slender fingers. Adults shook hands. Children did not. After a moment, John took the offered hand. Dania's skin was dry and warm. She squeezed just a bit, then let John's hand go.

She obviously knew who John was. Everyone who had been at the landing had seen John.

'May I talk to you?' Dania said. She didn't seem at all uncomfortable with John's silence.

John shrugged.

She tugged a bit on her pants legs as she sat down. Her hair waved on top. Her eyebrows were as dark as the rest of her hair.

'I want to see my friends,' John said.

She nodded. 'I know. Have a seat, John. Let me explain what is going on here.'

John crossed his arms tightly as he had seen the guard do. 'I need to see Allen. I promised him that we would stay together.'

She sighed. 'Look,' she said. 'You're in a lot of trouble, and there's very little anyone can do to get you out of it. Right now, Lina Base's authorities aren't going to grant you many privileges. You scared them when you ignored your restraints and huddled in a group this morning.'

'We didn't do anything,' John said. 'Allen was upset.'

'It appears that you're all upset,' Dania said. 'And we need to work with that. Please, sit down so that we can talk.'

John sat on the edge of the cot. It tilted forward with his weight. He had to brace his feet on the floor to keep his balance. When he sat, he was directly level with Dania. The chair was so close her knees brushed against the cot.

'I don't think anyone's explained to you what happened,' Dania said.

'We know about the murders,' John said, his voice trembling. He still didn't think of their actions as murder. It had seemed so right at the time. Even that last time, when Michael screamed as the knife approached his neck . . .

Dania leaned back a little, as if she hadn't expected John to say anything. 'Well,' she said. 'I suppose you do. But all of you

73

were born on Bountiful, and you have never been to a base. Did they explain to you in school how Parliamentary law functions?'

John swallowed the lump that had grown in his throat. 'I've never been to school.'

'I see I'll have my work cut out for me.' Dania ran a hand through her thick hair. 'Briefly, then, the colonies have their own security forces, but follow Parliamentary law. If something serious happens, as it did in this case, it is tried on the nearest base, taking all factors into account. The fact that in this case, you are minors and admit to the crime simply makes matters more difficult. That, the involvement of the Dancers, and Justin Schafer.'

John frowned. This was making no sense to him. Tanner took care of punishing people on Bountiful. John hadn't even seen Tanner when the Lina Base people came. 'Look, I promised the others I'd help them. Allen is really upset, and he needs his friends. Please— '

'That's what I'm trying to tell you, John. You can't see your friends, at least for a while. You'll have a hearing in front of a judge to determine competency and whether you should be tried as adults. Then . . . '

It was as if she were speaking another language. John knew the words but not the meanings. The coldness in his feet had spread to his stomach. 'I don't understand,' he said. 'Why can't I see my friends?'

'Because, right now, the government thinks you're all dangerous when you're together.'

John opened his mouth and then closed it. The burning grew in the back of his eyes, and he rubbed them with one fist to control it. 'Allen can't be by himself. He needs us.'

She nodded. 'I understand. I'll do the best I can.' She folded her hands on her knees, then leaned forward. 'I'm your advocate here. I'm the one in the best position to help you, but you are going to have to help me. You'll have to be honest and cooperative, and willing to do as I say.'

John wiped the side of his fist on his cotton jumpsuit. The room felt smaller with her in it. He wanted to back away from her, to hide, but there was nowhere to go. 'I want to see my friends.'

74

'You will.'

'Now. I want to stay with them.'

'I'm sorry.' She ran a hand over her lips and leaned back in the chair, as if she were trying to figure him out. 'You have no understanding of this system, do you?' she asked as if she didn't expect him to answer. 'We'll have to make a deal, because I don't have time to explain the history of our legal system. Do as I tell you, and within three days, I'll make sure you see your friends.'

'Three days?' John leaned forward too far, and the cot tipped beneath him. It toppled to the floor with a muffled thud. He caught his balance, raised himself up Dancerlike, and put his feet on the floor.

Dania was watching him, her mouth slightly open. 'I've never seen anyone do that,' she said.

He picked up the cot and made sure it remained upright. Then he stood beside it. 'I need to see Allen right away. He hasn't been . . . well . . . since the people from the base arrived. Please.'

She stood, too. 'He's under observation, and I'll make sure he gets some extra counselling. One of the base psychologists will be coming to see you as well. His name is Harper Reeves. I want you to tell him everything – how you feel, what you're thinking. You can trust him. Like me, he's trying to help you.'

The chill was filling his entire body. 'The only way to help me is to let me see my friends.'

She shook her head. 'I know you don't understand this, John. But, right now, seeing your friends is the least of your worries.'

iii

After she left, he paced for what seemed like forever. Four short strides from one side of the room to the other. He ran her words back through his head, what he could remember of them, and they still made no sense. On Bountiful, Tanner told people when they did something wrong and asked them not to do it again. And they didn't. It was that simple.

He would never try Dancer rituals on his friends again. He

had told the Lina Base Authorities that, and they hadn't listened. They hadn't said a word.

When he had gone around the room for what seemed like the thousandth time, a servotray appeared in the wall above the cot. The tray was white. So was the bowl, and the food inside. They were trying to drive him crazy. They wanted to show him that there were worse places than Bountiful.

The food smelled rich and yeasty. His stomach growled. He took the bowl, and scooped up the mess with his fingers. It had the rough texture of the gruel his mother used to make, but it had a sweeter taste. He hadn't realized he was so hungry.

When he finished eating, he set the bowl back on the tray, and lay on the cot. They weren't going to let him out. They weren't going to let him see Allen or any of the others. They were going to keep him in here until he couldn't stand it any more. Dancers went crazy without the sun.

A thump made him start. He sat up, his mouth cottony and his eyes gummed shut. He must have fallen asleep. He looked over at the servotray. It was gone and the lines in the wall marking its place had vanished too. New lines were forming in front of him. The door was sliding back.

John ran his hand over his eyes, then rubbed the front of his jumpsuit. In all the time he had been here, he had accumulated no dirt at all. No colour, no nothing. It was as if he were the only real thing in the room.

The door slid back and a man came in. He had long dark hair, more brown than black, that went past his shoulders. His eyes were almond-shaped, wide and warm. He smiled, and John recognized him. The man who had looked at him with such compassion at the double doors.

'Hey,' the man said, extending a hand as Dania had done. 'I'm Harper Reeves.'

This time John didn't hesitate. He took Harper's hand, found it warm and welcoming. Harper wore a red shirt that accented his darkness, and brown drawstring pants that matched his hair. Like John, Harper was barefoot.

'Dania told you who I am?'

John nodded. Harper let John's hand go, and shoved his own hands in his back pockets. He paced around the room as

John had done. 'Small,' he said. 'And barren. But clean. You must hate it in here.'

The burning started again. John blinked, hard. 'I want to see my friends. Please let me out of here so that I can help them.'

Harper stopped pacing. He stood near the toilet hole. 'What would you do for them?'

'I'd be there. We'd be together. We're never really apart much. Please. I promised.'

Harper leaned back against the wall, his hands still in his pockets, his elbows keeping him upright. 'It's important to you, that promise?'

'I do what I say.' John felt a bit of anger rise. Who was this man to question John's ability to keep promises?

'That's an admirable trait,' Harper said. 'The problem is that here the base authorities have taken all control away from you. Dania didn't really explain that, did she?'

John could barely catch his breath. Somehow that sounded worse than anything he had encountered on Bountiful. He at least had control over his time there. 'No,' he said. 'She didn't say that.'

Harper pushed off the walls with his arms. 'Worst case you will remain in this cell until the hearing. If you work with me and Dania, we should be able to get you some time out of here, maybe even move you to a more congenial place.'

'She said she'd get me to see the others in three days.'

'If she can. You see, John, here on Lina Base, the deaths you caused are viewed as serious. Do you understand that?'

John half-shook his head. He hadn't caused deaths – not intentionally. He had been trying to help them. Trying to help all of them. 'They weren't supposed to die,' he said.

'What was supposed to happen?'

'They were supposed to grow up!' John's voice echoed in the small space.

Harper was staring at him, dark eyes sparkling with interest. 'Just like the Dancers?'

'Yeah.' John sat heavily on the side of the cot. The man was giving him sympathy, and he was taking it in. He had needed warmth so badly. 'Just like the Dancers.'

'But humans are different than Dancers.'

The words hit him like a slap. 'We have hands. We have

hearts and lungs. We grow up.'

'But we don't have two sets of hearts or lungs. And we grow up on our own.'

John was trembling. 'I don't understand,' he said, 'what makes you so sure.'

Harper Reeves

Harper's hands were still shaking when he arrived in the cafeteria at the end of the restaurant section on deck ten. The smell of roast beef and ham cooked with too much grease turned his stomach. He ignored the grime streaked plastic windows and went through the always open door. He threaded his way through the servo units, closed at this time of night, past the old-fashioned grill which was giving off the odours, to the booths beyond. Dania was sitting at her favourite booth in the corner, with windows that overlooked the bottom edge of the docking bay.

Her feet were crossed at the ankles, her pants tight across her thighs. She was clutching her hair with one hand, and staring at hard copy in front of her. Her small computer screen sat to one side, the cursor blinking.

Harper grabbed a cup of coffee with caffeine – this place was the only restaurant on the base that served the real stuff – and slid across from Dania. 'That last one's breaking,' he said.

She looked up at him, her eyes glazed. She blinked twice before he was certain she had focused on him. 'Who?'

'Allen. I don't think he's stopped crying since the authorities talked to him. His nose and eyelids are actually chapped.' Harper tugged at the drawstring on his pants. When Harper had offered just a bit of sympathy, Allen had clung to him and sobbed. Harper wasn't able to ask any questions. He just held and rocked the boy until the boy fell asleep.

'Did he ask after his parents?' Dania asked. She tucked a strand of hair behind her ear. Her fingers were smudged with ink. She usually scrawled all over hardcopy forms.

Harper frowned, remembering. 'No,' he said. 'None of them did.'

Dania nodded. 'Neither did the girls, according to Mariko.'

'Did she find that odd?'

'Did you?'

'I'm reserving judgment until I understand this situation better.' Harper picked up his mug and sipped. The coffee was strong and bitter. 'Will you be handling all the children, then?'

'I don't know.' Dania gathered the papers and stacked them together. 'Right now I am. I've asked Judge Puyi to assign other attorneys, but we're short-handed as it is. I suspect she'll rule that the cases are similar enough for me to handle them all.'

Harper's shirt was still damp from Allen's tears. He tugged the material away from his chest, felt a slight coolness as he did. 'I don't know,' he said. 'They seem different to me.'

'Brief me,' Dania said.

He glanced around. The other booths were empty. The cafeteria was empty except for the man in the stained apron who scraped at the grill with a flat silver pad. The snick-snick-snick sound rose above the drip of the coffee boiler. During the day this cafeteria was packed. At night, the restaurant a few doors down did most of the business. Both cooked food from scratch during certain hours, and both catered to different vices. He preferred the cafeteria because he liked caffeine and grease better than alcohol and sugar.

'I haven't made more than a handful of preliminary notes after each session,' he said. 'I can write you a report— '

She shook her head as he knew she was going to.

' —All right,' he said. 'This is first impression. You need to make your own record. I have had no time to think on this, so you have to clear it with me before using it officially. Agreed?'

'Agreed.' She moved the keyboard over and pushed two keys. The words VID RECORD appeared briefly on the screen, followed by his visage.

'This is first impression,' he repeated just to make sure she had it down properly. 'You have to clear this with me before using it officially.' He looked away from the screen, unable to watch himself when he was talking to her. 'I saw all the boys. Max is pretty quiet, but he's performing self-mutilation. He has bitten his lips raw and he's scratching through the skin on his arms, and he had treatment through the autodoc, so this is since he was incarcerated. I have to check the autodoc report, but from my own cursory examination, I would guess this mutilation is new.'

Dania nodded. 'Any danger of him harming himself?'

'Not seriously,' Harper said. 'But it's too soon to tell for sure. The one I'm the most worried about on that level is Allen. The boy is devastated. He's lost everything: his home, his friends, his family, and his tears suggest that he knows it – and that he understands his own culpability. I might be reading too much into this, but the tears suggest a deep anguish that neither of the other two boys are showing.'

'What do you suggest?' Dania said.

'We need to get him out of that sterile environment, put him in a room with soft things, like cushions, pillows, stuffed toys. Offer him as much comfort as we can, and make sure the people who are observing him know that he needs to be watched closely.'

With her left hand, Dania flagged the record. 'I'll see what I can do.'

Harper sipped his coffee. It had cooled. It soothed a rawness in his throat he hadn't even been aware of until that moment. 'The one who baffles me is John.'

'The leader.'

Harper shrugged. 'We only have Schafer's word on that. But John's actions seem to confirm it. He only spoke of himself once, when he thought I was accusing him of lying to his friends. We actually talked, unlike the others, but all he wanted was to be with the other children, particularly Allen, whom he professes to be frightened for.'

Dania nodded. 'He did the same with me. He seems remarkably self-possessed. He has a vocabulary that astounded me, yet he claims never to have gone to school.'

'I have no idea what's truth and what's not at this point,' Harper said. 'I don't even know where their perceptions are faulty. I need background materials. Then I would like to get together with Mariko and compare notes. I know we will have to let the children interact so that we can get a better picture of their interpersonal relationships, but that may have to wait.'

Dania sighed. She pushed a key on the pad. Harper's image winked off the screen, followed by the words END VID RECORD. She leaned back and brushed her short wavy hair out of her face. 'It's beginning to look more and more like we're going to have to try each one separately. According to Schafer, one of the girls,

Beth, broke with the rest and confessed. That's how he was able to track this down. She'll have to be handled differently than the boys, and they'll have to be handled separately, too.' She shook her head. 'It's a mess, Harper. This will be the first test of the Alien Influences Act.'

Harper started. The snick-snick-snick behind him had stopped. 'They're not going to trial, are they?'

'Doesn't matter.' Dania folded the computer and slipped it in her carryall. Then she slid the papers in the flaps. The man in the apron rounded the corner and switched off the coffee pot. 'We have to determine at the hearing how to treat them in our legal system. Do we treat them as children or are their crimes too severe for that? Do we treat them as human? Do we treat them as human under Dancer influence? Do we treat them as Dancers with human characteristics? Do we treat them as Dancers only? You and Mariko have your work cut out for you.'

'So do you,' Harper said.

Dania nodded. She ran a hand through her hair – and it was messy enough to look as if she had done that all day. 'I don't like this case,' she said. 'Every private attorney in the quadrant has been vying for it, and suddenly the judge gives it to me. I don't have the experience to try this, and when I told her, she smiled and told me to do my best. The government has been treating them like adults from the beginning. I put in a formal request that the guards' treatment be reviewed, but I know nothing will come of that.'

'You saying they're trying to bury this?'

'Clearly they want these children out of sight and out of mind. That impromptu press gathering at the shuttle bay really pissed off Werfel. It won't happen again.'

'Come on. They can't hide something of this magnitude.'

Dania shrugged. 'They hide lots of things. Did you know that four Salt Juice studies have been classified in the past year?'

Harper wrapped his hand around his mug. He felt a little thrill run through him. She had brought that up for a reason. Some kind of Salt Juice influence? He already knew of the motives that had come from Bountiful. He understood greed.

'You're going to have to get us all more time,' Harper said. 'We can't make judgments like that in the space of a few weeks.'

'I'll do what I can.' She reached across the table and took a sip from his cup. In the front of the cafeteria, the servo units hummed as they rose, their display pads switching on. She glanced that way briefly, then looked back at Harper. 'This is one of those times when I wish our legal system had developed differently when we went into space. We're using a system of jurisprudence that has its roots on Earth, in post-Reformation England, centuries of tradition and custom that simply do not apply to life out here. If I can't put those children in a context that the court will accept, Harper, they will be placed on a penal ship and sent to Reed or one of the other active mines. They're too young. Your Allen will shatter— '

'If he makes it to the ship,' Harper said.

'I'll do what I can for him.' She slid out of the booth and grabbed her carryall. 'I'll do what I can for all of them.'

She slung the carryall over her shoulder. Harper slid his cup across the fake wood surface of the table. The shaking had stopped, but not the fear in his belly.

'Harper?'

He turned. She was standing beside the servo units, which had risen to eye level in anticipation of her order. They looked out of place in the cafeteria, their tall, white stalks and blinking display pads destroying the historical ambiance the owner had tried to create.

'I will upload everything I have on the children, Bountiful, and the Dancers. It should be in your mailbox by the time you return to your office.'

He nodded. 'You need to send me text and analysis of the Alien Influences Act too,' he said. 'I have some stuff, but only the supposition that my colleagues have prepared. I need material on what the Parliament intended, and whether or not anyone has attempted to use it since the enactment.'

'Will do,' she said. 'I don't know if it will clarify or not.' She adjusted her carryall, and walked out of the cafeteria. The servo units lowered to their at-rest height, the displays sending a faint green light to the glass in the counter across from them.

Harper sipped his chilly coffee and leaned back in the booth. His shirt was dry, but he still felt the pressure of Allen's needy body against his. The boy's tears had shaken him more than anything. A need that deep didn't come from a single incident. The boy had acted as if he had never been held before.

But Harper knew that wasn't true. He had watched from the doorway as all the children huddled in a group. They had relied on each other.

Please, I promised.

He had the sense he was facing something larger than it seemed. Even Dania's outline of the subject of the hearing seemed simplistic. Something else was happening as well.

He had to find it. He had to find it quickly. He had the sense, from Allen's gulping sobs, that there wasn't much time.

John

His toenails had turned purple with the cold. He slept on his back, with his feet tucked under his thighs. He often woke with the straps cutting into his skin and his legs prickling and numb.

He counted the days by the meals he ate. Six meals: two days. He had seen Dania once and she had tried to explain the procedures to him. He listened intently, but couldn't remember what she said moments after she spoke.

Harper was clearer. Harper said he would never see his friends again if the case went badly. John had asked how to make the case go well, and Harper had told him to listen to Dania.

But Dania made no sense.

Despite the calls he sent, the Dancers only came to him in his dreams. They chirred and whistled, touched his face with their cinnamon-scented hands. He spent hours on his cot, thinking like a Dancer, floating ever so slightly above the ground, turning his thoughts toward the future.

But the future didn't seem clear any more. He was away from Bountiful as he had wanted, but he was even more trapped than he had been there.

And frightened. He couldn't tell anyone how frightened he was. He kept seeing Allen on the shuttle, asleep next to Skye, his small mouth open and moist, tear tracks marring his round cheeks. He felt the others too, but Allen's need was stronger, and no matter how much he asked, John wasn't allowed out of the room.

The thump he had come to recognize as the door preparing to open echoed through the room. He sat up on the cot, and shook out his legs, watching as the door's lines appeared in the white wall. The day before he had spent hours looking for those cracks and not finding them. They had placed some kind of barrier over the door, a barrier that disappeared with a thump when it came time for the door to open.

The big blond guard ducked through the door, the guard who had tossed John across the room on that first day. His heart pounded in his throat, but he made himself take deep breaths. *Cooperate*, Dania said, *and no one will hurt you.*

John resisted the urge to touch his cheek. The pain had been short that day, but intense.

'Put out your hands,' the guard said.

John did. The guard put wrist restraints on him, testing them once. A light jolt ran through John's skin, and he winced at the remembered force of the pain when he got off the shuttle.

'Follow me.'

John slid off the cot, nearly losing his balance because he couldn't use his arms. His legs were weak; he had been lying with his feet tucked under his thighs for too long.

The guard looked over his shoulder. His nose was flat and wide, digging into the flesh of his cheeks. 'You will keep pace with me.'

John nodded. He was shaking. Dania had said nothing about this. He didn't know where the guard would take him, or what the guard would do.

Bend over, son, this won't hurt a bit.

John closed his eyes, willing his father's voice to go away. Then he opened his eyes again and followed the guard out of the room.

The corridor was narrow, barely wide enough for him and the guard, and too bright, with the same white walls he had just left. As he stepped up, his chilled feet encountered carpet. Its soft surface felt warm against his toes. He shivered once, as the chill left him, then embraced the warmth.

The door did not close behind him, but remained open, revealing the simplicity of the cubicle he had just left. The familiarity of the room – he knew each space and corner – attracted him, and he wondered at it. He hated being confined, but he hated surprises even more.

Another guard appeared behind them, a woman who was as tall as John. But her arms were thick with muscle, and in her hands she carried a small snub laser. He didn't acknowledge her. They didn't need to protect themselves. He had nowhere to run.

There were no other doors. The walls were smooth, deceptively so, and he wondered how many invisible doors hid behind the clean surface. Probably quite a number. Guards could forget the doors were there, and prisoners would die inside, unable to get out, trapped forever.

This time, his shudder didn't come from the cold.

The blond guard followed the corridor to the right. Ahead was a third white wall, a dead end. The guard ran a thumb along his belt, something thunked, and then the door appeared, almost as wide as the corridor. The guard pushed against it, and the door swung open, revealing a world filled with colours and sounds and textures.

The walls were still white, but covered with paintings. Most were surreal – odd spaceships on black backgrounds with a dotting of stars. Green plants hung from the ceiling, and music, thin and joyful, was piped through some kind of sound system. The carpet was the light rose John's mother had coaxed out of her backyard flowers. The benches lining the walls were upholstered with flowering plants on a white linen.

John had to stop at the door. The sudden rush of colour and sound gave him a headache and made his eyes water. The guards stopped too, as if they had expected such a reaction.

Only two days. Only two days and he nearly drowned in sensation. What would it be like when he had been imprisoned for weeks?

He took a deep breath and stepped out of the white hallway into the colour. This carpet was a deep pile, the soft strands burying his feet. The guards took his arms and led him forward. Their fingers dug into his skin, as if they expected him to run now that he saw life again.

The corridor widened and, on the left, a large glass room jutted out of the wall. Green plants of all shapes and sizes pressed against the glass, their leaves in what appeared like painful agony. Whoever had placed the plants inside had no knowledge of horticulture. The blond guard let go of John's arm long enough to open the glass door. The woman put her hand on the small of John's back and pushed him inside. Then she took off the restraints and followed the blond guard into the corridor.

John hovered near the door. The plants blocked his view of

the rest of the roon. The air inside was humid, and sweat beaded on his brow. The warmth felt good. He pushed up the sleeves on his jumpsuit, and walked along the brown carpeted path.

It opened into a wide area filled with huge pillows. Plants hung from the ceiling, their tendrils reaching toward the ground below. The walls farther in were mirrored, so he felt as if he were in a large, tame jungle. Tension he hadn't even known he was carrying slid out of his back.

'John?'

The voice belonged to Skye. He whirled. She was standing behind him, her small frame half-hidden by a pile of pillows.

'Skye?' He trembled. She was smaller than he remembered, the angles on her face sharper. He was afraid to touch her, afraid that if he did, she would vanish.

'Come here,' she said. 'Everyone's here but Allen.'

Her voice rose just a bit as she said Allen's name, and he felt the worry, then, clear and strong. He crossed the warm carpet, ducking beneath plants until he reached her.

They had gone down into a square area, two steps below the floor he stood on. They had built a barricade of pillows, imprisoning themselves like Dancer children. Skye took his hand and led him down. He touched them all: Verity, her red hair tousled; Pearl who seemed paler than she had been just a few days before; Max, his chin smeared with dried blood from his scabbed lips; Dusty, arms wrapped around herself, still refusing to meet his eyes; and Beth, who launched herself into his arms as soon as he got close.

He pulled her tight. She was trembling as badly as he was. They were all wearing white jumpsuits and only Max's was stained. They must have been imprisoned in the same kind of rooms.

He smoothed Beth's hair. Her warmth calmed him. Being with the others calmed him. He reached out his hands and pulled them all in, until they came together in a group hug. After a moment, it blended into Dancer greeting ritual, hands stroking faces, refamiliarizing themselves with the texture, the smell of each other.

He had never been so alone as he had been those last few days.

After a moment, Skye pulled out. 'I'm waiting for Allen,' she

92

said, and went back to her post.

The group separated and sat, remaining close. John took the pillow in the middle. Beth leaned against his right, and Verity against his left. Pearl put a hand on Dusty, and Max leaned against Verity.

John took Beth and Verity's hands. He could scarcely breathe with all of the emotions running through him. He was glad to see them, and yet the burning had returned to the back of his eyes. He blinked it back. The others relied on him. They needed him to be strong right now. Fear still gnawed at his belly; he was not sure how long he could be with them.

Dania had done it, though. She had brought them together. 'Are you okay?' he asked, looking at Beth.

She nodded, her gaze flitting around the group. Her hand remained limp in his. 'They separated us in the corridor, and put us in different rooms.'

'They each had these cubicles with light beams . . . ' Verity shuddered. 'We've been talking about it. It seems they put us all in the same kind of place, but made sure we were apart.'

'I've been trying to contact someone,' Pearl said, 'but those walls are a barrier.'

'We always knew walls were barriers,' Dusty whispered.

'I hated my room,' Max said. His tongue played with his damaged lower lip.

Stop it, John thought, sending Max a wave of warmth. *Stop hurting yourself.*

Max shuddered a little, but continued as if he felt nothing. 'It was all white and all there was was this cot, and no one to talk to.' Finally he looked up, his eyes filled with tears. 'I'm scared, John.'

'He's here!' Skye cried. She scrambled up the pillows and ran into the centre of the room. John squeezed Beth and Verity's hands, then got up and hurried after Skye.

Allen was standing at the edge of the large pillowed space, his body half hidden by a nunner. Its broad flat leaves brushed against his skin, leaving a trail of light green dust. Tendrils from hanging plants brushed against his face, but he appeared not to notice them. His jumpsuit was askew and rumpled, his eyes glazed.

Skye reached him first. She wrapped her arms and legs

93

around him, clinging to him as if he were a tree trunk. He didn't move. His hands remained at his side and he continued to stare straight ahead.

Allen, John thought, sending all the love and concern he had felt. *Allen, we are worried about you.*

Two tears leaked out of Allen's eyes. Skye brought her feet down but, as she did so, he put his arms around her and buried his face in her shoulder, his body shaking. She patted his back as if he were a baby.

John reached them and pulled them both into a hug. Pearl arrived next and put her arms around them all. Then Dusty squeezed in. Max clung to Pearl, Verity clung to Max, and Beth wormed her way inside, next to John. The hug became warm and rich, humming with the tenderness that John had missed.

— If only we could be like this always, Beth whispered.

— Then we will know that someone loves us, Max said.

— We will always love each other, John said, and it wasn't until the whistles and chirrups came out of his throat that he realized he was speaking Dancer.

Hands had reached up, found each other, linking. The warmth John had felt had spread through his entire body, into his groin. His fingers found others, light and soft as the carpet beneath his feet.

— They would like us to think we are evil, Dusty said.

'We are!' Allen cried in English. 'We killed.'

The moment slipped as if it had never been. The hands fell, the warmth receded. John pulled the bodies nearest him close, but the humming link had died.

'Maybe,' John said, 'if we had had more time — '

Other hands, strange hands, reached into the circle, pulling them back. John clung to the children around him, but he wasn't strong enough. The strange hands yanked until he stumbled backwards, into the arms of his guards. The blond guard held him while the other put on wrist restaints.

John struggled. They couldn't take him now. Not when he got close again. Not when he saw the others for the first time.

Beth wasn't fighting with her guards. Allen stood in the centre, abandoned, head bowed. Max had crumpled in a heap and his guards were picking him up. Skye was struggling, all elbows and knees.

'No!' John cried. 'Not yet. Please. Let us stay.'

The guards pushed him forward, but he locked his legs. They kicked the back of his knees and he fell, his toes curling at an odd angle, sending pain through his shins. Pearl was crying for Allen, Verity was screaming, and Dusty had landed beside John, kicking and flailing, rolling from side to side so that they couldn't put restraints on her.

Two big hands encircled his waist and picked him up as if he were sand. The blond guard threw John over his shoulder, his face slamming into the guard's back, and someone grabbed his ankles, putting other restraints on them. Still he squirmed, trying to free his body. The restraints grew tighter, and then the waves of pain started, running through him, squeezing his chest.

Allen's guards had taken him by the shoulders and were pushing hm out of the door. He was the only one who was docile.

Allen, please. Allen. You're a Dancer. Remember, you're a Dancer. John had to stop struggling to send the thought, but Allen didn't acknowledge it. He kept walking, head down, until he made it through the door.

The blond guard started forward too. John bucked, shoving his knees into the guard's chest. The restraints became white hot heat, searing his flesh. Tears prickled and his breath was coming in short gasps. His own cries had joined the others, incoherent words of protest and loss. As the guard carried him through the door, he stopped, collapsing against the guard's hard frame, pain throbbing through him.

'No,' he said into the smooth fabric of the guard's uniform. 'Please take me back. Please.'

But no one heard him, no one acknowledged him. For a half second, he thought he felt Beth inside him, her words faint. . . . *sorry, John. So sorry* . . . but when he tried to catch it, the message and Beth were gone.

The restraints remained hot until the guard left the corridor and entered the white prison space. The bare walls seemed even starker, the air colder. John buried his face in the guard's silver uniform, unwilling to look. They were taking him back. Back to that room. Back to the cold.

Something thudded up ahead, then the guard stopped. The

woman removed the restraints and the guard tossed John. John flew through the air, caught a glimpse of the door, sealing the guards behind it, the cot barren and alone against the wall, the black toilet hole the only spot of colour —

— and then he hit the far wall, his skin slapping against the smooth surface, pain shimmering through him. He slid to the floor, cracking his right elbow as he landed, the air leaving him in a sudden whoosh.

He couldn't breathe.

He.

Couldn't.

Breathe.

Panic shot through him before he realized he was taking shallow breaths, not enough to replenish the loss, but enough to keep him alive. The ache in his elbow was exquisite: sharp and intense. He focused on it, using it as a centre until the oxygen filled his lungs.

Then he sat up. He was dizzy, and his right arm hung limply at his side. What had gone wrong? One minute they were close and the next guards were pushing them apart. For a half second, he had allowed himself to believe he would live in that warm, soft place, filled with greenery and his friends. One brief, happy moment before he lost it all.

Again.

Dania Zinn

The lift didn't move fast enough for Dania. She stood in front of the thin crack in the doors, carryall over her shoulder, foot tapping impatiently against the metal floor. When the lift eased to a stop, and the doors began their slow side apart, Dania slipped through the crack and into the Security Chief's central office.

Two dying palms stood like sentries in the middle of the waiting room. A thin young man, his dark skin pocked with acne scars, huddled over a slanted desk. The desk held eight viewscreens and twenty-five non-view access lines, almost too much for one receptionist to handle.

Dania gave the receptionist only half a glance, enough to note that each of the screens was lit. Only one showed the now-empty group room. She shoved on the heavy doors – made of real North American oak – and stepped into the chief's office as the receptionist stood behind her.

'Hey! You can't do that! Hey — '

The doors closed, cutting off his reedy voice. The chief's office was dark. A huge oak desk dominated the room. The chief's overstuffed chair was turned to the side, his body hidden in the textured blue fabric. Fake oak pannelling hid four walls covered with flat screens. Only the left wall showed anything now: fifty screens, some showing the children, some showing the guards, and two still focussed on the group room. One screen showed Harper and Mariko, deep in discussion in the corridor outside Harper's office, and another tracked Dania, showing her small and lost in front of the chief's oak desk.

She didn't like that picture.

She leaned forward and slammed her hands on the desk, making sure her palms left prints on the polished surface. 'What the hell is this?' she snapped. 'I ordered that meeting for my consultants so they could watch those children interact. You break it up with guards and destroy any — '

'Perhaps you didn't see the infra-red scan.' August Werfel swivelled his chair until he faced her. His eyes were flat and narrow, his skin tough and carved with deep frown lines. She had never seen him smile. 'Something happened when they gathered like that and started to chant.'

'That's precisely the kind of thing we wanted to observe. You are interfering with my case.'

Werfel folded his hands over his flat stomach. 'And you, Ms Zinn, forget yourself. Those children are hostile and dangerous, and I must protect the base from them at all cost.'

'Those children are *children*,' Dania said.

'Those children committed the most brutal murders I have seen in my tenure as chief.' Werfel's lip curled slightly. 'I will not have them loose their powers on this base.'

'They used native equipment. They didn't do it with their minds. As long as they're guarded, we will all be safe.' Dania leaned as close to him as she dared. He didn't flinch. His gaze remained steady.

'What makes you so certain?' he asked.

Something in his voice made her freeze. They weren't always on opposite sides of a case. He had saved her, twice, from a manic client, and he had stopped a riot that started in Judge Ni's courtroom before it spread to the rest of the judiciary. Often, she used him as a source. He used his informant's tone now.

'What do you know?' she asked. She kept her position, but she no longer felt as fierce. Just by asking the question, she had lost ground to him.

'I know you haven't read your history.' His chair creaked as he pushed even deeper into it. 'The miners on Bountiful over 100 years ago nearly exterminated the Dancers. After a series of murders.'

Dania stood slowly. She had read her history. She had seen nothing about this. 'Murders?' she asked.

Werfel nodded. 'Young boys. Shaft watchers, you know, down there to monitor the equipment, make sure the oxygen kept flowing through the salt caves. Half a dozen found in the space of a week, hands, hearts and lungs missing.'

'Did Schafer know this?'

'Wouldn't matter if he did,' Werfel said. 'Those kids of yours confessed. Just like a group of miners did. But no one listened to them. The miners slaughtered the Dancers. It wasn't the usual thing you see in colonization where the native species just gets in the way. The miners waged a full scale war – and if it hadn't been for a few of the remaining shaft watchers contacting Lina Base, there wouldn't be Dancers to this day.'

Dania grabbed the heavy oak chair to the side of the desk, and pulled it forward, sinking into it. 'This isn't in the records. I did look. I've been reading about Bountiful for days. How'd you know about this?'

'Because,' Werfel said, his frown lines digging deeper into his skin, 'the first man I ever killed in this job was one of those miners.'

Dania felt as if she were floating. Events were happening too rapidly for her to grasp. She paused, took a deep breath, and did the maths. Werfel had been on the job for forty years, ever since he was fifteen. 'That miner had to have been pretty old.'

'Ninety-five. He'd been a shaft watcher, one of the group that confessed. Only no one knew it.'

She shook her head a little. He was going to make her pry this story out of him. 'I don't have a lot of time, Chief. Explain it so that I can verify and see if it's relevant to the case, and to your actions this afternoon.'

'Go ahead. Verify. You'll need some security clearance which I'll be happy to give you. Everything got classified when they discovered Salt Juice.'

Salt Juice. Dania ran a hand over her face. It all came back to Salt Juice. If only she could get her hands on those buried Salt Juice studies. Maybe if Werfel gave her the clearance, she would find both the history and the studies. 'What will I find in those histories?' she asked.

'You'll see that same infra-red energy that was appearing around those children of yours. I tell you, it's not something I ever wanted to see again.' He hadn't changed position, but his body seemed tenser, more alert. He sighed, pushed his entwined hands forward, and stretched. Then he leaned his elbows on the desk.

She waited.

'Okay,' he said. 'Here's what happened. I'm new, barely five weeks on the job, as pimply-faced as Roy out there. We're

101

scanning the screens toward the end of second shift, keeping an eye on Uma's – a bar near the docks – long gone now. Seems there's a bunch of old men in there, and the more they have to drink, the weirder they get. They make these noises, and the infra-red scan starts showing some strange fluctuations. The men start grabbing people around them. My partner alerts some other security teams, but we're the first to arrive. We burst in just as this one guy pulls a Dancer knife and goes for another old guy, slashing his arm off with one movement. We order him to stop, he doesn't; I shoot but not to kill, and the guy collapses. Suddenly he's older than he looks, tons of wrinkles, brittle bones. The weak shot I hit him with will stun a man my age, but kill a guy over ninety.'

Dania tried to picture it: Werfel making the kind of mistake that would cost a man's life. She couldn't. He had become the sort of man who never made a mistake, who, in fact, ridiculed others who erred in any way.

'Thing was,' Werfel said, 'he didn't look that old. Neither did the other guys. Every one of us involved swore to that, including the bartender. But when you look at the cordings, you see a bunch of old geezers acting weird. That's not what it looked like on the screens.'

'Sounds to me like you panicked this afternoon based on an old memory,' Dania said. 'Those children were in your custody. There's no way they could have weapons. No way at all.'

Werfel studied her for a moment, his cool eyes even flatter than they had been. 'Maybe,' he said. 'But I've been on this base long enough to know that there are things in this universe we can't understand. The Dancers are tapped into some of that. Those old guys had a history of acting strange when they were together. People died around them. Now people are dying around these kids. I don't want to take any chances, Counsellor. I can't.'

She nodded. He was frightened. She could hear it in his voice. She had never heard fear from him before. 'Still, Chief, that interaction could have taught us something.'

'Maybe. Maybe it would have given the kids the kind of power they needed to be free of us. Use the clearance. I left a badge for you with Roy. Check the records, Zinn. Read your history. Then talk to me.'

She knew dismissal when she heard it – and for once she was willing to go. She grabbed her carryall.

'And Dania?'

She stopped. Werfel was looking at her, a frown on his face. 'No more problems, all right? The base is tense enough with these kids here, and I have to monitor that sort of thing. If we have anything else weird happen, I'll ask Judge Puyi to render a decision so fast those kids will be on Reed before you even hear they've left the base.'

Her body stiffened. 'Is that a threat?'

He shook his head. 'A warning. You have to know what you're up against. I'm up against a base that believes those kids are dangerous. The government is using any excuse it can find to get those kids out of the public eye. No one wants this case as the first test of the Alien Influences Act. It's too messy, and Schafer is unreliable. I got word from the Base Command. Any more problems with those kids, and I have the government's permission to take care of them myself.'

Dania didn't grace that comment with a reply. She didn't dare. Everyone was making it quite clear that she had one chance and one chance only with those kids. She let herself out of the door. Roy, the receptionist, glanced at her as she walked through, but said nothing. She stopped long enough to grab the clearance badge off his desk. His monitors were on the cells, as well as on the corridors through the children's deck. She had never seen such security – not even when they had had a serial killer shipped in from Minar Base for special evaluation.

Werfel was spooked, and the feeling was catching.

She hadn't liked those group hugs either, and when the kids started that whistling, it had unnerved her. It felt otherwordly, as if she were watching one of the native species specials the Alliance put on the nets.

She stepped into the lift. The doors closed before the connection hit her. The kids frightened her because their behaviour was alien.

Not human.

Like the Act specified.

Dania ordered dinner at the small take-out place next to her office. Then she rode the lift to her apartment, unlocked and opened the door. The smell of almond chicken and fresh tea greeted her: the take-out order had arrived only moments before she did.

Her apartment was small, but built on two levels – an unusual luxury at the base, and one she was willing to pay dearly for. She slept on the second level in an airbed built into the floor. A Jacuzzi bath and shower were also on the second level, with a double row of windows that had a view of the vastness of space. She supposed that when she used the facilities, a passing shuttle's crew might see her, but the chances were slim enough that she kept the curtains open most of the time.

A functional kitchen stood on the first level. But the large main room was her pride and joy. Three floor-to-ceiling foot wide windows graced the wall opposite the door. She had worked them into the room's design. The artwork on the remaining walls matched: long and narrow, also running floor to ceiling. She had had them especially commissioned to match the space.

She had also covered the white floor with thin black runners, anchored by the black-and-white furniture she had chosen. Now she pulled off her shoes, set down her carryall, and crossed into the kitchen.

The food sat on the servo unit built into the side wall, the bill hanging from the bottom of the food plate and marked paid. She took the hardcopy receipt and tossed it in the recycler: she hated excess paper, always had, thought it a waste of the base's resources. A sign of ostentation, just like Werfel's oak furniture. She had kept her place decorative, but light and functional, easily mobile, should she ever transfer to another location.

She grabbed the hot plate, a fork, and the large thermos of tea, and carried them to her easy chair in front of the windows. She sank into it and stared into the darkness, letting her mind process the information she had gathered during the day.

In the four hours since she left Werfel, she had dug into the classified files. She still hadn't been able to access the Salt Juice studies, but she had been able to go into the histories, studying everything she could find about mining, the Dancers and

Bountiful. The miners weren't the only ones who had problems associated with the Dancers. The early Salt Juice entrepreneurs lost a child to the same bizarre death. Instead of attacking the Dancers, though, they had blamed the situation on a bad batch of Juice, thinking that the killer – who had been caught in the act – had lost complete control of herself.

The almond chicken had a smooth glaze, and rested on a bed of fluffy rice. The chicken was fresh and the almonds added enough flavour. She washed her first bites down with tea; she hadn't realized how hungry she was.

The Dancers. Schafer's report, skimpy as it was due to his grave physical condition, made no mention of them at all. In her public statements in preparation for her own trial, Netta Goldin had mentioned the undue influence of the Dancers, but Dania had thought it some kind of defense ploy. Still, she had received a message just before leaving her office, letting her know that the Provisional Parliament of the Territorial System was having an emergency meeting to examine the efficacy of the immediate shut down of the colony on Bountiful. Not only did a shutdown mean the redistribution of lifelong Bountiful residents, it also meant significant financial losses for Salt Juice manufacturers and others with a stake in the colony.

Such an action made no sense – unless they were covering up something.

She finished the chicken and set her plate on the floor. The history of Bountiful showed that the Dancers had some kind of impact on the humans around them. The defective Salt Juice argument didn't stand, because Salt Juice hadn't been invented during the mining era. But there were other factors to consider as well. Did something on the planet cause a kind of insanity that manifested itself in an imitation of the Dancers' actions? Were certain groups susceptible to it? Unlike most of the current colonists, the children had spent a great deal of time with the Dancers – and the children were the only ones since the dome had been built to exhibit this kind of behaviour.

Dania sighed and sipped her now-cold tea. In moments like this, she still missed Nicky intensely. He would have debated the issues with her, forced her to think of things she hadn't considered before. He used to pad around their huge one level apartment in his bare feet, the cat trailing after him like a puppy, and he would spout legal theory as if it were poetry.

Her throat was constricting. According to Harper, three years was more than enough time to recover. But Harper wanted to see her outside of work. He didn't know – no one did, not even her grief therapist – that when a man touched her, she flashed on the body they had sent back from Ifor, the skin she had loved to caress in tatters, only his face remaining, eyes closed as if in sleep. The officials in charge of the body had told her that Nicky had made a mistake, attempting to do field work with a native race without enough preparation. But he had thought it so important. He had been one of the originators behind the Alien Influences Act, and he thought it necessary to know the laws – if any – of the natives who had worked with the clients Nicky was defending.

Since his death, she had ignored the work on the Act, and had barely noticed when it passed. She had tried to beg off the case for personal reasons, but Judge Puyi wouldn't let her. Then Dania had gone to her therapist for a medical discharge, but her therapist refused, claiming such work would be cathartic.

Cathartic. If Dania had been Nicky, she probably would have gone to Bountiful herself, to attempt to understand the Dancers. But she wasn't. She would rely on the experts here, and make what decisions she could.

The thing she had to remember, the thing she couldn't forget, was that eight children depended on her. For their very lives.

iii

Despite an intention to take care of her physical needs, she was in her office before first shift. Five hours of sleep rarely sufficed, but her dreams were filled with Nicky and headless children. The rest she got working seemed better than the rest she got while trying to sleep.

Her office had the same functional black-and-white design as her apartment. She had redecorated after Nicky's death. Harper said the black and white was representative of her new and improved vision of the world. His sarcasm was something she didn't like about him.

As if on cue, a bell sounded and the security system

announced Harper and that he was unarmed. Ever since the manic client had attacked her, Dania had a state of the art, extra sensitive system installed in her office. She got rid of her human receptionist, and let the system screen all her calls and visitors. Her legal secretaries didn't like the change much – they said it made her unapproachable – but she did. She knew that nothing could happen to her without warning.

'Open,' she said.

The door swung out, and Harper stepped inside. He wore a red sweatshirt and tight cotton pants. The bags beneath his eyes suggested that he hadn't slept well either.

'You get my report?' she asked before he could say anything.

He nodded, running his hand through his already tousled hair. 'I'm not sure if an ancient bar fight among old men is precedent enough to mess with a sanctioned suspect evaluation. Mariko's thinking of getting a ruling.'

'Werfel says the patterns are the same.' Dania saved her place in the file reviews and pulled the cover over her desktop screen.

'Yes,' Harper said. 'And it could have retriggered the stress of the trauma of his first on-the-job kill. It might have nothing at all to do with the infra red scan or the kids. Sure wish someone in this base had enough clout to send Werfel in for a psychological review.'

Dania smiled. They both knew that she could make such a request – any official of the court could – but that she wouldn't. 'You did get the cording, though.'

'Oh, yeah,' Harper said. 'There are people here from the Extra Species Alliance on Bountiful. The Dancer expert, Latona Etanl, is being held in protective custody. The Territory is charging her as an accessory to murder, and so I couldn't approach her. But her assistant, Daniel Vincour, has more knowledge of the Dancers than anyone else on the base except her, so I spoke with him.'

Dania leaned forward. 'And?'

'He says they were performing a Dancer greeting ritual, although he claims the use of the hands was more sexual than normal greetings— '

'Sexual?'

Harper nodded. 'Dancer genitals are in the hands. Anyway, that's not the most interesting part. He said that when they

107

spoke of past events, they used English, but anything to do with emotion, the present or the future was in Dancer. He said it makes perfect sense: the Dancer language has no past tense, and that the Dancers think only in the present and future.'

The security bell buzzed. Dania tapped the system, requesting that it hold all appointments until she was done with Harper. 'What were they saying?'

'Here's his translation.' Harper pulled hard copy from his pocket. He held the paper in front of his face as he read, his fingers making dents in the page. 'Beth: "If only we could be like this always." Max: "Then we will know that someone loves us." John: "We will always love each other." Then they touch for a moment before Dusty says: "They would like us to think we are evil." And that comment provoked Allen's outburst.'

Dania leaned back in her chair. The soft plastic cushions held her, eased the tension rising in her back. 'What do you make of that?'

'At this point, I don't know,' Harper said. 'The one clearly in the most distress is Allen, although I am worried about Max. Max, at least, remains calm for long periods of time. His incidents of self-mutilation might be controllable. But Allen has been crying and sleeping since he got here. The only time he seemed to come alive was with the others.'

'He's feeling guilty.'

'It's more than guilt,' Harper said. 'It's as if everything has been tainted for him. They were talking about love, and he couldn't see it without the deaths involved. I think he's your link, Dania. The problem is that he's sinking so far into himself that he may not be of any use to anyone soon.'

She sighed and swivelled her chair. Love. Something about love. There was a point there that she could use. 'You have a plan.'

'I have an idea, and it's based on supposition. What if these kids can't talk about their emotions in English? What if they need Dancer?'

'It would explain why you and Mariko keep hitting dead ends when you try to bring the conversation toward feelings.'

'Yes, it would,' Harper said. He folded the hard copy and stuck it in his pocket. 'And here's my proposal: I know Werfel won't let us put all of the children together again, but what about

108

three? Say, John, Beth and Allen?'

'What about Skye? She appears to be very close to him.'

'Too close,' Harper said. 'We may not learn enough. They may have developed an intimate shorthand. With Werfel so spooked, we may only get the one chance. I want an opportunity to understand what's going on.'

Dania nodded. She placed her fingers on her desk. 'What about Allen? I thought the meeting was to help him.'

'I can't help him unless I know exactly what's wrong. He can't help you unless he can communicate with me. I think this is the best solution.'

'Have you discussed this with Mariko?'

'Yes.' Harper adjusted the legs of his pants and slid forward. 'She agrees. She's coming to see you this afternoon. You might check with her then.'

'Oh, I plan to,' Dania said. 'And I'll have to clear this through Werfel. It might be even more detrimental to have guards break up a second meeting.'

'Exactly.' Harper stood. 'Thanks, Dania. I'm glad that we agree on this one.'

'We agree,' she said. 'I just hope to hell this meeting helps.'

John

The guards had taken him out of his cell twice since he last saw the others. Once they took him to that plush room with the autodoc. He had climbed inside the cubicle and waited while the light played over his arm. It had ached with a fierceness he hadn't known before, and the probing warm light seemed to make the aches worse. Toward the end of the session, John had passed out. When he came to, he was lying on one of the couches, his arm held by a steel brace and completely numb.

The second time they took him out of his cell, they brought him here, back to the garden room where he had last seen his friends. He sat alone, breathing in the humid air, lying against the soft pillows and staring at the refreshing greenery. Just having his senses stimulated was enough. He never wanted to go back to his cell again.

They had left him in his cell for almost a day after the first meeting, the pain nearly knocking him flat. He found that the best thing – the only thing – he could do was lie on the cot and sleep. The pain would wake him if he turned and bumped the elbow, but at least he didn't have to think about the meeting, and trying to discover why the guards had broken it up.

No one had come to see him since. Not even Dania. He thought his entire future might be in that room, alone, with only his memories for company.

He hadn't believed it when they brought him to the garden room, restraints tight on his arms, four guards instead of two. They brought him inside, took off the restraints and set him free.

Immediately he had gone to the pillows in the centre of the room. The trip had left him exhausted, his arms sore. He lay on his back with the sweat trickling down his face, the plants swaying above him.

They would like us to think we are evil.

We are! We killed

In his fevered dreams, Katie had come to him. She had sat beside his bed, wearing a long sleeved jumpsuit, tiny new fingers poking through the sleeves.

Should have waited, John. Everything would have been all right if you had waited.

A hand touched his arm. He started. Beth's hair brushed his face. Her dark skin had grown paler in the last few days. For a moment, he thought she was a dream, then he realized he hadn't closed his eyes.

He reached up with one shaking hand, and tucked her hair behind her ears. Then he pulled her close. She crawled beside him and buried her face in his shoulder.

So sorry, John. So sorry.

She hadn't said anything, but he felt her inside him, felt the sorrow and guilt sliding off her in waves. He put his arms around her and held her. He was sorry too. It seemed that nothing in their lives had gone right, and even the precious moments, the ones with the Dancers, now had a vile taint to them.

It's okay, he thought to her. *We will come through this.*

Especially now. Now that he could hold her.

No. She pushed against him, trying to sit up. He kept his hands on her waist, unwilling to let her go. *You don't understand, John. That man on Bountiful, I told him. I told him I thought that Michael would never grow up.*

Her feelings invaded him, an intensification of his feelings. The responsibility. The fear. The self-blame.

Bethie. He sent her love with the words. *They knew anyway.*

She shook her head. *I told them. I told them that it didn't work.*

And you were right. It didn't. Just thinking that made his heart ache. He tightened his grip on her waist, put pressure on her back and pulled her back down. Her body was stiff, but he didn't care. He needed touch. He had been without touch for so long he was starving.

She put her hands on his face, touching his eyes, his cheeks, his nose. Her eyes were closed, but she was open to him. Her need to be touched was as strong as his. He slid his hands up her back, felt the bony outlines of her ribs. She had grown thinner. This was eating her up inside. When he touched her neck and her jaw, she relaxed against him.

114

The guards were watching, but he didn't care. He needed touch so bad—

Then he felt another presence, tentative and pain-filled. Beth must have felt it too, for she froze, her body growing rigid all over again. They looked in the same direction, their heads moving in unison.

Allen stood beside the same plant as he had stood by before. Its leaves brushed him, almost hid him from their view. The tendrils from the spidering plant above him caught in his hair. He was staring straight ahead, but John could feel him inside, tiny and frightened.

—Allen, John said in Dancer. Beth echoed his name, only in thought.

Allen looked over. The skin hung in folds on his face. He hadn't been eating. His cheeks were chapped and his nose was red and raw.

—Jonny? Allen said in the same language. —I keep thinking I will die.

No. The thought was Beth's but John could feel the pain echoing through it. *No more of us can die.*

John stood, and pulled Beth up beside him. *We're Dancers,* he thought to Beth. *The only way through the pain is to be Dancers.* He made his body light and he floated to Allen. Allen watched through red rimmed eyes. John touched Allen's face gently, in greeting. After a moment, Beth was beside them. Her fingers did not brush John's for that would be rude. Allen tilted his head back and the muscles in his face went slack. His presence inside John became stronger, not as tentative.

After a moment, he brought his hands up, and they stroked John's face. Allen's hands were warm and moist, like the air in the room. He smelled faintly of sweat and fear. John brushed Allen's hair back and sent as much comfort as he could. Then Allen took his fingers from John's face and put them on Beth's. She closed her eyes, as if doing so could made her absorb the touch even more. John dropped his hands – the pain had returned to his elbow – and waited until Beth and Allen were done.

Finally, they stepped back from each other. Beth and John wrapped their arms around Allen and pulled him forward to the pillows. His body was shaking and twitching as if he couldn't

115

control it. No tears lined his eyes, but his breath came in short sobs.

John felt the grief resound in him. He hadn't allowed himself to think about what their failure meant – that he would never talk to Linette, never plan anything with Katie. They would never sneak out of the dome together in a tribe nor see the Dancers again.

Let him go. The words were Beth's, inside him like fresh water. *You can't hold on so tight. We will all drown.*

John gasped and pulled back just a little. Allen reached for him, his eyes hollow. 'It was wrong, John,' he said. 'It was all wrong.'

John understood that, but he didn't feel it. If they put him back in time, back on Bountiful, he would have done the same thing all over again. He and Katie had tried so many things. They thought Dancer magic was the only option left.

Beth glanced at him and nodded. She was reading him, even though he wasn't sending. But Allen wasn't. Allen still had that faraway look on his swollen face. He took John's hand and rested it on his knee.

Remember the transformation of the Useless Ones?

John tightened his grip on Allen's hand. He remembered. It had been hard to determine who was a Useless One and who was not. The Dancers seemed to know. There had been no ceremony, really, just general acknowledgement of the up-coming sacrifice. Then, by the time the children made another visit, the Useless Ones would be gone.

'I remember,' John said, suddenly wanting out of Dancer mode. Beth had taken Allen's free hand, a frown on her tiny face.

I understand it now, Allen said. *We should have taken that jar, John.*

On the visit before Linette's . . . ritual, a Dancer had pressed a jar into John's hand. The insides had glowed and shifted, and he had handed it back, remarking on its beauty.

'I don't understand,' Beth said. Apparently she, too, was unnerved by Allen's sudden calm. 'How does it link?'

I've been thinking about it since we left Bountiful. Allen kept his head down, but his thoughts were clear. *I know now. Watch.*

He raised their hands above his head, and started to chant.

116

The words were Dancer, the same chant they used to open the puberty ritual. He only made it to the third repetition when his body convulsed.

No! Beth and John's thoughts tangled together. They released his hands, but it was too late. Allen convulsed again and fell back, his eyes half open.

He wasn't breathing.

John leaned over him, not knowing what to do. He grabbed Allen's shoulders and started to shake them. *Allen! Allen, please. Allen!*

Allen's slitted eyes glowed silver. Beth grabbed John's bad arm and pulled him away. *Get back, John.* The silver light whitened the entire room.

Then the guards were inside, knocking back plants, their footsteps loud in the silence. Four guards grabbed John and slammed him into the glass wall, putting restraints all over his body: his wrists, his ankles, his knees, and binding his arms to his chest. Pain shot through his damaged elbow as they pushed on it. Then they shoved a restraint in his mouth. The light was warm. He didn't try to struggle against it.

They were doing the same to Beth. Her gaze was on him, her presence strong in his mind, even though she was reaching for Allen.

We're not Useless. Allen, come back. We're not Useless. We need you.

The silver light had faded. Two guards were bent over Allen. They touched his neck, feeling for a pulse. One of the guards shook his head. The other scooped Allen's body in his arms. Allen hung limply, his head lolling to one side. His eyes were dark, his hands trailing on the floor.

Allen, John thought, reaching, but he felt nothing inside that body. Nothing but emptiness. Then his gaze met Beth's. She was watching him, holding herself motionless against the restraints.

We're not Useless. Her thought was strident and pleading at the same time. With it came a request for reassurance. But John had none to give. Allen was gone and he had done it on his own. Dancer magic.

And in the jar, silver light, shifting.

We should have taken that jar, John.

117

Then he understood. The ritual wasn't done. 'No, wait!' he called to the guards, his words clear around the light. 'Please!' They had to bring Allen back, quickly, before it was all in vain.

Instead, they turned on all his restraints at the same time. Intense heat shimmered through his body, making him ache. The restraint in his mouth became so tight that it pushed his tongue against the back of his throat. He choked, panic rising in him. He flailed, feeling the oxygen leak from his muscles. The guards watched him, no expression on their faces, and then, as black spots appeared in his vision, they turned the restraints down.

He sucked in air, feeling the terror subside.

Beth was watching, her eyes wide, her face pale with fright.

The pain was still sharp from the other restraints. He was going to pass out anyway. He had energy for one last message.

We lost him, Bethie. Allen's gone.

Dania Zinn

She ran out of the listening room, leaving her carryall and her shoes, the carpeted floor soft against her stocking feet. Her hair slipped its bun and fell in pieces across her face. She pushed open the emergency door and took the ladder stairs because she didn't want to wait for the lift. She reached the group room just as the guards carried Allen into the hall.

His arms and legs were bouncing as if he were a stuffed toy. His head was tilted back, his mouth open. His eyes were slits, filled with darkness. The guards were running with him, although he didn't appear to be breathing.

'Why didn't you call for Medical?' she asked. She had to jog to keep up. Her breath was coming in short gasps.

'Too dangerous,' said the guard beside her. He was a tall, slender man, whipcord thin and not winded. 'Don't know what caused this. Could have been anything.'

'I contacted Medical on the way in,' said a female guard, flanking the boy's other side. She was blonde and cute, too tiny to look powerful. But she, too, was running with ease. 'They'll meet us halfway '

Dania wanted them to stop moving. She wanted to see if Allen was still alive. But she knew, from the moment she had seen him convulse, that everything had gone wrong.

The corridor veered to the right and the carpet became tile floor. The paintings disappeared, and the walls were bare. The double doors in the centre of the hall burst open, and four people wearing Medical light blue ran toward them. They were carrying hand-held monitors, and one of them was wheeling a smart cart.

The guards stopped and put the boy on the cart. His arms hung off the side. They had to adjust his body; it had no will, no volition. The team from Medical were all female and as tiny as the blonde guard. They moved with an efficiency that put Dania

121

to shame.

She leaned against the wall, grateful for its coolness. Sweat trickled down the side of her face, and her hair clung to her skin. She brushed the strands away, and watched.

'No vitals . . . '

' . . . cortex unresponsive . . . '

The Medical in charge, a woman with dark hair cropped short against her scalp, opened his mouth and examined the interior quickly with her minidoc. Then she shoved the light up his nose, and finally used her fingers to spread his eyelids apart.

'I thought you said convulsion,' she snapped at the female guard. 'What happened to his eyes?'

'Eyes?' The guard peered over, then looked away, her skin turning green. 'The other boy bent over him, but I didn't see him touch—'

'Send a message to Werfel,' said the reedy guard. 'Have that prisoner searched.'

'For *eyes*?' Dania asked. Bile built in the back of her throat. She had to swallow to keep it down.

'They're missing,' the woman in charge said. She held the lids open, examining with the minidoc. 'But nothing's ripped here. No blood. Everything's hooked up as if the eyeballs were snap-in replacement parts.'

Everything was a nightmare. Dania leaned against the plastic wall for support. Allen was dying; his eyes were missing. The children killed him and they had met on her orders. She couldn't remember so many things going wrong since they called her to identify Nicky's body.

'He's hooked into the couch,' said one of the other Medicals. 'But he's not responding. Nothing's wrong with his body. It just refuses to work on its own.'

'Keep using artificial stimulation. *Make* it work.' The chief kept peering into the empty eye sockets.

'Doesn't matter,' said another Medical. 'There's no activity in the brain. We shut the equipment down, we shut the kid down.'

The chief pulled back. She glanced at her wristputer and sighed. 'Record death at 15.03, and send a copy of the cot record to the appropriate data bases.'

Dania swallowed, and pushed off the wall. 'What killed him?'

'She's his lawyer,' the female guard said softly.

'Counsellor, if I knew that I might have been able to save him.' The chief put the minidoc back in the pocket of her smock. 'If his eyes weren't missing, I would say there's absolutely nothing wrong with him. And if I didn't know better, I would have said that he was born without eyeballs. Someone want to tell me what happened?'

'He was holding his hands over his head with two other kids and chanting,' the female guard said. 'Then he convulsed twice, and fell backward. One of the other kids leaned over him, and now he's dead.'

'We have a cording,' Dania said. 'I'll make sure you get a copy.'

'Do that,' the chief said. She grabbed the edge of the cot and pulled. She and three others dragged the cot – and Allen's body – through the double doors.

Dania leaned back against the wall. Werfel had been right. He had warned her that kids would be dangerous together. She had chosen not to believe it.

She had been wrong.

Harper Reeves

Harper pressed the heels of his hands into his eyes. The plastic chair in Observation dug into his buttocks. The air was cool but sweat dripped down his back. He played the scene over in his mind, the scene he, Dania and Mariko had watched:

Allen entered and hid among the plants. The others noticed him. They touched. They exchanged a few words, and sat down. Then John and Beth looked agitated. Allen appeared calm for the first time since Harper had seen him. They said two or three sentences, non sequiturs, and then held their hands above their heads. Allen's body convulsed, John bent over him, and Allen died.

Allen died.

Mariko's hand brushed Harper's shoulder. Her touch was light, but he jumped anyway. 'I was speaking to Medical,' she said. 'They'll make sure the death report is in our files.'

Harper rubbed the bridge of his nose with his thumb and forefinger, then sat up. The room was dark, as it was supposed to be, the view into the plant-filled Group room below still clear. The pillows were mussed; otherwise there appeared to have been no disturbance at all.

Mariko took her chair beside him, then captured his right hand. She was as small and delicate as a child herself, her black hair cut like a cap to fit her head. 'There was nothing we could have done.'

He pulled his hand from hers. She was a therapist. She should have known better than to utter platitudes. 'Werfel warned Dania. He said something like this could happen.'

'Something like what?' Mariko said. 'We don't know what happened.'

But they did know. The children had some kind of interaction, and Allen was dead. The court would not go easy on them now. Harper stood. He couldn't remain here, wrapped in his own sense of failure.

People were relying on him.

He had to get out of this tiny room with its glass walls. He closed the lid on his wristputer – he would make reports later – then picked up Dania's carryall and her shoes. They were cool and soft, like she was. He had never seen her so upset.

That wasn't true.

He had seen her that upset once. When Nicky died.

He took the lift out of the booth. The lift went down quickly, and the doors opened into the corridor across from the Group room. Figures moved inside the room, stalking something in the plants. His heart pounded. He took a step forward before he realized that the figures inside were Werfel's people starting their investigation.

He walked down the hall toward Medical. The interior designer had ignored these corridors. Workspace was supposed to be functional. The empty walls and the constant white reminded him of the children's cells.

John had been screaming as they restrained him. *No, wait! Please!* Who had he been speaking to? The guards? Or Allen?

The double doors separating Medical from the rest of the floor stood open. Harper went through. Dania leaned against the wall, her shirt askew, her hair mussed, and her stockings in tatters around her feet. Her legs barely seemed to support her and her eyes were damp with tears.

He set her carryall and her shoes next to the door. 'Dania?'

'He's dead, Harper.' Her voice was flat. She didn't look at him.

'I know.' He leaned against the wall beside her, careful not to touch her. 'Do they know why?'

'No.' She swallowed, her adam's apple moving in her long neck. 'But they know it wasn't natural causes.'

A tremble went down his spine. He hadn't realized how much he had been hoping for a natural death. 'How?'

'His eyes are missing.'

'Oh, god.' The tremble became a full-blown shudder. 'You made sure the vidnets aren't going to get ahold of this, didn't you?'

'And how do you expect me to do that?' She pushed away from the wall, suddenly full of energy. She had, apparently, needed

128

somewhere to direct her anger. 'I counted twelve guards and four doctors. Not to mention you and Mariko, and Werfel's people. Out of that group, someone will talk to the vidnets. Your bright idea has probably cost those children their future.'

'You're overreacting, Dania.'

'No, I'm not.' Her eyes were flashing, her cheeks flushed. 'These children confessed to murder on Bountiful, and now they're involved in another death. Do you know what that means, Harper? The government's been looking for something like this. Base Security has the right to get an immediate judge's order deporting these kids to a juvenile penal colony, to protect the base and prevent more killings.'

Harper hadn't known that. There were a number of features of Parliamentary law that he didn't know or understand. 'Can't you get a stay?'

'Should I?' She ran her hand through her hair. It tousled along her face, clinging to the skin near her ears. 'Another child's dead. His eyes are missing. Maybe everyone was right. Maybe these kids are dangerous. Maybe we should get them off this base as quickly as we can.'

Harper grabbed her shoulders. 'Did you see John take his eyes? Or Beth?'

She was shaking. 'No.'

'We were observing. Don't you think we would have seen it?'

Dania blinked at him. The colour was receding from her cheeks. 'He could see when he got there.'

'I know.' Harper let her go. 'We need to review the cordings of the session. You need to get that stay.'

'What do I tell the judge?'

Finally he understood the look on her face. The incident had sent her on some kind of personal spiral. Some memory from her past had gripped her, and she was helpless – as helpless as she had been after Nicky's death.

The mutilation. Nicky had been mutilated.

'For god's sake, Dania. Think. This is what Nicky was working for. That's why this is so important. Human beings can't rip each other's eyes out without drawing blood. There was no blood. There was nothing. They didn't even speak coherently to each other. This is not normal behaviour, Dania. It's not human behaviour.'

129

The intelligence flooded back into her face as she worked the puzzle. 'We don't know enough about the Dancers,' she said, 'to know if this is Dancer behaviour. This could fall in the centre of the Act.'

'Exactly.'

Dania combed her hair with her fingers. Then she picked up her shoes and slipped them on, bracing herself with a hand against the wall. 'I'm going to go to Judge Puyi for the stay, then I will meet you and Mariko at the diner this evening. We'll map out a strategy.'

'Great.' Harper felt relief flood through him. She was clear again. He didn't like the way she had gone vacant on him. 'We'll be there.'

She scooped up her carryall and slung it over her back. She started down the hall, then stopped. 'Harper?'

'Yeah?'

'Thanks.' The word was soft. She knew he had pulled her out of that hole she was sinking into.

'You're welcome,' he said. Then he watched her go, her hair swinging. She adjusted her shirt. With her shoes on, the carryall, and the clothing back in order, she looked like Dania the attorney again, one of the most competent women he knew.

Just like she had to be.

ii

Mariko had already made copies of the cordings and given them out. Harper made sure that Daniel Vincour had one so that he could analyze the whole thing from a Dancer perspective. Harper's own notes were important, but he only made a few verbal jottings in his wristputer before taking care of his most important task.

He found it odd that no reporters greeted him at his office. He also saw no signs of the media frenzy that should have accompanied this whole event. Werfel seemed to have it all under control.

Harper had to talk to John before Werfel's people got to him. Perhaps John could tell him what had happened and what it really meant.

Harper felt a prickle of unease as he headed for the prison wing. For the first time ever, guards were posted outside the door, and the security lights flashed red around the frame. Harper ignored them as he punched in his security code and ran his voice and retina scans.

The door didn't open.

'Sorry, sir,' one of the guards said. 'This area is off-limits to all outside personnel.'

'I'm not outside,' Harper said. 'I have clients in there.'

'You an attorney?' the second guard asked

'Forensic psychologist. I need to evaluate the boy who was involved in the incident today.'

The guards glanced at each other. Something passed across their faces, but Harper didn't catch the emotion.

'You're too late, doc,' the first guard said. 'They're gone.'

'All of them?' Harper asked.

The guard shrugged. 'The kids involved in that murder a few hours ago. Sent outta here so fast that we haven't even had time to get their possessions.'

Harper felt a chill run through him.

'Orders are,' the second guard said, 'no talking to the press, no talking to anybody. Except you, the other counsellor and that attorney. After today, those kids don't exist.'

Not yet. They couldn't be sent away yet. Not when Dania and Harper had finally found something on which to pin the defense. 'Where did they go?'

'We took them down to Docking fifteen minutes ago.'

'Docking?' He didn't like the way this was going.

The first guard's smile grew wider. 'Don't worry, doc. They're gone. Werfel made sure they had private shuttles. Small ones, all separate. He didn't want those kids together, so they're all going to different facilities on Reed.'

Reed. Reed was maximum security for juveniles. All hard-core criminals with no hope of redemption. The planet had some psychological facilities, but they were little used and known for their poorly run research. Werfel had to have been planning this. Just as Dania had said.

But he couldn't have done it alone. Harper felt a heaviness fill his limbs. Dania had been right. The government wanted these kids hidden. They had never wanted this case tried.

'Sorry, doc,' the guard said. 'No more clients. Hope you still get paid.'

Oh, he was still going to get paid. That wasn't the issue. The issue was those children and the mysteries they held.

He had to find Dania. He had to see if there was something they could do.

Part Three

Beth

i

Either she never slept or she slept too much. Beth pressed against the cool plastic walls in the far side of her private cubicle, her knees drawn to her chest. She picked at the skin beside her thumbnail, the other fingers already red and raw.

The room was sparse, and three times the size of her cell on Lina Base. A sleep couch floated in the centre, mimicking the weightlessness of space. The floor and walls were bare. Only the closet door and the door into her private bathroom marked the white surface.

She had lived here for five years and had done nothing to make the room her own. The other contract employees bartered their services for decorations – her next door neighbor, Suni, had holos hiding the plain white walls. But Beth preferred the whiteness. It reminded her of Lina Base and of Bountiful. Sometimes, when she rested on the couch, she could almost see the Dancers walking through the walls.

Dancers. Hard to imagine she had not seen them for eleven years.

She wasn't even supposed to think about them. But she did. Every day. And Allen, his eyes glowing silver.

His words haunted her dreams. *I know now. Watch.* He had seemed so calm. She hadn't been calm since she was twelve years old.

A chime sounded throughout the room. The kitchen staff had prepared employee breakfast. She only had fifteen minutes to make it to the staff lounge. She opened her closet door, pushed past the costumes and toys until she found a clean white shift and pulled it over her head. Even though she had showered last night, the faint scent of earth still clung to her. It had taken most of the night for her to come back to herself. She still felt as if bits of her personality were missing.

She opened the door and stepped into the hallway. It had

been decorated in light greens. Branches mimicking earth trees and vines climbed up the walls, with the yellow of sunlight floating through. She loved this place when the hotel was full, and each sector was turned on. The forest came alive, birds chirping in the trees, the sun beating down, a slight breeze blowing. The carpet had the texture of grass. She had thought herself so lucky when her services were bought by the Hotel on Orda Base, the only base established by private interest in this sector.

She didn't consider herself lucky now.

She followed the corridor to the stately mahogany doors that opened into the lobby of the human section. The hotel was huge – running through all forty levels on the base. Each lobby had been designed to resemble colonial periods on individual planets. The human section looked like an English hotel in Africa in the early twentieth century. The doors opened to the fake veldt. Ceiling fans wove lazy patterns in the cool air. The furniture was sturdy white wicker with colourful cushions. The wood trim was dark, giving everything a heavy feel. Glass chandeliers hung from the ceiling as if they provided the artificial light. Huge plants dominated the furniture groupings, and ivory carvings sat on the tables.

Beth could explain the history of each piece, as could all the staff members. Should any guest find the symbolism distasteful, the staff was quick to assure them that the hotel used colonial decor as a reminder of the excesses of the past, excesses that the Provisional Parliament was determined not to repeat.

She could say those words without flinching. Now.

As she went through the heavy doors, she stopped. Someone had erected a large glass case in the centre of the lobby. The case had replaced two furniture groupings. The interior of the case was full of water, except for a large flat rock in the centre. Waves rippled on the surface, as if something were moving in the case.

She glanced around. No one stood behind the long mahogany desk. The remaining furniture groupings were empty; all the doors were shut. The entire staff had decided to attend breakfast this morning, apparently.

A sleek white head popped above the water and peered at her. A Minaran. Its little fingered fins were pressed against the glass, the rest of its body wriggling as it held itself in position. How odd. It had to be travelling with a human companion to have its own place in this part of the hotel.

She crossed the room and touched the warm glass. The Minaran's gaze met hers, its ice-blue eyes open and friendly. The poor little thing had to be lonely. If she could hold it, and feel its warm, wet fur against her skin, she might be able to ease the loneliness – both of their loneliness – for just a short time.

'Beth!'

Roddy's voice, harsh and nasal. She jumped away from the window and stood, hands clasped behind her back. She kept her gaze trained downward, on the thin patterned rug, away from the Minaran in the cubicle. Roddy hated it when she ogled the guests.

'What are you doing in the main lobby?' He stood beside her, the heat from his thin body brushing her skin. He wore a long black waistcoat, matching pants, and a starched shirt. A gold watch fob glinted over his stomach. His breath smelled of peppermint. He had just had a cup of his favourite – expensive – tea. 'Did someone call for you?'

She shook her head. She always crossed the lobby on the way to breakfast, but she would never tell him that. He would give her a demerit for every day she had done it, just like he would give her demerits for looking at the Minaran. Or maybe he would take a week's worth of tips. Not that it mattered. She kept her tips in the hotel account, untouched since she had arrived. Someday, maybe, she would get enough money to buy herself free.

'You know I don't like having the personal staff in the lobby. It creates a sleazy atmosphere. Some of our patrons would prefer to ignore people like you.'

As he would. She finally raised her head, and saw Carla behind the desk, watching the entire exchange. She wore a morning gown, its muslin fabric tight over her bosom, the fake, built-in corset drawing her waist into a small circle.

'I was walking through,' Beth said, 'and I saw the Minaran. What's it doing here?'

'That's none of your business.' Roddy clasped his hands behind his back, puffing out his small chest. His dark eyes looked moist, his narrow features sharp in the bright light. His muttonchop whiskers overpowered his thin face. 'When you were hired on, you were told not to ask questions—'

'Beth was not hired,' Carla said. She lifted the small hinged door that connected both parts of the desk, and walked through. Her gray dress swished as she walked, the toes of her narrow, high buttoned shoes peaking out from beneath the skirts.

Roddy didn't move. He froze, just like Beth had, when faced with his boss.

Carla stopped when she reached them. She stood half a head taller than both of them. 'Let's not have this discussion in the lobby, hmm? My office, please.'

Carla walked back through the desk and opened the door to the maze of back rooms. The colonial design disappeared outside of the guests' view. Computers, white walls, and space art dominated the hotel's back.

Carla had a corner office. It had two wide windows that looked out on the docking ships and the stars beyond. If a person stood close to the windows and looked down, she could see the edge of Orda, looking blue and brown, with white swirls along its top. Beth had never been there. She never wanted to be.

The office was done in tans, and everything was made of colonial plastic, except Carla's chair which was upholstered and moulded to her form. Security screens hid in the back wall, and four different computer screens bleeped beneath the glass covering on her desk. Carla ignored them as she walked around. She looked out of place here – a powerful woman who stopped in at the office on her way to a costume ball.

'Sit down,' Carla said as she slipped into her chair. Beth didn't want to sit in the colonial plastic – such chairs made her think of Bountiful – but she did anyway. Roddy sat beside her, perched at the edge of the chair as if he were going to spring up at any minute.

'The lobby is not a place for dressing down an employee,' Carla said, folding her jewelled hands together and leaning forward on the desk. She was looking at Roddy. 'We are striving to make our guests as comfortable as possible, and they don't need to see dissention among the staff. Is that clear?'

Roddy nodded.

'Good,' she said. 'You may go.'

Roddy leapt out of the chair, moving faster than Beth had ever seen him move. He was gone from the office by the time Carla turned to Beth. 'You know better than to stand in the lobby when you're not working.'

'Yes.' Beth looked at her hands. They would never be as groomed as Carla's. The years of hard labour would always remain in the form of yellowed calluses, bent nails, and scarred skin.

'The Minaran fascinates you.'

Beth didn't answer. When she stared at the creature, memories crossed within her. Memories of that investigator – what was his name? Schafer? the one she had confessed to – who had killed so many Minarans and who had destroyed her world too. Memories of being trapped, naked, in a cage much smaller for her first real journey into space, the other prisoners passing her, jeering, and tapping on the clear plastic. She had hated it, hated it, and not even the memory of the Dancers got her through.

All that combined in loneliness so deep that sometimes she thought nothing would fill it.

'Beth?'

Beth looked up. Carla's voice was harsh, but her eyes weren't. Carla was the only nice person Beth had met on the staff. The rest treated her like dirt, like she was worse than dirt, like she had no value at all.

'You have more demerits than any other staff member. Your ten-year service contract has grown to sixteen. If you don't watch yourself, you could be indentured to the hotel for life.'

Beth shrugged. She had nowhere else to go. Bountiful was closed now, and no one would ever give her dispensation to return. Meagre as it was, the hotel was more home to her than any other place she had lived. Any other place except Bountiful, among the Dancers.

Carla stood up and adjusted her bustle to make sure it was straight. 'I would like to make you a project, Beth. I think you're smarter than any other person on staff. I can send you to an alien no one knows anything about, and you can discover its sexuality and please it in a matter of hours. If this system ran on merits instead of demerits, I suspect you would have been out of here by now, instead of accumulating enough trouble to keep you here indefinitely. But I need to know if you're willing.'

141

Beth didn't move. When people had wanted things from her in the past, they had taken. Even when the offer had sounded good, it had turned out poorly for her, made her feel even more useless and alone. 'What do you want from me?'

'I want to train you to become my assistant. You could act as liaison between all branches of the hotel, and it would free me up to work more with Orda on coordinating restaurant work, shopping and other activities for those who've docked here. I would put you in New Species Contact. You would discover what a species needs to feel most at home and work with the design and personal staff to accomplish that.'

Beth clasped her hands together. If Carla had seen her room, she would never have considered Beth for this assignment. She couldn't work with people. She barely spoke to them. Imagine if she had to talk to other species. Normally she went into their rooms and became a Dancer, absorbing the emotion of the other beings and flowing with them until she found what they wanted. Then she would leave and, Dancerlike, put away everything that had happened. 'I don't know design or diplomacy.'

'I would train you.'

Beth shook her head once and stood. 'If you knew about me, you wouldn't offer this.'

'I know that you came to us from a penal ship. I know that you were in for murder.'

'No.' Beth reached out and touched the edge of Carla's desk. The plastic was smooth and warm, like the glass around the Minaran's cubicle. 'I'm one of the Dancer Eight. Our crimes were so big we were shunted off Lina Base without a trial, and each subsequent petition has been denied. Because of us, the Provisional Parliament shut down its second planet, and ordered that humans never contact the Dancers again. And the remaining seven of us were scattered into isolation, away from aliens. That's why the hotel had to get special dispensation to buy my indentured servitude contract.'

Carla studied her for a moment. Nothing flickered in Carla's face, but her gaze flattened for a moment. Everyone had heard of the Eight. New hotel staff members – hired, not bought – saw the history cordings, warning about intimate contact with aliens, and those cordings contained the history of Bountiful.

'Well, no wonder most of your file is under wraps.' Carla smiled, a thin, tight look. 'But you've managed to keep yourself clean here. No alien has influenced you.'

'That's because,' Beth kept her voice soft, 'that's because I haven't let them.'

ii

Beth went to her room the back way, taking hallways only used by the staff. She didn't want to see the Minaran and be tempted to stop again in the lobby.

Her stomach growled. She had missed breakfast altogether, a mistake after last night's client. Her hands were shaking. She had never told anyone of her past, for fear of the very reaction she had gotten. A lowering down, a dismissal, a re-evaluation of who she was. Carla hadn't retracted the offer, but she hadn't pushed either.

They both knew Beth couldn't take the position. If the territorial Government's security wing found out, they would fine the hotel or close it down for carelessness. The hotel ran a risk giving her any alien contact at all. Putting her in a position of power after that contact would be ruinous.

She was doomed, forever, to live like this.

She hated Carla for making the offer, and then for retracting it. Hated even glimpsing the opportunity.

The hallway outside her room was quiet. She pressed her finger against her door, and it slid open, revealing her haven. Her prison.

The sleep couch floated just above her head. A great tiredness overwhelmed her. Now she was ready to sleep. After all the stresses of the night and morning, her body was finally prepared to let go just enough, to hide.

She pulled off her shift and waved to the bed. The motion made it float down to her, and she climbed on it, letting the softness take her. She closed her eyes, and felt the bed rise to its place in the centre of the room.

The Minaran swam behind her closed eyelids, its little white body begging for her attention. Minarans were not space-faring creatures, so they had no place in the hotel. Therefore, the hotel

143

would have to build something special.

But why not put it in one of the water wings, where creatures whose bodies needed moisture resided? Why bring it here, to the human quarters, where the special accommodations would be even tougher?

Someone had to have brought the creature here. Someone had to travel with it, to provide it with accommodations, to alter a vessel to carry the creature in space. Someone had a lot of money invested in that Minaran.

Odd. Too odd.

Beth opened her eyes and stared at the blank, white ceiling. Still the sense of the Minaran did not leave her. Minar had been closed like Bountiful. The Minarans were an endangered species, like the Dancers.

She sat up so fast the bed rocked and nearly tossed her out. Like the Dancers! The Minarans were a protected species – no one was allowed to remove them from the planet. And this one was a baby, since it was the size of a cat. Adult Minarans grew to the size of small humans.

That's what had been striking her as odd, more than the cubicle in the lobby. The entire staff knew about the Minarans – they learned about them in the same cording that spoke of the Dancers. The staff knew about the illegality of transporting Minarans, and still gave this one a place of honour in the lobby.

She had seen a lot of strange things in the hotel, and she had ignored most of them. She couldn't ignore this one.

The Minaran's wide round eyes haunted her in a way no one had since Allen died.

iii

Before she could figure out what to do about the Minaran, three chimes sounded inside her apartment. Her mouth went instantly dry. A summons from Roddy. So soon after the last one. Usually she had two or three days to recover.

He was probably angry that she had got him in trouble. Well, he wouldn't have to worry any more. Carla would never take her side in a case again.

Beth waved the bed down, slipped on her crumpled shift, and

144

brushed her hair out of her eyes. She didn't care how she looked for him. She was beginning to care less and less about everything. Someday she might go the way of many other contracts: dead by their own hand.

Beth let herself out of her room and took the two flights down to Roddy's office. The door was open, and she walked in. His office smelled of tobacco and liquor, both substances banned outside of special permit areas, like restaurants. He got them in the hotel because the hotel had to be prepared for a guest's every need. Or a manager's every need. But he never told the authorities that.

Roddy kept up the Victorian motif, even though he didn't need to. Rich reds and dark woods covered the walls and carpet. The furniture was heavy, so heavy that Beth wondered how it met regulation. Roddy's stiff suits and muttonchop whiskers looked natural here, as did his distaste for her and the others like her.

'We had a request from Amphib,' he said, his back to her. Steam rose from a cup on his desk, and she recognized black tea, as difficult to get as the peppermint stuff he usually drank. 'I've forgotten. Do you swim?'

He hadn't forgotten at all. He liked to toy with her. She wouldn't give him the satisfaction of emotion in her answer.

'Yes, sir.'

'Good.' He turned. Between his fingers, he held a pipe, unlit, of course. His gaze was cold. 'We wouldn't want you to drown, like Tina did. We can't afford more scandals like that.'

'Good swimmers can drown in only a few inches of water if they get knocked unconscious,' Beth said. Keeping her tone flat had become more difficult. Tina had taught her how to swim when she first came to the hotel. Careless sex, violence, or some kind of accident had caused Tina to die.

'I suppose.' Roddy leaned against a shelf filled with paper books. 'We had a request from a Tritoid. Seems it heard about our interspecies service from a satisfied friend. I have a cording in the next room if you would like to see how it's done among consenting Tritoids—'

She shook her head. She had discovered that information often interfered with her flow, her opportunity to do her work. 'What room is it in?'

145

He handed her a card with the floor plan and a duplicate of the print that would open the Tritoid's lock. 'In all fairness,' Roddy said, not sounding fair at all, 'I should let you know that Tritoids achieve orgasm underwater. I trust you can hold your breath for long periods of time?'

Beth bit back a response – she usually held her breath the entire time she was in his office – then snatched the card from his hand and left.

She took the staff hallways, which grew narrower the farther she got from the human quarters. The white walls closed in like a tunnel, and the carpet thinned to a bit of fabric that stifled sound. The air grew humid and dank. At least the Amphibs were close to the human quarters. The atmosphere, oxygen levels, and room design weren't all that different. She hated going deeper into the watery bowels of the hotel, where moisture dripped off the walls, and the pressure made her ears hurt.

Finally she pushed open the door leading to the correctly numbered area, and climbed a series of rocky steps. The air that greeted her was thick with humidity and smelled faintly of stagnant water. The Amphib section had several kinds of water pools – stagnant, spring-fed, salt-water, acidic, and fresh water. Some Amphibs did well with chemical water treatments. Others died.

The walls were covered with wet, glistening stone – probably fake because real stone would be too heavy for regulation. Bent tritons hung over each door, much like the ivory sat on tables in the human lobby. Silvery scales glittered behind the rocks, and in the distance was the sound of a burbling stream.

The door she was supposed to enter was already partially open. She pushed her hair back with one hand and paused, taking a deep breath. Stagnant water. Yuck. Then she closed her eyes and reached to the part of her mind that was still Dancer.

Immediately the longing came, and with it a warmth that went down to her crotch. She hadn't been touched, really touched, since Allen died. Maybe this time . . .

She floated inside, anticipation hovering in her belly. The fetid smell made her stomach turn. Part of her brain woke, the part that pulled memories and stored them so that she wouldn't have to look at them. Then she became fully Dancer, all emotion, existing in the moment.

Before her, a large creature shaped like a melted triangle sits in front of an algae filled pool. The creature watches her with matching patterned eyes. Its skin sparkles like jewels.

Not jewels. Water dappled. Air smells rank. Stagnant water. It speaks – a rumble she does not understand. But its emotion comes to her, complete with pictures:

She steps forward, rubs her hand on its jewelled skin, feeling water, feeling coolness, feeling slime. Her entire body heats. She loves touch, wants touch, craves touch . . .

She pulls off her shift, and presses herself against the creature. Together they dive into the green algae floating on the surface of the pool . . .

iv

And when she came to herself, she was standing outside her apartment door, her clothing clinging to her wet body. She smelled ripe – decayed water and something else, something even more foul. Her body felt heavy, tired, used, like it always did when these things ended. Not touched. Aching for touch even more. She lifted a hand and found it coated with black slime. A shudder ran through her, and she pushed open the door to her apartment.

Three chimes echoed. Roddy. He wanted to see her humiliation. Odd he could think that after all these years she could still be humiliated. Odd that she could. So many of the others shut off their skins as if their brains had developed with an on-off switch. Hers must have malfunctioned. She always came to herself frightened and disgusted.

And empty.

Inside, she discarded her shift and climbed into the bathing cubicle. She set the water temperature near scalding. Washing didn't make the feelings go away, but it did give her some of her dignity back. She never could remember what happened – it had been stored in a part of her memory she had denied herself access to – but that never changed her feeling that what did happen was wrong.

The chimes sounded again. She put on a long sleeved shirt

147

and long pants to cover any bruises that might show up on her skin. Then she brushed her hair out of her face and checked herself in the tiny mirror. No trace of the Tritoid remained, except in the wary look behind her eyes.

She was about to let herself out when the door swung open. Roddy stood there, his cheeks red above his bristly whiskers, his hands on his narrow hips. 'I've been summoning you.'

Even his sharp tones didn't make her feel anything. 'I just finished,' she said. 'I was coming.'

'You finished almost an hour ago.'

He had been watching, then. She wondered how many times he watched, and how it made him feel. She shuddered. The idea that he watched made her feel even more used. 'I don't know what couldn't have waited until I got cleaned up.'

'The Tritoid wants you back this evening. It is bringing in a number of guests, and wants you for entertainment.'

Finally emotion got through – a stab of pain so sharp she nearly doubled over. Remembered pain. The last time she had participated in an interspecies orgy, she nearly died. Roddy knew that. He knew how she feared another encounter. Maybe he was still punishing her for the encounter with Carla, earlier.

She put one hand on the undecorated wall to steady herself. The plastic was cool, soothing, against her palm. 'It's against regulations to perform with an alien twice in one day.'

'You're in too much trouble to quote regulations to me.' His jaw was set, his mouth in a sideways line. She didn't like the way his eyes glittered.

'The regulations protect the hotel.' She kept her voice soft, but the muscles in her arm tensed. After the talk this morning, she doubted she would get any more protection from Carla. Beth would have to fight this one on her own. 'Too many humans die from repeat contact. Sometimes the alien touch is like a slow-acting poison. I remember when Steve died—'

'I had the autodoc check out the Tritoids,' Roddy said. 'You'll be fine.'

'No.' Beth felt dizzy. She had never stood up to Roddy before – to anyone before. She wondered if the Minaran swimming in its little tank felt the same trapped anger that she felt so dangerously close to the surface. 'No,' she said again.

'This kind of action will allow me to hold your contract

forever.'

For a brief second, she forgot to breathe. Forever letting Roddy tell her who could touch her and who couldn't. Forever trapped by his petty perversions and mean-spiritedness. As if she had a place to go even when her contract expired. She was banned from the only place she wanted to be.

Remember the Transformation of the Useless Ones? I understand it now.

She made herself take a small breath and focus on Roddy. 'Forcing me to stay here forever really gives me a lot of incentive to work harder,' she said and pushed her way past him. She brushed against his scratchy wool suit as she did so, and she shuddered all over again.

The hallway was alive, birds chirping and a gentle breeze blowing. Sunlight fell on her face, warming her skin, but not her heart. She walked toward the lobby, looking over her shoulder once to check where Roddy was. He had gone the other direction, probably to report her. Fine. Let him.

The doors to the lobby were open. Four humans wearing matching red robes and tiny red hats clustered at the reception desk. Four more sat in the wicker chairs, luggage scattered around them. Another ship must have landed.

She didn't look any of the humans in the eye. Instead she walked to the Minaran cubicle. The Minaran slid off the rock and swam to her when it saw her, putting its little black baby fingers against the glass. She put hers against the glass too, as if they could touch. They would touch, if she could get rid of the glass.

She leaned her forehead against the warm surface, and stared into the wide blue eyes. For the first time since Allen died, she reached. *I know how you feel,* she sent, packing the message with the feelings of being trapped, of being lonely. The Minaran blinked, then scrambled up the side so that its face was directly across from hers.

She felt a faint thread of fear that was not hers, a wish for someone warm and shaggy to sleep on, for a nipple that would fit just right in the mouth.

She nodded, then sent back as much warmth as she had.

'Pretty, isn't it?'

The voice made her jump. It was soft, deep and human. The Minaran tumbled backwards in the water, its little fins peddling

149

as fast as they could. It swam behind the rock, leaving a faint residue of terror in its wake.

Beth turned to see what had caused the commotion. A woman stood behind her. The woman's hair had been painted in small geometric squares of black and silver, and her skin in complimentary shades of brown and cream. She wore a deep purple dress that accented the bizarre geometry of some distant fashion. Beth stood up straighter. Women guests intimidated her more than any others, with their wealth and their self-assurance. This one probably wanted to take her back to the room.

A splash sounded behind her. The Minaran was sitting on the rock, pushing at the water with its fins. When Beth's gaze met its, it dove off the side of the rock again, hiding. With all the motion, the feeling of terror grew.

As did her understanding.

'You brought it here,' Beth said. The words slipped out and she wanted to clap her hands over her face in childlike fashion. The woman had brought the Minaran here, and it was terrified of her.

The woman shrugged, a delicate movement of one large shoulder. 'It's on its way to a new home.'

'A new home?' Beth was trembling inside. 'Wasn't it home on Minar?'

The woman laughed, but her pale eyes glistened with chill. 'Sometimes,' she said, 'creatures don't know what's best for them.'

Beth remembered what it was like, being told she didn't know what was best. It had placed her here, ultimately. 'You're a psychologist?'

'So sweet and amusing.' The woman reached over and tucked a strand of hair behind Beth's ear. 'No, darling. I specialize in rare objects.'

Beth winced and pulled away. The woman let her hand drop. 'I thought you were the one who liked touch,' the woman said.

Beth stiffened. This was a guest. A guest who knew about the employees at the hotel. She couldn't contradict someone that important. 'I'm off-duty,' Beth said.

The woman's eyes twinkled for the first time. 'I thought the staff never went off duty.' Her smile grew wider. 'Would you like to please my little Minaran there? It looks quite lonely.'

Inside the cage? Trapped behind invisible walls? Beth pushed away, trying not to be rude, but her entire body was shaking. She bobbed her head once, and walked away. Once she was out of view of the lobby, she started running and didn't stop until she reached the safety of her own tiny room.

v

In her dream, she dove into the Minaran's tank. The water was cool against her skin. The creature rubbed its furry face against her breasts, seeking comfort, seeking milk. She pushed it away. She wanted friendship, not touch.

Not that kind of touch.

She swam underwater to the rock in the centre of the pool. Then her fingers gripped the hard surface and she pulled herself up. Artificial sunlight caressed her body, warmed her, comforted her as she hadn't been comforted since she left Bountiful.

The Minaran pushed its face against her arm. Its muzzle was wet, blue eyes liquid. It chirped at her like a Dancer making a nonsense sound, then dove under the water. When it rose again, it was on the other side of the rock. Loneliness radiated from the Minaran. Its round eyes were sad.

She rolled over on her stomach, covering herself as best she could. The Minaran used its fins to pull itself on the rock and cuddle next to her. She tried to push it away – it was too human, too cute. She didn't want touch, didn't want touch, didn't want—

Beth woke up, heart pounding, skin crawling. She put her head between her knees, and made herself take deep breaths. Ever since she saw the Minaran, the nightmares were coming thick and fast. Opening a little door that would best remain closed.

Behind it was a despair she thought she had buried. When she fell into it, it would be deeper than any pool in the hotel.

She would never surface.

I know now. Watch.

She raised her head and opened her eyes, forcing herself to concentrate on the rocking motion of the bed.

151

Trapped. The little creature was trapped. No being deserved to be imprisoned, bartered and sold. No being. No one.

Not even her.

She eased the bed to the ground so that she could climb off. Then she stood barefoot on the cold floor, hugging herself as she stared at the four blank white walls surrounding her.

vi

She hadn't been outside the hotel in almost a year. After the opulence of the hotel, the plainness of the rest of Orda Base always startled her. She never took the main doors out, so that she could avoid the shopping district and not be tempted. She always took the freight exit that crossed into the ports.

The hallways were wide, the ceilings high. They were gray with dirt and smelled of rust and soured perfumes. The lighting was thin and pale, barely enough for humans who occasionally had to lead cargo through. Usually the hotel employed top-of-the-line servobots, since they were cheaper than organic labour and twice as reliable.

A year ago, she had practically lived in these corridors. A year ago she had actually had a purpose – until she realized that Willis wanted more from her than sex. More than she would ever be able to give.

He told her it didn't matter, but it did. Buried in that secret part of her brain were Dancer rituals. Her friends had fallen victim to them before. They would again, if she allowed it.

The freight tunnels opened into the docking bays. Orda Base now had the highest traffic of any base in the system, but when it had been built, it had been built small because it was on the edge of the colonized sector. Orda Base had also been an experiment, funded by private industries instead of the government. That meant retail, commercial and for-profit space had once been easy to obtain here, instead of regulated almost to death as it was on the other five bases. The availability of all kinds of unregulated goods, foods, and services made Orda Base grow quicker than any other base, and brought colonists in to the nearby system so that they could use the facilities without staying more than a few nights in the exclusive, but extremely expensive hotel.

The bay, originally built for four shuttles, had six crammed in non-regulation format. The air had the sharp tang of chemical exhaust from the oldest shuttle, shuddering near the closed bay door. The floor was black with skid marks, the steps leading to the upstairs offices corroded and nearly falling apart. Just because Orda Base made money didn't mean that it spent the money wisely.

Beth rounded the shuttles, pushing the hair out of her face as she walked. Technicians bent over a shattered navigational computer removed from the third shuttle. Servobots removed cargo from three shuttles and scattered the packages in various directions. Lights reflected from the line of windows up above, and Beth could see shadows moving.

She stepped over cables as she made her way to the stairs. Once there, she gripped the handrail and felt the ancient metal flake against her fingers. Her footsteps rang against the stairs, which she took two at a time. She hated the way they shivered with her every movement, as if they would tumble around her at any moment.

When she opened the door to the offices above, Willis was standing near the reception desk, his hands clasped behind his back. He was the only person there. He had probably seen her coming up the stairs, and had asked for privacy.

'Going to take me up on it?' he asked, his voice jaunty, his eyes filled with too much hope.

She let a breath out slowly. In all her concern for the Minaran, she had forgotten her promise: she would see him again when she changed her mind. She stared at his expectant face, his compact body with its broad shoulders and comforting arms. She could teach him, she supposed. He had long slender fingers. He could learn Dancer touch.

Then Michael Dengler's face flashed through her mind: the terror permanently etched on his forever eight-year-old features.

No. She couldn't risk it.

'I'm sorry, Willis,' she said. 'I can't.'

· He nodded, then leaned against the metal desk. 'Knew it wasn't my charm,' he said.

'It's not you,' she said.

He smiled then, a soft look that didn't quite reach his eyes. 'I know that now. Took me most of the year to figure that out, but I know it.' He stood and took her hand. A tingle went through her that she couldn't completely suppress. 'What do you need?'

She glanced around. She didn't like this room with its functional chairs, too large desk and windows open to the entire bay. 'Can we go to your office?'

'Sure.' He let go of her hand and put his on the small of her back, propelling her with him as he had done a hundred times in the past. No one in the bay offices would think anything more than what they had already thought – that Willis was one of the lucky few that got a freebie from a hotel employee.

His office was a small dark cubicle in the centre of the bay's infrastructure. Because he worked in communications, the powers that be figured that he didn't need amenities like windows and light. He barely had enough floor space to accommodate two naked bodies. A single chair on wheels slid around a desk that stood out on all four walls, carrying displays and lights and equipment that Beth didn't even pretend to understand.

A soft female voice echoed in the corridor. NEXT ARRIVAL IN 36 MINUTES. NEXT ARRIVAL . . .

Willis closed the door on the sound. He took his hand away from her body, pulled over the chair and grabbed its back for support. 'Something's happened,' he said.

She nodded. 'I need to get a message to the nearest Security Division Headquarters. Can you do that for me?'

Willis leaned forward, the chair sliding beneath him. 'You all right?'

'It's not for me,' she said purposely avoiding his question. And then she told him. Everything.

vii

It took two days before there was any response. She spent most of her time hovering near the lobby, but she didn't need to. Word hit all corners of the hotel almost an hour before Security Division arrived.

She sat in one of the wicker chairs, half hidden behind a

154

potted palm so that no one at registration could see her. The Minaran swam in its cage. Its fur had grown coarse, its eyes less bright. It still swam up to her when it saw her, but it no longer pressed its fins against the glass. Whenever she tried to read it all she got was a deep despair that mirrored her own.

The lobby was full – people trying to get out of the hotel before the Security Division arrived. Beth watched them too, wondering what they all had to hide, why they had to run away so quickly. Most could have gone down to the shopping district in Orda Base and spent the day there. Security Division only had orders to come to the hotel.

Carla's voice echoed over the din of other voices, making arrangements, clearing out customers. Her neat topknot was coming askew and the lines on her face were deep. She, too, knew Security was coming, but she didn't know why, and she couldn't leave.

The cushion on the chair was soft, but the wicker edges rubbed against the back of Beth's legs. Her body was sore. Roddy had sent her into the bowels of the hotel the night before, to a creature that preferred darkness. She had come to herself with unusual bruises and a limp on her left side.

She could no longer justify what she did. It was masochistic. She was a willing participant in a perverse sort of torture. Even if she had bought her freedom like she once planned, she had no training, no ability, no way to improve her own life. If the plans she had made with Willis worked, this moment would be the highlight of her entire existence.

She brushed her hair away from her face with her left hand, and noted a slender man dressed in black standing in the shadows beside the Minaran's cubicle. Another man appeared, also dressed in black, on the other side of the cubicle. Beth glanced around. Slender, muscular humans with stun rifles cradled in their arms blocked all the exits. They had arrived without triggering any alarms or sounding any buzzers.

The lobby grew slowly quiet as people realized they were surrounded. Patrons stood rooted to their places, their gazes riveted on the doors. Beth rose. Carla lifted the lid on the reception desk and walked through.

'Officers?' she asked, her voice calm.

The man Beth had noticed first, the slender one near the

Minaran cubicle came forward. He pulled a computer clip from his pocket. 'Ma'am.' He nodded once, as a person did when meeting someone he respected. 'I need to see the Manager on Duty or the highest person in charge of the hotel.'

Carla's height matched his. Her old-fashioned outfit made her look larger than he was. 'In this wing, that's me,' she said. 'I could contact the hotel CEO if you would like.'

'Not yet.' The man's voice boomed in the small area. The Minaran had stopped swimming and had retreated to its rock. Beth wished she could do the same. 'I came to inform you that you and your Hotel are in violation of Section 1.675 of the Territorial Legal Code.'

'Violation?' Carla's voice actually trembled. Beth's mouth was dry.

'Yes, Ma'am. Kidnapping, imprisonment, and trafficking in an endangered species.'

Carla's expression was blank.

The man inclined his head toward the tank. 'The Minaran, Ma'am. It belongs on Minar. Nowhere else.'

A lump had risen in Beth's throat. It was working. Someone would actually defend the Minaran.

Carla's face had gone pale. She tugged on the neck of her tight dress.

'We're also looking for a human,' the man said. 'A woman named Carla Arrowsmith.'

Carla's eyes widened. She smoothed the bodice of her dress, then let her hands fall to her side. 'I'm Carla Arrowsmith.'

The man grinned. 'Then you shouldn't look so shocked, Ma'am. You will receive a commendation from the Security Division for risking your job and contacting us. The Minaran will be returned to its rightful home, and the guilty parties will stand trial.'

And after Security Division left, Carla's job would be up for review. All hotel employees had to put the guests' needs above all else – even above the hotel.

Carla's gaze searched the lobby, and stopped when she saw Beth. They stared at each other for a moment, and then Beth let her guard down. Anger, fierce and pure, slipped in, accompanied by a trapped feeling that Beth knew so well – a feeling Carla had never experienced before.

No one deserves to be imprisoned, bartered or sold, Beth sent to her. *No one.*

Carla looked away. A flush in her cheeks meant the message had been received.

A black-uniformed member of the security team touched the leader's arm. 'She's gone,' he said softly.

'Damn,' the leader whispered. 'We were so close.'

Beth ignored them. She limped over to the Minaran's cubicle. It was watching from the rock. She put her hand against the warm glass. The Minaran inclined its head so that it could see her better, but it did not swim toward her.

They've come to save you, little one, she sent to it, along with as much joy as she could manage. *They're going to take you home.*

The Minaran lifted its head, its round eyes open. She felt a longing that was not hers, a longing for someone warm and shaggy to sleep on, for a nipple that fit just right in the mouth. She nodded.

Soon, she promised. Then she smiled. *Ah, little one. At least one of us is free.*

viii

She left the hotel by the front door for the first time since she had arrived on Orda Base. It no longer mattered what regulations she had broken. Carla was angry with her, and would give her enough demerits to enslave her to the hotel for another decade. Roddy would exercise his perversions on her until he lost interest, and she would die in some stagnant pool of water, unwanted, unloved.

Useless.

The front doors of the hotel were made of ivory columns. Intricate carvings graced their sides, and matching carvings covered the doors. The taste and beauty of the hotel were mimicked in the shops closest to the hotel's entrance. Shoppers from all different walks browsed through the windows or drank from tiny, thin cups in the 'outdoor' cafes that lined the walkway.

Beth browsed too, her hand constantly brushing the pocket stuffed full of money. One purchase for herself, her first and

157

only.

Ahead, four musicians stood in a circle and played a jaunty tune, all light and air and magic. Farther down, a woman sang, her voice warbling like a bird. Even farther, two men clowned for a small audience. The entire atmosphere was lighter than anything she had ever known.

She stopped in the centre of it and let it wash over her, pretending, for half a minute, that she was part of the privileged who could live in such a world. If she got caught down here, though, she would receive even more demerits and the hotel would own her forever.

Not that it mattered.

For the last two nights she had been dreaming of Allen. *We're Dancers*, he said in one dream. In another, he took her hand, and led her to the edge of the children's pen. *They're trapped*, he said. *But inside they hold the secret to being free. We all do.*

I'm not Useless, she said to him.

He smiled, his little boy face round with a kind of joy. *None of us are*, he said, *in the right form.*

She found herself outside a store whose clear windows were full of ceramics and blown glass. Sculpted Minarans climbed out of a pool, a Siska held a fish in its ten-toed paw, and a group of tiny, thin Dancers reached up to the sky as if they saw her peering at them. She pulled open the door and went inside, hearing a bell tinkle above her.

A square old man with a sand-blasted face sat at a work table toward the back. Around him were sculptures in various states of completion. Behind him was a shelf of bowls, all white and unpainted. His skin was dark, the kind of dark created by a too-harsh sun.

'You've been to Bountiful,' Beth said.

The man set the piece of glass he held in his fingers down. 'I grew up there,' he said. 'Left when I was eighteen.'

And now he was probably four times that, judging by his build and the wrinkles on his face.

'You've seen Dancers.'

'Only once,' he said. 'Never forgot them, though. You've seen them too?'

Beth nodded.

The old man smiled. 'They were beautiful. I got some in the

window.'

'I know,' Beth said. 'How much are they?'

The price he quoted her was nearly the amount she had in her pocket. It didn't leave her enough. She bit her lower lip.

The man tilted his head, Dancerlike, and watched her from the corner of his eyes. 'What's wrong?'

'I came to buy a jar,' she said. 'I can't buy it and the sculpture.'

'Jars are cheap, missy,' the old man said. 'Tell you what. You take those Dancers and I'll throw in a jar like the Bountiful miners used to make at no cost.'

He stood. He was half a head shorter than she, and his movements were slow and creaky. He shuffled to a shelf near the back of the room, grabbed something and stood. Beth suppressed a cry. The jar was shaped like the jars of her childhood, the ones that stood on Dancer shelves. Its glass was full of impurities, small bubbles that looked like eyes.

It was perfect.

'I'll take them both,' she said.

The old man smiled. 'It's always nice,' he said, 'to have a little bit of home.'

ix

She took them back to her apartment and set them on the floor. If she squinted, the Dancers looked almost real. She could smell their cinnamon tang, feel the touch of their rubbery fingers. Seeing the old man was a sign, buying the jar was a hint. She had given someone notice.

If she stayed here, she would be useless. If she left, she had nowhere to go. No one loved her. No one cared. Her life had no meaning.

Saving the Minaran was the best thing she had ever done.

The Hotel would watch her from now on. She would never get another chance. She only had freedom today because every-thing was in flux.

She clutched the jar to her chest and reached inside, to that blocked wall of memories. The voice she heard was John's, a tenor stuck halfway between childhood and adult. *Be a Dancer, Bethie. We're Dancers.*

159

Then Allen's: *I know now. Watch.*

She had watched and not even realized it in her human self. But her Dancer self knew. The jar was hard against her chest.

She closed her eyes and reached, convulsing once.

Twice.

But there was no pain. The jar slipped from her hands, and bounced against her thighs before rolling to a stop near her ankles.

She held it in place and reached for it from inside, with the knowledge Allen had sent her at the end.

And as she did, the air turned silver.

Part Four

John

i

The lights flickered. John knelt on the webbed metal, the pattern digging into his knees. In this back tunnel, behind the pilot's bay, the air processor worked poorly. Sweat dripped down the side of his face and slicked his fingers. He leaned as close as he could to the display panel, a small light wedged against the side. He could barely see well enough to do the task – replacing microchips with the latest models, adding more memory, more function. The near-robotic feel of the work was all that mattered: pull, grab, replace; pull, grab, replace. They should have had a droid doing this, but they gave the work to John, a sure sign that his contract was nearly up.

He didn't mind. He didn't need the money. He had several credit accounts established in several different identities, partly for his work, and partly as a protection against a future catastrophe. He worked odd jobs like this and stashed the credits in a particular identity's account. This job's money went to his Sean persona. John had hoped for more cash, but what he had would do.

He had been on the trader ship for a month, and it was making him nervous. Thirty-five people, crammed in close quarters. State rooms around the side, pilot's bay up front, cafeteria/play area in the middle. All the cargo was stored below. Even though he was maintenance and janitorial, he still had to mingle with the rest of the crew.

They watched him as if they expected him to go suddenly berserk and murder them all in their sleep. His reputation as a member of the Dancer Eight always preceded him, no matter what he did to hide it. Twenty years, and his childhood still flashed before him, like a beacon.

Footsteps rang along the webbed floor. He didn't move, figuring that whoever it was would have nothing to say to him. A faint whiff of cologne, sharp and spicy, and expensive, illegal tobacco. The captain.

'John, someone to see you.'

John looked up. The captain stood on the other side of the corridor, the overhead lights strobing his face as they flickered. His skin was pale from too much time spent inside, his dark eyes narrow and filled with mistrust. Once John had fancied this man his friend, but John didn't have any real friends. Not since he was twelve years old. The day Allen died.

'I will not see anyone,' John said. Sometimes he played the role, the Dancer child everyone thought he was. The one who never spoke in past tense, only present and future, using the subjunctive whenever possible. The one who couched his thoughts in emotion because he had nothing else, no memory, no ethics, no soul.

The captain didn't even blink. 'She flew in special from Rotan Base.'

John stood, his scalp brushing the ceiling in the narrow corridor. His knees ached from the pressure of the webbed floor. He closed the display. She was a client, then. His time on the trader ship would end sooner than he expected.

The corridor widened as it reached the play area, but the heat remained fierce. The cafeteria was empty except for two red-faced techs sprawled in one of the booths, sipping coolers. Apparently the ventilation system was out. They were discussing whether they wanted to fix it or whether they wanted to wait until next planetfall. John would have argued for fixing it. The entire ship smelled of dirty, wet socks and unwashed bodies.

The captain led him through the booths, past the food displays, and beyond the couches to the door leading to the state rooms. The captain stopped at his personal suite and keyed in the access code. John had never seen this room; it was off limits to all but the captain himself. John stepped in, but the captain remained outside. The door snicked shut.

Computer-generated music – technically proficient and lifeless – played in the background. The room itself was decorated in whites, but the lighting gave everything a reddish cast. The couch was thick and lush. Artwork stood on stands around the room, and the small dining room had an art-deco design. Through open doors, he could see the bed, suspended in the air, cushions piled on top of it. A practical suite that could, in turns and with a flick of the light switch, function for business and pleasure.

Odd that the captain had the lighting set for pleasure.

A woman stood behind the dining room table, gazing out the thin portals at the stars. Her shoulder-length black hair looked dyed; no strand appeared to be the same shade. She wore tight, expensive black-and-white silks, wrapped so that the black and white material formed triangles on her torso, and revealed the shape of her breasts, the curve of her hips. She looked the part of the seductee, although she was the one who wanted to hire him.

John never hired out for personal jobs other than bounty work. He would tell her if he had to.

'I would like you to work for me, John.' She didn't even turn around to acknowledge him. He felt his hackles rise. She was establishing herself as the adult, him as the child in this encounter. He hated being treated like a child. The claustrophobia inched back on him, tighter than it had been in months.

He leaned against the door, feigning a casualness he didn't feel. He wanted her to turn around, to look at him. 'Why should I work for you?'

'Forgive me.' This time she did turn, smoothing her hair as she did. Her face was stunning: full lips, painted red; long nose that accented her high cheekbones; wide eyes enhanced to match her hair, in variegated shades of black. Her face was also familiar. John squinted, puzzling. He had seen her before.

'I'm Anita Miles,' she said. 'I run an art gallery on Rotan Base. We specialize in unusual objects d'art . . . '

He stopped listening, not needing the explanation. He recognized her face from hundreds of cordings, from vids, and announcements in the net. She was perhaps one of the most powerful people in this section – controlling trade and commodities. Her gallery sold anything that could be considered art. Once she sold a baby Minaran, claiming that, since the species was nearly extinct, the Minarans could only be appreciated in an aesthetic way. He couldn't remember if she won or lost the ensuing lawsuit.

Baby trader. The entire galaxy as an art object. If she had been in business when he was a boy, what would she have done with the Dancers?

'Why should I work for you?' he repeated.

She closed her mouth and gave him a once-over. He recognized the look. *How much does he understand? I thought I was explaining in clear terms. This is going to be more difficult that I thought.*

'You're the best,' she said, apparently deciding on simplicity. 'And I need the best.'

He often wondered how these people thought he could bounty hunt with no memory. He shook off the thought. 'What will you pay me?'

'Expenses, of course, a ship at your command because you may have to travel a bit, and three times your daily rate which is, I believe, the equivalent of four hundred Rotan credits.'

'Eight hundred.'

Her expression froze for just a moment, and then she had the grace to flush. John crossed his arms. Too many clients tried to cheat him. He took them on any way. If he tried to avoid those who treated him like a Dancer, he would have no business.

'I'm not a Dancer.' He kept his tone soft, but made sure. 'I wasn't even raised by them. The court says I wasn't even influenced – at least in the legal sense. I've served my time. When they released me from that hell hole on Reed, they declared me sane. Sane for a human being means an understanding of time and an ability to remember. After your little stunt, I won't work with you for anything less than five times my rate, one month payable in advance.'

The flush made those spectacular eyes shine brighter. Not embarrassment after all. Anger. 'You tricked me.'

'Not at all.' John didn't move. He felt more comfortable now with this little hint of emotion. He could ride on emotion, play it. That was one of the few things he had learned from the Dancers which he kept. 'You had expectations. You shouldn't believe everything you hear.'

For a moment, she drew herself up as if she were going to renounce him and leave. But she didn't. She reached into her pocket and removed a credit pouch. She had to have needed him badly.

She handed him two chips, which he slipped into his own pouch. When he was alone, he would place them in his private account, under his own name. One hundred and twenty Rotan credits. Perfect. He smiled for the first time. 'What do you want from me?' he asked.

She glanced at the portals, as if the stars would give her strength. The story was an embarrassment then. An illegality perhaps or some mistake she had made. 'Several weeks ago,' she said, 'I acquired a Bodean wind sculpture.'

Awe rippled through him. He had heard of Bodean wind sculptures. The Bodean deserts were full of them, swirling beautifully across the sands. No one knew how to tame them; they remained an isolated art form, on a lone planet. Someone must have figured out a way to capture them, wind currents and all.

'That's not the best part,' she said. Her tone had changed. She still wasn't treating him like an equal, but she was closer. 'The best part is the mystery inside the sculpture. My equipment indicates a life form trapped in there.'

—If we grow up, we'll be able to leave. We won't be trapped here. With them. On Bountiful. If we grow up . . .

He shook the memory voices away, made himself concentrate on her words. Something inside the sculpture. A bodeangenie? But they were the stuff of legends. Traders to Bodean claimed that the sculptures originated to capture little magical beings – 'genies', the traders called them – to prevent the creatures from causing harm to the desert. When the Interspecies Alliance went to study the sculptures, however, they found no evidence of life in or around them.

Strange stories had come from Bodean; odd visions and beautiful lights in the sky. None of the stories could be traced or documented.

But that didn't mean they weren't true.

His hands were shaking. She trapped things and called them art. 'You don't need me,' he said. 'You need a specialist.'

'I need you.' She whirled, her hair spiralling around her. Beautiful. Dramatic. 'The wind sculpture's been stolen.'

ii

Sleep. Narrow trader bunk, not built for his long frame. Dream

169

voices, half remembered:

> . . . *we'll be able to leave* . . .
> . . . *the Dancers do it* . . .
> . . . *You'll grow up* . . .
> . . . *Stop, please* . . .
> . . . *Just another minute* . . .
> . . . *Stop!!!* . . .
> . . . *the other hand* . . .
> . . . *Stooooop* . . .

He forced himself awake, heart pounding, mouth dry. The trapped feeling still filled him. He rolled off the bunk, stood, listened to the even breathing of his three cabin mates. He hadn't had that dream since – when? the penal colony? the last trading ship? He couldn't remember. He had tried to put it out of his mind. Obviously that hadn't worked.

Trapped. He had started the spiral when she said the word trapped. He leaned against the door, felt the cool metal against his forehead. The memory voices still rang in his head. If someone had listened, then maybe . . .

But no. The past was past. He would work for her, but he would follow his own reasons.

iii

Her gallery was less than he expected. She brought him there immediately after their arrival on Rotan base. Shoved into a small corner of the merchant's wing on deck sixteen, the gallery had a storefront of only a few metres. He had to duck to get in, and he was not unusually tall. Inside hung the standard work by standard artists: an Ashley rendition of the galaxy, done in blacks and pinks; a D.B. portrait of the shynix, a red-haired, catlike creature from Yster; a Degas statue of a young girl dancing. Nothing new, nothing unique, not even in the manner of display. All the pieces were self-illuminated against dark walls and stands, a small red light beside each indicating the place for credit purchases.

The gallery was even more of a surprise after she had told him her tale of woe: she claimed to have the best guards on Rotan, an elaborate security system, and special checking. He saw no

170

evidence of them. Her storefront was the same as the others in a government-funded base, complete with a plexi-glass wall that descended precisely at 21:00 each evening.

The dry, dustless smell made him want to sneeze. The air's cleanliness, at least, was unusual. He would have to check the filtration system. The sculpture probably didn't disappear at all. Some over-eager viewer might have opened the container, letting the wind escape, and the sculpture returned to the grains of sand it was. No great mystery, certainly not worth 120,000 credits. But he wouldn't tell her that.

Anita threaded her way through the displays to the back. He felt himself relax. There he would find the artwork he sought – the priceless, the illegal, the works which had made her famous. But when the door slid open, his mood vanished.

Crates, cartons, holoshippers, transmission machines, more credit slots. The faint odour of food. A desk covered with hardcopy invoices and credit records. A small cache of wine behind the overstuffed chair, and a microprocessor for late night meals. A workspace, nothing more.

She let the door close behind them, her gaze measuring him. He was missing something. He would lose the entire commission if he didn't find it.

He closed his eyes and saw in his imagination what his actual vision had missed. The dimensions of the room were off. The front was twice the size of the back. Base regulations required square sales – each purchased compartment had to form a box equal on all sides. She had divided her box into three sections – showroom, workroom, and special gallery. But where?

Where something didn't fit. The wine. She sold the wine as art – nectar of the gods, never drinking it, always collecting it. Wine didn't belong with the boxes and invoices.

He opened his eyes, crouched down, and scanned the wine rack. Most bottles came from Earth. They were made with the heavy too-thick glass that suggested work centuries old. Only one didn't belong: a thin bottle of the base-made synth stuff. He pulled it, felt something small fall into his hand. He clenched his fist to hold it as the wall slid back.

Inside was the gallery he had been expecting.

Holos of previous artifacts danced across the back wall. In those holos, the baby Minaran swam. He wondered where it

171

was now; if it could feel happiness, or exploitation. He made himself look away.

A tiny helldog from Frizos clawed at a glass cage. A mobile ice sculpture from Ngela rotated under cool lights. Four canisters in a bowl indicated a Colleician scent painting. He had only seen one before; all he had to do was touch it, and he would be bathed in alien memories.

More valuables drifted off in the distance. Some hung on walls, some rested on pedestals, and some floated around him. None had the standard red credit slot beside them. They were all set up for negotiation, bargaining, and extortion.

'Impressed?' She sounded sarcastic, as if a man with his background could not help but be impressed.

He was, but not for the reasons she thought. He knew how much skill it took to capture each item, to bring it on to a base with strict limitations for importing. 'You have your own hunters. Why hire me?'

She tapped on the helldog's cage. John winced. The dog crouched against the other side. 'I would have had to hire a hunter no matter what,' she said. 'If I removed one of my own people from a normal routine, I would have to hire a replacement. I choose not to do that. My people have their own lives, their own beats, and their own predilections. This incident calls for someone a bit more adaptable, a freelancer. A person like you.'

He nodded, deciding that was the best answer he would get from her. Perhaps she had chosen him, and not one of his colleagues, on a whim. Or perhaps she thought she could control him, with his Dancer mind. It didn't matter. She was paying him. And he had a being to free.

iv

Working late into the night so that the dreams would stay away, he did the standard checks: exploring the gallery for bits of the sculpture; contacting the base engineers to see if sand had lodged in the filters; examining particulate material for foreign readings. Nothing. The sculpture appeared to have vanished.

Except for the small item he had found near the wine cache.

He set it in the light, examined it, and froze. A sticker. Lina Base had used them for temporary i.d. for the past ten years. Stickers weren't the proper term. Actually, they were little light tabs that allowed the bearer to enter secured areas for brief periods of time, and were called stickers because most spacers stuck them to the tops of their boots.

He hadn't touched one – he had only seen them, fading remnants on a forgetful spacer's boot. He hadn't been to Lina Base in twenty years.

The memories tickled around his head: Beth, her eyes wide, hands grasping, as the guards carried her away; sitting on his own bed, arms wrapped around his head, eyes burning but tearless; the cool scent of processing mixed with the faint odour of piss that always brought back that sterile white cell; and Allen, his body convulsing, as the room filled with silver light.

Dancer mind. He snorted. If only he could forget. He was cursed with too much remembrance.

He set the sticker down, made himself move. He had to check arrival records, see who had come from Lina Base, who frequented it. Then he would know who took the sculpture.

v

The next morning, he walked into the gallery. The showroom was filled with Elegian tourists, fondling the merchandise. They were human, from a successful colony which had become a city state, but their customs were strange. They wore thick fur coats despite the warm temperature on the base. The security system had to be elaborate to allow such touching without any obvious watchful presence. The room smelled of animal sweat and damp fur. No wonder her filtration system was good. He pushed his way past a cluster of five, and let himself into the back.

Anita was cataloguing chip-sized gems that had arrived the day before. She was sitting at the desk, its surface clear except for the equipment she needed for the immediate task. She wore a jeweller's eye, and didn't look up when he entered. Her hair was tied back; the severity of the style made the colour of the various strands fan like a painter's palette.

'I need that ship,' he said.

173

'You found something?'

He nodded. 'A lead. Some traders.'

This time she did look up. The jeweller's eye gave her face an alien cast. 'Who?'

A small ship out of Lina Base named *Runner*. Owned by a man named Minx. He worked with four others on odd jobs no one else wanted – domestic cats from Earth to a colony of miners on Calmium; a cargo of worthless moon rocks to scientists on Mina Base. No records older than twenty years. No recording of illegal trading of any kind. But he didn't tell her that. He still wasn't sure if he was going to tell her anything.

'No one you'd know,' he said. 'If it turns out to be the people we're looking for, I'll introduce you.'

She removed the jeweller's eye. Her own eye looked less threatening. 'You're working for me, which gives me the right to know what you've found.'

'You *contracted* with me,' he said. 'And I have the right to walk away any time I choose – keeping the retainer. Now. Do I get that ship?'

She stared at him for a moment, then put the eye back in. 'I'll call down,' she said.

Justin Schafer

He adjusted the lace cuff of his sleeve so that the ruffle covered the back of his hand. His fingers, long and supple, the skin that still looked shiny and new to him, peeked out from the white froth. Then he tugged the high, ruffled collar and peered in the mirror hanging on his bathroom wall, wishing that there was some way to hide his face and still be seen in polite society. His doctors, colleagues, and friends all swore that he had no scars, but he could see them below the soft, baby fresh skin the doctors had grafted on twenty years before.

Bountiful would haunt him forever.

He tugged the waist of his black pants, put on the matching waistcoat, and adjusted the sleeves once more. When he could be objective, he knew he looked good enough. The doctors' magic ensured that he would have no wrinkles – that he would look forever thirty-five, even though his curly hair had long ago gone to silver. After living through five years of testing, mixing and matching skin colours, of growing and regrowing healthy tissue, he understood now why so few chose to use the process to keep the age off their faces. No beauty was worth that kind of pain.

He slipped an ear cuff on his left ear, the embedded sapphires winking in the light. Then he smoothed his hair back one final time and walked into his bedroom.

The room was wide and spacious. An entire wall of portals looked out over Bountiful, which looked golden from this distance in space. The bed took up most of the floor, its black cushions rising only a few inches from the surface. The walls and ceiling were painted an Earth sky blue, since dreaming of Earth was one of the only things that had carried him through those five years of agony.

He never went back, though. By the time he was fully healed, Lina Base had become his home. He had regained friendships, and professional status. Being an expert witness at three high profile trials, continually publishing monographs about his discovery of the Dancer Eight, and the work he had done since on the legal definition of Alien Influence had made him a minor celebrity. After all the years of loneliness, he welcomed the attention.

Craved it, in fact.

But he didn't crave the continual round of speeches, talks and public appearances. He refused to leave Lina Base, thinking that would cut down on the request for his services, but it didn't. Tonight's speech would be the fourth he had given in so many weeks; and because a lot of his local colleagues attended all of them, he couldn't recycle, but always had to write something new.

A chime sounded in his living room. He sighed. He still had fifteen minutes to prepare, and he liked to spend those alone. Obviously, though, tonight he wouldn't get what he wanted.

He went through the double doors into the public room of his suite. The furniture was low-slung, understated and comfortable. The rug, done in a tan, never showed dirt. He covered the walls with framed sections from his monographs, and miniaturized holos of him with dozens of honoured guests. The room was his proof that he had become someone, his way of showing that he had become the most famous psychologist on the base. He kept the proof in his home instead of his office because he needed to see it more than the colleagues who had snubbed him after Minar did.

The chime sounded again. He sighed and ran the security profile. It revealed Lewis, his assistant, tugging on the collar of his formal shirt. The door slid open, and Lewis walked in.

The formal clothes were baggy on him, as if he couldn't find a tailor on the base who could adjust clothing for his small, compact frame. His black hair was slicked back, and a spot of hair grease remained on his chin. He had shadows under his tiny eyes, and his thin lips were drawn into a line.

'We've got fifteen minutes,' Justin said.

'I know.' The door hushed shut behind Lewis. 'But I thought I should tell you here instead of at the banquet. You always say you want to know when I have news.'

Justin froze. Lewis looked like an overgrown puppy and had

178

the social skills of a newborn baby, but he knew how to uncover information. And the only information crucial enough to tell Justin immediately had to do with the Dancer Eight.

Justin had been following their lives ever since he came out of his first operation. By that point, the inexperienced counsel had already botched the legal side, and the sorry excuse for a child psychologist had screwed up any chance at documentation. If any group deserved to be tried and freed under the Alien Influences Act, it had been the Dancer Eight, and despite the appeals that Justin had filed through a different attorney, nothing could be done to change the sentence. The stupidity of allowing the children to get together not once but twice, and the resultant death made the sentences immutable. The best he had been able to do was to get each case reviewed five years down the road. That had allowed all of the children to be released on rather stringent parole.

The difficulties smacked of government intervention, but he had never been able to prove it. On paper, all the reasons seemed rational and clear, except for the extreme urgency with which the children had been dispatched to Reed. That had taken some planning and some strings that a base security officer, a judge, or an attorney did not have the ability to pull.

He tapped his wristputer and notified the banquet organizers that he would be late. Then he turned to Lewis. 'What do you have?'

Lewis ran a hand through his hair, and Justin winced as the grease dripped on to the back of Lewis's waistcoat. 'Another death.'

'John?' Justin kept tabs on all of the children. Two had died rather horribly and three had died quietly, leaving only John and Dusty to attempt to live regular lives. Justin had been surprised at John's longevity. He had always seemed, by the profile, to be the one who would do things first.

Lewis shook his head. 'Dusty. Locked room on Orda Base. I've been doing some checking before I brought it to you. She was trying to get passage to Bountiful, but the courts denied it. She had made her appeal to Judge Dania Zinn.'

'My God.' Justin sank into a chair, not caring that he crushed the back of his waistcoat. Dania of all people should have understood what Dusty was trying to do. But Dania had allowed the death of the fragile boy, Allen, to shatter her. She had stopped believing in the innocence of her clients, no matter what the appearances – and unlike many lawyers, such innocence mattered to her. She moved to prosecution, and later to a judgeship known for its harshness against anything to do with aliens and alien influence.

She should have refused the case on the grounds of conflict of interest. But when it came to the Dancer Eight, nothing Dania did made sense.

But Dusty couldn't have known that. All she would have known was that Dania had once tried to defend her. And then Dania had turned her down.

'What are the facts?' Justin asked.

'I've already loaded them into your files,' Lewis said, 'but here's the short version. She was running a scrap yard on Orda, with a small cabin behind the yard. Her partner, who made it quite clear to authorities that he was not her friend – he said she was too strange to have friends – saw her go into the cabin after she received the news from Zinn. He heard some strange sounds, thought she might be in trouble, tried the door and couldn't get in. The cabin had no windows. He called for help with the lock but didn't leave the door. By the time he got in, she was dead.'

'Like Allen?' Justin asked.

Lewis nodded. 'She was autopsied on Orda Base, and they have no idea what happened to the eyes. Say it's not possible – especially when someone is alone in a room.'

'Apparently it is possible – at least for these kids.' Justin sighed, and leaned back. The chair swung beneath him. 'Do me a favour. Send the report to Dania Zinn, compliments of me. Ask her to review the gag order on Latona Etanl. The woman's been out of prison now for ten years. The least the government could do is let her talk about her experiences. And I need to talk to an expert on the Dancers. Daniel is good, but he doesn't have the depth of knowledge that Latona does.'

Lewis frowned. 'You've been denied this request before.'

'Yes, but not by Dania Zinn, and not so close to a request from one of the Eight. Dania can only blame herself for Dusty's death. That might motivate our judge to do the right thing for once.'

'What does it matter?' Lewis asked. 'Only one of the eight is still alive.'

Justin stood. 'I'm not doing it for John. I'm doing it for precedent. The Alien Influences Act has only been used in cases where children were raised by aliens. It has been tossed out in cases that mimic the Eight. And I don't think it should be.'

'I don't know,' Lewis said. 'I still think you're tilting at windmills.'

Justin started. Leave it to Lewis to use an expression that was old when the first colonists left Earth. But it was strangely apropos. Justin was tilting at windmills, but it was the only thing he could do to make up for all the destruction he had caused in his short life.

'I'll meet you in the hall,' he said, adjusting his waistcoat, and smoothing the wrinkles out of the back. 'I'll just be another minute.'

Lewis nodded and left. Justin put his hand on a highly polished onyx table, and rotated his shoulders, trying to ease the tension out of them. He still dreamed about those children and the interviews, little Beth's face with its wide eyes and trembling lips. *But he's not going to grow at all, is he, Dr Schafer?*

Is he?

And now they were all dead. All but one. The leader. The mastermind behind it all.

If they had stayed on Bountiful, they would have died, too. It was an untenable situation. No matter what choice he had made, the children died.

Horribly.

That was why he no longer travelled off Lina Base. He would never investigate another case. Both on Minar and on Bountiful he had learned that he was not cold enough to play with other lives.

John

i

The shuttle was nearly a decade old, and designed to carry less than five people in comfort. The seats were four wide booths that John could not stretch out on. Their plush velour reminded him of the shuttle he and the other children had taken off Bountiful. The pilot's bay was sealed with double locks. If he wanted to contact her, he had to do so through the computer link.

He was the only passenger, and he spent the first hour on board trying all the different seats, hoping that one would be comfortable enough to sleep on. No luck. But they all had computer access, games and holos. In the back was a food terminal which provided all the food and drink he wanted. The only rules, made clear in a loud, flat, recorded female voice as he entered, were that he was not to disturb the pilot – for any reason. He guessed she had found out about his past and wanted nothing to do with him.

After another hour he found a way to curl on a booth so that his body wouldn't cramp too badly. He then slept most of the way to Lina Base. Sleep was his way of escape on ships. When he was awake, they reminded him of the penal ship, of the hands grabbing, voices prodding, violence, stink and finally isolation, ostensibly for his own good. When he was asleep, ships were the only places that allowed him rest without dreams.

His puter alarm went off an hour before landing. He woke, smoothed his unruly hair, and then paced down the narrow aisle. He hadn't been to Lina Base in twenty years. He had blocked most news of it, not wanting to know that the cold white cells still existed. He knew that the other children were sent to the same place he was, but when he had tried to find them, he had been beaten within an inch of his life. His elbow rebroke, and it wasn't fixed until the administrators discovered that he

185

couldn't work with a broken arm.

Strange things served as compassion in his life. He had always been grateful to the administrators for what little care they had shown him. If he had been an adult, they would have forced him to work, broken arm or not.

Ultimately, that compassion had trapped him. The little acts of kindness became more important than anything else. So important that he stopped looking for the other children. When he was finally released, he decided not to search for his old friends. The little acts of kindness had already moulded him into the cold, lonely man he was. He saw no need in dredging up the past.

Finally the warnings sounded and he sat down, strapping himself in. An odd flutter floated in his stomach, and bile rose in his throat. He swallowed it down. He was crazy to go back, crazy to look at the past he had been avoiding. No job was worth that, especially a job he only half-believed in.

The shuttle banked and turned. The feeling was so familiar that he felt he could close his eyes and open them to find Beth, Allen, and the others scattered in the seats around them.

With guards up front.

He was arriving without guards. He had been free for a long time.

With a thunk and a bang, the shuttle stopped. A headache, newly formed, pounded against John's skull. He should have bowed out when he saw the connection to Lina Base. He should have told Anita to hire someone else.

The door slid open, but he didn't move. Outside were the echo of old voices:

. . . *did you kill them* . . .?

. . . *feel to slice someone's hands* . . .?

. . . *any remorse* . . .?

. . . *murderers* . . .

. . . *children* . . .

With a hum, the door to the pilot's bay opened. She was slight, with almond eyes and dark skin, her long hair piled on top of her head. She stared at him. John stared back, unable to move.

'We're here,' she said.

'I know.' The words rasped out of his throat. He had to force

186

them out. He could barely breathe.

She crossed her arms in front of her chest. She wanted him off her shuttle.

He had to go into the base.

He drew himself to his full height, and stepped out of the booth. He was half a head taller than she was. As he approached the door, he looked down on her.

She didn't move. She didn't even flinch. Her eyes were a light blue and they were cold.

You will move in a group. You will make no sudden movements. You will do as we tell you. Walk down the stairs, across the floor to the open double doors directly in front of you. You will answer no questions and speak to no one in the crowd.

He took a deep breath and gazed out the door. The docking bay was smaller than he remembered. Only two shuttles fit comfortably inside. It had shiny new walls, painted a gray that hid streaks. The flooring was the webbed metal now favoured over the colonial plastic. The double doors at the end were painted black, not the brown of his memory. Shuttles scattered across the floor in a haphazard pattern, and workers milled around them. There was no crowd, no curiosity seekers, no one staring at him, waiting for him to slip.

'You okay?' the pilot asked.

He nodded and gripped the railing. The steps felt wiggly beneath his legs. The metal stairs still ran up to the second floor, and the observation windows were opaque. He had seen a hundred bays like this in a dozen different bases. This one was no different from any of them.

Except for the smell. Dusty, tangy, harsh with chemical cleaners. No other place in the colonized sectors smelled like this. The urge to sneeze rose in him. He breathed shallowly until it went away.

With the smell came the press of bodies, the pressure of the light cuffs against his wrist, the feeling of floating, like a Dancer, something he hadn't allowed himself to do for twenty years.

. . . look . . .

What's he doing?

. . . aren't on the floor . . .

. . . flying . . .

He made himself walk down the stairs. His boots clanged

187

against the metal webbing on the floor. He blinked. No crowds, no reporters, no friends trapped with him, no guards. No Harper, standing near the door, looking like a saviour he could never ever be.

John was thirty-two years old. An adult. A man who could handle himself.

And Lina Base had changed in twenty years. He knew it, had looked it up when he knew he was going to come. Now it had three docking facilities instead of one. It was one of the main trading bases in the sector, and had grown instead of declined when the officials closed Bountiful. He stopped, remembered: if he went to one of the portals, he would be able to see Bountiful, its deserts and mountains etched across the surface like a painting, the Singing Sea adding a touch of blue to the art.

Odd that he missed the place when, as a boy, all he wanted to do was leave it.

'You seriously okay?'

'Yes!' He whirled, expecting his anger to deflate her worry. Then he understood that she was speaking from obligation. He was her charge until he left the docking bay, and she didn't want the responsibility of handling him.

She stood at the top of the stairs, hands resting on her hips. 'Then get to Level Three for inspection and hosing. They need to clear this spot for other arrivals.'

He nodded, feeling a bit numb at her lack of concern. Procedures. After an outbreak of Malanian flu almost three decades before, Lina Base had become fanatic for keeping unwanted elements off the station. In the days before the hosing procedures, traders were quarantined on their ships or forced to stay in segregated decks for three months.

He turned his back on the pilot, glanced at the black double doors leading to the prison wing, and then sought the lift that regular folks used. It stood, as he expected it to, at the base of the metal stairs.

The lift was an older model, still made of the colonial plastic that had been jettisoned from the rest of the bay. The lift's sides were gouged from too much equipment, and near the floor the plastic had beaded as if something too hot had been pressed against it for much too long. The chemical smell was strong in there, and he was glad that the ride to Level Three was short.

The doors opened to a corridor decorated in browns and greens. Plants stood beside doors like sentries, their ceramic pots blending in with the thick brown rugs. A door on the left slid open for him, and he went in, amazed at the computerized efficiency of the base.

This room was nothing like the cheesy examination room they had put him in as a child. This one was a full suite, obviously designed to hold someone who had to remain in quarantine. Two couches flanked a wall that opened to a large screen, surrounded by holochips, a netlink and a wide ranging sound system. Above him a bed floated, its long flat surface and thick pillows looking inviting. Toward the back was a servo unit with a food display that showed holographic replicas of the choices.

A square servobot on tiny wheels rolled in the room from behind the food display. It carried a clear glass filled with pink liquid on its top. John sighed. He knew the procedure. He had just been through it on Rotan Base, but here it felt different. It felt intrusive.

He stripped, then took the glass off the tray and guzzled the sour pink juice. Some enterprising scientist had discovered that the stuff helped the autodoc in diagnosis. He set the glass back where he found it and the bot disappeared where it had come from.

He walked over to the mirrored cubicle and stopped. His body was lean, and corded with muscle, the skin still dark where Bountiful's sun had touched it all those years ago. He looked like his father, like the man who had turned his back on John, and disappeared into his Salt Juice, never to be seen again. His father had been about John's age at that point, on the verge of losing his career, his home, and eventually his wife. John had looked up the records soon after they freed him from Reed. All of the parents were charged with negligence and fined. Those with children still at home, like the Denglers, had those children taken away. Then the entire colony was closed after Netta's conviction. The colonists were scattered all over the sector. John's father had died in a detox centre on Lina Base, going through a withdrawal the doctors didn't know how to treat because they had refused to believe, even then, that Salt Juice was addictive.

How wrong they were.

It wasn't until years later someone reevaluated the events on Bountiful with Salt Juice addiction in mind. They had used the records on parental negligence cases as evidence that Salt Juice was not only addictive, but that its high destroyed the deeper human emotions. Like love.

He had always believed, although he never had proof, that the government had known this when the Dancer Eight were arrested, and that was why the Eight were hidden away as quickly as possible.

With his left hand, he pushed his long hair out of his face and stepped into the chamber. Nerves fluttered in his stomach. The door closed and he braced himself. He had never got used to the autodocs, not after the first time. It had been less invasive than the docs on the ship and on Reed, but it had seemed worse, probably because it had been his first time.

Light strobed beneath his feet, then opened like a shower into multifaceted streams. They invaded his orifices, tickling with the warmth of their touch. He closed his eyes, holding himself still, knowing that on some of the outer bases, hand searches were the norm. He didn't know how he could stand that, when he found this procedure so invasive. Then an entire band of light held him in place while the autodoc searched him for viruses, traces of alien matter, alien materials, and – probably – alien thought.

Alien influences.

A shiver ran through him. He had been twelve years old. Twelve years old, not realizing what they had done was abnormal, not human. Yet he was still human enough to feel terror at separation from all he knew. Knowing, deep down, that the horror was only beginning.

The autodoc was beeping and, for a long moment, he was afraid it had found something. Then he realized that it wanted him to leave its little chamber. He stepped back into the main room and retrieved his clothes – now cleaned and purified – dressed, and pressed the map to find out where he was and where he wanted to be.

Because he had come as an employee of Anita Miles, the Base protocol officers assigned him a guest suite near the main activities centre. The suite had a bedroom, living room and its own separate bath. The computer equipment and networking facilities were state of the art, and he silently thanked Anita for both her reputation and her influence.

He hoped he would not have to use the suite long, but if he did, at least he would live on Lina Base in comfort.

Unlike the first time.

He clamped down on the memories, refusing to get locked into them again. Then he sat at the desk and logged onto the net, requesting all available information on Minx's ship, *Runner*.

He found no extra files. And all the docking records were classified. He sighed. Nothing was going to be easy, just as he expected.

iii

John huddled in the shuttle records bay. Dark, cramped, smelling of sweat and skin oils, the records bay was as familiar as any other place on the Base. Only this was a different kind of familiarity. Every base had a records bay, and every base had an operator like Donnie.

He was small, wiry, scrawny enough to be comfortable in such a tiny space. His own stink didn't bother him – he was used to being alone. He monitored the traffic to and from the base, maintained licenses, and refused admittance if necessary.

'Left just as you were docking,' Donnie said. His lips barely parted, but his teeth were visible – half fake white, half rotted. 'In a hurry, too. Gave 'em the day's last slot.'

The day's last slot. No other craft could be cleared for leaving then, until the next day. John clenched his fists and pushed them against his thighs. So close.

'Where did they go?'

Donnie checked the hard copy, then punched a button. The display on the screen was almost unreadable. He punched another button, lower lip out, grimy fingers shaking.

'Got a valid pass,' he mumbled.

John shivered. Something was off. 'Where?'

'Bountiful.'

The word shimmered through him. Heat, thin and dry; deep flowery pefume; the rubbery feel of the Dancer's fingers . . .

'You done?' Donnie asked.

John took a deep breath, calmed himself. 'You need to get me to Bountiful.'

'Nope.' Donnie leaned back in the chair. 'I checked your records. I know who you are. Even if Bountiful were open, I couldn't let you go there.'

Trapped. This time outside of Bountiful. John's fingernails dug into his palms. The pain kept him awake, sane. He made his voice sound calmer than he felt. 'Where do I get this dispensation?'

Donnie gazed at him, scared of nothing, so secure in his small world of records and passes. 'Level five. But they won't help—'

'They will,' John said.

iv

He went back to the room and paced on the thin, hand-woven carpet, trying to think of a way to do this on his own. His mouth was dry. He was shaking with excitement, and he could feel his Dancer self struggling against the barriers he had erected in his brain.

Struggling to get free.

He clamped it back. Now was the time to let someone else do the job, let someone else catch Minx, find the bodeangenie.

Then someone else would return the genie to Anita, and she would sell it, continuing to enslave live beings to make a profit.

But what if there was no genie? All of this agonizing would be for nothing. He would go to Bountiful, and bring back a sand sculpture, nothing more.

He would go to Bountiful.

He sat down on the overstuffed couch, letting its softness encase him.

He would go to Bountiful.

He would go home . . .

192

John spent the next several hours in his suite. He put in a call to Anita and told her to hurry or she would never get her sculpture back. If she pulled the strings and doled out the cash, he would spend his time digging out information about the traders.

He did most of it on the computer in his suite. Although the records of docking systems and cargo hauls were classified, information about personnel, for the most part, was not. Lina Base's paranoia about its traders led to a wealth of information. Lina Base's records on Minx and his crew were more complete than Rotan Base's.

Perhaps that was because Lina Base was their main area of operation. They were well known here, but not liked. Two men worked with Minx: Dunnigan – trained as a linguist, and Carter – no formal training at all. The women, Parena and Nox, provided muscle and contacts. They had gotten the jobs on Calmium and Mina Base. And they had all hooked up eighteen years before.

After Bountiful had been closed.

When Minx had to expand his operation.

When Salt Juice became illegal.

Salt Juice. That little piece of information sent ripples of fear through John. Food. He had to get food. Take care of himself. He stood, unable to stop his mind.

Salt Juice had started it all.

The very smell of it gave him tremors, made him revert, close all the doors on himself, close out the memories and the emotions and the pain. He would focus on the future for protection, Dancerlike. No one had ever been able to get in. He had learned, over the years, the only way to keep himself intact, human, was to take care of his body so that the damaged part of his mind could recover.

He stopped in front of the servo unit and stared at the food display. The food had come to him on a small tray that jutted out of the wall. He would take it and eat it, no matter what it was, no matter what they put into it.

And the little cell had smelled of chemicals and piss.

His piss.

He had to get out of the suite. It didn't matter that it was big

193

and colourful and unlocked. He couldn't stay inside a room in Lina Base. Not now.

His heart was racing as he opened the door. For a half second he thought he wouldn't be allowed out. He still needed the food. His mind was trapped in his past and, if he wasn't careful, it would take hours before he could come out.

He followed the corridor to the activities centre. Double doors opened into a wide hallway, covered with lists of all his choices of activities. He had noted before that there were restaurants here. He picked the one at the edge of the centre, knowing the layout, knowing that that restaurant would have portals with a view of space.

Of freedom.

He hurried past the arcades and the virtual reality suites and the sex vendors till he found the restaurant he was looking for. It had no human employees. A line of servo units stood at the door, advertising the restaurant's lack of individual cuisine.

He didn't care. He didn't want to eat in his room, alone. He couldn't face it.

Behind the units were rows and rows of wooden tables, four matching chairs surrounding them. Behind the tables was an entire wall of portals open to space, with hanging plants on all sides. He ordered off the servo, picked a table near the window, and ran a credit voucher through the servo's payment slot. His food appeared on the table almost before the voucher stopped running.

He walked over, passing half a dozen tables with Base employees eating alone. In the corner, two women were in deep conversation. No one looked at him. No one even acknowledged his presence.

He liked that. He sat down at his table and looked at his tray in awe.

Roast chicken, steamed broccoli and mashed potatoes. Not a traditional servo meal. He had thought that when he ordered, expecting some poor rendition of a beloved meal, but no. The food was rich and well prepared. He picked up his fork and made himself eat slowly, feeling the food warm the cold places inside him. As he nourished himself, he allowed his mind to roam.

Salt Juice had been one of the most potent intoxicants in the sector. It was manufactured only on Bountiful, using the herbs grown by the Dancers. The main reason for the dispute with the Dancers, he learned later, was those herbs. When the colony finally discovered how to grow them without Dancer assistance, the colonists, led by Netta Goldin, had tried to wipe out the Dancers.

With the help of the children. Poor, misguided children. Lonely little children, who only wanted to leave the hell they were trapped in.

John finished his chicken and moved on to the mashed potatoes. If he reached, he could still feel the shock he had felt when he read Netta's trial records. She had shown no remorse. Neither had the security officer, D. Marvin Tanner. Only Latona Etanl, who was determined to be an accessory in all the murders for introducing the children to the Dancers without protecting those children from Dancer influence, had shown any regrets at all.

She had had poor counsel. They all had.

But at least Netta and Tanner were locked away for good. And if the trials had waited a few more years, they probably wouldn't have been. Long term exposure to Salt Juice, especially the chemicals used in the manufacture of the Juice, cause a kind of mental illness that showed itself in extreme narcissism, to the point of believing that nothing existed outside of the needs of the self. The children could be used – or abused, as most of the parents had done – because they didn't really exist.

The food sat like a lump in John's stomach. Later studies also showed that young children were often immune from the effects, and that the immunity gradually disappeared after puberty.

He hated that fact. He always wanted to believe he and his friends had followed the Dancer lead because they were suffering from long term exposure to Salt Juice. He had yet to find any excuse for their behaviour.

Except that deep childhood belief that what they had been doing was right. That it would work, though all the evidence was to the contrary.

John pushed the tray back. Salt Juice. Minx traded in Salt Juice.

Then moon rocks, cats. Worthless cargo. But Calmium's

northern water supply had a drug as pure as crystal meth. And the Minaran skin was poison which, taken in small amounts, induced a dangerous kind of high. Get the balance off in any direction, and the addict died.

Minx's crew were drug runners. Good, competent, skilled drug runners.

So the bodeangenie had more than artistic value to them. It also had some kind of stimulant value. He leaned back, the chair's wood digging into his spine. He wondered if that information was in Lina Base's net, or where he would find it.

He stood and then froze. A man leaned over the servo units, staring at the choices. John hadn't seen that face since he was a boy, but he remembered it clearly. The face haunted his dreams.

What did the Dancers teach you?

We only saw them once.

Why didn't you want Michael Dengler to play?

He was too little.

But he was with you the last time I saw him.

He followed us around.

The man who had betrayed them. The man who had set everything in motion, who had stolen their freedom, and had ruined their lives.

Justin Schafer.

John swallowed. He knew, on a rational adult level, that Schafer had probably saved their lives. But the child in him had always blamed Schafer for his insight.

Food appeared on a table near the front. Schafer walked over to it, and sat down, not seeing John. John waited until Schafer was bent over his meal, then got up and went out the side door, making sure he was never in Schafer's range of vision. John looked very different now, but he wanted to give Schafer no opportunity to recognize him.

He didn't know what he would do if he ever saw Schafer face-to-face.

vi

John went back to the suite to find a message from Anita. She had bought him a window – three days – and she let him know that it had cost her a fortune. He smiled. He was glad to put her money to good use.

He located the pilot and together they flew to the place from which he had been banned for life.

Justin Schafer

The crowd for the morning roundtable was large. Some of the colonial psychologists who were on the base for the annual continuing education seminar that Justin had spoken at two nights previous were scattered around the room, looking shy and out of place. The roundtable had been held ever since psychologists arrived at Lina Base. The same restaurant sponsored it from the beginning: a Chinese place in the old Earth section that, rumour had it, served the best dim sum on all the bases.

The restaurant was grimy and old, with cracked plastic tables and chipped china plates. The servo units up front dated from the Base's early days; the food they served often didn't match the food ordered. It didn't matter. No one came to the restaurant for the servo units. They came for the home-made items that were served from six a.m. until midnight. On Saturdays, the psychologists dominated the place, so that they had first pick of the dim sum that the restaurant specialized in.

Justin sat in his favourite booth, a large faded red corner section that sat five comfortably. He was wedged into the corner, just past the crack in the colonial plastic table, taking his first bite of pot sticker and relishing the doughy taste. Two colonial psychologists sat on either side of him, and Lewis sat at the edge of the booth.

The two psychologists were gushing about Justin's speech, and he was wishing he was somewhere else. He had long since tuned them out, knowing that they couldn't say anything he didn't already know or give him compliments whose sincerity he doubted.

Harper Reeves slid in the remaining side of the booth, and Justin stiffened. Reeves grinned at him. The look made his face cascade into wrinkles. Reeves was Justin's age, but stress and hard luck had made Reeves look at least ten years older.

'I'm amazed you're here this morning,' Reeves said. He picked up a spoon and scooped a pot sticker off the pile in the middle, dumping it on the plate in front of him.

The colonial psychologists shut up and sat at attention, obviously feeling the tension Reeves had brought to the table. Lewis shot Justin a glance over the petite colonial's head.

'I haven't missed a roundtable in years,' Justin said. He took a last bit of his pot sticker then delicately touched a napkin to his lips. He wouldn't get into another fight with Harper Reeves. Reeves hated him, and believed that the career Justin had made on the Dancer Eight belonged to Reeves himself. But Reeves had lost his license to practice for five years after the death of young Allen, and had had to go through training and a residency all over again. Even then he was no longer allowed to practice on children.

'Your watchdog hasn't been doing his job.' Reeves stabbed the pot sticker with one chopstick and put the entire thing in his mouth. He chewed for a moment, then spoke around the food. 'I'm amazed you let one of the Dancer Eight get on Lina Base without setting up an interview with him.'

The food made a slow turn in Justin's stomach. He took a sip of weak black tea to stall for time. Did he admit his ignorance and find out what Reeves knew? Or did he play it cautiously and try to save face? He grabbed the metal teapot and poured more warm tea into his cup. 'I'm supposed to see John this afternoon.'

'Well, you blew it then.' Reeves picked up his other chopstick and stabbed another pot sticker off another tray. 'He left for Bountiful last night.'

'Bountiful!' Justin bumped the table. Plates and cups rattled. Conversation died in nearby booths and people glanced over to see what had caused the commotion. He no longer cared about saving face. 'How the hell did he get passage to Bountiful?'

'Apparently he has a very well connected patron, who paid an excessive amount of money to get him three days dispensation. And the patron herself is quite interesting. Seems she grew up on Bountiful herself.' Reeves bit into the pot sticker and some of the insides fell to his plate. The rest of the dough balanced precariously on his single chopstick before falling as well. Reeves pushed the pieces around before setting the chopstick down. 'I don't think they should have let him go to Bountiful, do you, Justin?'

Justin didn't care what Reeves thought. 'Lewis, would you check into this, please? Let's see what we can track down.'

Lewis slipped out of the booth.

The two colonial psychologists looked surprised and confused. Justin could imagine the conversations they would have when they returned to their peers. *He didn't even know. One of his specialties and he didn't even know.*

Justin smiled at the petite colonial. 'Excuse me,' he said. He couldn't stay there any longer. John had been on the base, and he had missed him. Justin had missed his opportunity to interview the remaining member of the Dancer Eight. And now John was returning to see the Dancers.

'Who gave him clearance?' Justin asked.

'Government permits, like usual,' Reeves said. He was grinning, enjoying this bit of power over Justin.

'Is that how you found out?'

'Come, come, Justin. Do you think my sources are as mundane as all that?'

Justin clenched his fists. A rage was building inside him. This felt like those years after Minar, when the others would taunt him, and he would always be one step behind. He made himself take a deep, calming breath. 'Yes,' he said. 'I believe your sources are as mundane as that.'

Reeves grinned. 'Well, then, maybe you should get them to work for you too. Obviously my mundane sources are quicker on the uptake than Lewis's.'

Justin made sure his smile was civil. 'Thank you for the information, Harper. You've been invaluable.'

'I'm sure you'll remember that,' Reeves said, 'come time for the meeting of the review board.'

Justin turned away and hurried through the crowded tables. Oh, he would remember all right, but not necessarily in the way that Reeves wanted him to.

But Reeves was not his most important problem at the moment. John was. The Dancers had meant death for the children. Who knew what they would mean for a maladjusted adult.

John

i

He closed his eyes as the shuttle broke through Bountiful's atmosphere. His whole body was shaking. He had managed to remain calm throughout the entire trip, but now that Bountiful loomed, fear was threading its way through him.

He didn't want to be here. He didn't want to see the desert, the dome.

The Dancers.

He had successfully put their ways out of his mind. He had worked hard at becoming separate from them, at learning how to integrate his entire self, past, present and future. He knew how to remain in the present and still hold his identity from the past. They no longer held him. And he no longer wanted them.

At least consciously.

On a subconscious level, they still existed for him. Part of him still loved them. Maybe if he didn't see them, he wouldn't have to think about them.

He would grab the sculpture, and leave.

John leaned forward, wishing the pilot would open her door. He needed human contact right now. But this was the same pilot, the same ship, he had had from Rotan Base and, if anything, she was even more wary of him.

He bent down, opened his duffel and pulled out the sand scarf. They were being sold as fashion items in the handful of clothing stores on Lina Base. No one seemed to recall that sand scarves were once necessary clothing on Bountiful.

He held the scarf to his chest, feeling the soft weave. The material was warm and familiar, a bit of the past. As children, they had stopped wearing sand scarves, and he had got so crisped by Bountiful's sun that his skin had never recovered. He doubted he could survive such intense sunlight now without protection. He wasn't going to test it.

He also pulled out the bottle of cream which he had had to

207

have mixed specially for him at the pharmacy. Between his knowledge and the pharmacist's, they might have got the formula right. The cream had a different odour and a slightly different texture: over the years, the pharmacological industries had made modifications in burn protection. The cream didn't have the force of memory the scarf had.

His throat had gone dry. Three days alone on Bountiful. The pilot wouldn't stay – he knew that without even asking. She hadn't received a dispensation that allowed her to remain planetside. He strapped himself in, knowing it was too late to turn back.

The shuttle bumped and scuttled its way to a stop. Already the temperature inside had changed from cool to the kind of almost cool developed when the outside air was extremely hot. John unstrapped himself, put on the sand scarf, and rubbed the cream all over his exposed skin. The cream was cool and sent little shivers through him. The scarf fitted better than they had in the past. He didn't have to use the old ways of wrapping it so that parts wouldn't drag on the floor. As it was, it barely covered his long length.

He felt like two people: an adult with adult burdens, and a frightened child hiding under the skin. He had to be an adult here. Everything he had been frightened of as a child was gone.

He slung the duffel over his back, got up, and knocked on the pilot's door.

For a moment, he didn't think she would answer. Then the door slid back. She stood there, arms crossed, blocking his entrance.

But not his view. Through the windows, the white Salt Cliffs, bits of salt rolling like dust in a wind. Beyond them, the Singing Sea looked golden in the heavy light. It looked different through the glass, brighter than anything he remembered. He hadn't expected brilliant colours, or perhaps he had forgotten them. Since Bountiful, he felt as if he had been living in shades of gray.

'Familiar?' the pilot asked. Her expression was wary. She knew his history. Perhaps she thought that once he set foot on Bountiful, he would pull out a Dancer ritual knife and cut her heart from her chest.

'We're on the edge of the desert,' he said.

'Regulations prevent landings anywhere else.' Her tone

implied that he should know that. And maybe he had. The Lina Base Authorities had brought the children here that last day. No one had come with them. No one had been allowed to come. The children had had no adults to see them off.

No adults. There were no adults here now, at least not in the sense that he remembered. There was no colony, no human presence except for the five traders, and now him. 'You're coming back in three days?'

She nodded. Her hands clutched her arms so tight that her skin was turning red. What kind of lies had the authorities made up about Bountiful to keep the curious away? That one touch of the desert sand would lead to madness? That one view of the Dancers would lead to murder?

'Wait for me. Even if I'm not here right away, I'll be coming.' The words sounded hollow to his own ears. She nodded again, but he knew at that moment that she wouldn't wait. He would have to be here precisely on time or be stranded on Bountiful forever.

Trapped.

The child inside him shuddered.

He tugged on the duffel strap, then turned away from her. She pressed a button that made the door slide back. Immediately heat poured into the shuttle. There was no bay crew, no one to attach stairs to the shuttle's outer side. He would have to grap the roll bar, and use the built-in lip to get down.

'It'll be too hot to touch,' she said, meaning the metal rollbar.

He nodded as he wrapped a bit of the sand scarf around his hand, thick, like a protective glove. He gripped the bar and used it to swing to the hard-packed sand.

The heat was a live thing, sinking into his pores despite the cream. The mines of Reed had been cold and damp, and since then he had lived on ships and bases, in controlled environments. He hadn't experienced heat like this since he was a child.

Sweat had already formed on his face and back.

The air smelled like flowers, decaying flowers left too long in the sun. Twelve years of memories, familiarity and fear rose within him – and suddenly he didn't want to be there any more. He turned to the shuttle, but the door had already closed. He reached up to flag the pilot down – and turned the gesture into a wave. He was not twelve any more. The adults were gone. The colony was gone. He was the adult now, and he wouldn't let himself down.

ii

The path was long gone. Sand had brushed over it as if it had never been. Small plants, brown and spiny, snagged at his shoes. He made sure he walked slowly, hating the heat of his clothing yet glad for the protection. Ahead, the dome shone like a glass in the sunlight. The walk wasn't as long as he remembered it, but he took it slowly, stopped every few minutes to sip from his warm water bottle.

The heat had not affected him like this when he had been a child.

He closed his eyes and stopped, feeling the breeze blow sharp grains of sand over his face. He would not think of the past. He would think of the future, of his plans when he met the traders.

The traders. He opened his eyes and marched forward as if this were some other place – a place that had no history for him.

The traders had made a brilliant decision to come to Bountiful with the wind sculpture. Here they had a ready-made empty colony, a desert filled with sand, and winds aplenty. They could experiment until they were able to duplicate whatever effect they needed, or they could use the planet as a base from which to travel back to Bodean. No one would have caught on if Anita hadn't started the search for her sculpture.

He should have called her and told her to send someone else.

The dome loomed in front of him like a bubble in the sand. The dome was smaller than he remembered. The prisoners' compound which he had been assigned to on Reed had been twice this size. He would be able to walk the length of the dome in fifteen minutes – and at the edges he would have to duck to avoid hitting his head on the dome's plastic ceiling.

Once he had thought this place the world. In his dreams, sometimes, he ran forever past the green plants and well tended gardens, trying to escape the dome.

He stopped in front of the dome, stunned to see it covered with little sand particles. In another generation, the dome would be a mound of sand, with no indication that anything had ever

210

existed beneath it. The desert reclaimed its own.

His hand shook as he extended it toward the dome. He brushed the sand aside, feeling the grains cling to the oil on his skin. The dome was hot, hotter than he cared to touch, but still he felt for the fingerholds that he knew would be there.

And found them. Smaller than he remembered, and filled with sand, but there. He tugged, and, with a groan, the section moved. He slipped inside, bumping his head on the hard surface. He was a man now, not a boy, and crawling through small spaces wasn't as easy as it used to be.

The ground inside was packed, but had no sand. His hands gripped the dirt, and pulled him forward until he collapsed on the hard surface. The air wasn't as stale or as hot as he expected it to be. It tasted metallic, dusty, like air from a machine that had been turned off for a long time. Decades, probably.

The traders had been in here. Of course they would know that the dome could be breached from the outside. Bountiful's colonists had had a terror of being trapped in the desert.

He sat up. The sweat was dripping off him and disappearing into the cracked dirt. The coolness of the air was welcome, but made him realize just how hot he had been out there. He took his water bottle from his duffel and sipped. Three days' supplies. He had to be careful with them.

He got to his knees, grabbed the inside of the hatch and pulled it closed. The force of the slam shook sand off the dome, and he could see the desert through the clear plastic, a sea of white against a brilliant sky.

Then he got up and turned around. He had entered in the centre of the dome, near the Food Dispensary and the Bartering Post. Beyond them, the houses stood in their perfect rows.

Nothing had collapsed. It looked dusty, empty, abandoned, but that good old regulation colonial plastic had held up to decades of neglect. The gardens hadn't been so lucky. The plants were dead. They must have stood, perfectly preserved, until the traders turned the air back on. Now the plants were crumbling all over the carefully nurtured soil.

It looked like a parody of his childhood, like all the decay and corruption which had existed in Bountiful had finally risen to the surface and overtaken the colony.

He started to walk. The sound of his feet, shuffling against the

211

earth, was the only sound he heard. No voices, no hum of the Salt Juice plant, no movement. Only John on a long, empty street, facing long, empty ghosts.

The houses looked odd to him now. He had lived most of his life in places with windows. These homes looked deformed, plastic shells that hid rather than protected.

At the end of the block, the park started, and in its centre stood the morgue. His mouth was dry. He wondered if anyone had bothered to turn off the cryogenic units or to remove the bodies.

He didn't want to find out. He turned left, toward Command Central. Chances were that the traders were there. They had turned on the air from there, and Command Central had the best equipment, the best facilities for most anything. The traders would remain in that part of the dome.

So easy. Then they would have to wait three lousy days together for the shuttle pilot to return.

The houses looked more and more familiar. Over the next block, his parents' house hid. He didn't go to it. But the route he chose led him past the Dengler house. He had heard through his various sources that the Denglers lost their remaining children. The government had levied charges of neglect and sent the children to foster care. Most of the colonists had lost their families that way.

He hoped it had worked. He hoped the other children had had a better life than he had.

He stopped in front of the house, with its dead rose bushes in front. They had brought Michael's body there in the daylight, leaned him against the door as they had done the others so that the parents would see and understand, so that they would know that they had to care for their son until his new organs appeared. But the adults hadn't done that. They had screamed and carried on.

John remembered his thoughts clearly. It had seemed so logical that if they removed Michael's head along with his hands, heart and lungs, that Michael would grow taller and stronger than the adults. But like the others, Michael hadn't grown at all.

John sank to the ground, and wrapped his arms around his head as if he could shield himself from his own memories. All he

212

and the others had wanted to do was escape. And they thought the Dancers held the secret to that escape.

He remembered huddling behind the canopied trees, watching the Dancer puberty ritual, thinking it made so much sense: remove the hands, the heart, and the lungs so that the new ones would grow in. He had been the third generation born in a new world. Of course he hadn't grown up. He hadn't followed the traditions of that new world.

The judge had asked him over and over if he believed that, why hadn't he gone first? He wanted to go last, thinking that the ultimate sacrifice. Dancer children didn't move for days. He hadn't understood the adult reaction – the children weren't dead. They were growing new limbs. Or at least, that was what he had thought. Until Michael Dengler. Then they made John understand what he had done.

He stayed on his knees for a long time. Then he made himself rise slowly. He did bounty now. He travelled all over the sector. He had served his sentence. This was done, gone. He had a wind sculpture to recover, and the people were within his grasp.

He made himself walk, and concentrate on the future.

iii

He found where they got in. Another section had been dislodged, letting heat and too bright sunlight into the dome. Footprints marred the dirt, and several brown plant stalks were newly broken. Being this close usually excited him – one of the few excitements that he had – but this time he felt empty inside.

His breathing rasped in his throat. He had a dual feeling: that of being watched and that of being totally alone. The hairs prickled on the back of his neck. Something was wrong here.

The section of the dome had been moved near the guest apartments. The apartments were near Command Central. The traders had known what they were doing.

A shiver ran down his back. They had planned this for a long time.

He grabbed the dome door and pulled it closed. No sense in allowing them an easy out.

They had left shallow impressions in the packed dirt. Five

different sets of footprints, all heading towards Command Central. He traced them around the dead and broken plant stalks, then stopped. The six large buildings of Command Central faced him like a demon from a nightmare.

Those buildings lived in his dreams. They haunted his waking moments. In there, Justin Schafer had interrogated him, and in there, the authorities had told him that he would leave Bountiful in their custody. For committing murder.

He shook off the memory, and walked to the main building. The door was open – an invitation almost. He couldn't go around to the windows, since there were none, and most buildings didn't have another doorway. He braced himself and slipped in.

The silence was heavier in here. The buildings always had a bit of white noise – the rustle of a fan, the whisper of air filtering through the ceiling. Here, nothing. Perhaps they only found the controls for the dome itself. Perhaps they wanted it quiet so that they could hear him.

The walls and floors were that spotless white which he despised, so clean they looked as if they had been washed days before. Only the dirt-covered tracks of the traders marred the purity, a trail leading him forward, like a dog on the trail of a scent.

He followed it, willing to play out his little role in this drama. Some action would take his mind off the remains of the colony, of the hollow vestiges of his past.

He rounded the corner – and found the first body.

It leaned against the wall, skin toughened, mummified into a near skeleton. For a minute, he thought it had been there since the colony closed and the air shut down, then he noticed the weapon in its left hand. A tiny pen-sized laser, keyed to a person's print. The design was new; it had come from Rotan Base only the year before.

He made himself swallow and lean in. One of the traders. For a moment, he couldn't determine which one. He ripped at the clothes, discovered gender – male – then studied the wrinkled, freeze-dried face.

Not the old trader, Minx, who had run Salt Juice. One of the younger males. Tension crept up John's back. He had seen this kind of death before, but where?

The answer required that he let down some internal shields, and reach into the walled off portions of his memory. He did so slowly, feeling the hot spots, the oppression the colony imposed on him. Then it came:

A Cadmium miner on one of the many cargo ships he had worked for. The miner had slipped into the hold, trying to get safe passage somewhere, not realizing that to get out of those mines he needed a series of shots, shots that protected him from the ways that the mining had destroyed his body, processes that wouldn't start until the mining ended.

The captain of the cargo ship had leaned over to John, and expressed the view of the entire ship. 'God,' he had said. 'I hope I don't die like that.'

John touched the corpse again, figuring that if he were contaminated there wasn't much he could do about it. Amazing that the man hadn't died when he left Cadmium. The traders had been far away from that planet for years. Amazing that the death would come now, here, in this faraway place, with a weapon in his hand.

John took the laser from the body and ran the diagnostic. The laser worked. He pocketed it. Better to use this weapon than his own. Covered his tracks, if he had to.

The footprint path continued down the hall. He brushed off his hands, and followed it. All the doors were closed, locks blinking, as if they hadn't been touched since the colony was evacuated.

He followed the trail around another corner, and found a second body, this one a woman. She was sprawled across the floor, clothing shredded, blood everywhere, eyes wide with terror. No desiccation, no mummification. This time, the reek of death, and the lingering scent of fear.

The scent of fear made the hackles on the back of his neck rise. The first death had struck him as odd; the second made him more than uneasy. It terrified him.

She appeared to have been brutalized and beaten to death, but as he got closer he realized that she didn't have a scratch on her. John's hands were shaking. He had never before encountered anything as odd as this. How did people die on a dead planet? Nothing here would do this, not in this fashion, and not so quickly. He knew about death on Bountiful, and it didn't work

215

like this.

He pulled the laser out of his pocket and kept going. The trail didn't look like footprints any more, just a swirl of dirt along a once-clean floor. He half-expected a crazed trader to leap out from behind one of the doors, but he knew that wouldn't happen. The deaths were too bizarre, too different to be the work of a maniac. They had been planned. And a little scared voice inside told him they had been planned for him.

iv

The main control room covered the back half of the building. Most of the equipment, long ago outdated, was dark and silent. The station where dozens of people had worked sat empty. Only one grid was lit – the one directly across from the door. He slipped inside, disturbing dust on the floor.

The grid dated from the original colonists. Its design was so old he had to guess at its functions. He checked the patterns, figuring out how it should run on guesswork, experience with odd grids, and a half-worn down diagram near the top of the board. His instincts warned him to absorb the knowledge in this room – and he was, as fast as he could.

This grid operated the environmental controls and the dome.

A door slammed somewhere in the building.

His skin prickled. He whirled. No one visible. No sounds. Nothing except the slight breeze caused by his own actions. He moved slowly, with a deliberation he didn't feel. He checked the corridor, both directions, noting that it was empty. Then he left the main control room. There was nothing more he could do inside. He walked in the direction of the slammed door. Someone else was alive in here, and he would find that person. He didn't know what he would do then.

You should be able to do something, a cold voice, half-familiar, said to him. *You are a famous murderer after all.*

The thought brought back the terror of the building; the accusations once hurled at him here. His heart was pounding against his chest. He took a deep breath in an attempt to calm himself.

Death had never frightened him before. He had never felt it as a threat, only as a partner, an accident. He never saw the murders as deaths, just failed experiments. No one he loved had ever died. They had just disappeared.

Another body littered the corridor. Literally. It had been chopped into small pieces and scattered all over the floor in a square pattern that made the killing a ritual execution done by the Fetin. He had seen enough of those at Reed.

He continued to walk, his footprints mixing with the dust. When he looked back, the soles of his shoes were outlined in blood.

You should be able to handle this, that cold voice said. *You have bathed in blood.*

He shuddered. This was different. He had killed, but these deaths were different.

Is it a matter of intent, then? the cold voice asked. *It seems that they are all equally dead.*

Around the next corner, he came upon the fourth body. It was crucified against a wall, upside down, blood still dripping on to the pristine floor. The hands and feet were attached with long metal spikes, and another had been forced through the chest.

It would take an incredible amount of strength to do that.

Perhaps he had been wrong. Perhaps one man had done it. A madman with a lot of determination, and perhaps some kind of toxic brain poisoning from a drug he wasn't used to. One man, Minx, the old trader, under the influence of the Bodean wind sculpture.

John hated to think Minx had done this in a rational frame of mind.

Like you.

John shook the voice away, and concentrated on the corridor in front of him. He had circled the entire building. From his position, he could s∵e the door, still standing open. Minx had to be outside, waiting. John tensed, holding the laser, setting his own systems on alert.

The dirt spread all over the floor, and a bit on the walls. Odd, without anyone tracking it. Was Minx's entire body grimy? John crept along as quietly as he could, trying to disturb nothing. It seemed eerie, as if Minx had been planning for this. It felt as if he had been watching, waiting, as if John were part of a plan. Even more eerie was that Minx had managed to kill so many people in

217

such diverse ways, in such a short period of time, and without the others intervening.

It made no sense.

John reached the front door, and went rigid, except for a trembling at the very base of his spine. Minx was there, all right, waiting, but not in the way John expected.

Minx was dead.

The blood still trickled from the stumps where his hands used to be. His chest was flayed open, heart and lungs missing. Head tilted back, neck half cut, as if whoever had done this couldn't decide whether or not to slice it through.

He hadn't been there when John went into the building. Minx couldn't have died here – it took too long to chop up a human being like that, even with a Dancer knife. John knew. He had done it with willing victims. Minx didn't look willing.

The blood was everywhere, spraying everything. Minx had to have died while John was inside.

The shiver ran up John's spine, into his hands. *I didn't mean to kill him!* the little boy inside him cried. *We just wanted to grow up, like Dancers. Please. I didn't mean—*

He quashed the voice. He had to think. All five were dead. Something—

'John?'

He looked up. Allen stood before him, clutching a Dancer ritual blade. It was blood-covered and so was he. Streaks splattered his face, his hands. He was still young and pudgy, but the sadness was gone from his eyes.

'Allen?' John knew it wasn't him, couldn't be him. Allen was dead. John had watched him die. John walked towards him anyway, wanting to wipe the blood off Allen's face, to see if his eyes were still red rimmed from too many tears. John reached for Allen, hand shaking. Allen didn't move as John's fingers brushed the blood-stained cheek – and then went through it.

Allen was as solid as wind.

Wind.

Allen laughed and grew bigger, Minx now, even though the real Minx remained dead at John's feet. 'Took you long enough,' the bodeangenie said with a familiar cold voice. 'And you call yourself the best.'

John glanced at the body, the ritual knife, and found the laser in his own hand. A laser could not cut through wind.

'No,' the bodeagenie said. 'It can't.'

John stopped breathing. He took a step back as the realization hit. The bodeagenie was telepathic. It had been inside John's head, inside his mind. He shuddered, wiped himself off, as if in brushing away the sand he brushed away the touch, the intimacy he had not wanted. Had the others died of the things they feared? That would explain the lack of external marks, the suddenness. That would explain all except Minx.

Minx, who had died of something John feared.

But why now? Why hadn't the genie tried to kill Anita's people on Bodean, or the traders at Rotan Base?

Then the images assaulted him: The trader ship, full of sweat, laughter and drink, hurtling toward Bountiful; the traders themselves dipping into the bodeangenie in Command Central, using him to tap each other's minds, playing; the Dancers stalking out of the woods into the desert; John, sitting in the cafeteria, his memories displayed before him; Anita, counting credits, peering into the bottle; the trap closing tight, holding him fast, a bit of wind, a bit of sand, a bit of plastic . . .

John was the bodeangenie's freedom if Bountiful didn't work. He could pilot the traders' ship back to Bodean. Fear pounded inside his skull. He didn't want to die like that. He had never wanted to die like that . . .

He slid to his knees, hands around his head as if to protect it. He had been invaded like this before, as a little boy, voices dark and chirpy, images full of light, and they had built a wall in the back of his brain, a wall to collect his personality, his memories – him.

He slipped inside that wall.

The bodeangenie chuckled, Allen again, laughter infectious. He went to the dome, touched it, and John saw Dancers, hundreds of them, more than he had ever seen, their fingers rubbing against the plastic, their movements soft and graceful, the thing that had given them their name.

'Three choices,' the bodeangenie said. 'Me, or death, or them.'

A little light went on behind his wall. The bodeangenie thought the Dancers frightened him. The genie could only tap what was on the surface, not what was buried deep, no matter

219

what its threats.

Wind, and sand, and plastic.

John hurled himself against the dome, pushing out, and sliding through. The Dancers vanished as if they never were. He rolled in the sand, using all his strength to close the door. The bodeangenie pushed against him with the power of wind. John's muscles shook, his arms ached. The bodeangenie changed form, started to slip out, when John slammed the portal shut.

Trapping the genie inside.

The bodeangenie howled and raged against the plastic wall. The side of the dome shook, but the genie was trapped. A little boy appeared in John's mind, alone in a foreign place, hands pounding on a plastic door. *Let me out*, the little boy said with John's voice. *Please, I didn't mean to—*

His words. His past. Trapped. The genie was trapped. It had to be or it would kill him. Trapped.

John ran.

Across the white hot sands toward the forest, toward something familiar. The sun beat down on him, and he realized he had forgotten his scarf, his ointment, his protection. The little boy kept pounding, sobbing. Torture. He wouldn't be able to survive it. Two more days until the shuttle arrived.

He could take the traders' ship, if he could find it.

The forest still looked charred, decades after the fire that Justin and Latona had set. But the canopied trees had grown back, and John could smell the familiar scent of tangy cinnamon.

Dancers.

No!!!! the little boy screamed in his head.

They came toward him, two legged, two armed, floating like black wraiths above the white, white sand. They chirruped in greeting, and he chirruped back, the language as fresh as if he had used it the day before.

His mind drifted into the future, into emotion, into their world.

I would like to stay, John sent to them. *I would like to be home.*

Justin Schafer

i

Justin was waiting in the shuttle bay when the pilot returned from Bountiful. He sat in the second floor booth and watched as the alarms went off, sealing off the rest of the station. The bay doors rose and the shuttle glided in, a large silver beast trapped inside these walls.

He rubbed his eyes. He hadn't slept much since he discovered that John had been on Lina Base. Justin and Lewis had applied to every organization they could think of for a pass to Bountiful, but each application had been denied. Justin had offered all of his savings and a sum over and above that, worth half the cost of his art collection, and still the Lina Base officials had said no.

Anita Miles had paid a large fortune to get John on to Bountiful. She must have thought she would recoup the money easily. Justin wondered what she wanted. He knew she was a famous art collector. Perhaps she remembered something valuable from her childhood on Bountiful.

Something connected with the Dancers. Something only John could get for her.

The shuttle's roar sounded too loud, even behind the double glass protection. The bay doors eased closed and Justin stood, tugging on his pants legs so that they fell properly over his shoes. If John were on this flight – and nothing had been said either way – he needed to see from the front that he could trust Justin.

It would be the only way they could work together, perhaps to save John's life.

Sixteen servobots, painted yellow to show their disaster relief designation, surrounded the shuttle, measuring the surface for radioactivity, and other problems it might have brought back from Bountiful. Justin's hands were shaking. He didn't know what he would say to John when they first met.

Did you know you are the last one of the Dancer Eight who still lives?

223

Probably. Anita Miles had been adamant, at least, about that. *Don't let him fool you, Doctor,* she had said. *He has a good mind under there. He likes to pretend that he has no memory, but his is better than anyone I have ever met.*

Obviously John had made quite an impression. Enough that Miles would pay his passage and warn others against him.

The warning light shut off over the door. The red colour disappeared, leaving the room a cool gray. Justin hadn't even realized the light was on until it went off. He grabbed the knob and tugged the door open, wondering for what must have been the thousandth time why the shuttle bays preferred old fashioned door knobs to the computerized equipment.

He stepped into the bay and felt the dry heat emanating off the shuttle. The air smelled of chemicals and something else, something that almost smelled of flowers. The scent was familiar; it was the scent of Bountiful, but he knew that smell had to live in his imagination.

The bots had pulled away from the shuttle, and the stairs wheeled themselves to the shuttle's side. Justin hurried down the metal steps to the bay floor. His breath was coming in small gasps. This would be the first time he had seen John since John was a boy. Justin wondered if John would even recognize him.

Justin doubted it. His heels clanged on the metal webbing, and he stopped several feet away from the shuttle itself. The door made a humming noise as it eased open.

A woman stood there, wearing a silver pilot's jumpsuit. She was petite, her skin naturally dark, her long hair piled on top of her head. She stepped out and the door closed behind her.

Justin swallowed hard. Perhaps John had gone crazy. Perhaps she had him imprisoned inside and she was just going for help.

He hurried across the floor, no longer concerned about his appearance. The pilot stopped on the first stair, watching him warily.

'Where's your passenger?' Justin asked.

A flush rose in the woman's cheeks, adding a light dusty rose colour and giving her a delicate beauty that her face hadn't had a moment before. 'He wasn't there.'

'Wasn't where?'

'At the landing site.'

'Did you search for him?'

She gripped the metal railing so hard her knuckles were white. 'Who are you?'

She hadn't searched, then. She wasn't going to answer any more of his questions without coercion.

'You didn't search?' Justin snapped, hoping he sounded official. 'You mean he could be down there, injured or dying, and you didn't check?'

'I ran a surface scan.' Her voice had a tone of defensiveness to it. 'I didn't find him that way.'

'Exactly,' Justin said. 'If he had been in the dome, you wouldn't have picked him up on that scan.' He approached the base of the stairs. 'I want you to take me to Bountiful.'

She stared at him for a moment, as if she were wavering, and then she extended her left hand. 'I need your pass.'

'Don't you understand that this is an emergency situation?'

'Perhaps you don't understand,' she said. 'I am a private pilot. I work for Anita Miles, not for Lina Base. I must follow the rules or lose my access to the base. Unless you identify yourself and give me your pass, I can't help you.'

Outgunned. She was more cautious than the average shuttle pilot. She probably had to be, with her employer.

'All right,' Justin said. 'After you go through quarantine, I want you to make a full report of the situation, including your negligence, and send it to all offices connected with Lina Base, and Bountiful security.'

She hadn't moved. She was looking down her nose at him. 'I'll do so,' she said, 'but I'll have to report your strange request. And I'll need your name.'

He stared at her for a moment. She was smarter than he would have liked. 'Fine,' he said. 'My name is Dr Justin Schafer. I am a well known xenopsychologist, and I am one of the few people who understand what kind of jeopardy you placed John in. You probably cost him his life. I hope you realize that.'

'I only do what I am told,' the pilot said. She walked the rest of the way down the steps and pushed past Justin.

He stood before her shuttle for a long time, wishing he knew how to pilot it himself.

*

The rest of the afternoon, he traced a frustrating trail through Lina Base's bureacracy. He went from Security to Regulations and Permits, from Special Dispensations to the offices of both representatives of the Provisional Parliament. He ended up waiting in the Governor's office on a chair upholstered with material that felt like metal, his stomach growling because he had missed both lunch and supper.

The receptionist didn't appreciate his presence any more than Justin appreciated the receptionist's. Justin had been the last supplicant to arrive late in the afternoon, and if he hadn't been personal friends with the governor, the receptionist wouldn't have allowed him in the office at all. As it was, he got to exchange the basic facts with the governor before being asked to sit in reception while the governor reviewed the files.

The receptionist was a thin man who affected spectacles as part of his tweedy 19th century retro outfit. Each time Justin had come into the office over the years, the receptionist had affected the latest retro style, never wearing anything that dated from the modern era. The spectacles were made of wire and added an owlish aspect to the man's face. Unlike the real things, however, the spectacles had no glass or plastic, only the wires pretending to enhance the receptionist's vision.

Justin hated to be kept waiting, especially by a friend. If finding John weren't so important, Justin would have left hours ago.

But the longer Justin sat, the more worried he grew. Over the past three days, he had discovered that John was chasing a ship of traders connected to Miles, who were well known for operating on the shady side of the law. Perhaps John had got on their wrong side. Perhaps they had him.

Perhaps Anita Miles had not told Justin the truth. Perhaps she had sent the traders and John for something precious.

Or maybe he had gone to see the Dancers.

Justin's ability to guess what would happen faded whenever he contemplated that possibility. He had never completely understood the Dancer Eight's relationship to the Dancers – no one had. He didn't know if contact with them would make John psychotic, if it would heal him or if it would kill him. There were too many variables, too many unknowns.

The receptionist stood. 'The governor will see you now,' he intoned in his deep baritone. Justin wanted to say something witty, to shatter the man's self-absorbed image of himself, but this late in the day it seemed like too much effort. Justin said nothing as he slipped past, through the open door.

The governor's office was the biggest on the base. It was in the base's centre, so it had no windows at all, only holoprints of various relaxing scenes from nearby planets. The one that shocked Justin each time he entered was the one of the Salt Cliffs overlooking the Singing Sea. The print looked alive – the cliffs viewed from a distance, their edge eroding, as it always did, in little salt balls that fell into the sea.

In one corner of the room was a couch and two easy chairs facing a fake fireplace. Justin usually sat there when he visited, but today the governor waited in her custom-made chair behind the big beige desk. Her head rested on the seat back, her curls crushed against the leather. In the artificial light, her skin looked too pale, her lips too red. Her eyes almost disappeared into her face. 'This is a mess, Justin,' she said without opening her eyes. Her voice was husky and deep, at odds with the delicacy she always presented.

He took a seat in front of the desk. The chair was as hard as the chair in the waiting room. Perhaps they had been designed to discourage contact with the governor. 'I thought you were familiar with the Dancer Eight, Aisha.'

'Of course, but only as a history lesson.' She swivelled the chair until it faced him, and then opened her eyes. Their deep blue always startled him. He had not seen a colour like that on anyone else. 'We've gone through four governors since then.'

'We've got one of the Eight left. He could be in danger down there on Bountiful.'

'Do you believe that?' The governor rocked her chair from side to side as she watched him.

He hesitated for a moment. He didn't know how to answer the question. 'Sometimes,' he said, finally. 'Sometimes I believe he may have discovered his own personal heaven.'

'And we can't have that, now, can we?' The governor smiled to soften the effects of her words.

Justin flushed. He had already thought of that. If John had

227

finally gone home, then Justin's arrival would mimic the pattern from twenty years before. But no one knew much about the Dancers. No one knew what kind of danger John was in, if any.

The governor leaned forward and placed her elbows on the carpeted desk. Her shirt sleeves pooled around her upper arms revealing the rows of faint white scars she had acquired as a child in a shuttle disaster. Her family had not allowed doctors to do special grafts, and she hadn't done the reconstructive surgery as an adult. She always thought that people would respect her more if they thought she was human.

'I'm not sure it is in the state's interest to send you to Bountiful, Justin. You have become an asset to the base. You bring in a lot of revenue each year, and your specialized knowledge helps our understandings of the other cultures around us. I hesitate, quite frankly, in sending anyone to Bountiful, but I hesitate even more in sending you.'

Justin resisted the urge to cross his arms in front of his chest. 'I don't think there's a better choice,' he said. 'No one else is qualified to go to Bountiful. I know the lay of the land, and I know John. I have been with the Dancers and I have been to the dome. If anyone can find him, I can.'

'You nearly died the last time you were on Bountiful.'

Justin nodded. 'I know better now.'

'Can you give me guarantees?' the governor asked.

Justin stared pointedly at her arms for a moment, then eased his gaze back to her face. 'Aisha,' he said gently, 'you know better than any of us that, in this life, there is no such thing as a guarantee.'

iii

The governor gave him two days and the use of the base's most sophisticated shuttle. She also assigned three warm weather Security officers to go with him and she made sure they were all briefed in Bountiful safety precautions before they embarked the next morning.

The pilot was a hefty dark haired man who had never heard of Bountiful and didn't want to be informed of its particular history. He would wait on the shuttle for their return. If they didn't return, he would notify Lina Base for back-up. The governor was determined that Justin Schafer would come back alive.

Justin was determined as well. As he slipped into the plush seat, eyelids heavy from days with no sleep, he knew this was his last chance to redeem himself. He would find John and save him.

Justin would do everything he could to undo all the damage he had caused twenty years before.

If John was still alive. The whole plan depended on the hope that John had survived against the odds one final time.

John

i

John thinks in Dancer: his mind is full of chirrups and sighs. The air smells of cinnamon and the heat no longer bothers him. His feet rise above the hot sand, and he floats in the group.

A dozen Dancers surround him. They call him by name, touch his face, their rubbery fingers welcoming. He has never seen them before. Their knowledge is part of the Dancer mystique.

One Dancer, a young male, floats ahead of the rest. Soon he shimmers and disappears, like a mirage on the desert. The other Dancers ignore their colleague. They focus on John. They touch him everywhere, their breath soft on his face. He feels odd with them. He stands eye to eye with each of them, his own flushed face reflected in the silver lenses.

So happy, they say. *Your presence makes us so happy.*

The happiness waves off them, holding him up, giving him even more buoyancy. A joy fills him too, like a bubble inside his stomach that grows with each passing moment.

He is home.

He is home.

He is home.

They reach the edge of the canopied forest and the cinnamon scent disappears, covered by the ancient smell of a forest fire. Blackened limbs hang beside him, their edges charred and flaking. He brushes against one, and it leaves a black streak along his arm. He shudders: the limbs look like Dancer arms, decaying in the bright sunlight

The Dancers avert their gaze from the destruction. They bow their heads and follow the path, shoulders hunched, hands pressed against their slender stomachs. One Dancer, a female, sees that he has char on his skin. She shrieks in panic, and uses the edge of his shirt to brush the blackness off. Then she rips the shirt from his back and tosses it on the forest floor.

He glances at his arm, afraid, suddenly, that it will erupt with infection. She watches him for a moment, then crawls inside his head, feels his fear, and tosses it away, another imaginary bubble that lands on top of the discarded shirt.

He feels lighter.

A little boy's voice in the back of his mind screams. The Dancer hears it and gently closes an imaginary door. The screaming stops.

No sadness, she sends to him. *Only joy*.

Only joy, he repeats.

The path widens. Ahead, the real forest stands, offering shade, offering security. Green and white tendrils poke through the blackened soil, like pieces of the future on a scarred and ruined past. The green and white growing bed becomes a trail itself, hiding the charred ruins like a carpet covering a floor. Only the remains of trees show evidence of fire.

The Dancers still do not look up. The female grabs his chin with one hand and forces his head down. *Only joy*, she reminds him.

He nods, but he can still see the destruction out of the corner of his eyes. She slides into his mind, a full-blown presence: an adult female Dancer who tends the children. She calls herself Shwtza, a sound halfway between a whistle and a chirrup. She finds him fascinating, with his pale skin and odd coverings. She presses close beside him, her left hand toying with the fingers of his right.

He does not pull away, although he knows the touch is sexual. Somehow it feels right that she explore him, that she understand what he is.

Now, she says. *Look*.

He brings his head up. Canopied trees with their viney branches form a protective covering over the ground below. Most of the ground is dirt, but tiny green and white plants surround the base of the trees, while other plants grow in rows to his right. He sneezes the smoke from his lungs, and the scent of cinnamon returns, overlaid by the freshness of xaredon. The path winds and curves into the forest's darkness.

Home, she says.

He nods. He is thirsty and tired, but he says nothing. The joy bubble has filled him, and leaves room for nothing else.

234

ii

Deep within the canopied recesses of the forest, tents stretch between trees. The tents form a large circle and in the centre is a controlled fire in a deep pit. The fire gives off almost no smoke, and it is the source of the cinnamon scent. He longs to go to it, but Shwtza takes his arm and ducks inside the nearest tent.

It is cool and light inside. The light is silver: it comes from the jars that line the tent's edge on the ground. As he steps in, the jars on opposite sides of the door light. Then the others follow as if the sparks from the first ignite the others.

She makes him sit on a large pile of dead, woven canopy leaves. The pile is soft and mushy beneath his legs. The lights near the door go out, and gradually the others follow, leaving him to blink at the sudden darkness.

Then she puts something cool in his hands. Another jar. A shiver runs through him. What does she want with him?

Drink, she says, and he does.

The water is cool and refreshing. He drains the jar quickly, the water settling in his stomach and burbling like an entity in and of itself.

She touches his head with her soft fingers. *So much sadness.* Her voice is as gentle as her touch. *Sleep. Then there will be only joy.*

He lets her ease him back on the pile. The dead leaves smell ripe and green, pleasant in a soothing sort of way. He closes his eyes. The darkness enfolds him and he is gone.

iii

When he wakes, he is outside. Sunlight filters through the canopy above him in diamond shaped patches on the ground. He sits up, surprised to be alone among the trees. He rests on a pile of dead leaves. It is soft and comforting. Beside it are dozens of small circles in the dirt. They form a semi-circle, leaving a Dancer-sized opening near the path. Above him the tree bark is worn at the same level on four trees. Things change, but he has no desire to remember how.

Behind him, he hears scrabbling and grunting. He gets to his

235

feet, wipes the remains of dead leaves off his pants, then pauses. The pants are hot. And silly. He slips out of them, and takes off his shoes and socks as well, leaving them beside the pile. Then he follows the sounds.

The air is cool against his skin. He tilts his head back and lets the freshness wash over him. It feels refreshing, freeing.

The sounds lead him down a narrow footpath that winds through the trees. Pink flowers grow beside the trail. They give off a heady perfume that makes him shudder. A memory rises and he pushes it away. He can almost see it, drifting in the air, like breath on a cold morning.

The grunting grows louder. Ahead he sees a fence made of tree bark. The salty scent of Dancer piss is strong here, along with another smell, the spicy smell of unwashed bodies. His breath catches in his throat, and his heart pounds. He is somewhere forbidden; he knows it to the core of his being.

But he does not stop until he reaches the edge of the fence. Inside, on the packed dirt, Dancer children fight. Their tiny leathery bodies scrape the surface. Their eyes are blue and empty. They grunt as they toss each other, and occasionally they squeal in pain.

The wildness is catching. He feels it drawing him in. He grips the bark fence, letting the roughness dig into his fingers. A child slams against the fence, shaking it. The child grunts once then launches itself back into the pile of fighting bodies.

He keeps himself separate, unwilling to become part of a mass. He is adult, yet not adult; that wildness has not been bred out of him. It sings through his veins, like a melody he has long ago forgotten.

With a push, he steps away from the fence. The wildness loses its hold on him. He takes a deep breath, feeling as if he has dodged something dangerous. Then his gaze catches shadows in the corners.

The shadows are large, gray childish ghosts. They move sluggishly. They are Dancer children, but just barely. Their eyes are closed, their faces a mask of pain. Adolescents. Soon they will go through the change.

A wave of pain floods through him, so deep he nearly doubles over. Suddenly two adult Dancers are beside him. They grab his arms and hold him upright, sending joy into him as if it were food. They push the pain out and it floats away. Together they support him, as they move him away from the fence, and toward the tent village.

The tents are high on the trees and the bark here has not been scraped. The grass is newly trampled and two Dancers dig a fire pit. The two Dancers supporting him leave him on the ground near the pit. He sits upright, but just barely. It seems he has no energy, no will of his own.

—We need a consult, one of the Dancers says, and John recognizes her voice. Shwtza. She is speaking to the Dancers beside the pit.

—We would prefer to do consults when the sun is gone, the female Dancer says, her voice lower and full of clicks.

—We have enough darkness, says the other Dancer holding John. —We need a consult now.

The female sighs and stands. She has the red circle of a leader on her chest. She claps her hands and tilts her head back. A wail builds in John's head, deep and rich, almost a song in and of itself. Gradually he realizes that there are words in the wail, words he cannot understand.

Shwtza takes his arms and leads him to a nearby tree. With vines, she ties him to the bark, all the while soothing and sending him joy. She ties him loosely – he can escape if he wants to – but he understands that the ties are symbolic.

He does not move.

One by one, other Dancers appear, their arms cradling jars. They set their jars around the firepit, then return to the tents for more. John counts almost forty Dancers. The jars number in the hundreds. The Dancer leader sets the jars around the pit in a tight circle, several jars deep. The jars pulse silver and the light under the canopy is blinding.

The wail ends, leaving a silence that echoes through John's mind. Then the Dancers sit crosslegged behind the jars. They grab hands and stare at the pit. John catches odd snatches of thought, like a chant that he can only barely hear. The silver light bathes them all, turning the Dancer skin into an iridescent mirror that brightens the light, intensifies it until John can barely see.

Other Dancers float out of the jars, wispy gray Dancers, hundreds of them, floating on their bellies above the pit. Some fly over to John and touch his face. Their skin has the rubbery Dancer feel, but it has no smell. He bites back fear. Then they fly around the top of the pit, faster and faster until they appear to have one fluid body. The chant fades out and only a single, large silver Dancer remains, floating above the original Dancers. Its eye sockets are empty, black holes in its silver face.

It is human. The Dancer's voice reverberates in John's mind. The language is Dancer, but not Dancer. It has words that sound like variations of Dancer words, variations he has never heard before. Yet he understands them. He feels another presence in his head, plucking the meaning from the human dictionary in his brain, sending that meaning forward, overlaying it on the Dancer sounds. *It was with us when it was a child. It looked to us to save it then, as it does now.*

John leans back against the tree. *Not human,* he thinks. *Dancer.*

It has lost a legacy that it did not even know it had, the silver Dancer said. *It is incomplete, wounded. We have no power to heal it, but we can nurture it for the rest of its short days.*

The vines seem tighter around his wrists. He wants to talk to the silver Dancer directly, but something alien in his own brain holds him back.

Make a tent and jar for it. It is Useless now, but when it transforms it will bring us great knowledge.

It has no joy. The thought belongs to Shwtza.

It left its joy in the child's pen. Keep it away from the young for it seeks there what it already lost. And wait for the transformation, remembering that what was once Useless becomes the most valuable of all.

Useless. The word bothers John but he can put no meaning to it. The memories fly from him even as he touches them.

The silver Dancer floats over him. It caresses his face, its empty eyesockets a bottomless pit. *Such pain,* it whispers to him. *Such deep pain.*

Then it fades away. The lights glow in the jars, bathing everything silver. The iridescence blinds John. He closes his eyes. When he opens them again, the light has faded to a deep impenetrable darkness.

Hands loosen the vines from his wrists. Shwtza hovers over him. —You are mine, Useless One, she says. Her voice has a touch of menace to it, a sound he has not heard before. —Come. Together we will find you a beautiful jar.

238

She floods him with joy and he follows her. But he cannot shake the feeling that he is about to leave something precious behind.

Justin Schafer

He hadn't seen the sun in almost twenty years. Justin stood on the landing strip and tightened the sand scarf around his face. The strip still showed faint tracks from the landings a few days before, but they were like the footsteps of a lonely man in an uninhabited world.

Already his burns were itching with the memory of pain, and sweat trickled through his curls. The doctors said he would burn in the sun no more easily than anyone else, but he didn't believe it. He wanted to find shelter; he wanted to leave this place now.

Behind him shoes scraped along the metal ridge as the three security officers swung themselves off the shuttle. The pilot had offered to remain with his ship – to wait, he said with too much sarcasm, for John to return on his own.

A hot, dry breeze rustled Justin's scarf. The air smelled of daffodils. A feeling of déjà vu came over him so strong that he felt dizzy. Time had stopped here; everything was as he remembered it. The sand was dazzling white. The sun felt like a furnace; the heat reflected off all the nearby surfaces. To his left, salt continually eroded down the cliff face, little crystals rolling and tumbling to the white beach below. The Singing Sea devoured the crystals, leaving a salt scum that reflected the harsh light.

The sun was everywhere: a thick presence as palpable as the security officers he had brought with him. He had had to force them to wear sand scarves and reflective creams. Only when he told the story of his burns and subsequent hospitalization did they finally acquiesce. These people – two women and a man – were tough, and they made their reputations on being so. Their silent, stoic company should have eased his mind. Instead it made him nervous.

That, at least, was different. Now the government valued him so much that they sent people to guard him. They were afraid that John would go crazy and kill him, as if Justin's death would make a difference to the history of the sector.

People would merely note Justin's death, and few would mourn. Then life would continue as it always had.

As it always would.

'Don't see no dome,' Theo said. The pilot had shut down the shuttle's engines and Theo's voice echoed in the stillness. Justin pursed his lips. A few minutes alone with the place that had nearly killed him was not too much to ask. The problem was that he had never asked for it, only assumed he would receive it.

Justin turned. The footpath had long ago disappeared, and the wind had covered any tracks John might have made in the sand. Still, Justin could see the dome reflecting the sunlight. From this distance, it looked no larger than his thumbnail. With little effort, he could still imagine life in that place: a thousand people toiling away at the Salt Juice plant, making their children miserable.

All the lives that Salt Juice had wasted, all the poisons the adults had breathed in. He often wished he had the ability to do a controlled experiment, to see how much of the Dancer Eight's behaviour had been due to Salt Juice inhalation. Current pharmacological expertise suggested that Salt Juice only caused reactions in adults. But pharmacological expertise of twenty years ago said that Salt Juice had no side effects at all.

'The dome's that way,' Justin said, pointing. Theo adjusted his sand scarf before squinting. He was a big man, broad, with arms as thick as Justin's thighs. The women were the same size, their breasts pulled flat against their muscular chests. The women said nothing, only followed Justin's point with their gaze.

'Looks like quite a walk,' Theo said.

'That's why I would like to do it on my own,' Justin said.

'Sorry, doc.' Theo's sand scarf was glued to the side of his chin. 'We're supposed to accompany you everywhere.'

To prevent him from starting fires? From burning alive under Bountiful's hot sun? To help him find John? 'Checked the water?' he asked Semira. They all carried packs, with equipment and food divided equally, but Semira had double-checked the supplies before they left.

'Enough for two days,' she said in her flat monotone. Her face

244

reflected her voice. Her mouth moved, but her expression never changed. It was the rock-solid seriousness of a woman who saw herself as a stone.

'Good.' He started out across the desert in the place where he thought the path would be. His feet sank in the sand, and a small pink plant disappeared off to the right. They should have brought an aircar. With the path gone, the fragile ecosystem would get marred anyway.

Fear rose like bile in the back of his throat. With each step, he felt the sun beat on his scalp. Sweat trickled down his back and the itch in his exposed skin grew worse.

He remembered little after falling face down in the sand all those years before. Latona's voice above him, calling his name over and over. Hands touching his crisped skin, sending waves of pain through him. The creams, stinging and soothing at the same time. And the sun, always the sun, a force so hot and relentless he thought he would never escape it. He had described that feeling to his doctors and they had assured him the pain he remembered came from the fire in the canopied forest, not from the sun itself. Bountiful's sun was powerful, they had assured him, but the kind of burns he suffered had come from close exposure to flames.

They were wrong. His skin had felt burned before he had set the herbs on fire. Before he and Latona had forced the Dancers to leave their homes. Before the colonists attacked.

'You okay, doc?' Theo asked.

That shiver of annoyance ran through him again. He deserved privacy here. They should have remained at the shuttle. They should have left him alone.

'I'm fine,' he said.

'Not that far to the dome.' Theo hadn't been this conversational since they left Lina Base.

'It's closer than it looks.'

'Think he'll be there? Or you think he's dead?'

Justin glanced at Theo. All the other man knew had to have come from tabloid reports, history classes and net research. Nothing that said how unpredictable the Dancer Eight had been.

'I don't know,' Justin said, in a tone that brooked no more discussion, no more speculation. He didn't want to think about what he might find. Perhaps John had emulated the others and disappeared. Perhaps he had just found the ideal place to do so, on Bountiful itself.

He was breathing shallowly. The bright sunlight, reflected on the white sand, hurt his eyes. He had made a mistake coming here, a mistake exposing himself to this kind of danger again.

'Hnh!' The sound was soft, not a scream, not even a cry, more like a loud, uncomfortable exhalation of breath. Justin turned. The other woman, Ret, was struggling to pull her foot out of a small hole. The sand had collapsed in a straight line around her, and the edges of the hole ran off in two different directions.

She looked at him, her expression flat, as unchanged as it has always been. 'I'm stuck,' she said.

He rolled his eyes. Something niggled at the back of his brain. A memory. He had seen pictures of this. The colonists warned visitors to stay on the paths lest they disturb the sand devil nests. Too many colonists had died trapped in Bountiful's harsh sun.

He shuddered. He was glad it wasn't him.

'The first thing to do is to relax,' he said. 'Then you need to ease the weight off that foot. Theo, carefully clear the sand around her shoe, see if she's trapped in a hole or something else. Do not get your hand trapped.'

Ret leaned all her weight to the other foot. Grains of sand rolled precariously into the hole. Theo crouched down. He removed a small shovel from his pack and dug slowly. Ret's shoe was stuck in clay that had hardened like a mould around it. Theo opened the shoe, and Ret pulled her foot out.

'Don't set your bare foot on the sand,' Justin said. 'It'll burn you.'

Semira held Ret up. Theo worked quickly to free the shoe. Only the edges of the clay had any give at all. Then the shoe came free. Ret grabbed it, and leaned against Semira while putting it on.

Justin let out the air he had been holding.

'What was that?' Semira asked.

'Sand devils,' Justin said. 'They have warrens that run beneath the surface. Those little traps are designed to prevent unwanted visitors from dropping into the nest.'

He no longer wanted to be walking on this surface. He didn't

246

want his foot trapped in the sand.

'I'll go first then,' Theo said. 'That way we'll root these little suckers out.'

'Better to let me,' Ret said. 'My shoes is already damaged, and you know how to dig cautiously. That way no one will be trapped for too long.'

Justin glanced up. Small white dunes studded with pink led to the edge of the dome. It was much larger now. Their walk would be shorter than he expected. 'The original path ended in the centre of the dome. We're too far to the right.'

Ret led them off, stepping gingerly over the cave-in. Theo followed her, then Justin. As he stepped over the small hole, tiny white hands pushed the sand back into position.

His throat was dry. He made himself swallow. It hurt against the dryness of his throat.

All they had to do was find John. Once they did that, he could return to Lina Base, to his work and his precious career.

The sand shimmered in front of them. Sweat ran down his back and pooled in the depression caused by the waistband of his pants. The sand scarf stuck to his skin, and the cream on his hands seemed to be melting.

He had to get out of the sun. He had to.

He reached into his pack and pulled out his water bottle. It was warm. He uncapped it, careful not to spill any, and took a long drink. The water was warm and tasted of the plastic bottle. He didn't care. The action calmed him.

'Be cautious with your water, Doctor,' Semira said. 'We don't know if the dome's wells are working.'

He didn't need the reminder. He had only taken the drink because he needed it. Weren't the others sweating?

Their skin had a sheen to it, but that could have been caused by the cream. He smiled a little to himself. He had always suspected they weren't real, that they were some kind of bot the governor had sent along to protect him. The bots could go in all kinds of conditions that humans couldn't.

'Something funny, doc?' Theo asked.

Justin shook his head. Unfair thoughts. He needed to turn his attention to the business at hand. He had to prepare himself to see John.

They reached the dome two long drinks later. Even the bodyguards had had to drink. Justin was finally convinced they were human.

He had forgotten them, though, as he approached the dome itself. Parts of it caught the sun, sending hot white light out like a beacon. But most of the dome was covered with sand. Farther to his right, someone had brushed the sand away from a dome hole, and left prints around it. He had checked it out, peering through the scratched plastic, seeing no one inside.

Whoever had gone in had remembered to close the door.

No one had touched the regular dome door in a long, long time. The sand appeared glued on to it, as if the desert windstorms had blasted the grains in place. Some sand fell along the side, like the erosion on the Salt Cliffs.

His heart was pounding in his throat.

He wanted to get out of the sun, but he had run from this dome all those years ago, with people behind him, wanting to kill him. He understood the human mind and he knew that until he faced his fear, he would always believe the killers remained inside.

But that first step was the most difficult of all.

'How do we get into this thing?' Theo asked.

'There's a little latch on the side,' Justin said. His voice was as flat as theirs. The fear was behind it; he could barely block the sound of it.

Theo brushed sand off the dome and swore. 'Damn thing's roasting.'

'It's stood in the sun for generations,' Justin pushed him aside. There was a trick to the latch; he wondered if he could remember it. He put his finger in the little depression and pushed up.

The door blew open, nearly hitting Justin in the face. A cold wind assaulted him and knocked him aside – he had to take two steps backwards to keep from falling. The others were blown back too. Theo hit the dome and cried out from the heat.

Then the wind left them and blew away. The hot, dry air returned, negating the instant cold. Sweat dripped down Justin's face, and he staggered once more before catching his balance.

'What the hell was that?' Semira asked.

'I don't know,' Justin said. It was as if someone had built up a lot of pressure inside, and opening the door had released it. 'Perhaps John didn't know how to use the environmental controls.'

The wind kept moving, a little swirling trail of sand marking its passage.

'Never felt anything like that before,' Theo said, puzzled. He was standing upright, rubbing the side of his right hand. A small blister had formed. The sight of it made Justin ill.

'You need to put cream on that now,' he said.

Theo nodded and reached into his pack. Justin turned away from Theo's wound, and peered inside the dome. The air was cooler there and had a fresher smell than he expected it to have. He was about to step inside when a hand caught him on the shoulder.

'We should go first,' Ret said.

They couldn't take this moment from him. He shook her hand off and stepped over the threshold into the dome itself.

A wave of dizziness hit him as his body realized it was no longer in the hot sun. He lurched once to the side, then righted himself. Inside, the air's freshness was gone. It had the ripe, fetid smell of decay – a faint scent, but enough to make the hackles on the back of his neck rise.

So did the vision in front of him. Dead, brown plants, withered across pristine plastic fences. The ground was hard and cracked. The buildings looked the same: terraform plastic was designed to withstand all sorts of harsh conditions. But with the death all around, the buildings looked like tiny protective shelters that hid all survivors.

Only there were no survivors. Bountiful had been evacuated shortly after he returned to Lina Base.

'What a mess,' Theo said. He had crawled in beside Justin. The women followed.

'Phew, this air makes me sick,' Semira said.

Ret came in and touched the inside of the dome. 'How come there's dirt on these walls but none on the buildings?'

Justin turned. Dirt had been layered on the side of the dome as if forced there by a strong wind. But the houses were clean, that stunning shade of white which the children had remarked on in interviews months later.

And the silence. He hated the silence. Lina Base always had noise of some sort, from the humming of machinery to the rumble of voices. Here there was nothing, except the breathing of his companions.

'Shut the door,' Justin said. No sense in tipping John off that they were here sooner than they had to. 'Let's head down to Command Central. They should have equipment there that will help us locate other life forms. And we can also do something about this smell.'

iii

The walk depressed him. The empty houses, the ruined plants, the destroyed dreams. What would Bountiful have been if he hadn't come here and discovered Netta's scheme? A large, thriving community that extended across the desert? A place where children continued to kill each other in order to be free?

He shivered. Places like this carried their own harsh ghosts.

The bodyguards were strangely silent. When Justin glanced at them, he found them peering around corners, moving softly, as if they expected something to jump out at him at any moment. Only his memory of this place kept him moving forward – and the memory was imperfect. He didn't know whose houses he passed. He didn't know if he walked by the doorway where Michael Dengler's body had been propped. He wasn't sure he would recognize the site of such trauma if he saw it.

He knew that he would recognize the Office of the Extra Species Alliance because it had windows. But the office was on the other side of the dome, away from Command Central. He would find Command Central, too, because it was large and shaped differently from the homes.

The smell grew stronger as they walked. Ret sneezed, then wiped the back of her hand over her nose. A frown grew on Semira's face. Theo brought his palm up and spread it across his mouth as if that would block the odour.

Something had died.

Recently.

250

Justin kept walking, his feet making soft thuds on the dirt. Nothing surprised him, at least not any more. The smell was coming from a decaying body – probably John's. He had probably used Anita Miles' money to come home and kill himself. The pattern was consistent with the disappearances of the other Dancer Eight. Only John had the opportunity to get to Bountiful itself.

They rounded a corner and Justin bit his lower lip. The guest building stood to the left looking much as it did when he last saw it. The plants outside were dead and crumbling, the dirt was brown, and the grass was dead, but the steps were clean and swept, and the door stood slightly ajar, as if it were awaiting his return. He had never again seen the personal effects that he had brought to Bountiful on that first trip. He wondered if they were still inside, gathering dust.

Theo and the others had gone on ahead. Justin was about to pry himself away from the guest house when he heard that small 'hnh!' he had heard when Ret fell into the sand devil trap. He turned and saw them, standing in a semi-circle a few metres ahead, their backs to him and heads bowed. He had noticed the similarity in their builds before, but never so much as at that moment: the top of their heads in alignment; their shoulders equal width across; their waists tapering into narrow hips. The white sand scarves accented the similarities, making them look like three members of a religious order, their heads bowed in prayer.

Part of his mind registered an urgency, but he didn't run toward them. He walked. His mouth had gone dry again, and the sweat had returned; this time it was a cool, nervous sweat, not anything caused by heat. It took him only a few strides to reach their sides.

And to see the source of the odour.

Dried blood covered everything. It was black and flaky like the plants. The bodyguards stood outside the blood spatter as if it would get on their shoes. But the blood was nothing.

The body was partially decayed. Blood had dried along the edges of where the hands used to be. The chest was flayed wide, heart and lungs missing. Head tilted back, neck half cut, eyes open and staring. The body was male. It was an adult, and it had only been dead a few days.

And it was not John.

Justin sank to his knees. The possibility he hadn't let himself imagine lay before him.

'Oh, John,' he whispered while the bodyguards gathered protectively around him.

John

i

She gives him water. He drinks greedily, absorbing the coolness, letting it refresh him. He lies in the shade, but even there it
is too hot. His skin is on fire and nothing he does seems to put it
out.

A wind has started. In the distance, someone shouts: *Sand
storm!* The Dancers run for their tents. John tries to stand, and
loses his balance. He would like more water, but Shwtza is gone.
He staggers forward and the wind hits with a force that shoves
the tents against the trees, bends the canopies almost to the
ground. Dancers scream and lie flat as sand pelts them like rain.

Only John remains standing, in the eye of an impossible
hurricane, a calm centre in the middle of the worst storm he has
ever seen. Sand swirls around him until the entire world
becomes his patch of ground surrounded by a white eddy. If he
stares into it, he will grow dizzy. He clutches at a nearby tree,
and the centre of the storm moves with him. With an audible
snap, the tree returns to its upright position, and he balances
against the trunk.

Another body appears in the centre of the storm with him. It is
a human body – male, pudgy, young, half his height. He
recognizes it, realizes —

— that in Dancer his mind has no words for this. Remembered words break through and he realizes —

— that the body belonged to Allen and Allen was dead. John
stood in the centre of a swirling sand storm, next to a canopied
tree, and felt fear envelope him.

He didn't know how he got there or what he had been doing.
His skin was burned raw and he needed medical attention. How
long had it been since he had eaten? He didn't know. He didn't
know anything.

'Not true, bucko,' Allen said, but the voice wasn't Allen's. The
voice was older, wiser, without the pain that Allen's voice

255

always had. 'You know. You just choose not to remember.'

John stared at him. It was important that Allen was dead. It was important that this being in front of him was not Allen. He knew this being. It had —

— nearly killed him inside the dome. He had run away from it, here, to the Dancers. He turned, but the swirling sand stopped him.

'I'm not going to kill you,' the bodeangenie said. 'That would be fairly stupid on my part.'

The genie stepped closer. It smelled of little boy sweat and sand. 'Listen closely, bucko, because I can only say this once. Those Dancer friends of yours are letting you die. They consider you Useless, and feel that you're worth more to them dead than alive.'

Bits of the last few days came to John like a hand through fog. Useless. Something had been useless. He certainly was. He had finally come home, home to a place where he was not needed.

'Point A,' the genie said, 'this is not your home. It has never been your home. It was always your haven, and there is a difference. Point B, you are certainly not useless. Your employer kidnapped me, and I am trapped on this godforsaken place unless I have the use of your hands.'

Trapped. Trapped. John frowned. He wished he weren't so weak and dizzy, so foggy in his mind. He had been somewhere else for days, somewhere he wasn't sure he wanted to return to. Trapped. 'I trapped you in the dome.'

'Oh, yeah.' The genie smiled. The look was predatory on Allen's innocent face. 'Four humans arrived at the dome and let me out by accident. They'll find Minx and company soon enough. I suspect they will blame the deaths on you.'

John leaned his full weight against the tree. The last time he had done something wrong on Bountiful they had come after the Dancers. 'On me?' he asked.

The genie nodded. 'If they catch you here, who knows what they'll do to your precious Dancers. I don't understand why you care for the creatures anyway. They were going to let you die.'

Useless. Useless. Useless Ones transformed.

The genie took a step toward him. Allen's body was slightly transparent. Through it, John could see the swirling sand. 'I *need* you,' it said. 'If you make me stay here, I'll kill your precious

Dancers myself.'

A lump had formed in John's throat. 'Four humans are here?'

'And they'll come after you once they see the mess I made of Minx.'

'What's to prevent you from killing me?'

The genie shook its head. 'You are dumber than you look, boy. I *need* you to get me out of here and take me home. I can't pilot a ship myself. I can blow on some of the controls, but I can't push. There is a limit to the abilities of the wind. Now, let's get out of here.'

'Ship?'

'Yes, ship.' The genie's voice was filled with sarcasm. 'I know where Minx left his ship. No matter what, you need to get out of the elements, boy. You need to care for that skin before you crisp completely.'

He was weak, he was ill, and he was naked. He could tell he hadn't eaten for a long time.

'There's food on the ship. Come with me, boy.'

He glanced around. The storm had worn a groove in the dirt around them. 'What about the Dancers?'

'Without you here, they can take care of themselves.' Then Allen disappeared, the storm ceased, and the sand fell to the ground. Dancers lay still for a moment, then they started to pick themselves up. John groped for words to ask them if they were okay when something pushed at his back.

He turned. Nothing.

The push came again. He was surrounded by wind. It lifted him off his feet and carried him through the forest, uprooting plants as it went.

ii

Minx had landed the ship on a rocky flat area that John had never seen before. North of the Dancers' forest, the rocks began just as the canopied trees ended, gray footsteps on white soil. The rocks slanted upward to a flat surface that overlooked a large carved valley. He could tell at a glance why the colonists had never used this as a natural landing base: it took great skill to make sure a craft didn't land wrong and fall into the valley

257

below.

The ship was outdated two decades ago, larger and more scarred than the holos he had seen of it. It could easily have held double the crew members and a big cargo. John had served on ships like it, but he had never piloted them.

The genie set him down at the base of the steps. John glanced up. The ship's hull had seen little or no repair during its lifetime. The name, *Runner* was scraped and almost unreadable. He only hoped the inside was in better shape.

He climbed the stairs, feeling the genie's wind at his back. When he pulled the door open, it moved easily because the genie helped. John stepped inside and immediately wished he hadn't. The ship had been sitting in the sun for days; the heat was almost more than he could endure.

He pushed through the narrow corridor to environmental controls and switched them on. The genie followed him, visible again, this time in a body he didn't recognize – that of a slender, boyish man with dark eyes and clothes that favoured ruffles and lace.

'One of the traders?' John asked.

'Carter,' the genie said. 'His tastes suit me.'

John's hands were shaking as he pushed a few more buttons. He didn't like seeing the genie as a ghost of a man newly dead.

'Doesn't it bother you to wear the body of a man you killed?'

'Should it?' the genie asked. It leaned against the door frame, arms crossed in front of its chest. Its sleeves hung down almost to its waist.

'Yeah,' John said. At least in his world. He had lived with guilt over murders he had not realized he had caused since he was twelve years old. The genie had killed intentionally, as if such a thing were natural and commonplace.

'Misconceptions,' the genie cautioned.

'Stay out of my head!' John snapped.

The genie sighed. 'It is the only place of interest available.'

'It's not available.' John pushed his way out the door, his hand passing through the genie's body, making his stomach turn. He knew that the genie was wind, but it still sickened him to see his hand pass through the genie's form.

The air had begun circulating, cooling almost instantly and leaving a pressure behind John's eyes. He climbed the stairs into the pilot's bay and glanced around. He had flown similar ships, smaller ships, but similar ones. He could handle this.

He slipped into the pilot's chair, the upholstery rough against his buttocks, and followed the sequence that the grid showed as engine start-up. In a moment, he would ransack the ship for clothes.

'Shouldn't you be running through the autodoc?' The genie was sitting in the co-pilot's chair as if it had been there all along. John hadn't seen it come up; but then the genie had the power to lose form at any moment.

'I thought there were people chasing us.'

'I can take care of them. I don't want you to lose consciousness between here and Rotan Base.'

'Doesn't matter,' John said, continuing the sequence. Tiny beepings indicated that he was following the right trail. 'This thing has an autopilot. It'll follow any course I set.'

'But you can't land that way.'

'No,' John said. 'You can't. I would just feel safer if we leave here now.' Then he wouldn't have the temptation to return to the Dancers, to allow himself to transform as they wanted him to.

The ship shuddered as the engines reached full power. A slight whine recorded at the edge of his consciousness. The interior was in perfect condition, another ruse perpetrated by Minx. John ran only a cautionary diagnostic out of habit. He found nothing.

He strapped himself in, and was about to tell the genie to do the same, when the genie disappeared. He sighed. It would take him a while to fully comprehend that something which looked human had no solidity at all. He pulled back on the thrusters and the ship sailed over the valley, then veered upward into space.

John glanced down only once. He saw the half-burned forest, the sand-covered dome, and a shuttle resting on the landing space. Around that the desert glistened. The rest of Bountiful was a mystery to him. Only that small portion had any meaning at all. He hadn't known there were rocks or valleys, and he didn't know if there was an end to the Singing Sea.

Perhaps he had done it wrong all along. Perhaps, instead of trying to leave the planet, he and the others should have run away.

259

The rest of Bountiful might have welcomed them. Somewhere out there, among the rocks and the valleys, the children might have actually made a home.

He would never know. All he knew now was that he was running away physically for the first time, from Bountiful, from the Dancers, and from five murders that would get blamed on him. Before, he had only run away in his mind.

'I don't like you,' he said to the genie, knowing it was somewhere in the room.

'Humans.' The genie's voice reverberated in the small space. 'As if liking mattered.'

The words stopped John for a moment. The ship broke out of the atmosphere and he adjusted the controls. 'It does matter,' he said quietly. 'Usually, if I don't like you, I don't help you.'

'You liked that kidnapper then?'

'Anita?' John leaned back in his chair. She had started this. He had forgotten that. 'No. She had taken you against your will. No one has the right to do that.'

'So you always planned to rescue me?' There was a plaintive note in the genie's voice, as if for the first time it spoke without irony.

'Yes,' John said slowly, marvelling at the way his life had brought him full circle. 'I suppose I did.'

Part Five

Anita Miles

Lina Base lacked the class of Rotan Base. Anita peered into the mirror in her isolation suite, carefully combing each strand of her hair into place. Imagine making all of the visitors go through decontamination and an autodoc inspection. If she had known that when she left Rotan Base, she would have sent someone in her place.

As if any of her assistants could have done the job.

She sighed and patted her dress along her thin form. The dress's multicolored weave matched the pattern in her hair. She hadn't had time to do her eyes properly, but their natural hazel usually adapted well enough. As if the yokels on this base would notice at all.

Her possessions rested on top of a servobot which she had already programmed. It would take her belongings to the suite she had been assigned and, with the help of a more sophisticated bot, make sure everything was put away properly. She hated things to be out of place.

She didn't have time to do such things. She had an appointment with the representatives of Lina Base, including the governor herself.

Anita pushed the lock beside the door and watched as it slid open. Then she stepped into the hallway, and looked both ways before she crossed it to get into the lift. The lift was small and cramped, smelling vaguely of human sweat and dirt. Nothing like it would ever have been allowed on Rotan Base.

She sighed, resisting the urge to pat her hair a final time. She was being critical because she was out of her element. Two of her hunters had already warned her that the governor would not accept bribes – of any size – and her other sources had told her that she had got five high ranking officials fired for allowing John to go to Bountiful.

As if she had known what kind of havoc he could wreak. A

man like that should never have been allowed out of the penal system. The responsibility lay on the government, not on her.

She would tell them that.

The lift stopped on the governor's floor. She tugged on her dress, wishing she had had more time to prepare. But the shuttle had arrived only two hours before the scheduled meeting, which had given her just enough time to go through decontamination. Her lawyer's shuttle had been delayed – some case he had to finish defending on Minar Base – and he had offered to assign one of his colleagues to her. She had declined. Lawyers usually mucked up the first round of negotiations. If she needed him, she could always bring him in later. He had done a good job on cleaning up the mess left by the confiscation of the baby Minaran; if he could handle that, he could handle anything.

The lift doors opened into a carpeted reception area. The chairs were cheap government issue, gray to match the dark tones of the carpet, with regulation upholstery that was meant to stiffen the spine instead of relax it. The prints hanging on the walls were poor reproductions of centuries old Earth art, most of it two-d, and most of it second rate when it had been done. Either the decorator had no taste or the governor had problems with theft. Given the limited resources of Lina Base, Anita would have suspected the former instead of the latter.

The receptionist was a thin man whose attempt at 19th century retro was poor. His spectacles dated from the United States circa 1970, his vest a copy of a German model from the early 21st century. His suitcoat was close – it belonged on a middle class Britain and dated from 1910. The shirt was the affront: it had a polyester weave and plastic buttons. She hated people whose affectations were improperly done.

She stopped in front of his imitation wood desk and looked down her nose at him. 'My name is Anita Miles,' she said. 'I have an appointment with the governor.'

The receptionist didn't even look up. 'Yes, ma'am,' he said in a baritone voice as poorly matched to his frame as his clothes were to their retro period. 'If you don't mind having a seat, the governor will see you shortly.'

'Oh, I do mind,' Anita said. The young man looked up. There was no glass in his spectacles and his eyes were a deep purple,

266

obviously dyed to match a retro style he no longer wore. 'I have just flown across the sector to attend this meeting. The least the governor could do is see me on time.'

She stepped around the desk toward the door, but the receptionist was quicker. He barred her way. Standing up, his reedy form was considerably taller than hers. 'I wouldn't do that, ma'am,' he said.

His posture was vaguely threatening. Adrenalin pumped through her. She hadn't had a challenge like this in a long time. 'Do you know who I am?' she asked softly.

'Yes, ma'am.' He crossed his arms and looked down his nose at her. 'I have already alerted security. They're watching. Make any threatening moves toward the governor or her office, and they will be here promptly.'

Anita frowned. She had not had a reception like this in decades – not since she became famous. Something was off. 'Instead of alerting security,' she said, 'you should have alerted the governor. I'm sure she wouldn't want to keep me waiting.'

'She knows you're here, ma'am,' the receptionist said. 'She will see you when she is good and ready.'

Good and ready. A phrase she had used herself on clients she had wanted to string along. Anita stepped away from the door. This encounter with a poorly dressed man was beneath her. She paced around the reception area, unwilling to sit in those cheap, uncomfortable chairs.

Perhaps she should wait for her attorney. But he wouldn't arrive until the next day at the earliest. Damn him and his so-called integrity. He demanded on seeing a trial through once he made his opening arguments.

Through the soft leather of her shoes, she could feel the hard weave of the carpet. How anyone could work in these conditions she had no idea. Nothing beautiful to look at, nothing comfortable to sit on. She had done her time in a place like this as a young girl. She had vowed to get out and out she got. Too late, of course. She would bear the emotional scars of that final encounter for the rest of her life.

'How much longer is it going to be?' she snapped at the receptionist.

Her tone didn't seem to disturb him. 'I don't know,' he said. 'She had another meeting before yours.'

Anita continued her pacing. From the lift to the desk and back again. If she wasn't careful, she would wear a hole in the too-thin carpet.

Lawyers. If hers hadn't been so good, she would have fired him a long time ago. Making her wait on an important night like this one. He knew she would have to do this first meeting alone. The Provisional Government had stressed its need to talk to her, and she couldn't contact to any of her hunters. She didn't know what kind of surveillance she was under, and she didn't want the government to have access to a trail. Their rules about art were petty and lacked vision.

She hadn't even had time to send someone else to Bountiful to locate the bodeangenie.

Damn creature. It had almost cost her more than it was worth.

Then she smiled. Actually, the bodeangenie was so rare that even if she had a hundred hunters searching for the next ten years, the amount she would receive from the creature's sale would more than cover her expenses.

And then some.

'All right, ma'am,' the receptionist said. 'The governor will see you now.'

ii

The minute Anita had walked into the governor's office, she knew she had made a mistake. The governor sat behind her beige desk, hands templed beneath her chin. Standing, flanking her, were Lina Base's two representatives to the Provisional Parliament. And, seated on the manufactured couch in the left side of the room was the chief of Lina Base's Security. One of the holos on the wall had been moved aside, and behind it, on a flat screen, was a view of the reception area.

They had watched her humiliation and done nothing about it.

The door closed softly behind her. On that screen, she saw the poorly dressed receptionist bow slightly as he pulled the door shut from the outside.

The only thing she could do was go on the offensive. 'I don't appreciate being kept waiting.'

'That's understandable, Ms Miles,' the governor said. She

brought her hands down until they rested on the desk's carpeted surface. She was slight. Her features would have been attractive if she had enhanced them, but she clearly belonged to the school that believed in natural looks. Her curly out-of-control hair reflected that quite plainly.

She did not apologize, so Anita decided to remain standing, near the door. 'You called me here. You must have something to discuss.'

The head of security leaned back on the couch. It groaned beneath his weight. He was a big man with no fat on his body, only muscle. His tight black regulation suit showed each bulge and ripple. She recognized him from the net files she had been sent when she knew she was going to go to Lina Base.

He put an arm over the back of the couch as if he expected her to sit beside him and cuddle. 'It has come to our attention,' he said, 'that you paid a large sum of money to let a convicted felon loose on a protected planet. Your action has resulted in five murders.'

Anita shrugged with one shoulder. 'He had a hunting license from the Provisional Government that permitted him to work all over the sector. I thought nothing of hiring him and extending him the same privileges I extend to my other employees. It is not my fault that the government allowed a dangerous man to go free.'

'Bullshit.' The word was soft. Anita turned. One of the representatives, the woman, had spoken. She had long blonde hair, black skin and white eyes with no pupils at all. She wore tiny chains draped over a see-through white sheath. Her attire attested to her constituency: the young radical factions that seemed to be growing on all the bases. 'Your methods are well known all over the sector, Ms Miles. When you hired John, you knew his background. You merely expected it to work for you instead of against you.'

'It seems that you all know my mind better than I do.' Anita approached the desk. The male representative, who wore a conservative gray silk robe and had his sharp features surgically enhanced, took a step back. She made him nervous, did she? If she was lucky, she would make them all nervous. 'My regular workers were busy. I needed someone quickly. I asked around, got recommendations, and acted on them. That it ended so badly is not my fault.'

'Actually,' the governor said, 'it is. He worked for you, Ms Miles. You sent him in pursuit of five traders who had allegedly stolen something from you. I assume in assigning the task, you gave him no boundaries, no limits? This is a man who had killed in his past for his own ends, and would do so again.'

'Oh, for heaven's sake,' Anita said. 'He was a misguided child when he killed before, and he's been clean for twenty years. You have no proof he would kill again.'

'So,' the governor smiled as she spoke, 'people from Bountiful stand up for each other.'

A chill ran through Anita. She hated it when someone knew of her childhood. 'I am simply tired of your implications that I hired the man to assassinate people.'

'He was forbidden to go to Bountiful. He was assumed to be Influenced, and that Influence would reoccur with any contact with the Dancers,' the governor said. 'You, with your reputation for hand-selecting your employees, knew that.'

'Then explain,' Anita snapped, 'why he has disappeared? Explain why I have not received my property back. Explain how I could have known all of this.'

'Rumour has it, Ms Miles,' the head of security said slowly, 'that those traders stole a Bodean Wind sculpture from you, and inside it was a bodeangenie.'

'Nonsense,' Anita said. 'We all know that bodeangenies are trader rumours.'

The chief of security smiled. 'Nice try, Ms Miles, but one wind sculpture with a bodeangenie inside was traded almost fifty years ago. The records are on file. Catching a bodeangenie is nearly impossible; containing one inside a wind sculpture the only way to transport it. If you have done so, you are sitting on a fortune. An illegal fortune. You have been warned against the capture of live beings before, Ms Miles.'

'If you remember,' Anita said, turning on him, 'I was acquitted of those charges.'

'Ah, yes,' the male representative in the silk robe finally spoke. 'On Minar. Your attorney got you off. Supposedly. But we have sworn affidavits here from jurors who claim that they received some interesting gifts from Rotan Base just before the decision. Gifts they were able to sell for a great deal of money.'

'Are you saying I bribed them?'

'Your attorney is in custody right now,' the governor said. 'He's been charged with all sorts of crimes connected to you. At the least, he'll be disbarred. At the most, he'll be imprisoned. The judge is looking over the records of your cases now.'

They had detained her attorney. No wonder his secretary had brushed her off. They had intended to meet her, alone, knowing that she would come without him. Their information had to be very good. 'Obviously,' she said, keeping her voice calm, 'you want something from me, and you are doing a good job of making sure that I will provide it for you. You have detained my attorney, you are implying that I hired John as a hit man, and you have made it clear that you will review all the charges on which I have been acquitted. I prefer my business to be conducted in the open. Tell me what you want and I'll tell you whether or not I can provide it.'

'Oh,' the female representative said, 'you'll provide it all right.'

Anita clenched her teeth so that she would not respond.

'Your hit man,' the governor said, placing an emphasis on the words, 'is very dangerous, and an embarrassment to Lina Base.'

Anita straightened slightly. So that's why the representatives were here, and why the governor had taken personal interest in the case. Their careers were on the line. Stupid. Her own vanity had led her to believe that they were there for her. She needed to keep an open mind. She needed to think clearly since she was on her own here.

'We want him found before he kills again.'

Anita crossed her arms in front of her chest. The movement strained the fabric over her shoulders and ruined the lines of her outfit, but for once she didn't care. 'So find him,' she said.

'We don't have the resources,' said the chief of security. 'That kind of manhunt is beyond our capabilities and would require approval from the Provisional Government.'

'So get it,' Anita said.

'That would take enough time to allow John to disappear forever,' the female representative said. 'We want to catch him now.'

'Without embarrassing yourselves.' Anita smiled at them. 'So you want me to help you.'

'You have the funds. You would search for him anyway.' The chief of security hadn't moved, but his body tension grew.

'Would I?' Anita now felt like she had the upper hand. She could sit. She chose a chair near the door and lounged in it, as the chief did. 'You're assuming that I believe he's worth chasing.'

'He has your sculpture,' the chief said.

'I have no proof that he has anything of mine. For all I know, my property could be somewhere on Bountiful.'

'You wouldn't let something priceless disappear,' the governor said.

Anita shrugged. The chair was uncomfortable, but she didn't let that show. 'You're assuming that I value it enough to chase after.' Then she let her smile widen. 'You're assuming that I lost it.'

Her words hung in the silence. The four government officials stared at each other. Finally the governor spoke. 'If you don't cooperate with us, Ms Miles, we will charge you with being an accessory to murder, bribing governmental officials, raiding a protected planet, and endangering protected species. We will confiscate your possessions and bankrupt you. We will start the proceedings tomorrow.'

'I do believe I'm entitled to an attorney,' Anita said.

The security chief leaned forward. 'If you do not have one by 9 a.m. base time tomorrow, one will be appointed for you.'

'We already have you on several of the charges, Ms Miles,' said the female representative. 'We have proof that you bribed officials here on Lina Base. The bribery occurred to send John to Bountiful, and he had contact with the Dancers, a protected species. If nothing else, Ms Miles, everything you own will become property of the state.'

Anita felt herself grow cold. She had been incautious in the methods she had used to get John to Bountiful. She had wanted that sculpture back, desperately. She had not taken the time to cover her tracks properly. She had figured that it wouldn't matter.

'What makes you think I can find John?' she asked.

'Finding things is your business,' the security chief said. 'You are set up for it.'

'What happens if I do find him for you?'

'We bring him in, charge him with the murders, and make sure that your name remains out of it. We reinstate your attorney and allow you to continue doing business in this sector,' the governor said.

'What kind of guarantee do I have that you will do these things?' Anita asked.

'My word,' the governor responded.

'That's not good enough,' Anita said.

The security chief chuckled. 'It will have to do, Ms Miles. You're not in a position to negotiate. The fact that we offer you this much shows how generous we are.'

'How desperate you are,' she said, crossing her legs. 'Suppose I leave this meeting and go to the news net? Suppose I let the sector know that Lina Base allowed a convicted felon to return to the scene of his original crimes? Suppose I mention your attempts at bribing me?'

'It would change nothing – for you, anyway,' the governor said. 'It would merely make things uncomfortable for us. We would still confiscate your property and charge you with every crime we can think of. People would eventually see your visit with the reporters as a desperation move on your part.'

'You think you have me,' Anita said.

'No,' the governor replied. 'We know we do.'

Justin Schafer

The forensic teams no longer needed him, but he remained on Bountiful anyway. He stationed himself at the edge of the detail, as an observer, although he did work if someone directed him toward it. A part of himself remained shut off and distant – he could stare at the bodies now without feeling shock or revulsion. They had become objects, pieces of a puzzle that had to be put together without aid of a guide.

Justin had spent two days on Bountiful and felt no closer to the answers than he had been before. He had taken his old room in the apartments – his clothing still hung in the closets where he had left it – and, if he tried hard enough, he could see that time had stopped here. The tragedy of the children had left an indelible mark on this place. The death of the traders would do the same.

At that moment, he sat on the packed dirt. He wore an old jumpsuit he had left on Bountiful twenty years before. It fitted as if no time had passed. He had't gained a middle-aged paunch; his body hadn't settled as so many bodies did. Perhaps retaining his thirtyish face had allowed him to retain his thirtyish body as well.

One of the medical technicians had got the dome to function properly again, and it was running through its cycle: rose for early morning; blue for mid-day; sepia for late afternoon. The cycle didn't jibe with Justin's memory of the events of the past, and he wished there were logs to check, to see if the colonists had followed a schedule other than the ones prescribed.

It wouldn't surprise him. They had done everything oddly.

Voice buzzed around him. Techs walked in and out of the Command Central. Yesterday they had made holos of the bodies and the surrounding area. They had also spent much of the night scraping nearby surfaces for evidence. Before Justin woke this morning, Lina Base's coroner had finished his last autopsy. He preferred to conduct them on site so no evidence would be lost.

Now the techs were bagging Minx's body – carefully, trying to keep it in the same position it had been found in. Justin had asked what was going to happen to it, and had been told that it would be stored in Morgue 3 – the evidence room – until John's trial was over.

They all believed John had committed the killings.

But Justin was beginning to have doubts. Sometimes, when he stared at Minx's body long enough, the body appeared to be whole, with no parts missing. Only the eyes were wide, indicating fear and death. He had had the same thing happen with the other bodies inside, but he had told no one. Somehow, with donning the clothes from his past, he had returned to his past. He was no longer Justin Schafer, one of the most respected psychologists in the sector. He was Justin Schafer, outcast, the man Netta had hired because she thought him incompetent.

Finally the coroner, Mór Kai, came out of the building. He was a large man with a two-day growth of whiskers on his florid face. His hands were wide and covered with tufts of white hair, as if aging had moved his hair from his head to his hands. His eyes were small and buried in wrinkles. His was a face that had seen a lot of pain and very little joy.

'Mór,' Justin said. 'May I talk with you?'

Kai blinked at him, as if he were seeing Justin for the first time. 'Thought you left already, Schafer.'

'No,' Justin said. 'I don't feel as if I'm completely done here.'

'Not much mind-reading you can do on dead folks,' Kai walked around Minx's body and stopped in front of Justin. Kai smelled of unwashed flesh and sweat; he had worked steadily since he had arrived on Bountiful the day before.

'I can do some,' Justin said. 'Sit with me for a moment.'

Kai swayed on his feet. 'I would like some sleep, Schafer.'

'You can sleep on the shuttle. Give me just a few minutes, and then you can go.'

Kai sighed and slid down to his knees. 'You'll probably have to help me up,' he said. 'I might fall asleep right here.'

'Only a minute,' Justin repeated. He helped Kai ease into a sitting position. 'I'm trying to figure things out. Were the bodies moved?'

Kai shook his head. 'Blood pattern shows they died where they lay.'

Justin frowned. He had been afraid of that. 'Speculating now, how long would it take to kill five people in such drastically different ways?'

'How the hell should I know, Schafer? I just examine 'em. I don't kill 'em.' Kai ran a thick hand over his face, as if he knew Justin would press for an answer. 'I don't know, really. Maybe an hour a person, give or take.'

'Five hours, give or take,' Justin grabbed his knees and rocked backwards. He had thought that it would take less time. His level of unease rose. 'What were the others doing while he killed their friends, do you think?'

'What are you, Schafer, a prosecuting attorney? How should I know?' The bags under Kai's eyes seemed to get deeper. He pushed himself to his feet, his joints cracking as he did.

'No, I'm not,' Justin said, ignoring Kai's movements, 'but any good prosecutor would ask the question.'

'I doubt it, Schafer,' Kai said. He straightened his body and stretched as if it were the only way to ward off sleep. 'I saw that vid of your boy's last murder. Twenty years ago, he killed a kid without even touching him. Who knows what he could do now, after years of practice.'

Kai walked away and trudged up the steps to the guest apartments. His room was next to Justin's.

John seemed the obvious choice for the killer, but Justin had learned, graphically, on Minar that the obvious choice wasn't always the right one. He had learned on Bountiful that identifying the right choice wasn't always the best decision either. He often wondered what would have become of the children, what would have become of the colonists if he had remained silent or allowed them to blame the Dancers.

He knew what would have happened to the Dancers. They would have died. But who knew how many human lives would have remained intact?

He took a deep breath and then realized what had been nagging him most about the colony. It smelled different. Even though the colonists had specialized in flowers, the colony had always been overlaid with the sickly sweet odour of Salt Juice manufacture.

The homes and families had looked well-formed here, but something had had to prompt those children to such drastic action. Something inside the colony; something that would have broken up the families anyway.

Something that wasn't very obvious.

Had the Dancers got into the dome to kill Minx and his crew? The dome doors had all been closed. But no one had been able to explain the rush of air that had greeted him when he opened the door. If it had been some kind of odd pressure, it would have dissipated when the traders arrived.

No. There was something here he was overlooking, something they were all overlooking in their rush to convict John.

Life had given Justin three chances to make the right decision in a major event. He had made the wrong decision the first time. He had made a questionable decision the second. This time, he had to make the right one. Not just for himself, but for a little boy he had failed twenty years before.

John

The genie knew where to land the ship. It even knew how. It reminded John to keep the nose flat and to decelerate at the proper speed once they came through the atmosphere.

John listened to its instruction. Over the last few days, he had learned that the genie's knowledge was true. The genie had no desire to kill him – at least none that had evidenced yet. In fact, it had guarded the controls while John used the autodoc after they left Bountiful, reporting back with readings every few hours so that John could make assessments.

He had let himself go farther than he ever had before. He hadn't eaten since he arrived on Bountiful, and he was dehydrated. He was burned badly enough to form small blisters on the skin, but not badly enough, according to the autodoc, to need more than minimal medical attention. He found clothing in one of the lockers, but didn't wear any until the day they landed. The material rubbed against the burns. Everything ached or itched. He wasn't sure which was worse.

They had landed on a mesa, high above the only desert plain John had seen as they drifted down to Bodean. Most of the planet was water – large oceans with small land masses poking through. As they orbited, he noted that the land masses were mostly made of rocky cliffs and were too tiny to support life. Only the continent with the desert – a continent which stretched for thousands of kilometers – had any biological diversity at all. The northern regions had forests, and green expanses the likes of which he had never seen. Only the southern peninsula was desert. It had looked so tiny before they landed. Now it stretched as far as the eye could see.

The genie had assumed Carter's human form. It sat in the co-pilot's chair without moving – as motionless as John had ever seen it. The inside of the bay had grown hot.

John cleared his throat. 'Okay,' he said. 'Now what?'

The genie looked up at him. John could see the chair through the genie's thin face. 'You believe my people are without honour,' it said, 'because I can wear the form of a creature I killed. But I will show you that we have more honour than anyone – anything – you have encountered before.' The genie stood. 'Come with me.'

John stood too. He was shaky, not entirely healed, and uncertain. He hadn't realized until the second orbit of Bodean that he had no plans. From the moment he had left Bountiful until the moment they landed, all he had concentrated on was getting the genie home.

They took the ladder out of the pilot's bay, the genie pretending to climb just as John did. When John reached the bottom, he found the genie waiting in front of the main hatch. John had to open it, or the genie would remain trapped inside.

The genie immediately disappeared. A wind so strong that it nearly knocked John over held him in the doorway and made him unable to drop the stairs. The mesa top was flat and brown – no plants grew on it. The wind kicked up brown dirt in little swirls that resembled miniatures of the storm that the genie had created among the Dancers.

He didn't know how long he stood there while the wind whipped and whirled around him. Sometimes it blew gently, touching strands of his hair and rearranging them on his head. Sometimes it blew so hard that it rocked the ship.

Finally the wind stopped and the genie appeared in human form again. Carter's clothes looked incongruous on this plain surface. 'Come with me,' the genie said, and it walked to the edge of the mesa.

John threw the stairs down, then gripped the metal railing that extended from the side of the ship. Bodean's sun was not as harsh as Bountiful's but it still irritated his skin. He stepped on the ground, surprised to find it as hard as rock beneath his feet.

The walk to the edge of the mesa was short. The sun was setting; the horizon reflected pinks and golds strewn with gray clouds. The vista was lovely enough, but John gasped when he looked at the desert below.

Unlike Bountiful's, this desert was golden – the colour of the Singing Sea. Brownish green plants dotted its surface like small sentries. Dunes rose and fell like waves and, in the distance, another mesa rose – a tower overlooking the tranquil scene below. Sand devils swirled, appearing to move closer, half a hundred of them, following their own individual current.

'It's beautiful,' John said.

The genie smiled. It clasped its hands behind its back, surveying the scene before it as if the desert were its domain. 'This is how your people see my home,' it said. 'But this is how it really looks.'

The genie swept one hand over the view. John blinked and took a step back. Ghostly towers rose as tall as the mesa. Each sand swirl turned into a paper-thin city floating just above the desert's surface. Wind blew through it all, wind with voices as individual as the genie's. The bodeangenies were everywhere and nowhere; their presence invisible, even to John's newly-opened eyes.

'How did she ever catch you?'

The genie shrugged. 'I was a curious fool. I allowed myself to be trapped. The Ancients had warned me, but I was too young to listen. I have since learned.'

'No wonder you wanted to come home,' John said. 'I have never seen a place so beautiful in my entire life.'

'The beauty matters less than the company. Everywhere else, I would have been the only one of my own kind.' The genie's smile was gentle. 'You understand that, don't you, John?'

John made himself look away from the etched world in front of him. The genie was not toying with him. The genie was being serious. 'I understand that too well,' John said.

The genie sat at the edge of the mesa, swinging its legs over the side. It patted the ground beside it, bidding John to do the same. John sat, feeling the hard dirt bite into his buttocks. Sweat ran down his back, making his blisters itch.

'Let me tell you about honour,' the genie said. 'Honour is not about doing what others tell you is right. It is about doing what you believe to be right . You have honour, John. You have had it since you were a boy.'

John shook his head. The sun had nearly set. The towers were glowing white against the darkening sky. 'I killed six of my friends.'

The genie leaned forward, its hands clutching the edge as if it were going to push itself off. 'You didn't kill them,' the genie said.

John glanced sharply at it.

The genie shrugged. 'It amazes me that you do not under-stand, for you, of all humans, have evidence of this. You wondered, back in the dome, why I hadn't killed my tormentors sooner, why I hadn't attacked the kidnapper on Rotan Base to gain my freedom. I didn't answer you then – at least not directly. But you need to listen to me now.'

The genie eased back from the edge and pulled its legs up until it sat crosslegged. The darkness was nearly complete. The only illumination came from the cities floating around them. John pulled away from the edge too, and mimicked the genie's position.

'We are telepathic. We slip into the mind and slip out, like wind, able to echo thoughts and to learn the manners of the creatures around us. We have the powers of the wind, the strength to blow, the strength to destroy and the strength to uplift. For the briefest moment, and with the right kind of creature, we have the power of illusion.'

'Your definition of moment is different from mine,' John said.

The genie held up its hand to silence him. 'I doubt that. Remember: we learn the manners of those around us. I chose my words with care.'

Another breeze tickled the hair on the back of John's head. He felt other presences, but he leaned forward to concentrate on the genie.

'Your Dancers have many rare abilities that serve them well. They are not telepathic as we are – their abilities in that direction are limited. Your language has no words for many of their abilities. They are not empaths, since they can create emotion in their subjects. They are not telepaths since they have no memory of what they have learned. They are enhancers. They take the magic they find around them and increase it, sometimes in factors of a hundred. It is what they did with me. I come home stronger than any genie has been before. I killed Minx and his crew on Bountiful because I had power there for the first time.'

Enhancers. John frowned. 'But they enhanced nothing in me.'

The genie laughed. The sound was like a gale blowing through a portal. 'That is where my understanding of you fails. Humans are the most complex creatures I have ever encountered. You have the ability to be anything you want to be – you are only limited by your beliefs. So, as a child, when you believed that you would become adults by using a Dancer ritual, you made truth. Had the adults around you not interfered, your friends would have grown new hands, new lungs, and new hearts.'

John was shaking. He couldn't catch his breath. 'But they didn't interfere until later.'

'No,' the genie said. 'They changed the ritual up front. They put the bodies in a freezer – and you were still human enough to believe that nothing can grow in the cold.'

John leaned back. He felt as if he had been stabbed through the heart himself. 'If we had taken them out – if we had taken them out — '

'They would have changed,' the genie said.

'Even Michael?'

'Even Michael.'

John stood up. He staggered away from the edge. His eyes were burning, and his face was wet. 'Why tell me this now?'

'Because of honour,' the genie said. 'Because you saved my life. Because you wanted to save my life even before you met me, even before I slipped into your mind. I really didn't have to influence you, John. The compassion was already there.'

John sat in the darkness, away from the breezes, away from the floating lights. The ground was like a board against his back. 'But you might be telling me this because you know it's what I want to hear.'

'I tell you the truth,' the genie said. 'And I can prove it. Think, John, as an adult human with all your limitations. What child can wield a knife – even an exceptionally sharp knife – and behead another child? You did it with a single stroke. Such a thing is impossible. You cut through wrist bone as if it were soup. John, human children do not have that kind of strength. Yet you never questioned it, and always believed it. And because the adults believed in the power of the knife, your abilities were never challenged, your faith never called lies.'

John lay on his back for a moment, listening to himself breathe.

'No, no, John, it will be easy,' Katie said, her eyes flashing. She brushed a strand of hair off Linette's face. 'And it won't even hurt.

287

When you wake up, Linny, you will be big enough to fight back.'

'Maybe I should go first,' John said.

'Linny needs to go first.'

And he knew that. He knew how bruised and battered she was: how the night before they went to the shuttle pilot, Linny had staggered into the park bleeding from every hole in her body.

'We could have changed it all by believing that they loved us, that Salt Juice had no power,' he whispered.

'No,' the genie said. 'The Dancers enhance. You have little ability for illusion, and you only seem to be able to affect changes in your own bodies. You might have stopped your own pain, but not the circumstances that caused it.'

John propped himself up on his elbows. All these years. All these years, he had believed he had committed murder because he had been told that he had. If he had only followed his own convictions, he would have saved lives. Linette and Katie and Michael would still be alive now.

'But they aren't,' the genie said. 'And nothing you can do will change that. You have believed in their death for too long. But here is the second part of my gift to you. You have learned much magic from your Dancer friends. You could have become one of them once, but no longer. Now you must use what bits you have. You must find your friends, the others who went to Lina Base with you, for in them lies your future, your salvation, and your haven.'

The genie's face was lit from within like the cities floating off the side of the mesa. 'You have given me my life. I give you yours in trade.'

John stared at the ship, a hulking shadow in the darkness. 'I need to disappear. They think I killed those traders.'

The genie shrugged. 'If you run, you will die. You cannot sustain your misery much longer. You must find your friends, for in them lies your only hope.'

The genie's words had truth. John couldn't take more blame, more accusations. 'They'll find me in that ship,' he said.

The genie stood, then floated like a brilliantly illuminated ghost. It left tiny reflections across the night sky. It touched the edge of the ship, and suddenly John saw a shuttle.

'I give you one last illusion,' the genie said. 'Your Dancers have made my illusions last forever for those who want to

288

believe. Believe that this ship is your own craft and it will be.'

Then the memory came clear to John: 'That's how you killed Minx, isn't it? You made him believe he was dying, so he did.'

'It was quite simple,' the genie said, hovering on the side of the shuttle, 'and quite cruel. Minx had killed many times in his life. He had ruined many other existences in ways that make death pale. My only regret is that I lacked the time to kill him more than once.'

A shudder ran through John.

As the genie smiled, its face transformed going from Carter to Linette to Katie. It stopped finally on Allen, features pudgy and soft, expression gentle. 'You have honour to avenge, John. Good luck.'

John stood, feeling himself dismissed. He walked to the shuttle, grabbed the side rail he knew had to be there and swung himself on to the lip.

The genie floated beside him, and little wisps of a breeze caressed his face. 'You will live forever on Bodean, John,' the genie whispered, 'And you will be forever remembered.'

Part Six

Dania Zinn

Her office was dark. Judge Dania Zinn closed the door, turned on a reading lamp over her desk, and pulled off her long black robe. She straightened the vest of the silver suit she wore beneath it, then slipped off her shoes and lay down on the couch, one arm over her eyes.

During the last week, her caseload had been heavy, but she hadn't been able to ignore the news reports about the murders on Bountiful. The news of the murders had arrived the day after Justin Schafer's snide little note about Dusty.

As if Dania hadn't been bothered enough. Dusty's death had left her with a vague feeling of unease, a lost-and-all-alone feeling that recalled the days after Allen's death. Then the murders, and John's implication in them. Somehow that hadn't made Dania feel any better about denying Dusty's petition to return to Bountiful.

Under the law, neither Dusty nor John had any right to return to Bountiful. The planet was sealed and no one except a few experts were allowed to set foot on the planet at all. That, coupled with the Dancer Eight's history, and the fact that they were convicted felons more than contra-indicated any return to the scene of the crime.

That hadn't stopped her nightmares, though.

Dania hadn't slept well since seeing the petition. The children, looking as they had when they got off the shuttle, sitting around her in a circle, crying with their hands over their faces. When they finally looked at her, their cheeks were tearstreaked, but their eye sockets were empty. Nicky stood behind them, his skin flayed, his face gone. *They want someone to care what happens to them*, he said. *Why don't you care?*

She sat up, the weight of her dream making her nauseated. She *did* care. Nicky, of all people, should have understood that. She cared so much that she had to leave the practice. Her failure with the children – causing Allen's death – had been the final straw in a law practice determined to break her. If her clients were innocent, she had to face watching them go to prison for crimes they didn't commit. And if they went to prison as innocents, the fault lay with her. If her clients were guilty, she still had to fight for their release, and if she won, she lost.

She preferred being a prosecutor, where the world could dissolve into shades of black. She had no trouble believing that everyone she prosecuted was guilty, that all of them deserved to be punished, and she went after them with a single-minded zeal that had surprised her. She had expected more of the same when she had become a judge, but found herself responsible again for decisions that affected innocent people's lives. At least, this time, the outcomes were not usually based on her mistakes, but on her beliefs. She had found, in the last five years, that she could live with that.

A headache was building in the bridge of her nose. She rubbed it with her thumb and forefinger. She wasn't quite sure why the murders bothered her so much, but they had. She had read everything she could find, even using her security access to allow her to see the holos of the bodies.

We need to understand the beliefs of the natives if we are to understand if the people they have influenced have broken any laws. It is our duty, as human beings. Nicky had said, that last morning before he left for Ifor, before his death. He had done so much early work on the Alien Influences Act and he had believed in it so fervently. She often thought it ironic that she had lost the case which had undermined it.

Justin's petition to review the gag order placed on Latona Etanl sat on top of Dania's desk. She looked at it each time she turned on the small reading light. Only one of the Dancer Eight remained alive. What would it hurt if Latona spoke now? It certainly wouldn't interfere with Dania's career. Her association with the Dancer Eight was not widely known outside of Lina Base. If anything, it would harm Justin, show that his theories and the basis of his career since Bountiful had been wrong. It might even provide help to the experts who were trying to figure out what had happened to John when he reached Bountiful, why a man whose record had appeared to be clean since his release from Reed would kill again.

296

Dania stood, feeling the weight of all those years on her frame. She had not had a relationship since Nicky, and hadn't been close to anyone since Harper self-destructed after the Eight left Lina Base. She had borne the weight of the last twenty years alone. Her body showed it. She had become stocky like her mother, and her hair had turned silver before she was forty. She had frown lines running from her eyes to her lips. The write-ups and profiles always said she had character, but she was still shocked when she looked in the mirror each day and saw a sour middle-aged face staring back at her.

She moved over to the desk and sat down in her plush, upholstered chair. Her office was usually her haven. She had picked an office that had no windows, and she had covered all the walls with bookshelves, spending her vacations travelling to flea markets and dumpbins, and once every two or three years, to Earth, returning with books that had not yet been destroyed. They covered her walls, some books made of leather, some of paper so thin that it crumbled beneath her touch. She liked the idea that knowledge could fit into the palm of her hand. It stopped the confusion she felt each time she logged on and began research on some point of law. There was too much to know. She longed to return to a time when knowledge was finite and decisions were easy to make.

Dania sighed and pulled the hard copy of Justin's request over to her. She scanned it one final time, seeing nothing in the write-up that made it particularly objectionable. All he wanted was the gag order on Latona Etanl lifted so that she could talk about the Dancers, their rituals and their practices. Finite knowledge that many people did not have. Knowledge that Justin believed might have prevented deaths like Dusty's or Allen's.

Or maybe ever the deaths of those five people on Bountiful, just a few days before.

Dania logged on and with a stroke of a finger added Justin's request to the next day's docket. She could make the change in less than five minutes, and she wouldn't have to think about it again.

The Dancers, the Eight, and Nicky might leave the realm of her nightmares and return to her subconscious, where they belonged.

John

The shuttle was state of the art, top of the line, the best John had ever seen, with a computer system that rivalled any base's. He spent his first day alone in orbit around Bodean, feeling awkward and vulnerable, but having nowhere else to go. He hoped that the new design of the ship would throw off the authorities long enough for him to find at least one of his old friends. He spent the day searching files and discovering that records kept on released felons were haphazard at best.

It seemed odd to him that he put the genie's injunction before his own safety. He probably should have hired an attorney and turned himself in, fought the charges of murder he knew they were going to place on him. But there was a subtext to the genie's words, an emotional underpinning laden with an urgency John didn't yet understand. Part of him believed that if he found his friends, he would have his freedom.

Belief. According to the genie, belief was all it took.

It took him only a matter of minutes to find his own record. The files had his release date from Reed and the site of his first job. Then he had to go to passage records and employment records, all made easy because he knew what jobs he had held. The difficulty would be in finding his friends, of whom he knew nothing after they left Lina Base.

To his dismay he learned that they had all been shipped out to the same penal colony, but kept in different sections of the sprawling compound, hundreds of kilometers apart. He had known that they had left together, but he had assumed everyone else had been assigned to different penal colonies, like Kirst. He found a copy of the judge's order, accidentally posted with the shipping orders, instructing Reed that none of the children ever see or spend time with each other.

They had all been shipped to Reed. They had been together for years, and had never known it.

After discovering that, he had logged off and wandered to the back of the shuttle, trying to keep his emotions in check.

During his first year, he had worked the ice mines deep below the surface. He, a boy who had grown up in one of the warmest places in the sector, now worked in the coldest. He wore a thermal suit with its internal heater, but that was never enough. He was too young to go into the mines themselves, so he worked in the factory, looking through the iceblocks for small gems and fossils frozen into the crust. His fingers were continually numb and his lips a permanent blue. If he spoke to anyone he was placed in isolation, so he learned how to be quiet and how to focus on the task at hand.

By the time he was fifteen, he was considered a model prisoner and, as a reward, he was trained to run the heating systems. Years of deep cold had left him thin and shivering. Any warmth seemed like too much, so the switch, in its first few months, had seemed like another punishment. But the skills he learned there got him on his first assignment as a repairman in a trader ship, and helped him learn everything from ship maintenance to bomber detail – and the skills to pilot, a job forbidden to him as an ex-convict.

They figured him to be a murderer now. Getting caught piloting was a small crime in comparison.

'John.' A female voice filtered through the sound system. It took him a minute to realize the voice belonged to the computer. 'Your scan is complete. The information you need is available in the pilot's bay.'

When he had left the pilot's bay, he had instructed the computer to search for any reference to the other Eight. His heart stuck in his throat. When he saw them, he had no idea what he would say to them.

Hi. A bodeangenie bade me to find you. It said that we made no mistakes, except the one children always make – to believe in the adult's version instead of their own.

As if that would work. He would be lucky to escape unharmed. The surviving Eight probably wanted nothing to do with him, wanted nothing to do with their past. He had no idea how he would have reacted if one had found him a few months previous. Probably with a bit of affection and a fear that ran as deep as a Reed chill. He could almost imagine it: instead of

302

finding Anita in that captain's boudoir, he would have found Beth.

And ordered her to get out.

He stepped through the door into the pilot's bay. The computer screen was up, a facsimile of a hard-copy record visible on the flat surface.

A death certificate.

He had seen enough of them in his bounty work. He sat down in the curved navigator's chair, his hands shaking, and stared at the screen.

Skye's name was on the top of the form, and a badly reproduced tiny holo of her as he had last seen her graced the right-hand corner. The holo looked flat and lifeless in its two-d reproduction. Her brilliant blue eyes were wide, her mouth curved downward. The holo had to have been made after they shipped off Bountiful.

He could barely breathe as he read. She had died in her isolation chamber on the penal ship. An investigation showed no foul play, although some of the circumstances of the death were unusual. The follow-up John did revealed that the details were classified.

He leaned back and swallowed, hard. She had been dead for twenty years and he hadn't even known. He had imagined her working somewhere, trying to forget the past, as he had. He had never thought she died.

Of the surviving Eight, only six were left.

He closed his eyes and then opened them again. At the bottom of the certificate was a tiny notation: c.f. Lieberman/ Reed/Case No. 223400.

With two quick strokes, he cited the reference number. The screen went blank for a few moments, then came up with four flat pages of news notes.

The case was nineteen years old, and was trumpeted as a victory for criminals' rights. Hans Lieberman, who was being sent to Reed for embezzlement and fraud, had been given the effects of a young girl who had died on the penal ship along the way. Reed tried to confiscate the effects, claiming that a convict had no right to possessions, but Lieberman contacted his attorney. The case held that a convict had a right to possessions obtained while incarcerated, as long as those possession were obtained legally. A bequest, such as this was, belonged to Lieberman. It would, however, remain in protective custody at Reed until Lieberman's release. The release date given was five years old.

The file search had given John the records of all the news and legal citations. He read through them with a growing headache. Most were full of legal notations he didn't understand, but finally, on the second to the last page, was a piece of information he could use.

Upon his release, Lieberman, who had proved himself a technical wizard on Reed, was indentured to Minar Base to upgrade and repair servobots.

Finally.

A destination.

ii

Minar Base was on the farthest side of the sector from Bodean. The journey took a day longer than John had expected. He used the time to search for news of the remaining Eight. They had all survived Reed, and most were indentured upon release. After that, he found no records at all.

The indenturing shocked him. He had not been indentured; had, in fact, been released with a small credit line, two changes of clothing, and a shuttle to take him to the nearest base. His service on Reed, according to his file, had been exemplary, and he would be used as inspiration for the remaining prisoners, showing them that model behaviour sometimes led to rewards.

What they didn't realize was that because he had been imprisoned as a juvenile, not as an adult, he had the opportunity for release. Had the judge not acted so quickly, she might have added another technicality and made John an honorary adult, and a prisoner for life.

He took a route tht skirted Bountiful and Lina Base, adding time to his journey. He didn't care. He assumed they were looking for him. Despite his imprudence near Bodean, he planned to be cautious. Fortunately he had memorized three different i.d. numbers for his emergency identities, and he tapped into the first. His account had enough credits to pay the tolls on Minar Base, and to buy himself a cheap room for a month. He hoped it wouldn't take that long.

When Minar Base finally appeared on his viewer, he was surprised at its size. It was one of the later bases, built nearly a hundred years after Lina Base, and he had assumed that Minar Base would be bigger. It was half the size, a tiny spiral floating out in space.

He used his i.d. number along with the shuttle's number in a request to dock. The Port Authority took so long to get back to him that he was afraid they had found that the shuttle didn't exist. But the genie's illusion seemed to work, even from this distance. When the Authority came back on line, they gave him a docking number and a time.

The first step.

He hoped they all would be that easy.

iii

No one questioned him. From the moment he arrived, he was a licensed bounty hunter named Sean. He had learned, over the years, that having a name which sounded like his own made things easier, made it less difficult to pretend.

Minar Base had only four docking bays which fitted five shuttles. Some ships weren't even cleared to land at the base – an odd set-up that John wasn't sure he understood. He was informed that he had to complete his business in two days because the Extra Species Alliance was holding a conference, and the base would need the docking space.

He wanted to be off the base before the Alliance arrived. He had had minimal contact with them since his release from Reed and he wanted no more. He didn't blame Latona for that first trip to see the Dancers, but the association made him uncomfortable.

Fortunately, it didn't take very long to find Hans Lieberman. He had his own office in the maintenance ring above the docking bays. The office was small, with a view of the shuttles below. The smell of chemical fumes was strong – mostly cleaners designed to scrub dirt off metal – and mixed with a heady cologne that should have been banned centuries ago. There

305

were no chairs – only a tool table that covered one wall. Bots covered the floor, dozens of them, in various stages of assembly. It took John a moment to see Lieberman.

He was tiny – about the size of a maintenance bot – with silver hair and white flesh that had gone gray. John recognized the disorder: Reed's ice miners gained it from a malfunctioning suit. Exposure to any kind of temperature extreme became very painful. The disorder could be treated with drugs that left the skin an odd gray colour. Lieberman had to have had it bad in order to have to take the drugs on a base.

'Hans Lieberman?' John asked. He stood in the open door, uncertain about how to cross the floor. 'I contacted you just after my arrival.'

Lieberman stood and brushed his hands on his gray coveralls, leaving black streaks that matched those on the chest and thighs. His fingers were long and slender with dirt-encrusted nails. His eyes were wide and bulged, another effect of the drug.

'You a reporter?' he asked.

John shook his head. 'No.' He glanced around. 'Is there somewhere we can talk?'

Lieberman grinned. 'This is the best I can do. This is about as private as it gets. No one thinks anyone who works with bots has secrets.'

John squeezed in the room, cautiously stepping over chips scattered on the floor. He pulled the door closed behind him. 'I understand you knew Skye.'

Lieberman's grin faded. He pulled over a servobot and sat on its flat surface, balancing precariously so that the wheels didn't slide out from underneath him. 'Everyone gets that wrong. I didn't really know her. She just cried on my shoulder one night. After that I kinda watched out for her. I don't know why they placed her on that shuttle. Most of the inmates were men, and most of them thought a little girl was there for them, if you know what I mean.'

John grabbed behind him, bracing his hand on the wall to steady himself.

'Nothing happened. I didn't let nothing happen. But I was scared for her, let me tell you.'

'Do you know what she did?'

Lieberman picked some dirt off his knee. 'Killed some kids on

306

Bountiful. Never understood that, really. She seemed like a nice girl, really broken up about some boy named Allen.'

'He died just before she was placed on the ship.'

'Yeah,' Lieberman said. 'I sometimes wonder if that's what caused her – you know.'

John glanced around. He saw an assembled servobot near him. 'Mind if I sit?'

'Be my guest.' Lieberman waved his hand. Below, a shuttle's engine started. The noise echoed in the tiny room. Lieberman was right; monitoring this place would have been silly.

They waited until the noise died down. Then Lieberman leaned forward, putting his elbows on his knees. 'Say, you never did say who you were with.'

'No, I didn't,' John said. He sighed. The genie's admonition had been too vague. Find the others, it had said. But Skye was dead. John wasn't sure how much he should risk with this man sitting across from him. Then he leaned forward, his position mimicking Lieberman's.

'My name is John,' he said. 'I was a friend of Skye's on Bountiful. I got transported to Lina Base with her. I served with you on Reed. Ice caves, right?'

'Damn body'll never be the same.' Lieberman said, but the words appeared to be a reflex.

John's heart pounded. Lieberman looked distracted. Maybe the authorities had let him keep Skye's possessions so that he would help them trap one of the Dancer Eight. But that made no sense. At the time Lieberman won his case, the seven remaining were imprisoned on Reed.

'Max, Verity, Pearl, Dusty, Beth.' Lieberman paused for a breath. 'And John.' It was a litany. 'Took you long enough. She told me the night before she died that everything she had left would go to one o' you. She made me swear it. That's why I fought so hard. Little girl had nothing. Every time I thought about giving up, she would come to me in a dream. Spookiest thing. "You promised," she'd say, and damn if she wasn't right.'

He tilted his head and his bulging eyes glared at John. 'How do I know you're one of them?'

John bit his lower lip. Anything he said would be hard to believe. 'You talked to Skye a lot?'

307

Lieberman nodded. 'She'd never talked to no one before. All she had was me.'

'Then maybe she explained being Dancer.'

'She tried. Made little sense to me.'

'Until she showed you, right?' John closed his eyes, hoping that Skye had shown him some of the Dancer ways. He reached —

— finding nothing but a wall, deep inside. A wall he had built, blocking himself from his Dancer self. That wall had crumbled on Bountiful and he had nearly died.

Useless.

Useless.

The word was not his. The word was Lieberman's, echoing in his head like a strong memory. It broke through John's wall and he floated, Dancerlike, above the servobot.

But John's ability to float only lasted a moment or so. He had never done it as an adult, never really supported his full weight above the ground – at least, not without Dancer help. He fell to the servobot with a thump, and the bot skidded beneath him. He had to grab on to the sides to keep from tumbling onto the floor.

'She thought she was useless?' he asked.

Lieberman's features were creased into a frown. 'She was just a kid. She didn't know . . .' His voice trailed off. 'You got that from me, that word, didn't you? And the floating. Damn. I thought I had made that part up. You got that from me!'

His voice rose with a kind of excitement. John had apparently confirmed something that Lieberman remembered, something that Lieberman had dismissed because he believed it crazy.

You are only limited by your beliefs.

'Can you stay here, like right here and not move?' Lieberman asked.

'Look,' John said, 'I'm in a bit of trouble — '

'I know. The Bountiful thing.' Lieberman grinned. 'We Reed survivors got to stick together. I figure if you were going to hurt me you'd have already done it. And if I was going to hurt you, I'd've found a way to signal for help up here. All it would take would be one yank on the back of one of these bots.'

John shivered. He was not being cautious enough. It was as if he had lost something since Bountiful, as if the cautious part of his mind were active elsewhere.

'I just want to get her stuff. It's in my stash, right next door. It's just that I don't want no one to — '

· 'I'm not going to steal it,' John said. Nor was he going to sit and wait. 'Or anything else you have.' He stood. 'We'll go in there together.'

Lieberman gave him a backwards glance, and then must have seen that John was determined. Lieberman opened a side door and slid inside, waiting for John to follow.

The room was little more than a closet. A single light illuminated shelves filled with all sorts of equipment, ancient and modern. Lieberman's stash mainly consisted of robotic and computer parts. A small computer blinked in the corner of a shelf. From John's understanding of the terms of Lieberman's release from Reed, Lieberman was not allowed any kind of computer equipment at all.

Good. Now they both had secrets on each other.

Lieberman moved some servobot frames. They made a scraping sound against the plastic. 'You know,' he said, 'there was another one of you on Minar, not too long ago. I remember because when he died I was a little angry. If I had known who he was, I would have given him this so it would have been out of my hair.'

Goosebumps formed all over John's skin. 'Died?'

'Yeah, few years back. Awful thing. I was glad I was taking my vacation. Guess it really upset the entire base.'

'Why?' John could barely get the word out.

'Because,' Lieberman said. 'I guess someone stole the corpse's eyes.' He shoved aside a glass bowl. 'Here it is.'

But John could barely concentrate. Max was dead too. What had the genie meant, sending him on this mission? How could he get his safety, his haven, and his future from childhood companions already dead?

Lieberman turned around. In his hands, he held a glass jar like the kind they had in the cook's quarters on the penal ship, the kind that was later banned when an uprising on another ship had used the jars to kill most of the crew.

'This is what she left,' Lieberman said. 'I don't know why it's so important, but she made me swear to give it to one of you. She said I had to because Allen never got a chance. I had to make

309

sure she had a chance. She said you would understand.'

The glass was sealed, and dark, filled with something. John didn't really understand at all. Allen never got a chance. None of them ever got a chance. They had been doomed from the moment they were born on Bountiful.

Lieberman extended the jar. As John took it, the entire glass seemed to pulsate. It grew warm and then a flood of silver light filled the room.

'Wow,' Lieberman said. 'I never saw it do that before.'

Anita Miles

She sat in her special gallery, feeling helpless. On the back wall, the holo of the baby Minaran swan. She watched it until she could stand it no longer; then she shut it off. She didn't need to be reminded of her first failure on the eve of her second.

The helldog was quiet. It slept at the bottom of its cage, as if it knew that any movement from it would disturb her. The Colleician scent painting occasionally erupted with an odour, as if it were trying to keep her entertained. She ignored it. She ignored all objets d'art, her attention focused on the empty platform that would have housed the Bodean wind sculpture.

The bodeangenie that started all of this.

She had pulled all her hunters off their regular routes and sent them after John. They had determined that he left Bountiful in Minx's ship and suspected he went to Bodean.

To return the genie.

She was such a fool. With his history, of course he would. The little girl who had blown the whistle on Anita's Minaran scam on Orda Base had also been one of the Dancer Eight. Anita hadn't seen the connection until she came back from Lina Base a few days before.

She was under admonition from the governor to find John and return him alive. She suspected that was the real reason they had sent her after him – to prevent her from killing him when she found him. She hated to be double-crossed. No one had done it successfully before. Not even that little girl on Orda Base. Anita had lost the baby Minaran – returned to Minar, damn it – but she had remained out of jail and free to ply her trade.

Unlike the little girl. The little girl had committed suicide a day later.

This, though, this could ruin her. If it reached the nets that she had lost a priceless art object, most of her sources would dry up, figuring their commissions forfeit when the object disappeared.

313

The most frustrating thing of all was that her attorney was still being held pending investigation, and the new attorney she had hired was too straightlaced for her tastes. He didn't understand that laws were meant to be broken as long as no one got caught.

At least she could be blunt with him. No matter what happened down the road, if he spoke out against her, she would sue him for breach of attorney/client privilege. That would ruin his career quickly and effectively.

The thought gave her no joy.

The scent painting sent out the odour of roses. Anita nearly gagged. She got up and left the gallery, hand clutched to her mouth.

Roses made her think of Bountiful.

All those year, trapped in that white, white world. Her parents had had no idea about beauty – their homes had had no decorations at all, only the flowers in the garden served as a break from the monotony.

Anita refused to have flowers in her gallery. She preferred to live on bases where greenery was prohibited. She hated gardens and fresh air and sunshine.

It all made her stomach turn, just like the scent of roses did.

But she had escaped. Unlike the Dancer Eight, who were ten years her junior, she had left her past behind her. Only occasional scents or visions had brought her any discomfort at all.

Her screen came up on her desk, blinking with a message. She took a deep breath to calm her nausea and pressed the vid display. Feodorovich appeared, his bald head and big ears nearly filling the screen. 'Want some coffee?' he asked.

Their code to talk in the gallery which she contantly swept for surveillance. She had paid the Rotan Base authorities years ago to ignore her little corner of the shopping district, but it was always good to doublecheck. She waited by the door of the main gallery, and let Feodor in when he arrived.

They said nothing as they walked through the main gallery, the back room, and the special door leading to the priceless displays. The helldog was standing as she walked in, but immediately lay down and hid its face in its paws.

'What?' she asked.

'The ship was sighted heading to Bodean,' Feodor said, 'and

not seen after that.'

'Yes?' Anita affected a bored tone to her voice. She had heard all of this before.

'Clay and his crew did a scan of the surface. No ship meeting that description. No ships at all, but they touched down just to make sure.' Feodor's voice was wobbling. Anita had never heard it wobble before.

'And?'

'Nothing. We lost contact. So we sent another shuttle, and they scanned the surface. All they found was Clay's shuttle.'

Anita straightened. She didn't like the look on Feodor's face. She didn't like the sound of his voice. She didn't like the feeling that was growing in her belly. Clay had been one of her oldest and best hunters. 'What happened to Clay?'

'Wind storm. Worst anyone had ever seen. Literally stripped the skin off their bones. All the crew had been outside and trapped in it.' Feodor ran a hand over his bald head. 'So the new crew sent a man down to investigate, and the moment he landed, the wind started up again, killing him too.'

'Intentional,' Anita said. Her throat was dry.

Feodor nodded. 'So it would seem.'

John had succeeded, then. He had brought the genie home, and the genie was free to protect itself. She glanced at the empty pedestal and resisted the urge to kick it over. The genie had been within her grasp. So close. So close and she had lost so much.

'Any sign of John?'

Feodor took a step back before shaking his head.

'Find him,' Anita said. 'Find him now.' And, government or no government, she would make sure that he paid. He would pay with something as priceless as the art object she lost.

He would pay with his life.

John

He set the jar on the floor of his tiny one-room rental, and stared at it with the lights out for hours. The jar pulsated and glowed, filling the room with a silver light. Lieberman had not been able to get over the change.

'Almost as if it knows you,' he had said.

John sat on the bed, pillows propped behind him against the wall, tucked in the corner with the blankets pulled up to his chin. He had left the bed on the floor afraid that some disturbance of the air function would make it land on the jar. He wouldn't be able to handle it if the jar shattered.

A memory tickled the back of John's mind. It was elusive, like a word he knew but couldn't remember. Flashes of it would touch him: blinding silver light with Dancers shrouded in front of it; hands caressing his cheek, smelling of cinnamon; a voice whispering, *Such pain, such deep pain.*

But the memories seemed unconnected, as if they had happened to someone else. As if they had been planted in his mind. Perhaps the genie – but he doubted it. He had believed the genie when it spoke of honour. The genie had nothing to gain from lying.

Gradually, sleep came. Deep, dreamless sleep for the first time since Bountiful. But through it all he felt a warmth that came not from the covers, but from a pulsating silver light.

ii

After Lieberman's comment, John's search for Max was amazingly easy. Max had been in charge of the garbage compacting and recycling centre. All waste was reused on a base like this; none of it was deposited into space as the old colonists used to do. Max had kept the systems running and made sure that everything which went into the garbage bins was recycled.

A lonely job, but that didn't surprise John. They all seemed to go for lonely jobs.

No. What surprised John was the way Max died. The records were quite detailed. John read them while eating off a servo tray in his room, his feet propped up on a stool, his back to the pulsating jar.

Max had always been quiet, but he seemed healthy, even jovial to his friends. As time went by, he got even quieter and he began a habit of biting his lips until they bled. One net report carried a 2-d photo of Max during his healthy period and Max when he started to change. The changed Max looked like the one John had last seen, hollow-eyed, blood staining his chin, his features gaunt and shadowed. He stopped talking altogether a week before his death. He put his affairs in order and made a list of recommended changes for his department, almost as if he knew he were going to die. Then one morning a colleague arrived after the shift change, to find Max dead, blood staining his torso, his lips almost gone, and his eyes missing.

The colleague screamed and sent for base security.

Base security ran the security vids of the area and found nothing. One spokesman later said he thought the vids had been tampered with. A blinding silver light had covered the crucial moments of Max's death.

A chill ran through John.

The silver light whitened the room.

Allen! Allen! No!

You must find your friends, the others who went to Lina Base with you, for in them lies your future, your salvation, and your haven.

But they were all dead. Or gone. Like Allen. All like Allen. What was the genie trying to show him? That his past continued to affect his present? He knew that. He knew that with each waking moment.

You are not Dancer. But you must use what bits you have.

What bits he had . . . The genie had given him a puzzle. The genie was telepathic, but not able to see the future. Had it known that so many of the others were dead? How?

John got up. Max had put his affairs in order, according to the net reports. That meant he had something to rearrange.

320

The bases were required by law to keep the effects of someone
who had died for five years. That gave the authorities time to
contact relations who might be a great distance away. The effects
were always kept to a minimum, chosen by the state if the
person had died intestate, the rest of the estate sold and put into
a trust account for the unknown relatives. If no one claimed the
effects after five years, they reverted to the state.

John had spent a week digging through the unclaimed effects
storage on Rotan Base once for a different case many years ago.
He figured the procedures on Minar Base would be no different.

He was right.

Oddly, on Minar Base, the storage was located beneath the
garbage recycling centre. As he took the lift down, the clunk and
drag of machinery grew. It seemed to invade the lift as he passed
the recycling centre, and then faded to a hollow roar on the
levels below. He got out, and let a shiver run through his body.
Poor Max. He must have been nearly deaf when he died.

The storage centre had a desk-sized waiting room where one
employee processed a stack of information and guarded the
locker codes. The employee was a woman whose white hair had
been shaved in tufts. She was young – maybe twenty – and
pasted on her beige uniform was a tiny insignia of one of the
radical political parties.

John hated politics and never understood how anyone got
involved in them.

The woman looked up. She had spent a considerable sum of
money to dye her eyes beige to match her suit. 'You the guy who
contacted my supervisor about Number 88790343?'

John nodded, his jaw tightening. He hated the impersonality
of the numbers. Max. The man's name had been Max. He had
been so terrified by what happened that he refused to let anyone
near him. He bit his lips until they bled. He never ate. He was
afraid his parents would punish him . . .

. . . and they had. Oh, they had.

John thought all that, and said only, 'Yes. I've come for Max.'

The woman touched her computer screen, then used an old-
fashioned keyboard to type in the numbers. A door panel slid
open behind them. 'Good thing too,' she said as she stood. She

was half John's height but perfectly proportioned. He wouldn't have known she was tiny unless he was standing beside her. 'All the 887s are scheduled for reabsorption at the end of the year. You barely made the deadline.'

Obviously Max's things were not worth much, for the supervisor had done only a cursory check of John's fake i.d. Max's parents had died two years after they left Bountiful and no other family members had come forward. John's claim of friendship was enough to get Max's entire estate.

Such as it was.

'Wait here,' the woman said. She went through the sliding door and, before it closed, John saw stacks and stacks of tiny black boxes, in rows barely wide enough to fit a human being. Now he understood why she was so tiny. She had to fit comfortably in those narrow spaces.

Bots couldn't do the job. It was too sensitive, and they were too easily corruptible.

John paced in the tiny space. The grind and thunk of the machinery above made him feel as if he were back at Reed. Trapped below something heavy that might fall through the floor at any moment. Trapped, and bored, unable to escape.

The door slip open. The woman came out with a white plastic box cradled under her arm. It must have been designed for transport, because it was the same size as the others but didn't look as heavy.

She set the box on her desk. 'I need your credit account,' she said as she slipped back into her chair.

John frowned. 'What for?'

'Storage fees. There wasn't enough money in the estate to cover four and a half years. If you want the box, you need to pay.' Her voice was flat. She didn't seem to care that she was giving him all that remained of a friend, someone with whom he had lived through one of the greatest traumas of his life. Perhaps she saw this too much.

Or perhaps her life had been easy, untouched by pain and death.

He hoped that were true, although he doubted it. He doubted anyone made it to age twenty without a lot of anguish.

He rattled off the account numbers and took the box. It was heavier than he expected. He held it gingerly, unlike the way she had done, and then got back into the lift.

His hands were shaking. He felt as if he were cradling Max's body. The thump of the machines sounded like the beat of his heart. The lift was too hot. Sweat ran down the side of his face and pooled in large drops under his chin.

He got off on his floor and hurried to his room. He was thankful that, although the room was small and cheap, it was not white. He had requested something beige, and received a room done mostly in tans. The jar was not glowing when he entered. It sat in the corner, looking like a food jar filled with some unidentified liquid.

He crossed to the bed and sat down, placing the box carefully beside him. He was breathing shallowly as he pulled back the lid. Three hardcopy letters, one in an old-fashioned envelope, several pieces of jewellery, mostly silver, mostly rings, and a shirt made of Lucian silk.

Two of the letters were from Verity. They had arrived e-mail over a decade before. The first was short.

Been dreaming about Bountiful. Scary things. The base psycho thinks they're repressed memory and I should check it out with someone else who was there. The only one I can find is you. It may hurt, Max, but the psycho thinks it will help both of us. Want to try?

There was no evidence of Max's reply, nor any indication which base the note was sent from. The second one was longer; it came from Orda Base.

I know you got my first letter. Systems here confirmed it. Please answer, Max. Please. I need help and you're the only one. I found Skye. She's dead. Everyone else has disappeared. Maybe we're crazy, but wouldn't it be nice to know we're crazy together?

I dream about Dancer rituals. Not the one that got us in trouble, but other ones. Sometimes I think if I try, I can see beyond myself. I hear Allen in my dreams. He doesn't cry any more.

Is that crazy, Max? Is it? Do you hear him too?

John shivered. He set the notes aside. He would check the mail records, see if any other letters were sent.

At least Verity had been alive. Ten years ago.

323

But then, so had Max.

On the envelope in cursive, someone had written 'Verity'. John debated leaving the envelope sealed. But he couldn't. Max had kept hard-copies because he knew that after his death his personal files would be destroyed. John had to know why Max thought all these letters were so important to keep.

Inside was a piece of thin paper. Hard copy readout of an e-mail letter.

Verity:
I send this to you and hope that you understand when you get it why I waited all these years. Your letters scared me. I had buried it all. People here thought I was a normal guy. I didn't really have friends, but people talked to me. No one knew that I had been to Reed, no one knew about Bountiful, and I wanted to keep it that way.

I didn't dream until your letters. I rarely slept at all. Now I dream all the time. I don't hear Allen. I hear Beth. She calls me from far away. She tells me I will feel better if I go full Dancer. She holds up a knife, covered with blood.

I hate the dreams. I have lost focus. My supervisor tells me I need to shape up, that my work is slipping. They send me to the autodoc every day to repair my mouth. I bite my lips again. I haven't done that since Lina Base.

I feel so useless now. Nothing I do will ever be right. I will slip, like I have now, to that dark place inside, with Beth, where she holds a knife.

We all have blood on our hands. Blood that light can purify.

I have put everything in order. It waits for you.

Max didn't sign the note. John's eyes blurred. Something had happened to them. To all four of them, from Allen on. They had found something, seen something, that he hadn't. He had been their leader and, in the end, they had failed to include him.

Hey, you guys. Wait up. Please. I want to play. Please. Can I play?

Michael Dengler. He hadn't thought of Michael Dengler as a child, an alive child, in years. Beth had begged that they include Michael.

He's so lonely, she said. *We have each other, but he has no one.*

Katie doesn't want him.

Katie's embarrassed because her parents broke the rules. If we let

Michael come, Katie won't care. Besides she's not here right now —

She's dead. They were all dead. Sometimes he thought *he* was dead. He probably should turn his attention away from this strange pursuit and find a way to escape the sector. Change his face, change his identity. Go back to old Earth or somewhere that they had never heard of him, so that they wouldn't kill him for murders that he – for once – didn't commit.

But he couldn't. Somehow the genie's words had bound him. He had to finish this task first. He had to put it all to rest.

Then he could move forward, into his future.

I have put everything in order. It waits for you.

There was something in the box beside the rings and letters. John pulled out the shirt. It was expensive, but an odd thing to keep. Beneath it was another hand-written note. *Save the shirt for my friends.*

As if he had known he was going to die.

John patted the shirt and found, inside the breast pocket, a small jar. A vial really, barely the size of his forefinger. The vial was made of glass.

His mouth was dry. He set the vial down on the silken shirt, and waited.

It took only a moment before the vial flooded the room with a blinding silver light.

Justin Schafer

It had taken him two days to get the officials on Minar Base to allow Latona Etanl to travel. Lina Base was too close to Bountiful, and the officials didn't want Latona to have any contact with the Dancers.

She might have been released from prison, but she had never been set free. The court had placed dozens of restrictions on her, even after she had been released.

The largest was the gag order. He had finally got that rescinded.

He expected to see the slender, attractive woman with hair that shrouded her like a scarf, the self-assured woman who had saved his life. When the officials showed him Latona Etanl on the security screen, getting off her shuttle on Lina Base, he almost told them they had the wrong woman. Then she glanced at the camera. Her dark, dark eyes were the same shape, but the pain in them was something new.

Because the release of the gag order was so new, the officials wanted to monitor the conversation. Justin was certain they wanted to learn everything he did about the Dancers.

They set up his meeting in a government place, near the cells in the wing where the children had been imprisoned.

He had to go through double security doors. He was warned that his entire conversation would be observed, and that several different cordings would be made. He didn't care. All that mattered to him was that he meet Latona in a neutral place, so that she wouldn't feel as if her tiny personal place had been violated.

The meeting room was small, half the size of his living room, with a regulation table and unbreakable plastic chairs bolted to the floor. Nothing sharp, nothing hard, nothing that could be used as a weapon.

And surveillance equipment everywhere.

The hair rose on the back of Justin's neck as he paced inside. White walls, no windows. Just like Bountiful.

He wondered if she would even notice.

The door slid back and Latona entered. She hunched, as if her back pained her, and her skin had gone from sun-black to a light brown. Her lovely black hair was gone. Her head had been shaved, and the bristles poking through the top were gray. She wore a white canvas jumpsuit, the cheapest clothing available. It suited her employment on Minar Base as a food supervisor.

All that talent wasted.

The door slid closed. Justin and Latona stared at each other from across the table. For the first time since the fire, he was conscious that his face hadn't changed. She had aged, but he had gained youth from the tragedy.

'I'm sorry I couldn't testify for you,' he said. 'I tried to, after I regained consciousness, after I found out. But they wouldn't take the evidence, said I wasn't impartial — '

She waved a hand, the movement fluid and dismissive. 'They needed scapegoats.' Her voice had lost its power. She spoke now in a husky near-whisper. 'I introduced the children to the Dancers, so obviously I was at fault.' She gave a small bitter laugh. 'Everyone ignored the parental involvement. Netta, Tanner and I took the blame for everything.'

'Like the children.'

'Yes,' she said. She pulled on the top of the chair nearest her. It swivelled and she sat. 'Like the children.'

Justin couldn't sit. He could barely breathe. Something in the back of his brain was trying to convince him that Latona was dead, and what he saw before him was an empty shell that had been kept alive by the vagaries of the state.

She sat with her head bowed, her hands clasped in her lap. Eighteen years of silence. Eighteen years when she could not speak to anyone about her life before imprisonment. Eighteen years when the word Dancer could not be spoken around her. Her access to the net was restricted, and her conversations monitored. She had spent thirteen of those years in prison as an accessory to murder, and the remaining five in food service on Minar Base, living her reduced life in a small apartment with no friends and no hobbies. He hadn't even thought, when he worked for the children's release, to work for hers as well.

He had taken her life too. She had helped him so readily, and he had repaid her by taking away her work, her passion, and her freedom.

'Were you able to read the materials I sent you?'

'And watch the vids.' She raised her head. Her jaw worked for a moment, as if she couldn't quite bring herself to ask the next question. 'Was there – did you? – was there no work on the Dancers since the trial?'

He didn't have to ask which trial. Instant experts had spent a great deal of time on the Dancers at her trial, trying to disprove all of her theories. Ultimately, the decision had been an emotional one: because the children had used a Dancer ritual on each other, she had been at fault for allowing the Dancers to influence them.

'No work has been done at all,' he said. 'Bountiful has been closed since we left.' He didn't tell her he had just been there. He didn't want her to know about the decay – about the scattered papers still on her desk in the Extra Species Alliance office, about the brown plants in vases on end tables, the sand scarves still hanging in the closet. He had spent the better part of an afternoon there, surveying the wreckage.

She let out a small sigh and looked down at her hands again. 'The deaths,' she said, 'the new ones? Those aren't Dancer. He had to have learned that somewhere else and even then . . .'

Her voice trailed off.

'Even then?' Justin prompted.

She shook her head, a slight, hidden smile on her lips. Her gaze remained on her lap. 'I was going to say that John would never do that. But that John – the one I remember – he's not a little boy any more, is he?'

'No,' Justin said. 'He's not.'

'I think about them sometimes. They were really happy that day, like I was giving them a treat beyond price.' That little laugh again. 'If only we had known. If only I had known.' She looked up at him then, and finally he saw her, in the spark behind her eyes. Just a hint of passion. Enough to know that some of her survived.

He wasn't sure if he was comforted by the thought or not.

'Amazing,' she said, 'how one choice can change everything so thoroughly.'

331

He wasn't going to get involved in what-ifs. He had promised himself that before he saw her. 'The vids,' he said, prompting her.

'The holos of the children were fascinating.' She rubbed her fingers along the edge of the table, as if she were cleaning it. 'The first was a greeting ritual. They spoke Dancer and talked about love. And it wasn't until Dusty said, in Dancer, that the people on the base wanted the chldren to believe they were evil that everything went wrong. Allen said they were evil. But then, the words everyone seems to ignore were John's: He said, "Maybe if we had had more time." Time with the children? Time alone? It's not clear. They haunt me, those words.'

She glanced at Justin briefly then, like a child seeing if an adult were paying attention. Her fingers kept rubbing the table edge.

'They were doing nothing wrong. Everything they said flowed from the greeting ritual. Perhaps if the guards had let it continue, everything would have been all right.' She sighed. 'Perhaps.'

Justin nodded. He finally sat across from her. It was obvious she wasn't used to speaking to anyone. Her discourse was disjointed, and had little regard for her audience. Her tone was flat, as if the subject did not excite her. But those glimpses at her eyes – those belied her effect.

'It is the second holo that makes no sense,' she said. 'After Allen says he thinks he will die, they speak in fragments, as if another conversation is going on that only they can hear. It is – eerie – given Allen's death.'

'Do Dancers die that way?' Justin asked.

Her fingers stopped their rubbing. She shook her head. 'Dancers kill the old members when the members decide, then stretch the skin and reuse the parts. Dancers believe in usefulness and practicality above all else. But something is missing.'

She spoke that last softly as if it were to herself instead of to him.

'What is missing?' Justin asked. He leaned forward, then hesitated when he saw her shoulders hunch up as though she expected him to hurt her. Gradually he leaned back.

'Sometimes when I would move from one group of Dancers to another, it was as if they knew I was going to do that, as if someone had sent a message ahead. Or like — ' she glanced at him, shy girl, under her lashes ' — that afternoon, with the fire. They all ran. Why would they all run? And how would they understand the threat? And why would they save the children?'

'I don't know,' Justin said.

'I kept thinking reaction to fire had to be instinctual, but I don't think so. There has never been that kind of fire in recorded history on Bountiful. And we threatened them. *You* threatened them.' That look again. 'And they understood. Understanding of that nature takes past experience. It takes a knowledge of the past and an ability to combine it with the present to look toward the future.'

'But you said the Dancers had no understanding of the past.'

'I know.' Her words were quiet. 'But I had eighteen years to think about it.' With her right hand, she adjusted the leg of her jumpsuit, then picked off imaginary lint. 'Something else happened. Something that I don't understand. And then Allen's death . . .'

She looked up, but her gaze saw past him, as if she were accessing a memory. 'In the Dancer tents are the little jars, remember?'

Justin nodded. The jars were crude, and she had said they had been made by the miners.

'The jars always had a faint glow, but sometimes that glow was silver and bright. When I brought the children the first time, the entire area flooded with light. Silver light.'

Justin sat up straight. 'Did a Dancer die?'

Latona shook her head. 'They all gathered in the light and sat in a semi-circle around the children. The light whirled and spun and heated the entire glade. It was the scariest thing I ever saw.' She laughed a little. 'At least, then it was.'

Justin frowned. He was trying to make sense of this. 'You're saying that silver light was connected with the Dancers?'

'What else would it be?' Latona asked. 'Silver lights like that usually don't emanate from humans.'

'Unless they're influenced,' Justin whispered. Finally. Almost twenty years too late, someone who would admit that the Dancers had influenced the children. But she had been in prison so long, he doubted anyone would listen to her. They hadn't listened to her twenty years before either. But she had been fighting for herself. The issue no longer was whether or not she caused the influence. The issue was whether the influence had occurred.

He looked up to find her staring at him. The passion was back in her eyes; the Latona he had known filling her face. Her cheeks were flushed, and it took him a moment to realize she was angry.

'I spent thirteen years in hard labour for doing something that is considered normal by the Extra Species Alliance. Taking children to meet the natives is a normal thing, a thing that is supposed to have the children learn tolerance. I used to tell myself that the conviction was okay; that you and I managed to save the Dancers so that made everything all right. But it is hard to live on altruism, Dr Schafer. I looked at everything you sent because you asked me to, and because I was curious about the information they denied me. But I will not work to clear someone else's name without clearing my own.'

The force of her anger hit him like a blow. He leaned back to get away from the energy she projected toward him. He took a deep breath and called on his training before he responded. 'Don't you think that clearing the children would clear you?'

'Not if they were influenced, Dr Schafer,' she said. 'Proving that would make any appeal I had impossible to win.' She stood up. He could almost see her long hair swirling around her.

'I have a suspicion that the rushed trials and the subsequent cover-ups were done by the government because they wanted to protect the Salt Juice trade.' Justin's words halted her. She towered over him, motionless, almost breathless, as if she waited to hear what he had to say. 'I think they knew, even that early, that Salt Juice had harmful effects and were covering it up. If I can prove that they were, would you help me then?'

Something passed across her features, a brightness, rather like hope. But almost as quickly as it appeared, it vanished. She pursed her lips, then spat out. 'I have told you everything I can. Get someone else to investigate the light.'

She turned her back on Justin as she took measured steps toward the door. A silent, hunched figure, a woman with a broken life, another person who would never forgive him. He wished he could explain that this time he was trying to do the right thing, but he doubted that would matter to her. He had done the right thing before, with her help, and destroyed her

334

life.

She was just beginning to rebuild.

She was obviously afraid he would destroy her again.

John

The psychologist who had treated Verity had moved from Orda Base to a new colony founded on Orda. The colony, called Riordan after one of its founders, was the first of its type. Most of the colonies to this point had been built around a natural resource, allowing the colonists to mine, manufacture or sell that resource. Riordan, on the other hand, was built around a manufacturing plant that imported most of its materials. The idea was that these would be the colonies of the future, tiny city states on the feudal model: the colonists would receive a high standard of living in return for a lifetime of service.

Riordan had existed for ten years now, and apparently the social services had moved in.

John had got clearance from flight control for landing, and had been surprised to receive a number. Shuttles landing near colonies usually were the only ones arriving. But the shuttle bays just outside Riordan were as busy as the bays on a base. John had landed and spent half an hour negotiating a docking permit before he was even allowed into the colony.

Riordan was like a place he had never seen. It made Bountiful look primitive. The colony stood in the open – Orda being one of the handful of planets in the sector that could sustain human life. Riordan covered an isthmus surrounded by three lakes. The city itself was built on several levels, with sky ways and underground wall.ways as accessible as the roads above ground. The decorations were metal and wood; no plants softened the appearances, and nothing resembled old Earth. Riordan was a city of the future and it looked like one.

John had an appointment to meet the psychologist at his office. He had been easy to trace because he had been the only psychologist on Orda Base at the time of Verity's letters. Of Verity, John found no reference at all. He went through all the public files he could think of pertaining to Orda, and she existed

339

on none of them.

He hoped the psychologist could help him.

The psychologist's office was on the top of a slender, spiral shaped building, with plastic windows and views of the skyways. The building had doors on all floors, with access from the skyways. John entered on the tenth floor, and opened the door to the psychologist's wing.

The reception area had been decorated in gray and blue, with a mural on the wall that gave an artist's fanciful representation of the skyways. The chairs matched the artwork – twisted, uncomfortable things that looked as if they should be floating instead of being sat on. There was no reception desk, no way to contact the doctor.

John jumped when a door panel he hadn't seen slid open. A short, dark-skinned man with auburn hair stood in the doorway. He wore a long white robe, in the fashion of other Riordans, and he smiled when he saw John.

'I'm Claude Larousse,' the man said. 'You must be Sean.'

John nodded.

Larousse clasped his hands behind his back. 'Please come into my office.'

John followed Larousse through the doorway and tried not to jump again as the door slid closed. The office was dark with curtained windows and heavy wood panelling. No artwork on the walls, and the desk, chairs, and couch were conventional except for their thick cushions.

Larousse sat in an easy chair next to the couch. John ignored the couch and sat in the chair across from Larousse.

'You are, I would guess, one of the Dancer Eight,' Larousse said.

A flush flooded through John's face before he could stop it. He had never been discovered so easily or so quickly.

'Young John, one of the leaders.' Larousse smiled. 'Don't worry. Everything said in this room is confidential. I would simply assume that no one else would be interested in Verity.'

John swallowed, feeling the heat on his face fade. 'Why would you assume that?'

'Her family abandoned her when the murders were discovered. She had kept in touch with one of her friends from Bountiful. They had met on Orda Base after they left Reed. The

340

friend had just died when Verity came to me. Verity had had to put the estate in order. I know of no one else in her life. She made no other friends on Reed, or on Orda Base. That, and the nightmares, were the reasons she first came to see me.'

John frowned. He wondered who Verity had kept in touch with. He would find out in a moment. He had another matter to clear up first. 'I thought you told me everything said would be confidential.'

Larousse shrugged. 'When a patient dies, it is up to me to determine what information would be useful to the survivors. After all, nothing but information lives after us. And if that information dies as well, the individual being is gone forever.'

Gone forever. John stood. He walked over to the curtained windows and peeked through the gauze. People walked along the skyways, talking and laughing. He had never had such ease with anyone. Except as a boy. Except with the children who were gone now.

Verity was dead. She had always seemed so alive to him, with her flaming red hair, as if the colour of her hair was indicative of a fire inside her soul. Then her letters, so plaintive: *I hear Allen in my dreams. He doesn't cry any more. Is that crazy, Max? Is it? Do you hear him too?*

Everyone else has disappeared.

He shivered. They all disappeared. Died. Without him. Was that crazy? Or sane? What kind of life did he have anyway? He was following a trail that was meaningless, refusing to protect himself from a crime he did not commit. Wasn't that, in itself, a kind of suicide?

'You didn't know.' Larousse's voice was soft.

John turned. He crossed his arms over his chest. His heart ached, but he had no tears. In the last few days, he had learned of the deaths of three friends and he had not cried at all. 'What happened?'

'I was hoping perhaps you could explain it to me,' Larousse said. He extended a hand. 'Please. Sit down.'

John made his way back to the furniture grouping. Leaving the window felt as if he were leaving a kind of security. He sat on the edge of his chair, his arms still crossed.

Larousse studied John's posture for a moment, then leaned back, the picture of relaxation. 'Do you know anything about me?' Larousse asked.

John shook his head.

'I am considered a maverick in my profession. I have a theory that the human mind assimilates and adapts, instead of being a predictable, stable machine. Children are the best test cases of this. Children raised in other cultures become part of that culture. Children raised near aliens adopt the behaviour of aliens. Sometimes these children can be humanized. And sometimes they can't.'

'So you took on Verity because she fit into your specialty,' John said. He couldn't keep the sarcasm out of his voice. He was sick of experiments. Sick of the pain they brought.

'No,' Larousse said. 'She was the one who started this diversion for me. She came to me because she could not be intimate with anyone. Closeness for her, I later learned, had an unspoken component, as if the other person could understand her thoughts. She often got angry at me for failing to know what she was thinking.'

Maybe we're crazy, but wouldn't it be nice to know we're crazy together?

John let out a deep sigh. He had never thought of it. He had never let himself think of it. That instant communication. That in-the-head Dancer speak. That in-depth knowledge of another person, so true that you almost knew what the person would do before she did it. He hadn't had that since Bountiful either.

The ache in his chest grew worse.

'Then the nightmares started.' Larousse's voice was soft, soothing. 'At first, she wouldn't tell me about them. But when she did, she told me her history, and I looked up the Dancer Eight, and found the question that no one had asked.'

John looked up, suddenly alert. Larousse's brown eyes were focused on each of John's movements. Larousse's features were softened with a compassion that seemed natural. John made a quick reach inside, and found no barriers. The words Larousse spoke were the words he thought.

'I thought: these children were not raised by Dancers. They were raised by human beings. Yet the children chose a ritual that made them instant adults. Gave them freedom, autonomy, and strength. What would make children from good homes, children raised with all their material needs, take such drastic action?'

A flash of memory ran through John's mind: Coming home to darkness, and the scent of Salt Juice. With that smell came fear.

'Verity and I started looking through her memories, using the nightmares as guides.' He shook his head, finally breaking his gaze away from John's. 'I later read about prisoners of war – almost any war would do – concentration camp survivors, stories of torture and brutality, and realized that I made the biggest mistake of my career with Verity. When she told me the truth through her dreams, I didn't believe her.'

John almost doubled over. He felt separated from himself, as if he were floating above the conversation, observing it.

Larousse hadn't changed his posture, but his cheeks flushed as he spoke. 'I think, perhaps, if I had believed, she would still be here.'

'What happened?' John whispered.

'She killed herself. Some strange way that no one completely understands. Somehow —

'Her eyes were missing.'

All the colour fled Larousse's face. 'How did you know?'

'Because Allen died that way. And Max, and probably Skye. I'm beginning to become afraid that I'm the only one left. That maybe they knew a secret that I didn't — ' John stopped himself. He hadn't expected to say so much, but Larousse's compassion warmed him. John glanced up, feeling like a little boy who had confessed to breaking a favourite toy.

'They died that way?' Larousse let out a small sigh. 'They all died that way?'

'She said she was useless, didn't she?'

'Many times,' Larousse said. 'Is there some kind of pattern here I should know? Some Dancer thing that I am missing?'

John shook his head. The ache in his heart threatened to overwhelm him. He swallowed, hard, to keep the ache down. 'I don't remember.'

Dancers, sitting before silver light.

Such pain. Such deep pain.

Larousse frowned. 'There's something there. We could work on it, you and I — '

'No!' John stood. He had to get out now. He didn't want any doors opened. He didn't want to know anything buried inside. If he did, he would go crazy.

343

Wouldn't it be nice to know we're crazy together?

'Wait,' Larousse said. 'You came for information. Sometimes I get overzealous. I'm sorry.'

John stood very still, watching Larousse. Larousse eased out of the chair cautiously, as if afraid sudden movements would startle John.

'The day before she died,' Larousse said, 'Verity gave me something. I think you should have it.'

He went over to the cabinet behind his desk and took down a jar. John recognized it. A Dancer jar, filled with bubbles and imperfections, made from white sand and blown glass. The insides were black.

Larousse held it out, but John didn't touch it. He wasn't ready to see the silver light yet. He had questions first. But he wasn't sure what they were.

'It's yours if you want it,' Larousse said. 'She said it came from her friend's estate. The gift reminds me of Verity, but it would seem that since it comes from a friend from Bountiful, it might mean more to you.'

John bit his lower lip, then quit, thinking of Max's scabbed lips and bloody chin. Max. A friend's estate. Not Max. Not Skye. John frowned. 'Verity gave you that *before* she died?'

Larousse nodded.

John could barely breathe. Perhaps Larousse was remembering wrong. 'Did they find one after?'

Larousse brought his arms down, and cradled the jar instead. 'What do you mean?'

'Among Verity's effects, was there another jar?'

'I don't know,' Larousse said. 'All I know is that she came in here the day before they found her. She handed me this jar, and told me that it was precious to her. When I tried to give it back, she shook her head, and said, no, that it belonged on my shelf. When I asked her to explain, she said I would understand in the morning.' He sighed. 'She showed no classic signs of suicidal ideation. Her energy level had not risen. She didn't have the desire to put her affairs in order. I wouldn't even have called her depressed, not really. More isolated, but I thought that was changing. She had said she was hearing from friends — '

'Who?' John asked.

Larousse shook his head. 'Old friends, she said. And that was all.'

I hear Allen in my dreams. He doesn't cry any more.

'This jar bothers you,' Larousse said.

John nodded. He licked his lips. Perhaps it only appeared full. Perhaps it was empty. Perhaps Verity had thought that, by giving it to Larousse, she wouldn't transform.

With a shaking hand, John reached out and touched the jar. The jar pulsed once, then silver light enveloped him. It didn't touch Larousse, although he continued to hold the jar. He squealed in fright, but didn't drop it.

John took his hand away.

The light faded, but didn't disappear.

'What is it?' Larousse asked, his voice filled with awe.

'It's Pearl,' John said, and closed his eyes.

Anita Miles

She dreamed she was on Bountiful again. The scent of roses overwhelmed her, filled her nostrils and made her want to sneeze. Beneath that smell was something else, the sharp, acrid odour of decay. She was lying in the park outside the cold sleep chambers, hiding from her friends. The other children her age frightened her; they were so intense. They studied and listened to everything their parents said, and they knew they would never leave Bountiful. They would grow up and work in the Salt Juice plant, like their parents and grandparents before them.

She would escape. She knew she would.

They made a mistake mixing the air. It was filtering wrong. The dome was sepia and she imagined the air to be the same colour. Thick and soupy and hard to breathe.

A Dancer stood over her. Thin, graceful, it chittered as it reached for her.

She screamed —

— and sat up in her own bed, her hands shaking. The lights had come up at the sound of her voice, something she had programmed years before when the nightmares plagued her, and she was childishly grateful. She drew her knees up to her chest and hugged herself. The newly remodelled suite, in its pinks, blues, yellows and greens, did little to cheer her. Only the fresh air was a relief.

She never had to smell the scents of Salt Juice and roses again.

She grabbed her satin wrap off the stand beside the bed, and got up. The thick pink and yellow carpet caressed her feet as the satin caressed her skin.

She was on Rotan Base.

Bountiful was far away.

But not really. It followed her everywhere. First that simple-minded slut at the hotel and now the murderous bounty hunter. Taking away her treasures, her reasons for being.

349

She ordered a sleeping mixture from her servo unit, wincing as she did. Her mother had used Salt Juice to help her sleep. But the sleeping mixtures made on Rotan were supposed to be harmless, with no side effects.

Like they once thought Salt Juice was.

She pushed the thought away as the unit slid a steaming cup that smelled faintly of mint on to its tiny tray. She took the foaming concoction and cupped it in her hands.

She was dreaming about Bountiful because of John. Because the bumbling hunters that she paid every week couldn't find him. The ship seemed to have vanished. There were no remains of it on Bodean, and no one had records of it landing elsewhere. His i.d. numbers weren't being used, and the credits she had placed in his account went untouched.

He had disappeared.

She needed to find him. She hated Dancers in her dreams. They scared her more than anything else. Ever since that night she had first seen them, when they touched her with their melted plastic hands. That night she had stumbled on them, alone and unprotected, on the edge of the canopied forest. The night that no human had heard her scream.

She gulped the sleeping mixture so fast that it burned the back of her throat. She set the dirty cup back on the servo unit until morning, then she staggered back to bed, huddling against the pillows while she waited for the mixture to take effect.

The memories rose: She had found them, sitting in a circle, weird silver light surrounding them, ghostly Dancers flying above them. An old Dancer sat in the middle. They were calling him Useless and she felt more than heard his resignation. He was going to become one of the ghostly ones, so that he could advise the others. She crouched behind a canopied tree and watched his body flatten as his soul flew from it. The other ghostly Dancers grabbed his soul and shoved it in one of the jars, trapping him, and she couldn't stop herself. She screamed . . .

. . . and they had found her, calling her Useless, placing her in the centre. The ghostly Dancers said they needed human knowledge and she kept screaming that she had none. But it wasn't until she broke down into huge gasping sobs, gulping out that she wanted to live, that she wanted a life, that they backed away from her. As they consulted among themselves, she had fled.

She made herself take a deep breath, reminding herself that she hadn't been to Bountiful in decades. But Bountiful – and the Dancers – had been with her all along.

Without the potions and the dream depressors, she wouldn't make another day. She would go as crazy as John, living in Bountiful forever – at least in her mind.

John

He ignored Larousse's questions and hurried to his shuttle, the jar cradled under his arm. He still had time on his permit; nothing said he had to stay outside the shuttle. There, in the tiny lounge, he folded back the seats and set the jar on the carpeted floor. Then he took out the other two jars and placed them beside the first.

He set them in a semi-circle because he knew that was right.

Then he turned out the lights.

For a moment, the shuttle was dark. Then a silver glow began in the jars nearest John. The third jar glowed and the lights travelled back and forth, growing with each movement. He knew them. He knew them like he knew himself.

Only he hadn't let himself experience it until he saw Larousse.

Skye.

Max.

Pearl.

He couldn't believe she was dead. He had asked Larousse what he knew, and he said that Verity finally admitted Pearl had killed herself. Verity had found the body. They had been sharing an apartment on Orda Base.

Pearl.

Max.

Skye.

They appeared before him, gray ghosts he barely recognized. Pearl's white-blonde hair looked yellow, her face pock-marked and scarred, her body long and thin and adult. Max was balding and had a paunch. Only the scabbed lips and the frightened features looked the same. And Skye, Skye had got smaller. Yet she was as he remembered her: her too-thin body at the very edge of childhood.

They touched his face, Dancer-like, but he felt only warmth. No fingers, no cinnamon smell. No real touch. He leaned into the fingers, wishing it could be different, wishing he could really touch them. They whispered his name as they floated by, and he knew that if he just reached, from somewhere inside himself, he could join them.

Skye settled in front of him. – No, she said in Dancer. – You must stay. You're not Useless.

– I have nothing. He was surprised that, even in Dancer churs, his voice could whine. – No one. When the authorities catch me this time, they will kill me or send me to Reed. It is the same as dying.

– We are not dead, Max said. He hovered behind Skye, hesitant even in death. – We are waiting.

For what? John couldn't bear to speak any more. He had to send his thoughts, try for the intimacy he had longed for.

Verity, Dusty and Beth are on Orda Base. Skye was inside his head, as she had been the last time he saw her. He could feel her, strong and secure, with no fear. He reached out, and his fingers slid through her gray form. She floated away from him, as if his touch hurt. *When you get them, we need to go to Lina Base, to the observation room.*

Where Allen died. Pearl's presence had pain with it, and years of living that had moulded her. He barely recognized her. He wondered if she recognized him.

You are not the same, she sent in response. *You have buried your Dancer. Once you were more Dancer than any of us. If you hadn't found them in Bountiful, you might have no Dancer at all.*

You must stay, Skye sent him. *You cannot follow us. We need you. They took us away from each other. And only you can put us back.*

– *Orda Base,* Max said.

Then Lina Base, Pearl sent.

And then, Skye's presence had such warmth, such enthusiasm, *And then, Jonny, we can go home.*

They faded away as if they had never been, leaving him in the darkness. He put his head in his hands, and the memory rose, of a gray Dancer, floating above him, probing him.

Such pain. Such deep pain.

His hands had been bound and he had felt no fear. But the rest of the memory wouldn't come to him. He was missing something important from it: an intent of some kind. She had given him water and the genie had saved him.

From what?
For this?
He couldn't touch them.
He was still alone.

Justin Schafer

Justin spent the next two days in his rooms, seeing no one, and monitoring the nets for news. He kept the lights low and stared out the portals into space, wondering where John was, and if he was afraid. The rooms were cool, but Justin did not turn up the heat. He wrapped himself in a satin blanket and moved only to get meals.

Latona's words haunted him. *I had eighteen years to think about it.* Over the years, she had thought, revised and changed her mind. He had given the same lectures over again, all the while searching for information, and telling himself he understood.

The children had seen a ceremony in which the Dancers were surrounded by jars and silver light. John shouting no as Allen's silver light faded. Allen died without eyes, and so did several of the others. Did that mean they had glowed silver as well? If so, what did it mean?

Latona had no answers, and she was an expert. He had sent a transcript of the meeting to Daniel, and had received a curt response back. *Latona was and is the expert. I gained all my knowledge from her. If she doesn't know, no one does.*

Justin didn't believe that. John knew. Maybe some of the former colonists did as well. No one had ever thought to ask how many groups of children the Extra Species Alliance had taken to see the Dancers over the decades. Was this group the first?

Perhaps the answer would be in the transcript to Latona's trial.

He sighed and tilted his head back, the blanket making a whispery sound as it rubbed against itself. Knowing the answer was moot, of course, if no one ever found John. He would be accused of a crime and never convicted, an escaped murderer on the loose in the sector.

Justin closed his eyes. He hoped John would never get caught.

361

Then, someday, the books would close on this and it would all end. He smiled a little, not liking the picture of himself that he was gaining. He wanted John to go free, because John's return would cause a reassessment of twenty years of work. Justin was the only person who had gained from the Dancer tragedy. If that tragedy were reassessed, Justin might look like a fool.

He had been a fool after Minar, and it had nearly destroyed him. He didn't want to be destroyed again.

John

Dusty was not, as the ghosts had told him, on Orda Base. She had never been on Orda Base. She had lived on Orda. He had spent several frustrating hours trying to get clearance to land on Orda Base before he realized that he should check to see if she had left. His records search turned up nothing. It wasn't until he misspoke, and forgot to mention the base, that Dusty's records showed up in legal documents from Orda itself.

Her partner was suing the state for her half of their business. Her death, it seemed, let the government take over her share, and the ensuing court action threatened to shut the entire business down. The partner was joined in the suit by three nearby colonies.

Her death. He had stopped work for a while after that, not mourning, really, not even in shock. Somehow he had known she was dead. He had felt, since he found out about Verity, that he was the only one left alive.

Dusty had run a dump and junkyard in the gravel pits equidistant from all three colonies. Orda Base itself used the yard to dump its waste instead of recycling it as the other bases did. The fact that Orda Base was privately owned caused it to follow all sorts of strange practices.

John stopped the search and slept for a few hours on one of the cramped seats, dreaming of the ghosts. He didn't know what else to call them, although they had seemed so real. The fright he hadn't felt when he saw them permeated his dreams, coupled with another voice, the sarcastic whisper of the bodeangenie: *They were wrong, you know. Dusty wasn't on Orda Base. You can't trust them. They were wrong.*

John thrashed on the seat, hitting his arm on the side, knowing it was a dream, but not wanting the dream to end. *You told me to come here*, he said to the genie, who was as invisible as wind. *You said to find them.*

365

I never said you should listen to them, the genie said, and then John popped awake. He was lying with his face pressed against the velour of the seat, his knees bent and shoved into his chest. His dream was right. The genie had not said anything about listening to his old friends. But he had no one else to listen to, and he was tired of listening to himself.

He got up to find that his permit to land on Orda Base had been approved. But he would not be given shuttle storage for twelve hours, which was fine with him.

He wanted to see Dusty's junkyard.

ii

He rented an air car in Riordan, pleased that Orda's ecology allowed for such conveniences. Travelling the distance to Dusty's any other way would have taken days; as it was, it took only a few hours.

The car was programmed to go to any settlement on the planet by the quickest route. So John had merely programmed his destination, watched the monitor show the money being deducted from his credit stash, and leaned back. The car took it from there, zooming over rocky terrain so quickly that John couldn't identify the little green shrubs poking through the cracks.

The farther he got from Riordan the smaller the rocks grew. Finally they turned into small bits of gravel scattered among weeds. This part of Orda had once been mined for its precious metals, but the mines were tapped out quickly. Only the gravel pits remained; small stones and dust were used in a variety of colony projects. The gravel pits covered hundreds of kilometers, and the junkyard was located in the very centre, on top of a site where the miners had once kept their garbage.

John could smell the yard before he could see it, the odours of decay and rotted organic materials permeated the air for nearly an hour before the yard appeared on the monitors. The car asked him if he wanted to bring his material into the yard proper or into the office.

He opted for the office.

The car parked itself on a flat rocky surface, and John got out.

The smell gagged him, and he wondered how anyone could stand being so close. The vista wasn't much better. Gray rock, gray pit walls, and ahead dark mounds of dirt and junk silhouetted against the gray sky.

The tiny building near the car was made of flat gray stones. The door was colonial plastic, but years of exposure had turned its white gray. John was about to knock when the door pulled inward.

A sweet smell John hadn't smelled since Bountiful wafted from inside. Salt Juice. John had to swallow hard to keep the contents of his stomach down.

The man standing in the door had the look of a Salt Juice addict, too thin, hunched, his skin darkened by the strange chemicals. His mouth turned downward as he spoke. 'I been telling you people we can't use the yard until the government comes to some kind of settlement. So go back, and send another petition. I'll be waiting here until something happens.'

'I'm not here to dump garbage or to go into the yard,' John said. 'I'm here about Dusty.'

The man closed the door and stepped outside so that John knew he was not welcome. 'She's the bitch who got us all into this mess. Wouldn't sell me her piece when she thought she was going to move, and then poisoned herself when that judge denied her passage.'

'Passage?' John shoved his hands in his pockets. He didn't want the man to see him shaking.

'Back to where she came from. Where she killed all those people.' The man bounced from foot to foot. In the thin light, his skin was sallow. He'd been on Juice for a long time.

Bountiful. Goosebumps rose on John's flesh. She had tried to go back to Bountiful.

The man squinted at John. 'I thought you were here because of Dusty.'

'I am,' John said. 'I used to know her a long time ago.'

'Then how come you didn't know about her leaving?'

'I just found out about her death,' John said quietly.

The man studied John with such an intensity, John almost took a step back. He remembered that look. With his father, it meant that the mood was about to change, something was about to erupt. Only later John learned that all Salt Juice addicts had

367

the look in one form or another.

'I was wondering,' John said, making sure his voice remained calm, 'if she left a jar. A poorly made jar with bubbles in the glass and some strange material inside that glowed.'

The man's lips were pinched into his face. He crossed his arms over his chest and stuck his chin out. 'I smashed it.'

The breath left John's body. For a moment, he had to struggle to inhale. 'You what?' he finally asked.

'I smashed it. When I found out I had to shut down this operation because of that bitch, I took the damn jar and I smashed it.'

'It's gone?' John repeated. His limbs felt heavy. This was how it had been when he was a child; the world shifting beneath him in the span of a single sentence.

'Yeah, it's gone,' the man said. 'I took the damn thing, threw it against the wall, and it exploded all pretty like. I figured later she probably left the damn thing so it would explode on me when I least expected it. Bright lights all over. Lucky for me that wall is made of rock or I think it might of blown a hole through the entire building.'

And then the light faded, and there was nothing. John wanted to sink to the ground and bury his face in his hands. *We lost her, Bethie. Dusty's gone.* The ghost scattered to the winds.

'What the hell did you want with it, anyway?' the man asked.

'Huh?' John barely heard the words.

'That jar? What'd you want with it?'

Then the anger surged through John like it never had before. He was as tall as this man. He was stronger. He could kill him with his bare hands, a luxury he never had with his own father. He had had to escape that man.

But he couldn't stand the idea of another death laid at his door. He took a step toward the man. 'Do you know who I am?' John asked.

The man shook his head, eyes wide at John's sudden shift in mood.

'I grew up with Dusty. I'm one of the Dancer Eight. And unlike Dusty, I've been back to Bountiful. I know how to use my power. All it takes is a single thought.' He reached out and caressed the man's leathery cheek with his fingers. 'A single thought, and you'd have no face left, no heart, no soul. Like you

368

did to poor Dusty.'

'I didn't do nothing to her,' the man said, backing away. 'Riordan Security, they cleared me. They said I didn't do nothing.'

'And I say you did.' John took another step closer. 'What kind of punishment does a man like you deserve?'

'I don't deserve nothing.' The man collapsed at John's feet, crouching and holding his hands over his head. 'Please. I don't deserve nothing.'

John stopped moving. He felt as if a bucket of ice water had hit him. He had crouched like that in front of his father. He had used the same words his father had used. John hadn't taken power. He had used power in the only way he knew how – the same way it had been used on him. 'I want the jar,' he said.

The man shook his head, keeping his face averted. 'I threw it out. The pieces are out in that junk heap. Long ago. You'd never find it. There isn't enough left.'

There isn't enough left. John took a deep breath. She had been so little and so quiet. The one member of the group he had never really paid much attention to. She had always been there, always helping, never saying anything.

Don't ask her about home, Beth said. *She's got it worse than any of us.*

And she still had. All those years escaping Bountiful and Salt Juice, only to end up with a man like this. 'I'll do everything I can to make sure you lose your lawsuit,' John said. 'You don't deserve anything of Dusty's. Not anything at all.'

iii

That night he flew to Orda Base. They gave him shuttle storage and he used the remaining credits in Sean's account to secure a nice room at the hotel. He had had a long, horrifying week. He deserved the luxury.

He had never stayed in the hotel. He had only heard of it, and had always wondered what it would be like to have all of his needs catered to, to have anything he wanted at any moment.

He had arrived late enough that most of the shops were closed. The bars and restaurants were still open along the strip.

369

Loud laughter and the clanking of glasses poured out of every doorway. The sounds grew quieter as he approached the hotel. When he reached its main doors, he stopped.

The doors were inlaid into wide ivory columns. The columns stretched as far as the eye could see, finally being encompassed by other decks. Carved into the ivory were figurines of humans speaking with aliens – all the sentient, space-faring races were represented. He had rarely seen the travelling aliens. Because of his past, he was always denied contact.

He went inside, and the doors opened automatically, guiding him to the human wing.

The air had a faint scent of sandalwood. He felt out of place here, as he walked its elegant carpeted hallways, looking at the murals depicting the hotel's history on the walls. They would discover that he was nothing more than a convicted felon, a man accused of yet five more crimes. They would know at a glance that he did not belong, that he was roaming in a world built for someone else, for more money that he could even dream.

But they already had his credits, and his shuttle port license. He would have to assume a different identity if he wanted another place to sleep.

As he approached the lobby, the hallway widened. The carpeting turned red, the fake artificial lights were made of gold and glass. The signs near the entrance proclaimed that this wing of the hotel decorated itself according to periods in human colonial history, all designs focusing on Earth. The hotel had just changed its decor from the Mongol period to the late 19th century – a period, judging from the holos, it had explored before. A female voice warned in soft tones that not all hallway programs were active yet, and apologized for the inconvenience.

Inconvenience. Someone should inconvenience him like that more often.

Two heavy mahogany doors stood open, revealing a lobby done in the rich reds of the hallway. The furniture was made of oak with matching red upholstery, and heavy red curtains hung on windows with a view of a fog-enshrouded city street. The walls were covered with flocked paper, and chandeliers hung from the ceiling, with candles producing fake flames. Small gas lights hung from the wall, also complete with fake flames and

370

soot stains above the openings. A fire burned in the grate that served as a focus for one of the furniture groupings, and real bound books stood in shelves on the walls, ready for someone to pluck them down and read.

A large portrait of a man with too-white skin and muttonchop whiskers hung over the fireplace. The portrait was done in an old-fashioned way. John could see the brush strokes on the canvas. Below, a little gold plaque identified the portrait as the owner of the human wing of the hotel, Roddy McNair.

John walked on the oriental rug that led the way to the registration desk. He leaned against the desk, and felt the polished wood against his fingers. A clerk, who wore a dark wool suit and gold wire glasses, stood from a chair in the back.

John introduced himself. The clerk smiled and leafed through a book filled with papers – the hotel's decor was perfect down to the last detail. John suspected that the closed door behind the desk hid the modern equipment that allowed the hotel to run smoothly.

'Ah, yes,' the clerk said. 'They brought your duffel up a few hours before, sir. Your room is ready and the sheets are turned down. Would you need anything else from the lobby?'

John didn't know what else the lobby could provide, and he didn't want to call attention to himself by asking. 'No,' he said. 'Just direct me to my room, and I'll be fine.'

The clerk smiled and handed John a gold key. 'Mr Simms will show you where to go.'

John turned to find a slender man standing behind him, smiling. The man wore a uniform with a high starched collar and a small hat. His grin made John nervous, almost as if the man had known that he snuck up on John.

He led John through a maze of hallways before taking the key from John's hand and using it to open the door. Then he had John press his thumb against the doorjamb before allowing the door to close. 'The key is safer than you'd think, sir,' he said. 'The door's coded to it, staff members, and now you, sir. No one else can get in or out.'

John nodded. He hadn't even thought about accessibility, had never really had enough possessions so that he cared. The only things of value he had now were the jars, and he kept them in the shuttle with the security system at full alert.

He closed the door and turned around. The room smelled of lavender. It had a sitting room suite, done in greens and browns, with the same heavy furniture as the lobby. The entertainment equipment was hidden behind doors in an oak cabinet. The bathroom had gold fixtures and a flush toilet complete with chain, which was just for show. The modern equipment had been given a Victorian air, so that it seemed to fit right in.

He went through the bathroom into the bedroom. The bed stood in the centre of the room, with four posters reaching toward the ceiling and a canopy on top. Big, plush pillows leaned against the wall, and curtains draped along either side. Rockers sat beneath the fake windows, a dresser leaned against one wall, and a wardrobe against another.

He opened the wardrobe to find his clothes hanging inside. The sheet had been turned down on the bed, and a mint sat on the pillow. Lilacs stood in a cut-glass vase on the dresser adding their heady bouquet to the room. He sighed and glanced at himself in the rippled mirror. His hair needed a trim and there were shadows under his eyes, but other than that, he looked fine. He had worried for nothing. He had to remember that confidence helped in the disguises. Confidence was, in fact, the most important thing.

Exhaustion from the day and from his anger overwhelmed him. He pulled off his clothes, set the mint on the nightstand, and crawled between the soft, cool sheets.

iv

He ordered breakfast through the servo unit tucked into a fake radiator in the living room. The meal came, complete with a steaming pot of caffeinated coffee that cleared the cobwebs in his head almost immediately. But the odd feeling he'd had since he lost his temper on Orda remained. It came with a restlessness that haunted him, and made him feel alone.

He finally decided that he wouldn't work that morning. He would explore the shops – and look like a leisurely guest of the hotel. He would do his searching later, when he felt a bit more like himself.

He left the hotel without seeing a soul except for staff

members, and let himself on to the strip.

It was a different place than it had been the night before.

Shoppers covered the streets. Some carried small baskets in their hands, others bags. They chatted and laughed, and spoke to each other as if they were old friends. He stood at the fringes of the crowd for a long time until he realized there were other loners, some walking intently down the walkways in front of the shop windows, others sitting alone on benches in the middle of the thoroughfare. He plunged into the crowd and felt a kind of comfort in it, something he had never felt in a group before. The voices carried over him, protecting him from his own thoughts, the merchandise in the windows gave him something to look at and the vendors on the thoroughfare sent food smells through the air that made his full stomach rumble.

The coffee shops, restaurants and bars, had all put tables on the walk outside. People sat in them, women with their hair down, men wearing hats against a non-existent sun. They laughed and talked and peered at each other in serious conversation as if they were enjoying outdoor air. The fiction seemed part of the posturing that was Orda Base, a place where anything could be had, for a price.

John felt no desire to sit with them. Even the food looked artificial, arranged in delicate swirls on plates with gold trim. The food from the vendor stands was more appealing – thick and juicy and sloppy, it was what unprocessed food should be, like playing in the mud or, John imagined, like sex. Still, he avoided the vending food as much as he avoided the restaurant food. Neither were really for him.

The shop windows showed everything from hair clips to multi-coloured shawls, jewellery for every conceivable appendage and furniture from each period of sector history. Trinkets from various colonies were displayed like lost treasures and, with little thought, John knew he could spend the credits of two of his other identities. He shoved his hands in his pockets and browsed, feeling more curiosity than envy at the eventual owners of these toys.

Finally in a recessed row of stores behind one of the bigger restaurants, he stopped. Glassware and pottery covered the window and through it, he could see a potter's wheel spinning in the back. Tiny sculptures lined the front, delicate things: a cat in mid-pounce, a furry Ayars cradling its young in its wings, and a circle of tiny, thin Dancers waving their hands in greeting. The Dancers took his breath away. He was inside the door before he realized it, his broad shoulders brushing against the shelves filled with fragile cups and bowls.

The potter's wheel stopped its whirring. The store smelled of dust and clay. John had never been in a place like this before. He came from behind the shelves to see the potter, a man with shoulders as wide as John's, a man shrunken, but not bowed by age. His hair was white, his skin darkened by a harsh sun. The man's fingers were gnarled and it looked as if it pained him to move them.

'Those Dancers in the window,' John said, his voice sounding odd, even to himself. 'Who made them?'

'I did.' The old man's voice was warm, his eyes warmer. It was impossible to guess his age. What time had not wrinkled, the sun had.

'You've been to Bountiful, then.'

'Grew up there,' the man said. 'Left a long time ago.' He grabbed the rim of another stool and pushed it forward so John could sit down. 'Your skin is sun-beaten too. More recently, I would guess.'

John touched his face. The burns were gone, the blisters healed. The exposure he had received on Bountiful was alien to him, as if it had happened to someone else. He had forgotten it. He had almost forgotten he had been on Bountiful recently at all. 'I grew up on Bountiful too,' John said.

'Hell of a place for a child.' The old man picked clay off his fingers. His arms were stained to the elbows. 'Trapped inside that dome with those fumes. Always thought I would live outdoors, where the air was clean and no one would bother me. Tried. Got so lonely I thought I would die before I saw another person.'

John almost blurted out his own loneliness, but stopped himself. The old man had been on Bountiful. They shared an experience, nothing more. 'What made you do the Dancers?'

'They were the only thing of beauty I knew from my childhood. That willowy grace. Can't smell cinnamon without thinking of them. Made that sculpture and had nightmares for weeks. Decided not to make any more.' The old man grabbed a wet towel from behind him, and wiped the rest of the clay off his hands. 'Strange history, that piece. Some woman wanted to buy it off me, but I didn't like the look of her – all expertly made up as if she were a work of art – so I told her it wasn't for sale. The next day this girl comes in, all battered and black and blue, acting as if she didn't even know she was injured – I knew right away she worked for the hotel – and I offered it to her at a quarter of its worth. Next thing I know, one of the hotel managers is giving it back to me, tells me to keep the money as a way of forgetting the incident.'

'But you didn't.'

The old man nodded. 'Couldn't. The girl was from Bountiful too. She died alone in her room. She came in here for one of my Dancer jars, and she had that willowy grace I hadn't seen since I was a boy. I gave her the jar and the sculpture.'

John bowed his head. He couldn't escape this quest even when he wanted to. It took several tries before the question came out of his mouth. 'Do you have the jar now?'

'No. They wouldn't give it back to me. Saw it though, and thought she had done something to it to make it more Dancerlike.'

She died, John thought. She died, and filled it with herself.

'But I got another one a few years back. Some poor girl killed herself in one of the apartments on Deck 23, and they were selling off her things. I bought it, and kept it. It's got something that makes it seem almost criminal to sell.'

John sat up straight. 'You have another Dancer jar?'

The old man waved. 'I always have Dancer jars, the ones made by the miners. No. I got one that's got the Dancer influence. In the back. You want to see it?'

John felt numb. His body was like a great protective shell around him. 'If I could.'

'Come with me,' the old man said. 'It's not something I want customers to see.'

He wound his way through half finished pots and broken statues, half curled hands, bent knees and frowning masks. The dust grew thicker toward the back, and John had to be careful not to step on anything as he passed. They went through a small door into an immaculate sitting room. Bits of dust hovered near the door, but the plastic floor was swept clean near the rope furniture. Through an open doorway, John could see a hall that split off into two rooms, a kitchen and a bedroom.

The old man went to a shelf and took the jar off of it. He cradled the jar against his chest and stared at John. 'I dream about it sometimes,' he said. 'A gray girl standing in front of me, half woman, half child, sobbing about the things she lost. She lives in the jar, but when I'm awake, I can't see her.'

His smile was wistful. 'I always think it odd how I see her. She should be Dancer and mysterious and beautiful, not human and fragile and sad.'

'May I touch it?' John asked.

The old man's eyes narrowed as if he were judging John's competence. Then he held out the jar. John took it, expecting it to pulse and fill the room with silver light.

Instead, a voice wailed in his head, and he nearly let go of the jar. The old man caught it by placing his hands over John's, then stared at John in awe.

Jonny. Jonny. Jonny, you came for me. I thought you'd all forgotten me. Even Max forgot me, and I've been so scared. Jonny. They left me all alone here. Don't believe them about the Useless ones. Once you're useless, you're always useless.

'Verity?' John whispered. 'Verity?'

He could half see her above the jar. The little girl he remembered with the flaming red hair, and the fragile, wispy woman he had never known.

Jonny, please, Jonny, let me out. Let me out.

Either the old man saw her or he heard her. His eyes had widened and his body was shaking. John sent to her in Dancer, to keep the response private. *I know where some of the others are. They did what you did. They found jars. They've joined.*

Can you take me there? Please, Jonny. Anywhere but here. I died here. I didn't expect to stay here forever.

I can take you, John sent. *If the old man agrees.*

Then I'm trapped here forever, she sent, and the little gray ghost popped back in the jar.

John and the old man stood there for a moment, their hands clasped over each other, warming each other on the jar.

'What did you do?' the old man asked. His voice sounded rusty as if he had never spoken before.

John closed his eyes against threatening tears. He willed them back. What did he do? He was wrong, from the start. He had thought, as a little boy, that the Dancers were freedom. All they had been were even more elaborate traps. What did he do? Over and over again, he led his friends into a kind of hell no humans should ever experience.

He opened his eyes. The warmth of the old man's hands wouldn't let John slip away inside of himself. 'Sit down,' John said. 'I have a story to tell you.'

Anita Miles

It drove her crazy, this not knowing. Each hour she expected to hear that someone had discovered John's trail, that someone knew where he was. But with her people dying every time they went to Bodean, she couldn't search for clues there, and there was no record of the ship. The governor of Lina Base had contacted her twice, the second time with a veiled threat, as if John's disappearance were Anita's fault. The governor wanted the murders solved, and the fact that the murderer was on the loose reflected poorly on Lina Base and all involved.

If John was not caught soon, the governor implied, Anita's reputation would go down with everyone else's.

She couldn't afford that. Her business was based on reputation. She thought of that each time she walked through the gallery, each time she looked at the treasures she kept in her own private stock. If she didn't have her reputation, she would never have discovered these gems. Without her reputation, her entire world would vanish.

That morning, she sat in her back office, wearing her jeweller's eye, studying a small mummified head that fitted in the palm of her hand. One of her operatives had brought it back from Kirst, one of the oldest penal colonies. If the head belonged to a prisoner, it was worthless, but the evidence showed that it was part of a burial process used by the tiny two-headed natives. Since the natives were now extinct, any relic brought a great price.

She took the eye out and set the head down. She was no expert on mummified remains, and she shouldn't have even pretended to be one. She looked at the handful of items in the storage boxes beside her desk and sighed. Examining them took too much work. She didn't want to work. She wanted to find John. She wanted to have her life in order again.

The door to the back room slid open, and Feodor entered.

'You're not paying attention to your link,' he said.

'Yes, I am,' she said. Her link was the most important thing in her life right now. Through it she would receive word of John.

Feodor shrugged. He pointed to her wrist. The tiny red light, used instead of the conventional voice notification because it was discreet, blinked rapidly. She hadn't noticed. She had been waiting and she hadn't noticed at all.

She was in worse shape than she had thought.

She shut off the light. 'Who is it?'

Since she spoke to the link, it responded verbally. 'A Roddy McNair, Orda Base.'

Anita frowned. Roddy McNair. She knew no one by that name. She was about to dismiss it when she remembered him. The supercilious hotel manager whose testimony exonerated her at the Minaran trial. Through her attorney, she had presented McNair with enough gifts over the years to enable him to buy the human wing of the hotel on Orda Base.

'Full link,' she said. The automated system kicked in. A small holo rose from the link surface on her desk. When she saw the rounded head and the high button collar, she wondered how she had ever forgotten McNair.

His muttonchip whiskers gave his face a florid look. His eyes were beady and too small, and he was too thin. He affected 19th century retro clothing – in fact, she had heard that he had redesigned the entire human wing of the hotel that way – but unlike most retrofreaks, he had an unerring eye for the original.

'Forgive me for cording this message, Ms Miles,' he said, his voice both prim and businesslike. 'But I speak better in a single burst. If you have questions, please let me know and I will be more specific if I can.'

The head turned to face her. It looked remarkably lifelike. She was pleased he had not called her directly. She didn't feel like talking to anyone but Feodor.

'You asked me,' McNair continued, 'to inform you should another "curio" turn up in my vicinity. Amazingly, one has. A young man who checked in last night bought it at one of the shops on the strip. Apparently the owner had been hoarding it. The owner was that odious old man who had refused to sell you the Dancer sculpture. He probably wouldn't have sold you this at any cost. But the young man is different. I checked him out.

He depleted his credit reserves on his trip to Orda Base, and his stay here at the hotel. Obviously he's here for business, but what kind I cannot say. I will make sure that his stay is pleasant and will keep him here for a few extra days. Please let me know when you can arrive, so that I can facilitate the transaction. I hope you're well.'

The image winked out. Anita let out the breath she hadn't even realized she had been holding. This was just the thing to get her mind off of John. She had only seen one Dancer jar with a soul inside. McNair had found it inside his hotel just after the Minaran debacle. She had purchased it at a ridiculously low price from him. Word in collecting circles was that such a jar was as valuable as a trapped bodeangenie and as rare. Collectors did not know that a filled jar contained a soul. They merely knew that the filled jars were different from the miner-made jars, and therefore more rare.

She had kept her jar because it represented her triumph over the place she had escaped. But a second jar. A second jar she could sell and replace some of her costs caused by the problem with John.

'Get in touch with McNair,' she said to Feodor. 'Let him know that I am interested in the curio and that I will be there as soon as I can.'

'What about the search?' Feodor asked.

'I am not conducting it,' she said. 'I am merely supervising it. I can supervise just as well from Orda Base as I can from here.'

Feodor frowned at her, but he left just as she had ordered. She stood and stretched, feeling more alive than she had for days. Even if she never caught John, this curio would represent the pinnacle of her career. Her reputation would remain firm, no matter what happened.

She would go to Orda Base and she would stay in the wretched hotel. And this time, no one would best her – at anything.

Part Seven

John

He didn't want the jar in the room with him. Verity's terrified presence had screamed in his mind all the way back to the hotel. He knew he must have had a strange expression on his face as he crossed through the lobby because more than one person stared at him and the jar cradled in his arms. By the time he got to his room, he was exhausted and emotionally wrung out. He set the jar inside one of the bathroom cabinets, and pushed Verity out of his mind. Then he closed the cabinet door, both bathroom doors, and crawled into bed, pulling the covers over his head.

She had gone crazy. No matter what she had been before she died, all those years in the jar had pushed the essence – the ghost – whatever she had become – over an unseen edge. She alternated between screaming, crying and pleading with him to make her feel better, and he had no idea how that could be accomplished.

So he abandoned her again.

If he were crueller, a different kind of man, he would take her back to the old man in the morning, but he couldn't. He had promised to show her the other jars, and he would. He hoped she would become their problem, then.

It took nearly an hour for the tension to work its way out of his shoulders and back, and another hour before he even felt drowsy. As he was drifting off to sleep the realization finally hit him: the girl who had purchased the Dancer sculpture, the girl who had arrived in the old man's store battered and bruised, the girl who had died alone in her room was the only member of the Eight John hadn't found yet.

Beth.

Beth was dead.

Long dead from the sounds of it. He hadn't pinned the old man down as to time, but the old man had called Beth a girl. If she had lived like the rest of them, if she had truly been battered

and abused, then she wouldn't have looked like a girl for very
long.

He put an arm over his face. Bethie. He still remembered the
feel of her body around his, the tight hugs that she used to give
him, the way her presence crept inside his mind. Somehow he
had hoped that she would have made it through unscathed.

But she hadn't.

He was the only one left – at least, as a living, breathing entity.
He didn't know what the four jars he had collected were, but the
beings inside – Max, Verity, Pearl, and Skye – had evolved into
something different. He felt odd being the only one still alive.
Before, even though he hadn't seen them for years, he knew the
others were still around. He was not alone in his past, or in his
pain. Now he was. He felt as if he had failed in not following
Allen's route on his own.

We should have taken that jar, John.

Beth had bought a jar just before she died.

Beth's jar was missing. The old man had had Verity, not Beth.
John sat up. The hotel had disposed of Beth's possessions.
Perhaps it had a record of what became of her jar.

ii

In the morning, John went to personnel and inquired about
what became of Beth's things. When he gave his name, the
personnel officer sat up a bit straighter and asked him to wait.
After a few minutes, a bellman came into the room, and led John
down a long corridor to a wide, plush office.

The Victorian motif seemed almost a caricature of itself in
here. Furniture crammed every corner. All of the sofas and
chairs had narrow feet and thick, stiff upholstery. The reds were
deep and rich, the woods grainy and highly polished. Books and
vases covered the surfaces, and pipes stood on a pipe stand. The
office smelled of tobacco and liquor, both forbidden substances
that John had brushed with more times than he cared to think
about. Underneath it all was the faintest hint of peppermint.

It took a minute for him to notice the other man in the room.
The man was thin and reedy, but his tailored, period suit made
him blend into the decor. When he turned to face John, John

390

squinted in recognition. He had seen those muttonchop whiskers just recently. In the portrait. The portrait above the fireplace.

This was Roddy McNair, the man who owned this wing of the hotel.

Something odd was happening. A routine inquiry should not bring John to the owner of the hotel.

McNair walked toward John, hand outstretched. 'Welcome to the hotel,' he said. 'I'm Roddy McNair.'

John introduced himself as Sean. He took McNair's hand. The man's skin was soft, his nails buffed and polished until they shone.

McNair took his hand away as soon as politely possible. 'I understand that you were asking about one of our girls. Young Beth. I don't suppose you enjoyed her services. She usually worked with aliens.'

John refused to let the confusion show on his face. He clasped his hands behind his back, trying to cover the urge he had to wipe them off. 'I have never stayed at the hotel before.'

'May I ask the reason for your inquiry then?' McNair asked.

'I knew Beth many years ago,' John said. 'I just discovered that she had died. In her possession at the time, she had a handmade glass jar. I had given it to her, and it had sentimental value. I was wondering what happened to it.'

'Ah.' McNair sat in one of the sofas, took an ivory pipe off the rack and rubbed its stem between his thumb and forefinger. 'When an employee of ours dies, as she did, with years left in her indenture, the hotels sells her belongings to recoup the losses engendered. She died many years ago. I doubt that we would still have records of the sales.'

There was something behind McNair's politeness, something John didn't like. 'I don't mind going through records,' John said. 'I would like to find the jar.'

'As you can well understand,' McNair said, 'hotel records are off limits to all but hotel staff. Still, I will instruct one of my assistants to look through the material from that year and see what can be found. If your jar still exists, I will do my best to locate it.'

'Thank you,' John said. The hair was rising on the back of his neck. He needed to get out of the room.

'Of course, you will remain a guest of the hotel until we locate the information you need.' McNair put the pipe in his mouth and smiled. 'And please, feel free to use any service we may have. All at the hotel's expense.'

John's nervousness was rising. 'You're being very kind.'

'We want our guests to feel special,' McNair said. 'I'm worried about finding this jar of yours. If you stay at the hotel's expense, then I am sure that we will at least satisfy you on that level.'

'I am already satisfied,' John said. 'This is a very nice place.'

'Yes.' McNair bit down on the pipe. 'Yes, it is. Thank you for your patience and willingness to work with us. I'm sure we will have something for you in a day or so.'

John smiled and took his leave. When he got out of the office, he breathed deeply. The scents of tobacco and peppermint were making him dizzy. Something was going wrong here. If the owner of the hotel had to speak to him, then something was off. Perhaps they knew who he was. But if that were the case, all they had to do was arrest him quietly and send him back to Lina Base.

No. Something else was going on. Something connected with Bethie. And he would do his best, with or without Mr McNair, to discover what it was.

Anita Miles

The Victorian decor was stuffy and oppressive, but most of the antiques were real. It must have cost Roddy a fortune to find and ship the furniture to Orda Base. Anita was impressed with the thoroughness and the exactness of detail. Few places in the sector went to this kind of trouble to impress their clientele.

She was impressed, although she felt out of place in her tight dress, made with fibre spun from six precious metals. Her hair had been coloured to match, strand by strand. She had needed the pick-me-up, and brought her stylist with her, to preoccupy her on the trip from Lina Base.

Still, as she waited in the lobby, examining the original editions of Oscar Wilde, Anton Chekov, and Emily Dickinson, she wondered what would ever induce anyone to evoke such a closed and façade ridden period of Western Earth history. When Roddy came out of the back, looking natural in his scratchy wool suit, his starched collar, and his bristly whiskers, she had a glimmer of understanding.

'Anita,' he said, crossing the room in two strides and taking her hand in his damp ones. He smelled of a rich perfume. 'It's been a long time.'

She smiled, and left her hand in his just long enough to be polite. Then she withdrew. 'What can you tell me?'

'I have sent him to our boardroom.' Roddy put his hand on her elbow and guided her toward a corridor. 'I led him to believe that you would provide him with information. You see, ironically enough, he is looking for your jar. He made some sob story about knowing the young girl who owned it.'

Anita stiffened. Very few people had known that girl. 'Do you have surveillance on that room?'

'Anita,' Roddy said, his voice so smooth it dripped from his mouth. 'Your conversation will be very private.'

'Don't lie to me,' she said, no longer caring about his feelings.

'I know you watch everything that goes on in this hotel. I would like to see this man before I meet with him.'

Roddy was a good manager. He slid with his customers' wishes. 'Do you think you know him?'

'It would be better to know before I walked in, don't you agree?' she asked.

Roddy nodded. He veered off in a small side corridor with no decorations on the walls, only small gas lamps. The faint odour of oil filled the hall, and Anita realized that even the lamps were real, as were the flames inside. Quite a risk in a setting like this one. A government-owned base would never have allowed it.

He unlocked a small door in the back of the corridor using voice, retinal scan and fingerprints. As he stepped in, he blocked her view.

'Shut down all but the boardroom,' he said. He was good, and smart. By the time Anita got through the door only one 2-d screen was on. A woman sat in the centre of the screen displays – which could go from 2-d to holo to special cordings with a single command to the computer. She was surrounded by bags of open food, and empty mugs with beverage stains on the bottom. Despite the food and the close quarters, the room had an antiseptic smell. The human monitor was not necessary, but a testament to Roddy's intelligence and paranoia.

Only one screen was on. It showed a room panelled in mahogany, with the rich red rugs that characterized the rest of the Victorian decor. The wing-backed chairs were brown leather, and they surrounded a long mahogany table. A man stood to one side, pouring himself a glass of water from a crystal decanter.

He was tall, dark-haired, and too thin. His movements were graceful. Anita held her breath. She was seeing John everywhere. He had no reason to be here. He was probably hiding on some rock somewhere in the sector, waiting for the commotion to die.

'Focus in on our young friend,' Roddy said.

The computer did as it was told. Suddenly the screen was filled with John's face as he sipped from the glass. He had circles under his eyes, and his skin was darker than she had ever seen it – probably from his days on Bountiful.

Her dress felt heavy and oppressive. She wished for the first time in years that she was wearing light, loose clothing that allowed her freedom of movement. 'He asked about my jar?' She kept her voice calm. She didn't want Roddy to know yet who his guest was.

'Yes. He said young Beth had left personal effects and he was wondering what happened to them. When I told him that they had been sold to fulfill her contract, he wanted to know if one of the items was a jar. I put him off, since I knew you were coming.'

She frowned. There must be something even more special about her jar than she knew. She would have to talk to him. She took a deep breath, and felt a deep surprise. She was looking forward to the encounter.

'Roddy,' she said, using her best master-to-servant voice. 'Do you know who that man is?'

'Certainly,' Roddy said. 'I had him checked thoroughly. His credit is good, although low, and I assume he has come here to make some deals.'

'Your thorough is not good enough,' Anita said. 'Did you hear of the recent murders on Bountiful?'

She felt Roddy stiffen beside her and a faint odour of perspiration mixed with his cologne. 'Are you saying — ?'

'You'd better call base security, and have them bring reinforcements. But they will need to wait until my signal.'

Roddy grabbed her arm. His slender fingers pinched her flesh. 'I can't let you go in there.'

'You can and you will,' Anita said. 'I need to know what he knows about the jars, and I want his before they confiscate it.'

'You can wait until after this is all over. I'll hold the jar for you — '

'No,' Anita said. 'John and I have business to finish. We will finish it alone. You will have your people stationed near the door, and you, young lady, will keep a close eye on me. If anything goes wrong, anything at all, Roddy, I will sue you for every credit you have. Is that understood?'

He bowed formally at the waist. The movement was sincere, not mocking. 'Yes, ma'am.' He stood. His normally ruddy face was pale. 'Let me call security, and then I will take you to the boardroom.'

Anita crossed her arms and waited for Roddy, staring at the screen, watching John pace in that overlarge room. She had

397

things to settle with him, all right. For damaging her reputation, for nearly ruining her credibility. For stealing her bodeangenie. He would pay. And he would know why he was paying before she caused the incident that would force Base Security to take his life.

John

The boardroom was cold. His fingers and nose were chilled. He poured more water out of the decanter and drank, wishing the air wasn't so dry. If he squinted, he could almost imagine rows and rows of woollen suited men sitting at the conference table, discussing the ways to maximize profits while increasing productivity.

The room had to be cold so people in those woollen suits wouldn't overheat. He was beginning to dislike this hotel's attention to detail. He didn't want to sit. Sitting alone at that table made him feel like he had been feeling too much lately, the only survivor in a room full of empty chairs.

He hated being in this room. He knew he was trapped. The owner was planning something. But the only way John would know that plan was to walk square into the middle of it. He knew they wouldn't arrest him. They could have done that at any point. No. This had something to do with Beth. No matter how he felt, he would see it through.

He glanced at the high ceiling and the narrow walls. He had learned over the years that it didn't matter how big the room, any place could be a prison. This just happened to be a cold one.

The curled gold door handle on the heavy doors turned downward. John set his glass beside the decanter and rubbed his hands on his pants. He took a deep breath. The game was about to begin.

The door opened, and a woman stepped in. The fibres of her dress glittered in the soft light. Her hair, loose around her shoulders, glittered in the same way. He hadn't seen her in weeks, but she looked the same.

Anita.

She was alone.

This made no sense. Had the owner contacted her? Was she going to do something to him? His palms were damp. This was a contingency that he hadn't thought of. He had never imagined Anita looking for him, although it made sense.

It made perfect sense.

She had paid him for a job he had not completed.

She pulled the door closed and leaned on it. 'What kind of game are you playing?' she asked. 'Did you kill Minx and the others to steal my bodeangenie? Did you think that a bodeangenie and a Dancer jar were enough to start a business that would go head-to-head with mine?'

She thought he was competing with her? She thought all of this a scheme to knock her out of business? He took a deep breath of the cool air. She was too smart to be that self-absorbed.

She had plans for him.

She wouldn't call security. She would kill him if she were double-crossed. There were rumours of it happening before.

He glanced at the door. She blocked his way to it. And he had found no other way out of the room.

She had him trapped. She was going to hold him in the room until her assistants came.

Trapped. Like the genie.

Trapped.

He needed time to think. He hadn't been prepared for this kind of contingency. He had planned to talk his way out of any situation with the owner. Maybe talking would work here. It would at least allow him to stall. 'Mr McNair told me he would have someone talk to me about Beth.'

Anita laughed. 'Beth. Yes. Little Beth.' Anita leaned her head against the door and watched him from her multi-coloured eyes. 'She was one of the hotel's pleasure girls, did you know that? Specialized in alien life forms.' Anita shuddered delicately. 'But I suppose the Dancer Eight always specialized in alien life forms.'

He would not be goaded. He had to think his way through this. There had to be a reason for Anita to come alone.

The jar. She knew about the jar.

He felt a flush rise in his cheeks. 'You have Beth's jar.'

Anita smiled. 'Served her right, the little thing. She was so self-righteous when she took my Minaran away. I was surprised she died. She won that battle. But then I took her most precious possession, although I never did find out how she got a Dancer

402

jar off Bountiful. I had been trying to for years, but my ships were always searched when they came back.'

John gripped the edge of the table behind him. She didn't know. She didn't know she had Beth trapped inside that jar. The chill in the room had grown. Now he had to save himself, and get Beth's jar. But even if he got past Anita, he still had corridors and corridors of the hotel to go through. And he knew that they had monitors everywhere.

'I took the genie back to its home,' John said.

'I know.' Anita said.

'It was furious at being trapped.'

Her smiled returned, small and cruel. 'Most beings are.'

She knew how he felt, then. She thought she had won. 'You wouldn't know,' he said. Maybe sheer physical strength could get him out. He could run to his shuttle —

'Oh, I know,' she said. 'Perhaps better than anyone but you. I grew up on Bountiful too. That's how I knew how rare a full Dancer jar is. The Dancers guard them with religious intensity.'

For a moment, he couldn't breathe. He wasn't sure he heard her right. But her voice echoed in his head. She had lived on Bountiful. Under the dome, in that sickly odour of Salt Juice. She knew —

The words exploded out of him as if they weren't even his. 'You grew up on Bountiful and you trap things for a living? You know what it feels like and you do the same?'

'I escaped,' she said. 'I survived. Which is more than I can say for you or your friends.'

Bethie, we lost Allen.

You don't understand, John. That man on Bountiful, I told him. I told him I thought that Michael would never grow up.

We should have waited, John . . .

When she died . .

When he died . . .

When they died . . .

We're Useless, John, don't you see?

If we're crazy, we're all crazy in the same way.

His whole body was trembling. Something inside him was straining to get out. 'You didn't survive,' he said. 'You perpetrated. You did the same thing that they did to us. You trapped, and tortured, and thought only of money.'

403

Her cheeks flushed, sending a pink colour through her face that clashed with her hair. 'I never drank Salt Juice. I never touched another being. I never intentionally harmed anyone.'

His father had said that. His father had said that on the last afternoon when the authorities took John away.

It's not my fault. I never knew what to do with the boy. He lies. He always lies. And now he's moved to killing —

The dam broke inside and with a rush of fury, he sent her everything he could think of, image upon image, memory upon memory. *Trapped in the house, listening as the door opened, as his parents came home, knowing most mornings he would wake up like the Dancer children, gray and listless, too battered to even move . . . white, white, white walls . . . the blood all over him, and Katie urging him on, her face cold and frozen in his mistake. He should never have let them trap her there before her transformation in that cold, cold bed, in that windowless building . . . Allen turning silver, the guards holding him pulling him away from Beth . . .*

Memories colliding with memories not his own: *Dancers hovering over her, their rubbery fingers cold, the silver floating around them. Voices she didn't recognize chanting Useless, Useless, Useless. No salvation there, no salvation anywhere.*

Then himself again. *The isolation on the prison ship. The cold of Reed. Trapped, his hands bound, tied to a canopied tree while Dancer ghosts touched him, calling him Useless. He was naked and they were touching him and the light, the silver light, was everywhere. Pain, such deep pain.*

He sent it to her, that pain, all the pain he had ever felt, sent it as Dancers sent things, in a bubble away from himself. She didn't have the strength to fight it, and he couldn't stop pushing once he started. He had to get it out.

Someone was screaming, high pitched and vulnerable. He grabbed the scream like a life rope and pulled himself up, out of the fury, the terrible feeling of being trapped. Anita was on the floor, holding her hands over her head, screaming —

— screaming —

— screaming —

Her memories were like his. The Dancers had sought out children. From the beginning. And she had escaped – to punish others as she had been punished.

Her screams had gone from piercing to guttural. She was

404

losing her voice. The doors opened and Base Security stood there, holding long thin silver lasers, training them on him. It would be so easy for them to kill him, and it would be wrong. He wasn't finished yet. He put up his hands.

'I didn't touch her,' he said. 'I swear. I didn't touch her. Please, don't kill me. Please.'

McNair stepped through the door looking more terrified than John had ever seen him. 'You kill with your mind,' McNair said.

'She's not dead,' John said. They were going to kill him and he would never finish. He would never have a chance to really live. 'See? She's not dead.'

He had to shout over her screams. One of the security people crouched beside her and tried to touch her, but she scuttled away from him.

'Please,' John said, hating that he had to beg. 'You can do anything you want to me, but don't kill me.'

One of the security people called for medical back-up. Another took out light locks. John winced when he saw them. He hadn't worn them since Lina Base.

The security officer approached, his face so pale with fear that John thought he would pass out. John eased his hands down in the proper position, and a dozen lasers focused on it. The officer held up one hand. 'If he tries anything or anything strange happens, kill him.'

Then the officer came forward and slid the locks on John's wrists. Anita's cries were undulating now, her hair tangled over her face, her dress ruined. She looked like a lost child, broken after her world had been destroyed.

'I think you should kill him.' Roddy's voice was shaking.

'You don't want that to happen in your hotel,' the officer said. 'And I don't want a blemish on my record. This is one for the courts.'

He took John by the arm, gingerly, as if John might burn him, and led him toward the door. The security officers parted to create a wide berth around him. He glanced at Anita as he passed. The self-possessed, beautiful woman was gone as if she had never been. The woman remaining had a glazed expression in her eyes, and so much terror inside that it screamed as it came out.

He had felt like that every day of his life, from the moment he was born to the moment he left Bountiful and sometimes beyond. Only he had remembered it. He had never allowed himself to forget. He had done many things, but he hadn't lied to himself about the horrors he had seen.

And he had never intentionally perpetrated the same crimes as his parents and the other colonists. Different crimes, yes. But his crimes. Made from his own mistakes.

Like this one.

They had him now. Forever. They would charge him with the Bountiful murders and he would not get free.

He glanced at Anita.

She was making little choking sobs, and lying on her side on the floor.

She had won. Too bad she would never appreciate it. He was trapped now, a rare creature, the only remaining Dancer Eight, worth at least as much as a bodeangenie, but not for sale.

Never for sale.

Only to watch and prod and poke and blame.

They would blame her breakdown on him, just like they would blame everything else.

They would send him back to Reed.

And five jars with human souls would be sold to the highest bidder.

Part Eight

Justin Schafer

Justin left Lina Base as soon as he heard of the arrest. The feeling that he was always late for or wrong about the important events of his life haunted him during the entire trip. The feeling intensified as the Orda Base authorities fought him over visitation rights. They seemed to believe that John could kill or maim with a single thought.

He spent the trip worrying about what he would say to John – how he would treat the boy. Justin had watched the holo of Anita's disintegration and it looked for a moment as if the two of them were engaged in mortal combat. Their common background had shocked Justin, and he had seen the fury on John's face.

Then, when the convulsions started, he thought they both were going to die the way that Allen had. But they didn't. Anita was broken, screaming, hysterical. The lead psychologist on Orda Base did not know how to handle her. She was lost somewhere inside herself, he said, and she couldn't seem to get out.

Justin reviewed his list of questions. No matter what happened, this meeting with John would change his life. Yet in some ways it was a godsend. John would go back to prison, and Justin's work would remain intact.

A twinge of guilt hit him with that thought. He was supposed to be open minded. He was supposed to be an expert in the human mind.

Sometimes he didn't even understand his own.

He took a deep breath. He should leave John to his own devices.

But Justin couldn't. Because, for the first time in his career, he knew that to do so would be wrong.

The cell where John was being kept was like nothing Justin had ever seen before. The walls were covered with dirt and grime, the floor had not been swept, and the mattress was old and covered with stains. The piss hole had backed up, and was giving off a stench that made Justin's eyes water.

He had had to fight six different administrators to get to see John alone. The battles began on the shuttle over, and continued until Justin agreed to sign a waiver, absolving Orda Base of all responsibility for his health.

He was willing. He had waited twenty years for this meeting.

The last time he had seen John, John had been one of a blur of faces, children who meant no more to Justin than the Minarans had on Minar. Only Michael Dengler had stood out from the crowd, and Michael had died.

Now John sat on the edge of the couch, not a little boy, but a man at his full height. His body was thin, but well muscled, his hair too long and dark. His eyes were shadowed, and his expression sombre.

'John?' Justin held out his hand as the cell door closed behind him. 'I'm Justin Schafer.'

John did not stand. He gave the hand a withering glance. 'I remember.'

The bitterness startled Justin. He had expected it from Latona, but not from John. John had been part Dancer to him, all grace and no memory. But the man before him had a memory – and it was a long one.

'I've come to help you,' Justin said.

John smiled, but the look did not reach his dark eyes. 'No,' he said. 'You came to gawk, and to help yourself. Don't think I haven't heard of your later work, Dr Schafer. At least you're rehashing your past and not making other people's lives miserable.'

Justin's heart was pounding. He didn't know how he had lost control of the interview so quickly. He had come with good intentions. For the first time he knew what he was planning was right. The fact that John didn't welcome him with open arms stunned him. 'You hold me responsible for what happened on Bountiful?'

'No,' John said. 'We all made bad choices in those days.'

Justin let out the breath he had been holding. Breathing hurt; the sharp piss smell assaulted his nostrils each time he inhaled. 'All right,' he said. 'Then let me tell you what I need to. I would like to hire an attorney for you. There are a number of people who do not believe you killed the traders on Bountiful. But your actions since have been odd, and we need you to explain yourself. There's interest in very high levels at seeing you convicted – you're convenient – but there's just as much interest in seeing that you get a fair trial.'

'So you can write more papers, Doctor?' John leaned back, his dark hair sticking to the wall. He looked both comfortable and in control. Each muscle of his body appeared finely tuned. ' "The Psychology of the Dancer Eight". I have never read such a bunch of garbage in my entire life. How can you purport to analyze people you have only spoken to once?'

Fear was making Justin's throat dry. Was this what John had done to Anita? Assaulted her verbally before the breakdown? The power in John's speech was something Justin was not prepared for. The Dancer children had been victims, unable to defend themselves – at least in Justin's papers. Somewhere John had learned how to attack. Justin would not fall victim to this man, in any way. 'I met you. I saw holos and cordings. I studied you and the Dancers. I interviewed everyone I could. It is a legitimate psychological profile.'

'And it's wrong.' John sat up. His movement was so quick that Justin didn't even have time to respond. 'You have never looked beyond the surface, Dr Schafer. Your entire career has been one of taking the illusions people present and going no deeper. When you realized that children – children! – were killing each other, you never asked why. You never looked to the true cause, the real motive.' John stood. The movement was quick and sharp. Justin had to freeze to keep from taking a step back.

John was taller than Justin was. John's height made him even more imposing. He was not a child. He was a very powerful – very angry – man. 'Think, Doctor. It would seem to me, although I am not an expert like you, that a basic tenet of human psychology is that when the children take drastic action, there is something wrong with the adults. You never looked at the families. You never looked at the community, although you did

413

us all a favour by breaking it up. You only looked at us as if we were diseased and because we imitated the Dancers, you and everyone else figured that they had influenced us somehow.'

'You chose their rituals,' Justin said. 'You chose them.'

'No,' John said softly. 'They chose us. But that's another issue and one I've only just figured out. No. The Dancers were never players. They were only a method of escape. And on other colonies, there are other escape methods – probably not as drastic or severe – but they exist. You don't understand your own world, doctor. How can you understand alien worlds if you don't understand your own?'

Justin felt very small in the face of that anger. The roles he had expected were reversed. John was the adult. Justin felt like the child – a recalcitrant child whose misdeeds had harmed everyone around him. 'I came here to help you,' Justin said.

'You came here to meet one of the Dancer Eight. The only surviving member. You said it yourself. You will help me if I only explain myself. I don't need to justify my life to you. And I wouldn't.' John sat back down on the cot and draped his arms over his legs. 'I wouldn't if it weren't for one last obligation I have.'

'Obligation?'

John clasped his hands together, and looked up at Justin. 'I will not explain that. But I met my court-appointed lawyer. She will crucify me like the last one did. I need your money and your help. I'll be your trained monkey, and answer every question you have, if you get me out of here.'

Justin felt as if he had been hit with a gale force wind. He could barely think. 'Why?' Justin said. 'Why would you do that?'

'Because I have a task to finish, and when it's done, maybe then I can put everything behind me.' John rubbed his thumbs together so hard the skin turned red. 'Will you get me out of here?'

'What task?' Justin asked.

John studied him for a moment, then a smile crossed his face that didn't meet his eyes. 'You wouldn't understand.'

Justin almost denied it. Then he thought of the mistakes he had made – mistakes evident to anyone who had met John, who had seen Minarans, who looked at the charred forest on Bountiful. No. He wouldn't understand. Time he shed the

414

arrogance that made him believe he could see inside everything.

'Will you get me out of here?' John repeated.

Justin stared at John for a moment, this stranger, this man, this member of a group Justin had thought he understood and hadn't at all. Justin had saved him and destroyed him in the same act over twenty years before. John was right; Justin owed him. 'Yes,' Justin said. 'I'll get you out.'

Part Nine

John

John sat on the landing platform at Bodean. The sun had set and the ghostly city had risen above the desert floor, its lights winking in the darkness. He sat, with his legs dangling off the side of the cliff, and felt the curious tendrils of wind playing with his hair.

If anything, Bodean was more beautiful than he remembered it. He had said so to the genie, who had welcomed him with such warmth that for a moment John had forgotten the three years that separated them. The year and a half long trial had been almost more than he could handle, but it had been the genie's corded testimony that had saved him. Fortunately, Justin had believed John's story, and contacted Judge Zinn, who decided to finally help a member of the Dancer Eight. She had allowed Justin to take John's ship to Bodean – after John had broken the illusion so that the genie would know Justin had come from John. Justin was still not a friend, but at least John no longer hated him.

John had spent a year fulfilling his obligation to Justin, answering every stupid question Justin could think of. John vowed not to read the resulting papers. Speaking to Justin was just another step in putting the past behind him. Justin would go on lecturing, his reputation as the expert on the Dancer Eight unshakable now.

Still, in three years, John had not felt content until this moment. He had told the genie that they were even now, a life for a life. The genie had offered to help John make Bodean his home, and John had refused. He had a future for the first time. He wanted to live it as a human being.

But he had an obligation to fulfill first.

Seven jars flanked him, their silver lights growing in the darkness. He had bought two more jars from the old man on Orda Base, and then had returned, at the ghosts' urgings, to

Orda and Lina Bases. He had used Justin's lawyers to defeat Dusty's partner. The site was abandoned when John finally made it to Orda. The junkyard had been in ruins, the building empty. It had taken nearly an hour to summon Dusty's presence from that wall her jar had been smashed against. John had to become Dancer, and chant the puberty ritual before she believed he wouldn't harm her.

And Allen.

He had moved inside the plants in the group room on Lina Base, a room no one visited because they thought they heard the sounds of a sobbing child. Only the Allen John had found did not sob. Allen claimed he had been waiting for the others to realize that they needed to transform.

'Time has no meaning here,' he had said when John found him.

Both Allen and Dusty had climbed in the jars as if they were long lost homes. He had reunited them with the other five, and brought them here. To Bodean.

The Dancers had been so clever. They had understood all along the threats that humans posed to them. But Dancer psychology was as sharply delineated as Dancer physiology. The Dancers put their pasts in jars and called on them only when they needed them. The useless Dancers became useful all through eternity, as wise gods to be summoned when the Dancers needed advice.

The Dancers had decided to use human souls to explain human lives. And what were more useless than children unable to grow up? John had no idea what Anita had seen as a young girl, but he suspected some of the Dancer jars on Bountiful already had human souls trapped inside.

He did understand why she broke at that moment, faced with what she had done, what she had lived through, and what she had seen. No mind could take the strain of that. He felt that was his only real crime: opening the door to Anita's dark soul.

For a while, he had thought of returning to Bountiful. But even if the law let him, he couldn't place his friends back on that world, in a place they had fought so hard to escape.

But they were no longer human. The genie had been right, all those years ago. They had become something other. Not Dancer. Not Useless. Not Human. A hybrid.

422

Only now that he was here, he didn't know how to set them free.

Gray ghosts swirled around him. Pearl with her old-young face, Max – his lips now healed, Skye as tiny as she had always been, Verity – her fears vanquished when she found her old community, Dusty – thin and silent, Allen, always smiling now as if he had discovered a great secret, and Beth, more beautiful than he had ever seen her, her bruises gone, the tortured look she had had when her ghost first appeared now part of the past.

What is this place? Beth asked, inside him, as she preferred to be.

The place I told you about. He tried to clear his sending of sadness, but he couldn't. The wind sent fingers through his hair, and he knew the genie was beside him.

It makes you sad. Isn't this a good place? Beth's confusion felt like his own.

You can be free here.

And that's good. Beth looked around. *I like it. It's beautiful.*

Yes. It's beautiful.

– Come with us, Max said in Dancer. – There's nothing for you now.

John stared at Max, then Verity, Pearl, Dusty, Skye, and Allen. There had been nothing for them because they had allowed nothing to touch them. Like them, he had never been fully human. Unlike them, he was willing to give it a try.

'Maybe I'll be back,' he said.

But you won't. Beth felt like another presence inside his brain. *That's why you're sad.*

He stood and brushed the dirt off his pants. The wind helped. The valley loomed below, lit by tiny thin lights. *I need to let you go, Bethie. I can't carry you all through my future.*

But Dancers bring their past everywhere.

John shook his head. *Dancers wall off their past. I'm merely setting mine free. I'll always love you and I'll always be your friend.*

Laughter made him look up. Verity and Max were floating toward the light, their jars dark. They were giggling and dancing on wind currents.

I've never seen her laugh before, Beth sent. Then she wrapped her spirit self around him in a full body hug. *Come back if you need to.*

I'll always know where you are. More laughter caught his

attention. Dusty, Pearl, Skye and Allen had joined the dance, forgetting to say their goodbyes. He watched them go. He hadn't set them free. They had chosen their own fate.

I'll always love you too, Beth said and then she pulled out of him. Her ghost watched him, without laughing, as she floating to join the others.

He turned away from the lights. He didn't know where he was going to go, he only knew it was away from here.

'You can never leave your past completely behind, you know.' The genie sat on the steps, looking like Justin.

'I don't like what you're wearing,' John said.

The genie shrugged. 'Spent so much time with him, I almost feel like I know him.' Then it laughed. 'You know, I could have said anything and convinced them to set you free.'

'Why didn't you?'

The genie's smile faded and its body slid into Allen. 'Because,' it said, 'our relationship is based on honour.'

It stood and held out its hand. John closed his hand around the illusion, wishing he could hold the wind. 'Will they be all right?'

The genie glanced over its shoulder at them. 'They still have their human minds. They believe this place to be heaven. And so it will be.'

John nodded. They needed heaven. So did he.

'There will always be a place for you here,' the genie said.

'I know.' John mounted the steps to the ship. He was grateful to have a place. But here he would have to give up his body to have a life. He wanted —

He wanted —

(short, pudgy arms reaching – like in his dreams, in his memories. His earliest moments)

He wanted to make a place for himself somewhere else, a place where he would have intimacy, where he would have love, where he would have himself. He had never done that before.

He believed he could now.